# What Reviewers Say about Gun Brooke's Fiction

### *Course of Action*

"The setting created by Brooke is a glimpse into the rarified world of celebrity and high rollers…and…witnessing the relationship develop between Carolyn and Annelie is well worth the trip. The novel is populated with a host of captivating…characters. Glimpses into the lifestyles of the rich and beautiful people are rather like guilty pleasures. The overall result makes for a most satisfying and entertaining reading experience."—Arlene Germain, *Midwest Book Review*

"Gun Brooke's international debut of the romance *Course of Action* is a winner. Brooke illustrates the struggle and complexities of not only a gay-straight relationship, but one that crosses professional boundaries as well. Both Annelie and Carolyn begin to go down one path only to find as they get to know one another, the path changes.I could not put this book down once I began reading the first page. It is tension-filled and fast paced. It is a wonderful romance."—K. Isserman, *Independent Gay Writer*

### *Supreme Constellations: Book One – Protector of the Realm*

"This sci-fi novel, the first of a trilogy of Kellen O'Dal, the lifelong protector of a small child with royalty running through his veins, and Commodore Rae Jacelon, who first meets her future wife in an altercation in the area of space she and her team are patrolling, is spell-binding, touching, amazing and incredible. Brooke is an amazing author and has written in other genres. Never have I read a book where I started at the top of the page and don't know what will happen two paragraphs later."—Anita Moyt, *Family & Friends*

"Gun Brooke has fashioned an enticing love story filled with electrifying conflicts to get this reader's heart racing. The action progresses from the rapid-fire battles, to a possible romance beginning with a forced marriage.…*Protector of the Realm* has it all; sabotage, corruption, erotic love and exhilarating space fights. Gun Brooke's second novel is forceful with a winning combination of solid characters and a brilliant plot."—K. Isserman, *Just About Write*

## By the Author

Course of Action

Protector of the Realm—Supreme Constellations:
Book One

# COFFEE SONATA

*by*

## GUN BROOKE

2006

THIS TRADE PAPERBACK ORIGINAL IS PUBLISHED BY
BOLD STROKES BOOKS, INC.,
NEW YORK, USA

FIRST PRINTING MAY 2006

**CREDITS**
EDITORS: JENNIFER KNIGHT, SHELLEY THRASHER AND STACIA SEAMAN
PRODUCTION DESIGN: STACIA SEAMAN
COVER DESIGN BY SHERI (GRAPHICARTIST2020@HOTMAIL.COM)

# Acknowledgments

Pol, USA, helped me research backgrounds and chisel out the back story of my characters.

Jay, Canada, read everything, commented on everything, and helped me keep track of the plot and stay in tune with the characters throughout the story.

G. J. Griffin, New Zealand; meticulous, patient, and with an eye for grammar, spelling, syntax, and style. This is the umpteenth story she has helped me with, bless her heart.

Georgi, Scotland, reader extraordinaire, gave me fantastic feedback and a lot of encouraging support.

Barbara, USA, read, commented, read again, and kept assuring me I was on the right path.

Lisa, Sweden, helped me keep my "Swedish voice" though I write in English. No-nonsense and grounded, my Swedish beta reader was invaluable to me.

Also thank you to Mom, Malin, and Henrik, for your never-ending support.

**Bold Strokes Books**

Radclyffe, publisher, thank you for the wonderful environment you create for us at Bold Strokes. I am blessed to belong to the best publishing house possible!

Dr. Shelley Thrasher, editor, thank you for making me look good! You make my voice stronger, and my stories better, and I love working with you.

Sheri, graphic artist, I loved the cover the moment I saw it, and didn't want to change a thing. You are a wiz!

Stacia Seaman, editor, thank you for your Argus eyes, with which you examine every single syllable. The quality of your work is amazing.

Connie Ward, publicist, Lori A, newsletter editor, thank you for all that you do to promote BSB books.

## Dedication

For Elon
Who loves coffee—and me!

For Joanne
Who showed me Rhode Island, and who loves coffee
and music—just like me!

For my family and friends…
Whether you drink coffee or not—your voices are music
to my ears.

Sonata
*so·na·ta*
Pronunciation: `so-'na-ta`
Function: *noun*
Etymology: Italian, from *sonare* to
sound, from Latin
: an instrumental musical
composition typically of three or
four movements in contrasting
forms and keys

Source: Merriam-Webster OnLine

Behind every successful woman...is
a substantial amount of coffee.
—Stephanie Piro


Coffee should be black as hell,
strong as death, and as sweet as
love.
—Turkish proverb

# The Taste of Your Name

For my love
I exhale your name out of gratitude
And passion
It rolls off my tongue when I am awake
And in dreams

I breathe it against your lips
Before the kiss
I want to taste your name
Across your skin

I will murmur it against your neck
Let it vibrate against you
Where as my voice is breathless
Yours is distinct and precise

You say my name like it was coffee
You know it throws me
It will be easy to hide in you
Wrap your love around me

Then when fire consumes us
I will bless us with your name

*Gun Brooke, 2001*

## PROLOGUE

"What do you mean, you want to cancel the tour, Vivian?" Malcolm Hayes said. "You're scheduled for concerts in Tokyo, Hong Kong, and Singapore. They'll claim damages and might damn well get them."

Vivian Harding turned from the window to her obviously stunned agent. "I don't care. I can't do anything about it, Malcolm." Impatient, she tapped the surface of the Venetian desk in her hotel room with perfectly manicured fingernails. "Just make it happen."

"But why so late? And so sudden?"

"I...I can't talk about it now. We'll discuss it in more detail when I'm back in the States."

"What's the matter? You don't have anybody to water your plants right now?"

"Don't be a smart-ass." Vivian pressed trembling fingers to her eyelids. "I fully intended to honor my contract, Malcolm. All I can say right now is that this is the only course of action."

"Dear God. You're serious, aren't you?"

Malcolm was also her friend, and Vivian watched with regret how utterly stricken he looked as he sank down on a chair behind the desk.

After a brief silence he cleared his throat and began again. "I'll take care of it, Viv. I promise."

## CHAPTER ONE

The bell above the café door gave a muted ping. As Michaela Stone glanced up from folding napkins behind the counter, she saw a woman she didn't recognize coming toward her.

Dressed in a casual yet elegant white and navy blue sweat suit, she looked like she'd just stepped off a yacht. Maybe she had. Her blond hair, kept in a loose twist, sparkled like it was alive. Mike found herself imagining how it would look if it were set free.

"Welcome to the Sea Stone Café," she managed, embarrassed to realize that she was staring. "I'm Mike. What can I get you?"

"Just coffee." The woman's voice was so rich and full it reminded Mike of a blend of espresso and smooth Belgian chocolate.

"There's no such thing as 'just coffee,' ma'am." Mike pointed at the blackboard over the counter with a grin. "We offer ten different beans, and you can have brewed coffee, boiled coffee, ice coffee, cappuccino, latte, macchiato…well, you see over there?"

"Ah…nothing ordinary will do, I see." Raising her porcelain blue eyes to the board, the woman read through all the coffee varieties. "Okay, a house blend cappuccino."

"Excellent choice. Coming right up." Mike abandoned the napkins and walked over to the espresso machine. While her hands automatically created the cappuccino, she thought about the woman waiting for it. It wasn't tourist season in New Quay, Rhode Island, and even then, she rarely saw anyone who looked like this woman just drop in. It wasn't just her clothes that suggested wealth and sophistication. The way the blonde carried herself, with ease and elegance, suggested a well-leveled self-confidence.

She placed an extra piece of chocolate on the saucer but stopped just as she was about to serve the coffee. "Would you rather sit at a table?" *Not just yet.*

"The bar's fine, Mike. I'm Vivian, by the way." She waited until Mike had put the coffee down before extending her hand and barely missed the cup. "Nice to meet you."

"Likewise, Vivian." It was surprisingly easy to call her by her first name. Vivian felt familiar. *People never feel familiar this fast. What's going on?* Mike cleared her throat. "Just visiting East Quay?"

"Yes, for a while. I'm on…hiatus."

*Interesting choice of words.* "Staying at the Marriott?"

Vivian didn't appear to mind the third degree. She sipped her coffee and looked relaxed. "No, I'm borrowing my friends' beach house with my two dogs. It's their summer home, but I look forward to sitting by the fire this winter."

"Ever experienced a New England winter? You may be surprised if you haven't."

Vivian laughed and the sound rippled down Mike's spine. "I know they can be brutal. I grew up in East Quay, a thousand years ago. The town has changed a lot, but I'm sure the winters are the same."

"We get snowed in all the time. As odd as it sounds, that's good for business."

"Yes, I bet people are even more interested in hot coffee when there's a cold wind outside."

"You got it."

Mike caught herself staring at Vivian and grabbed a new pile of napkins. She neatly folded one in three, turned it over once, and attached the simple brass napkin ring.

"You work here alone?"

Unexpectedly happy she hadn't bored Vivian, Mike shook her head. "No, I've got three part-time employees. One comes in for the evening rush."

"You're the owner?" A surprised smile revealed perfect white teeth when Vivian leaned forward, her fingertips playing with the rim of the coffee cup. "Well, I certainly admire what you've done with the place. It was already pretty run down when I was a child."

"It was condemned when I bought it, been sitting empty for several years. I had to renovate for six months before I could get a license to serve food."

"And look at it now."

Mike warmed to the approval in Vivian's voice, pleased that she appreciated Mike's hard work. She watched Vivian sip her coffee, closing her eyes as she tasted it, and she looked so sensual Mike wondered if that was how she looked when she made love. Shocked at her thoughts and disturbingly aroused, she stared at the napkin she'd unconsciously wrinkled beyond recognition. *Damn, what's wrong with me?*

"How long have you been in business, Mike?"

"Almost six years. I graduated from the University of Rhode Island, and then fate called me to this old marina. I fell in love with its beautiful vintage yachts and this abandoned building begging to become a café."

"And you listened." Vivian's eyes sparkled.

"I did. It's hard work, but I've never regretted that." *What I regret is all the years I wasted before that.* Despite Mike's best efforts, thinking about the past left her feeling naked and exposed. "This is also my home," she continued, and tried to find the security that thought usually carried. "I live in the basement."

"In the basement? In this old house? Is that…healthy?"

"Sure." Pulled out of the mood she hated for a few seconds, Mike laughed, again warmed, this time by Vivian's apparent concern. "I had it completely restored when the café started to make money. Before that I lived in a small apartment in town. Now I have lots of space. And it's not as dark as you'd think." *And there's really nothing wrong with darkness. You can hide well if you stay out of the light.*

Vivian Harding couldn't take her eyes off Mike's face and the shadows flickering in her eyes. She felt like a voyeur as she sat across the counter and wondered what had caused such torment.

The young woman, or perhaps not as young as she'd first thought, was beautiful in the darkest of ways. Her hair was so black that the highlights were blue. They emphasized her blue-black eyes, set deeply under black, full eyebrows. Her features were strong, with sharp planes and angles—a face full of character. "So you're like me, live and breathe work?"

"I guess that's true, to some extent." For a moment, Mike's

expression lightened. She placed a new pile of folded napkins next to Vivian. "I watch a lot of movies and play the drums. Especially if I'm angry. That's why I started—to get rid of stress in college."

"Ever play professionally?"

"No. Except for the gigs at college where they paid us in free beer."

"Beer?" Vivian couldn't stand the stuff. The smell, the taste; it was all bad. She wasn't about to insult Mike's taste, though.

"Yeah, there was a lot of beer, but I stayed away from it. I don't drink."

More shadows. Vivian leaned forward so she wouldn't miss any of Mike's facial expressions. "I don't drink much either these days. A glass of red wine on special occasions, that's all. I'm on, well…some medication, and the two don't play nicely together."

"I'd say so." Mike grimaced, making Vivian laugh. "I knew someone who mixed alcohol with a little bit of everything. Everything but food."

"Sounds like a careless person," Vivian suggested cautiously. *I bet that was someone close to you.*

"To say the least."

They exchanged another long look, and again Vivian felt something indescribable happen, something she couldn't grasp, but it was as tangible as the coffee cup in her hands. Mike's mix of dark wildness, combined with an undeniable vulnerability, stirred something inside Vivian and induced a faint tingle in her stomach. She was amazed at her own interest, and it did take her mind off the issues she was battling. Vivian welcomed the change of focus.

"You said you have dogs." Mike changed the subject, her eyes now black as thunderclouds. "What kind?"

"Great Danes," Vivian replied, trying to sound cheerful. She wanted to assure her she had nothing to fear from someone who was almost hiding in East Quay. Mike's look of relief and the disappearing tremors in her hands were worth the effort. "They're brothers, six years old, called Perry and Mason."

Mike laughed aloud and the irresistible sound produced goose bumps on Vivian's arms. "Perry and Mason! You a Raymond Burr fan?"

"Not really, but somehow the names fit. They're both nosy and stubborn." Vivian grinned. "They're also sweet and well behaved, most of the time. Since I'm alone in that beach house, they make me feel safe."

"Is your family still here in East Quay, Vivian?"

"No. I moved my parents to a condo near the harbor in Newport as soon as I could afford to. My mother always wanted to live near the water, and nowadays she loves to watch the ships come and go. Especially the QE2."

"What do you know." Mike sounded enthusiastic. "I went to Newport once, with a family I stayed with, and we toured the QE2. I was stunned, beyond stunned. I knew one day I'd travel on that ship and visit all the ports she went to." Leaning forward, she placed her chin in her palms. "I still want to."

"And you should, *cara*. You have plenty of time, but the sooner the better."

"Have you sailed with her?"

Vivian nodded. "Yes, but it was a working voyage."

"You don't exactly strike me as a sailor." Mike winked.

Laughing, Vivian shook her head, covering her forehead and feigning exasperation. "You found me out," she huffed. "Honestly, I was part of the entertainment."

"You're a performer?"

"Yes. I sing."

"How great. I play the drums and you sing—we have potential." A fierce blush crept up from Mike's neck and spread to her pale cheeks like wildfire. "Hey, I didn't mean—"

"I know, I know. But I see your point." Vivian smiled, charmed by Mike's apparent confusion.

The bell pinged and a young woman poked her head in. "Sorry I'm late for work, Mike! I'll just park my bike and be right in."

The mood between Mike and Vivian broke like a dry twig, and they both pulled back. Vivian slid ten dollars beneath her cup. "Well," she said with some reluctance, "I think that's my cue. It was nice talking with you."

"Thanks. The same to you. Do come back."

A quiet longing in Mike's voice made Vivian stop and turn. "Of course I will. You make excellent coffee, *cara*."

❖

"Hey, kiddo, drop what you're doing."

Eryn Goddard jumped when her boss's loud voice sounded just a few inches from her right ear. "Why?" She pivoted on the chair, meticulously preventing her disdain for Harold Mills from showing. He was a short, stocky man, and if his nonexistent social skills weren't enough, he wasn't running the local paper very professionally. She resented his lack of objectivity and his obvious pandering to some of the local politicians and merchants.

"Get down to the Marriott, pronto. Hernandez was supposed to go, but his wife's hatching their fourth." Harold obviously thought that Mrs. Hernandez should've thought better of interfering with business than to expect her husband at her side for the baby's birth.

"What's up at the Marriott?" Eryn was already on her feet, eager to get out of her bully of a boss's way.

"A press conference. The world press is there. Make sure you have your credentials. Security's bound to be tight."

"Are you going to tell me what kind of press conference, or will that be a surprise?" Eryn knew she sounded sarcastic and didn't care. Harold glared, and she felt a little wave of satisfaction.

"Our only freakin' diva is back for the first time since she skipped town some forty years ago. Do me a favor. Put East Quay on the map for a change. Ask a headline question. Anything."

Eryn's mind raced. Only one name came to mind, but was that possible? "Vivian Harding? The opera singer?"

"Bingo."

Eryn hated when he said "bingo" in that smug tone. *Overbearing prick.* "All right, I'll head over there now. When's the press conference?"

"In forty-five minutes." He checked his watch. "Make that forty."

"And that's cutting it a tad close." With her teeth clenched around a juicy insult, Eryn headed for the door, pulling her shoulder bag over her head as she strode between the desks in the small office. *Nothing like a little pressure!*

❖

Vivian applied her deep red lipstick with skilled precision. As she put it down, she leaned in closer to examine her reflection. It was important to look impeccable, today more than ever. She gently pressed a tissue to her full lips before applying a second layer.

Something stroked against her leg, and she looked down at the dog. "Do I look the part, Mason? Will I look enough of the homecoming superstar to fool the press?"

Mason sat down and tilted his head as if to ponder the question, making her laugh. His brother joined them and rested his large head on the dresser, reluctant as usual to take his eyes off her.

Vivian returned her attention to the mirror and made sure her hair was secure in its loose twist. She had chosen a red pantsuit over a white sleeveless blouse and her trademark three-inch-heel pumps. Colorful earrings and a matching necklace full of emeralds, topazes, and rubies glittered. *I dress the part, and they see what I want them to. So what? That's how you play the game.*

When she heard the cabdriver honk for the second time, she threw a multicolored scarf casually around her shoulders and patted Mason and Perry. "I won't be long, boys. Behave." Looking once more into the mirror, Vivian took a deep breath. *One last time. Surely I can pull it off one more time?*

❖

Eryn sat down in the first row, at the far left, and looking around, she realized she was lucky to get this seat. One of the more seasoned reporters, who'd been a close friend to her previous boss, had saved it for her since the conference room was packed. Media people lined all three walls in the large room.

The buzz from the audience rose and fell around her, but Eryn was busy opening her tablet PC and locating the files she needed from her wireless uplink. Many Web sites were dedicated to the world-famous mezzo-soprano, and she'd read reviews of Harding's performances and recordings before. Vivian Harding was one of the few classic divas in the same category as performers like Birgit Nilsson and Maria Callas.

Eryn wondered how such a talent could have sprung from East Quay. Few people in America, let alone outside the country, had ever heard of this little town. And despite Vivian Harding's fame, she hadn't put it on the map. As far as Eryn knew, this was the first time the singer had been back since she'd left East Quay immediately after Malcolm Hayes discovered her.

At the sound of applause Eryn glanced up at the podium, expecting the star of the media circus to appear. Instead a dark-haired woman in a dark blue skirt suit, her chocolate brown hair in a low, snug bun, climbed the few stairs to the dais.

She seemed familiar, and after a second Eryn realized why. Not only was Manon Belmont the owner of the venerated Belmont Foundation and considered East Quay's first lady, but she was Eryn's neighbor in the condo she'd inherited from her great-aunt. It was pretty mind-boggling to be living in the same building as the town's crème de la crème. They'd never actually talked; Eryn had only seen her from afar and doubted if Belmont would even recognize her. Not that it mattered.

Eryn settled back and prepared to take notes when Belmont placed some papers on the table in front of her and looked out over the audience. She had a commanding presence, Eryn noted absently.

"Hello, and welcome. I appreciate that so many of you could attend, and I know you're eager to meet the woman who made this possible. We're here for a very good cause, and having our town's most famous person on board is tremendously exciting." Her throaty voice easily carried throughout the conference room. Obviously Belmont was used to being in the spotlight. Eryn couldn't help but appreciate the confident way she carried herself. It was also hard not to notice how attractive she was when an inadvertent movement outlined her full, high breasts and the curve of a hip. "Please, welcome Vivian Harding."

Belmont clapped, initiating a new round of applause. The door opened again and Vivian Harding emerged, highlighted by the harsh spotlights aimed directly at her. She stopped just inside the door, her hand tucked over the arm of a man. She squinted briefly and hesitated, murmured to him, and he nodded. Then she joined Manon Belmont at the table on the dais, the spotlights dimming as she sat down.

Harding was not what Eryn had expected. She was taller than she appeared on TV and youthfully beautiful. Eryn checked the Web site she had just pulled up to confirm that she was actually fifty-four. She saw no signs of plastic surgery, and though Vivian possessed generous curves, nobody in their right mind would ever call her fat. Her red tailored suit complemented her full figure, and her brilliant blue eyes nearly outshone her dazzling jewelry.

"Thank you, ladies and gentlemen of the press."

There it was. The voice. Eryn was no opera aficionado, but no one on the planet who owned a radio or TV set could mistake Harding's voice for anyone else's. Eryn knew she'd never forget hearing it in real life, if only speaking and not singing.

"This press conference isn't just about me." Harding waved off the applause. "While I realize you're interested in my life and work, I'm actually here to support an extensive charity project, governed mainly by the Belmont Foundation." She glanced sideways, a smile on her bright red lips. "Manon Belmont has come up with a plan to raise enough money within a year to build a new wing at East Quay Memorial Hospital. In fact, the construction company is making initial preparations."

Everyone was silent for a few seconds, since the announcement had taken Eryn and her colleagues off guard.

"In what way are you involved, Ms. Harding?" a man sitting three chairs from Eryn asked.

"I will sing in a benefit concert at East Quay Hall, three weeks from tomorrow, with the proceeds going to the hospital."

Eryn caught Harding and Manon exchanging a furtive glance.

"The concert will serve a second purpose as well," Harding continued. "It will also be my farewell performance."

## CHAPTER TWO

After several audible gasps, a volcano of simultaneous questions erupted.

"Are you retiring, Ms. Harding?"

"Why have you returned to your hometown now? Didn't you once promise never to return?"

"Did Ms. Belmont contact you?"

"Are the rumors regarding you and Peter Ovolov true?"

"Ms. Harding? Over here! Is it true that you've fired Malcolm Hayes because of the scandal in Rome?"

Embarrassed, but not surprised, on her colleagues' behalf, Eryn looked over at Manon, whose expression had hardened.

"One at a time, please." Vivian Harding was clearly used to being accosted by the press on such occasions. "You in the yellow blouse, in the second row."

"Amy Torres, the *Boston Phoenix*. Why are you giving your last performance in a godforsaken little town like East Quay?"

Eryn groaned. *What an idiot. Doesn't she realize her question will alienate every citizen in this town?*

"I left this town exactly thirty-eight years ago, and it's high time I gave something back to it. After all, I went to high school here, and my parents lived and worked here for more than half a century."

"But why now?" The reporter was insistent, and something impertinent in her voice made Eryn want to muzzle her.

"Why not now?" Harding countered, her expression still friendly, but she spoke with an obvious bite. "This is about closing a circle. I've seen and played almost every major opera house in the world. Now I want to finish my career in my hometown where I started out. Or maybe you didn't do your research well enough to realize this fact, Miss…? I'm sorry. What was your name?"

*Ouch. Good for you, Harding. Don't take that kind of treatment from anyone.* Eryn thought she saw Manon nod approvingly before sending the reporter a cold glance. Eryn raised her hand.

❖

Manon Belmont could have throttled the *Boston Phoenix*'s reporter, but she also knew these types of questions were unavoidable. Vivian had assured her that after dealing with the European press, she didn't consider the U.S. media too bad.

She regarded the next reporter Vivian acknowledged. The woman was young, with stunning red hair in a long braid and a self-assured look about her. When she rose to ask her question, relaxed and confident, Manon leaned forward so she wouldn't miss her words. She managed to avoid frowning when her pulse quickened at the sound of the woman's clear, strong voice.

"Eryn Goddard, *New Quay Chronicle.* Have you collaborated with the Belmont Foundation before, Ms. Harding? You and Manon Belmont look like you know each other."

Vivian spoke in a low-key tone, unlike the confident onstage voice she had just used to address the other journalist.

"Ms. Goddard. Eryn, was it?" A faint tremor in the elegant hands, probably only visible to Manon, spoke of Vivian's inner turmoil. "I admire your perception. Yes, I've worked with Ms. Belmont on several projects, and we've had some success. We became acquainted when she came to Paris and I was performing at Opera Nationale. We spoke after the performance, and when I learned she was one of the New England Belmonts and how dedicated she was to her grandfather's legacy, the foundation, I was keen to help her raise whatever funds she needed." Vivian raised her hands, palms up, and gestured toward Manon. "So if you think I've done anything remarkable for this town, you should be a thousand times more proud of Ms. Belmont. *She* is this town's true daughter. I'm proud to call Manon Belmont my friend."

Manon was astounded. She'd never expected Vivian to say anything like that. Not that the part about how they met wasn't true…but the whole daughter-of-the-town business? And Vivian sounded almost regretful. *What was that about?* Manon glimpsed the reporter, Eryn, scribbling energetically on her computer as a forest of hands stretched toward the ceiling. With the autumn sun from a nearby window igniting her dark red hair, she appeared quite beautiful. Puzzled by the thought, Manon forced herself to focus on the other reporters. Then, to her annoyance, the insolent woman in the yellow shirt now blurted out the next question, without waiting to be acknowledged.

"Why haven't you let your fans know about your work for charity?"

Manon glanced at Vivian, who appeared remarkably calm. *She sounds as if Vivian is obligated to report every move she makes. No wonder she wants to retire.*

"It's quite simple," Vivian responded. "I'm doing this for personal reasons. Private reasons. I didn't want that misconstrued as some kind of bid for publicity."

The woman looked stumped at the reply, and in the back, someone began applauding. The sound grew stronger, and Manon saw Eryn rise to her feet, bringing others with her as the entire assembled press gave a now-flustered Vivian a standing ovation.

"Please, please," Vivian whispered, her eyes suspiciously bright, despite her brilliant smile. "Enough of this." She looked at Manon, pretending to despair. "What do I do?"

"Enjoy," Manon murmured. "You deserve it."

"Very well. I'll take a few more questions. You, sir, in the black suit on the first row. It's Dan, isn't it?"

"Yes, Dan Casey, *New York Times*. I'm flattered that you remember me and sad to hear you're retiring. Usually, at this stage in an opera singer's career, you're at the peak of your performance, with a lot left to give, vocally and artistically. Why end it now? Would you like to share any of your reasons with us?"

With no sound, more a faint twitch of leg muscles, Manon felt Vivian begin to tremble and watched her press her palms together tightly before answering.

"Mostly the reasons are private, and I do agree with you. I'm not ending my career as a performer for artistic reasons. But I can tell you this. I'll miss it a lot." The slight quiver in her smile seemed to quiet everyone. "Even the press, Dan."

"It's a tremendous loss for the music world."

Vivian murmured a thank-you, and then, with a hint of distress, she glanced at Manon, who gave her a reassuring nod and took over.

"I can answer the rest of your questions regarding our charity concert. The town has donated one week's rent for the concert hall, for rehearsals and the main event. Ms. Harding's performance will be the main attraction, of course, but we will have a full program, with several other local performers. An itinerary with all the details will be available when you leave..." She heard herself talk about these details with the press, but part of her alternated between making sure Vivian was all right and examining Eryn Goddard's reaction to what was going on. She was obviously eager to get everything down, since she wrote at an energetic pace and regularly glanced up at Manon and Vivian.

Manon eventually wrapped up the press conference with a sigh of relief and surreptitiously peeked at Eryn one last time. At the same moment, Eryn looked her way, and, to Manon's great embarrassment, lifted an eyebrow questioningly.

Manon groaned inwardly and quickly averted her gaze. *Oh, for heaven's sake. To be caught staring!*

❖

The taxi drove away with Vivian, and Manon walked back into the Marriott, intending to pick up her briefcase and talk to the hotel manager before returning to the office. Alone in the corridor, she coughed, her itching throat making her realize how exhausted she was. *Damn flu. I thought I was over it.* A coughing spell racked her, and she almost cursed aloud as she leaned breathless against the wall.

"Ms. Belmont, are you all right?" someone asked, and placed a hand on her shoulder from behind, startling her.

Manon saw first the green corduroy jacket and tan chinos. Then the red hair, gathered into a long, loose braid; the slightly freckled oval face; and golden butterflies glistening in small, neat earlobes swam into focus. Tipping her head back a little, Manon gazed into large, luminescent green eyes behind thin metal-framed glasses. It was the reporter from the first row, Eryn Goddard. A big leather bag was slung across her right shoulder and hung down to her hip.

"It's all right. I'll be fine," Manon wheezed, and hated how weak her voice sounded.

"You sure? That's a bad cough."

Determined not to show just how bad she felt, Manon let go of the wall. "I assure you, I'm fine, Ms. Goddard. Thank you."

"You're welcome, but there's no need for thanks." Eryn tossed her braid over her shoulder with her free hand. "Especially since we're new neighbors."

"Neighbors? I haven't seen you in my building."

"I just moved into the condo below yours."

"I see." Manon tried to think of something more interesting to say, but she was still annoyed that anyone, especially a reporter, had seen her in a weakened state. To top it off, Eryn was scrutinizing her unabashedly, her braid swinging slowly off her shoulder like liquid red gold as she tilted her head. *If I didn't know better, I'd say she's checking me out.*

Manon grew cold and breathless for a totally different reason. She stepped back, hoping the added physical distance would deter Eryn from seeing…too much. "I'd better be going."

"Okay. Hope you feel better soon."

"Thank you. For your concern." She winced when she heard her own starchy words. She couldn't afford to alienate the press. Although she felt ridiculous, Manon began walking toward the door at the end of the corridor.

"Ms. Belmont?"

"Yes?" Manon looked back over her shoulder. Eryn's eyes glittered as if she was hard pressed not to smile.

"You're welcome."

❖

As Eryn strolled down the street she wondered why she couldn't stop thinking about Manon Belmont. The extraordinarily poised Belmont onstage was a distinct contrast to the vulnerable woman she'd just seen in the corridor. Eryn wondered how someone could appear so collected every instant in public. She carried herself impeccably, wore her hair in a tasteful but restrained style, and dressed conservatively, no doubt from the most expensive boutiques in Providence and Boston. However, the woman Eryn had just encountered in the hotel hallway acted almost unsure of herself, as if she was afraid of saying the wrong thing.

A limousine passed her and then slowed. Eryn assumed it was because of the afternoon traffic, but no other cars were in the limo's lane. It stopped completely, and Eryn halted next to it, curious.

A back window lowered. "Are you on your way home, Ms. Goddard?" Manon Belmont asked in a reserved tone.

"Yes. The cab line was so long—"

"Would you like a ride?"

Eryn hesitated only a moment. "Thanks, if it's no bother. That'd be super."

The chauffeur, a distinguished-looking man in his sixties, came around to the passenger side.

"Ma'am." He politely removed his cap as she entered the car.

"Thank you, sir."

"Just call me Ben, ma'am." The corner of his mouth twitched, making his neat mustache quiver.

"Only if you call me Eryn. I'm not used to being ma'amed." Eryn grinned when he nodded. She already liked the chauffeur.

As they merged into traffic, Eryn turned to Manon, who was busy reading from a folder. She made no attempt to talk to Eryn, only glanced at her and nodded distractedly.

The muted light in the limo softened Manon's features, making her look different—less strict, younger. Eryn knew she was in her early forties and that she'd never married. In fact, she was supposedly a barracuda when it came to men. With a new man on her arm at almost every function, she teetered on the difficult edge of being envied or called a tramp.

As Eryn studied Manon discreetly she wondered if anyone who actually looked at this class act of a woman could call her a tramp. An aura of quality, of substance, permeated the air around Manon, as if she oozed old money, old values. *As if I'd give a hoot for old values. Old values crucify people like me.*

❖

"Thanks for the ride. Definitely better than a cab." As the old-style elevator stopped at the fourth floor, Eryn pulled the gate aside and hoisted her heavy computer bag farther up on her shoulder. "This is where I get off."

"My pleasure." Manon sounded strange. "And again, thank you for being kind to me."

"Hey, no problem. Just drink lots of fluids, okay?"

"Thank you. I'll remember that." Manon obviously had something else on her mind.

"Yes?" Eryn asked gently.

"You're a reporter…and in my position, I have to be careful."

"And you want to make sure this is all off the record." Irrational disappointment shot through Eryn, making it even hard to speak. *Why do I care what she thinks?* "I thought we were just chatting."

"The press hasn't given me many opportunities to chat, I'm afraid."

Manon's reserved stance spoke volumes. Obviously she wasn't going to encourage any warm and fuzzy heart-to-hearts between neighbors. The muscles in Eryn's stomach clenched into a tight fist. Manon's tone of voice, stiff, yet tinged with defeat, bothered her. *I wonder what she's trying to hide. She's clearly worried about something.*

Eryn was annoyed that Manon apparently lumped her in with all the other reporters she mistrusted. And what ticked her off even more was her own reaction, her urge to assure Manon that everything was cool, that she had nothing to worry about.

"I'm sure the media's given you a lot of attention. That can't be easy," Eryn said, and struggled to sound matter-of-fact. "Of course you're suspicious. But if I ever try to interview you, you'll know beforehand. Fair enough?" She tried a mischievous grin, which disarmed even Harold once in a while. "After all, we're neighbors and I may need a ride again."

A few seconds ticked by, then Manon smiled carefully and unfolded her arms. "You're right. Neighbors should have an understanding." She paused and checked her hair with quick, jerky fingers. Eryn wondered if she was *that* nervous. "If you need a ride and see Benjamin and the car, use it if it's convenient. Besides, I can tell he likes you."

*And you? Do you like me? Or was that just a clever brush-off?*

Eryn shook off her own bit of paranoia and waved to Manon before she closed the elevator gate. As the old monstrosity squeaked on up to the penthouse floor, Eryn stuck her key into her door lock and turned it absent-mindedly.

She simply couldn't figure her illustrious neighbor out and her reporter's antennae were buzzing. Manon was seen as a scion of the community, but there were suggestive whispers about her private life. She was also aloof, verging on rude. It didn't add up. What had Vivian Harding said? East Quay's true daughter? *Curiouser and curiouser. I'm going to do a little research and see what I can find out.* Eryn knew Manon was bound to be hiding something.

Tired beyond words, Eryn craved a hot bath and some red wine. *First things first.* Humming, as soon as she entered her apartment she walked over to her CD player and pressed play. *You can't soak in the tub without Eric Clapton.*

❖

Mike lifted a crate of oranges and started filling the basket next to the chrome juice press. If anyone ordered fresh orange juice at the Sea Stone Café, they could watch the staff squeeze it or they could suck it out of the orange themselves if they wanted it any fresher. Mike grinned and whistled almost inaudibly.

"Mike? Where do you want me to put these?"

Mike gasped at the sound of the unexpected male voice. With her hands in an automatic defensive pose, she jerked around so fast that Edward, one of her employees, almost lost his balance as he backpedaled, juggling a large melon under each arm.

"For crying out loud. I didn't mean to scare you." Edward put the melons down on a nearby barrel. "You okay?"

"I'm fine. I'm fine." Mike rubbed her bare arms. "Just a little jumpy."

"A little? Any jumpier and you'd end up in orbit."

"I'll send *you* into orbit," Martha said, nudging her husband out of the way. "Go out back and make yourself useful. It's garbage day, and I've got four bags for you to tie up."

"Yeah, yeah. Garbage." Edward rolled his eyes at Mike over Martha's head. "I'm going, I'm going."

Martha carried one of the melons to the area between the bar and the kitchen. When she returned, she put her hand on Mike's shoulder. "You look frozen. Why don't you pop down to your place and get a sweater?"

"I'll be okay. Just a tad chilly for a second."

"You almost did your karate stuff on Eddie. Not that he wouldn't benefit from some roughing up, but I'd kinda like for him to keep his teeth. Want to tell me what's going on? You've been somewhat tense lately."

"I…" Mike forced herself to ignore another shiver. "I can't talk about it. Not now."

"Oh, child, it's okay."

Mike saw nothing but unconditional kindness in Martha's eyes. Tears welled up when Mike thought how blessed she was that Martha and Edward had walked through the door and into her life five years ago. They were the parents she'd wished for throughout her teens, and not having any children of their own made it even better. *Maybe I should feel selfish for monopolizing them. But hell, I don't. I need them. I love them.*

"I understand. I do. Just so you know you can come and talk to me anytime."

"Thanks. I will. One day."

"Good." Something on the TV caught Martha's attention. "Oh, my! Look at that! It's her!"

"Who?" Mike turned around, curious since Martha hated the "dumb-box," as she referred to television sets.

"I adore her, Mike. Edward and I saw her in Italy when we were on that tour we won. In Milan at La Scala. He didn't want to go, he hates opera, but as soon as she started singing…he cried like a baby."

*Vivian!* Mike felt her jaw lose cohesion. The heavy makeup didn't hide Vivian's features, but all the bright colors changed her appearance.

Martha reached for the remote and raised the volume. "Oh, what a beautiful speaking voice."

"Her name's Vivian," Mike said, still under the spell of the woman she'd chatted with the day before. *And she's so damned beautiful.*

"That's right. Vivian Harding."

"I've heard of her. I think," Mike said dubiously.

"If you know her name's Vivian, how come you don't know who she is?"

"She was here yesterday having coffee. We talked some. She was nice." Seeing Martha stagger and grab for the counter, Mike had to smile, and she felt the shadows around her dissipate. "She promised she'd come back."

"She did?" Martha pressed a hand to her ample chest. "I hope she does. Soon. Today. No, not today. I look like hell."

"You look fine. But I don't think she meant today. If she did, it's not long till closing time."

Martha looked reassured. "What did you two talk about?"

"Nothing special. Stuff."

"Did she enjoy the coffee?"

"Very much." *I think she enjoyed chatting with me. If she wasn't just slumming, for kicks. It didn't seem that way, but…you never know.*

"You make the best coffee in town. It's sure worth coming back for. And, sweetheart," Martha added, circling Mike's waist with a strong arm, "so are you."

# CHAPTER THREE

Early-morning mist caressed the ocean. As Mike stretched her legs, she glanced at the trees farther up the shore. Soon their leaves would blaze against the azure skies. She loved fall.

Inhaling deeply, she jumped off the boardwalk and started her morning run in the cool, crisp air. As she approached the water she shortened her stride. The sand made her work hard as she deliberately stayed on the dry part of it. Eight or ten years ago she couldn't have guessed she would enjoy such familiar routines. She'd never controlled her time or her life, so making and sticking to her own schedule now empowered her. Back then it had been a struggle to move, to force the same body to obey that now responded so willingly.

Mike could almost hear Josie Quinn advising her not to beat herself up for what she went through before she got her act together. Mike thought fondly of her, the first adult able to reach her in years. At twenty-one Mike had been broken, disillusioned, undernourished, and full of hate. Josie, then in her late forties, volunteered at the Youth Center in Providence, and Mike learned to respect and finally love her mentor in just six months. They had always stayed in touch, but now it pained and worried Mike that she couldn't track Josie down.

Shaking off her sad thoughts, Mike inhaled deeply. *The scent of autumn, my favorite time of year.* Good for business too, but without the hassle of the summer crowd. The beach was almost empty. This was just how Mike liked it. She ran for another ten minutes before she spotted someone approaching. A breeze caught the woman's caramel-colored coat and pushed the morning mist farther out to sea.

As she jogged closer, Mike saw the woman wasn't alone; two huge dogs flanked her. Mike slowed so she wouldn't startle the two Great Danes, which she realized had to be Vivian's Perry and Mason. The breed wasn't unusual in New England, but as far as Mike knew, no one else in this neighborhood had dogs like that. Closer, she could see Vivian's long hair fanned out like a fair silken sail on the wind.

Mike slowed to a walk, then stopped next to her and stretched one leg at a time by tucking it up behind her. "Nice to see you again, Vivian."

Fighting to control the excited dogs and keep her windblown hair out of her face, Vivian looked like she needed a break. "Mike, you're up early."

"Habit. I always jog early. I haven't seen you on the beach before."

"Perry and Mason insisted on exploring today. I thought we better do it before the beach crowd comes."

"Smart move. So these are your boys. They're cute."

"Cute isn't the word I'd use, but they're being good right now. Sometimes they set each other off and can be a handful." Vivian laughed, eyeing the dogs affectionately.

Mike couldn't resist smiling. *Her laughter. I've never heard anything more beautiful.* Mike regarded the large dogs respectfully. "They're…wonderful. May I pat them?"

"Of course. They're friendly."

Carefully approaching the dog she thought was Mason, Mike looked into his dark eyes as she extended a hand. To her relief he licked it immediately and then trotted over to her, pressing his body against her hip.

"Good Lord, when I said they're friendly, I didn't mean *this* much. Mason never takes to anybody like that." Vivian moved closer. "He's usually very reserved, especially with strangers. Perry is the sycophant of the two."

"Ah, I know what it is. I smell like fresh pastry." Mike grinned, surprised at how much this eccentric woman and her dogs charmed her. "He must think I have something yummy in my pocket."

"That could be it." Vivian laughed again. As she stepped forward, the other dog moved in front of her and made her stumble. Staggering toward Mike, she fumbled for support but lost her balance. "*Merde!*"

"You okay?" Mike shoved Mason out of the way and slid her arms beneath Vivian's, stopping her from falling.

"Yes, yes. Thank you." Vivian sounded out of breath as she leaned against Mike. "Didn't pay attention, that's all."

Mike had a sudden, almost frightening urge to hold Vivian closer, to shield her.

Another nudge at Mike's legs made her look down. "Perry seems to like me a lot too," she said, changing the subject when Mason's twin sniffed at her pockets. "I'll have to bring some doggie biscuits in case we run into each other again."

Still half leaning on Mike, Vivian paused before she answered. "I'm sure we will. I plan to make this a routine for the dogs while I can. I don't know exactly how long I'll be in East Quay."

Mike hesitated but finally let go of Vivian. She didn't want to start jogging again; instead she just stood there, enthralled by Vivian's eyes. They reminded her of the ocean and were even bluer out in the open, without the excessive makeup Vivian had worn on TV. "I understand you're an opera singer."

"Yes. After I perform for the Belmont Foundation, I'm going to take a break. Believe it or not, it'll be my first vacation in two years." Vivian gazed at her gently. "You look like a hard worker too. Something we have in common."

"I guess so." Mike's cheeks warmed under Vivian's gaze. "Keeping the café profitable takes a lot of effort, so I have to work more or less around the clock. With a break for a short nap now and then."

The dogs began to pull in the direction Mike had come from. "They're impatient." Vivian paused and pointed to a house on stilts about fifty yards from the waterline. "My manager's house is just over there. Would you like something to drink? Juice or a cup of coffee?"

Mike started to use the café as an excuse to decline but changed her mind. *I never go anywhere, and she'll find out in a flash that I'm not very worldly. But I think she likes to talk to me. And I could sure look at her forever.* She returned Vivian's smile. "Thanks. Some juice would be nice."

As they walked toward the dunes, Mike realized that though she didn't know Vivian, she very much wanted to.

❖

Vivian unleashed the dogs before she climbed the stairs. Seeing how they had taken to Mike, she smiled. Their reaction was a good omen, since Mike was her first private houseguest, a nerve-wracking prospect. Even though she had entertained her colleagues for years in the opera world, that had been business. But to have a young woman over for an impromptu visit felt more daunting than even her upcoming performance.

Vivian gestured for Mike to sit down on the patio before she hurried into the house and grabbed a pitcher of orange juice from the fridge. She placed it and a couple of glasses on a silver tray, took a deep breath as she picked it up, bit the tip of her tongue for balance, and carried it out to the patio, hoping she wouldn't trip or spill anything. Successful, she placed the tray on the cast-iron table. "Here we go."

"Thanks." Mike was still patting the dogs. "Perry, Mason, down."

Vivian stared as her boys obediently lay at Mike's feet and gazed up at her, as if eager for her praise.

"Good dogs." Mike's words were met with adoring looks and wagging tails. "I'm glad you haven't had their ears cropped or their tails docked."

"Yes," Vivian said, her heart warming at this observation. "Personally, I find it unnecessary and unnatural to subject any pet to that kind of treatment."

"I know what you mean. You mentioned they're brothers. They look alike."

"Yes, some people warned me they might become hostile toward each other when they matured, but after six years they still only play."

"Best friends, huh, boys?" Mike ruffled the dogs' ears. "They're great."

Vivian sipped her juice and motioned for Mike to accept the other glass. She studied Mike—black hair, milky white complexion, and the darkest blue eyes she had ever seen. Tall, at least six feet, and slim, Mike appeared fragile, but the way she jogged suggested strength beneath her smooth skin.

She recognized an unexpected attraction, which was both puzzling and unwelcome. Granted, she'd been acting out of character lately, and with good reason, but she certainly didn't have time for any mysterious feelings. This called for casual conversation. "So, Mike, did you grow up here?"

"I lived on the other side of town most of my life. Was raised south of East Quay, in the outskirts four bus stops from the depot. Now they've built a whole new community there, kind of like a suburb, though it's silly to think of a town this size having one."

"Unless you consider the tourist season with all the summer guests."

"True. Everyone and their dog are here then." Mike winked at Vivian. "Present company excluded, of course."

"Of course." Vivian hoped her smile didn't look as forced as it felt. Maintaining a relaxed façade was more difficult than she'd anticipated. "I know exactly where you're talking about. I grew up not far from there, a bit closer to town, on Delivery Street, and couldn't get away fast enough. I hated it with a passion. It was so run down and depressing…" She grimaced. "I guess that's why—"

"What?"

"I'm shocked that coming back to East Quay is comforting. Like home, you know? It's odd, because I don't know anyone here anymore, except my manager and Manon Belmont."

"You're not exactly back in the sticks, are you?" Mike cocked her head and glanced around, gesturing at the luxurious interior. "This is definitely the more upscale part of East Quay."

"Like I said, it isn't mine."

"But surely you make more than your manager." Mike pursed her lips. "If you don't, you must be gullible or doing something else wrong."

Vivian tossed her head back and laughed aloud. "God, how true. This isn't a small apartment above a hardware store, that's for sure. Returning to 'the right side of Quay' and still helping the local hospital by doing what I do best feels okay."

"And it should. No need to go slumming to prove a point."

*She actually gets it.* Vivian wanted to reach out and squeeze Mike's hand in gratitude, but instead chose to cuddle Perry's silky ears. *If she gets it, perhaps I can really come home.* Some of the comments the reporters made during the press conference still stung, perhaps because she believed, deep down, that they were justified. *I did abandon this*

*place and didn't look back, until now, despite every attempt they made
to get me to perform here over the years. And now I need these people
a lot more than they need me.*

"You're performing for free, right?" Mike interrupted Vivian's
thoughts. "That's cool and very generous."

"Yes, I am. And thank you. Those $1,500 tickets should certainly
help build the new children's hospital wing. Manon Belmont expects
most of New York's opera community to turn out."

"That's great." Mike said. "With all the cutbacks lately, our
hospital needs the cash."

"I know." Vivian let her fingers trace the rim of her glass, creating
a delicate, haunting sound that made the dogs prick their ears. "After
Manon and I discussed this project, my manager took care of everything.
At first he was apprehensive, but I told him since I was going on leave
this was a fabulous way to end my tour. Honestly, Mike, I've traveled
for so long and…"

*There's more than I can handle alone now.* She was so relieved
to know Malcolm was taking care of things when she had to keep one
doctor's appointment after another. He was more than her manager.
Before she met Manon, Malcolm and his wife were her only friends
and had been since she was a teenager. The hordes of admirers and
fanatical opera fans that constantly surrounded her, as well as her
accompanist, makeup artist, and the paparazzi, weren't a good source
of new relationships. And besides, she had always been an ambitious
workaholic.

Vivian realized she was drifting and said briskly, "I have to make
some changes, so I decided to take a break here. Time will tell if it was
the right move." She sipped her juice again. "Exactly how did you end
up owning such a successful café?"

"Martha and Edward helped me turn an out-of-the-way café into
a popular place for the yacht crowd and, later on, the locals from East
Quay." Mike sounded cautious. "Lately, we've attracted a lot of out-of-
towners, thanks to some serious advertising. We couldn't accommodate
a bigger crowd until now. At breakfast and lunch, we have mostly
regulars, and in the evenings all sorts of people come in for a meal and
some coffee."

"Sounds like long days for you."

"Very long days. That's why my morning run is so important. It
gives me a chance to…breathe."

Watching the careful smile that flickered over Mike's features reminded Vivian of glimpsing a startlingly beautiful sunrise, only to watch it disappear as fast as it appeared. Uncertain why a mere smile had such an impact, Vivian struggled for something to say.

"I can imagine that. Most people don't realize what kind of physical effort being an opera singer entails. It's like being a lumberjack."

"A lumberjack?"

"Performing for an entire evening is hard on the body."

"I'm glad I ran into you this morning." Mike gestured toward the dogs, the glass, and the ocean view. "This was great."

"I agree. How old are you, Mike?" The question slipped out before Vivian could stop it. *Damn, where's my tact?*

"Thirty-four." Mike sounded unfazed. "You?"

"I'm fifty-three." Relieved, Vivian liked Mike's quick return of her frank question. "Actually fifty-four in a few months."

"You look a lot younger."

"Thank you, so do you. Age is really just a number. We opera singers aren't like many theater and screen actors. We can still find parts well into our sixties. Makeup helps, but our performance isn't about appearance. It's about the voice."

"You don't need any help in either department," Mike said impulsively.

Embarrassed but pleased, Vivian changed the subject. "I can certainly see why people eat at your cafe. It feels so warm and welcoming. Besides, you're bound to attract all kinds of coffee lovers."

"I know. Our Java lovers are very particular about how we grind and brew their coffee." Mike fiddled with her glass, flustered at the praise. "And being meticulous has paid off. My best investment, not counting Martha and Edward, was our state-of-the-art espresso machine. I stayed up the entire first night staring at it, making cappuccino, café latte, café mocha, and ten other specialties. Edward insists that he found me asleep with my arms around it, but I don't recall that."

"Well, you have a new customer to add to your regulars." Vivian smiled at her sudden commitment, limited though it was. "I love the ambience, and the view is wonderful."

"Thanks. That's the idea. When the sun goes down and the sky's all purple and orange, the marina is a pretty romantic place." Mike made a wry face. "At least if you believe in romance."

"And you don't?" Vivian's voice was gentle.

"No."

"Not ever?"

"I don't actively look for it." Mike shrugged and appeared a little uncomfortable. "I have a business to run."

Vivian recognized her own life all too clearly in that sentiment, and it saddened her. They had loneliness in common, it seemed. She watched Mike rise from her chair with Perry and Mason standing at attention. "You have to get back to work?"

"I'd like to stay longer, but…" She patted the dogs, which rose expectantly. "Now, boys, behave and I'll bring you doggie treats next time, if it's okay with your mom." Her cheeks reddened as she glanced at Vivian. "Damn. I didn't mean to invite myself…"

Wanting to erase Mike's mortification, Vivian placed a hand on her shoulder. "Just pop by anytime. I'll be here most of the time, when I'm not rehearsing."

"Okay, then. See you later!" Mike patted the dogs and stunned Vivian by gently touching her arm, the contact so brief it barely registered. "Have a really good day." Mike ran down the steps toward the beach and jogged at a steady pace along the water's edge.

Vivian touched her own arm, which tingled from Mike's touch. The sky was ablaze, but she resisted the urge to close her eyes. Instead she watched Mike until she disappeared from sight.

# CHAPTER FOUR

Manon sorted through the Sunday paper and tossed everything but the entertainment section on the floor by her bed. Noticing Eryn Goddard's byline, she tried to reconcile the professional-looking woman in the photo with the redheaded force of nature she'd just met. Now she understood why she hadn't recognized her, though she should have at least remembered the name.

Sunday mornings were the only times she indulged in personal luxuries. She'd already filled the tub with hot water, scented with honey oil and bay-leaf bath salts. She read on her way to the bathroom for a long soak, caught up in Eryn's article about Vivian Harding. Pleased by the publicity, Manon was relieved that the piece didn't speculate about Vivian's private life. Eryn had obviously done her homework too. She mentioned how much the opera world admired the singer but didn't just focus on her notoriety. Instead she provided facts about the person, the woman Vivian Harding. Eryn demanded her reader's full attention and some brainpower. Though Manon was neither a writer nor an editor, she took pride in being able to spot talent. And Eryn clearly had it.

Manon placed the newspaper next to the bathroom sink. As she removed her bathrobe, she scrutinized herself with unusually critical eyes. Though her full breasts were a bit out of proportion to her slim figure, as were her long legs, a college friend, Faith Dabrinsky, had once told her, "When you wear those preppie clothes, you hide your wonderful assets. You've got to learn to flaunt them a little…in a respectable way, naturally."

Manon knew she was only half joking. She climbed into the large tub and set the jets to maximum before she sank down into the milky bubbles. Leaning back she let the soothing scent and the massaging water engulf her.

Being head of the Belmont family and Jacques Belmont IV's only direct descendant had its moments, but it also created headaches and heartache. She wondered if her grandfather and father had routinely felt as tired as she did right now and how they had relaxed from the demands their positions placed on them.

She'd been only thirteen when the somber realization had struck that she would take over the family fortunes *and* the obligations that came with it someday. Fortunately, she'd had seventeen years after that to prepare for the legacy before her grandfather died. It had felt natural to take over the foundation, his heart's work. It had never felt like a burden. She loved it and had concentrated on learning everything she could about how to administer the many philanthropic programs. She hadn't expected to find herself at the head of Belmont Industries quite so soon, however.

Rubbing a soapy hand down her arm, massaging her tired muscles, Manon recalled her shock when her father had suffered a massive stroke four years after her grandfather's death and soon passed away. Suddenly she was responsible for running both Belmont Industries and the Belmont Foundation, two independent companies that needed full-time attention.

She couldn't have done it without her highly competent friend Faith, who took over the business side of Belmont Industries and breathed new air into the corporation.

Manon turned off the Jacuzzi's jets and welcomed the silence. As she sank deeper into the water, her chin just above it, she let her hands slide along her body and gently rubbed sore muscles. The image of a redhead with long, rich hair pulled back in an intricate French braid invaded her mind: Eryn Goddard, her new neighbor. Manon sighed and continued to explore her own smooth skin.

Eryn's eyes intrigued her. Shimmering, green, and luminescent, they were unwavering in their intensity. Manon shivered and slid farther under the water, only her face above the surface. Involuntarily she parted her legs, and the hot water flowing against her most sensitive parts made her gasp as if someone else was touching her.

It would be so easy to imagine she was feeling Eryn's caress, but Manon struggled against such fantasy, as she had always done. She could ill afford it now. As a Belmont, she had been raised from birth to be perfect, to behave immaculately. Though *she* saw nothing wrong with being gay, her legacy didn't allow her the luxury of putting her own interests and happiness first. All her life she had worked hard to fulfill her family's expectations, burying her need for personal fulfillment and learning to be satisfied with the rewards of the family business. Though she had found women attractive since she was seventeen, she couldn't act on her feelings. Absolutely not.

Eryn Goddard's face emerged again, and Manon moaned as one hand found an erect nipple and the other moved toward her swelling center. *I shouldn't.* But it was too late to stop; the startling rush of arousal was too strong. Pushing her self-imposed rules aside, she spread her legs and stroked down along her folds. The slickness between them was easy to spread over the aching ridge of nerves at the center. In her mind, she loosened the ribbon holding Eryn's braid, and fragrant wavy hair surrounded them...*Them? Oh, God. Stop it, you fool! Get a grip!*

Furious at herself, Manon rubbed harder, quicker, as if getting the orgasm over and done with would erase Eryn from her mind. With agonizing slowness, she moved toward climax, her clitoris swollen and hard where her fingers pinched it. Images of Eryn's tongue sliding between her fingers to soothe and entice came and went. Manon whimpered and muttered incoherent words, sometimes cursing under her breath. Unsure if she struggled toward, or against, her pending orgasm, Manon finally went rigid, convulsing as wave after wave of lonely pleasure surged through her.

The water sloshed around her, and for a moment it wasn't foamy water at all, but long red locks and the soft skin of a freckled cheek that touched her. Manon cried out, muffled, close to mortified, when her orgasm began to wear off. Silent tears ran down her cheeks and blended with the water, and she had no idea where the tears of sadness ended and the ones of fury began.

Eventually the water became so cool she started to shiver. Her legs unsteady, she rose and took a quick, hot shower. Afterward, she rubbed her skin vigorously with a terry cloth towel, determined to wipe the thought of Eryn Goddard off her skin and out of her mind.

❖

The Sunday brunch crowd occupied almost every table in the Sea Stone Café. Vivian moved between them with calculated ease as she kept her eyes on a vacant table by the far wall. She reached it with a sigh of relief and sat down, adjusting the scarf covering her hair, which she had pulled back into a French twist for the day.

"Vivian," a familiar voice greeted her from behind. Mike showed up at her side. "Perfect timing—I was just thinking about you."

Vivian smiled at the spontaneous comment and promptly saw two red spots appear on Mike's high cheekbones. "I was thinking of you too—and your coffee," Vivian teased, delighted at Mike's reaction. Then it occurred to her that Mike might be making polite conversation with yet another customer, and the possibility erased her smile.

"Of course," Mike countered, "the way to a lady's heart is through caffeine in appropriate doses."

Reassured, Vivian felt her cheeks warm under Mike's gaze. *Me—blushing? Now that's one for the tabloids!* "Well, if you want to stay on my good side," she said, "you can bring me a double espresso latte and a baguette with lettuce and tomatoes...and perhaps a sprinkle of Parmesan."

"My pleasure." Mike smiled, but then she wavered. "Want some company? It's time for my break. Or are you waiting for someone?"

As Mike straightened her back and shoved her hands into her apron pockets, her obvious discomfort piqued Vivian's interest. "I'd love some company, Mike. I'm here by myself."

"Great." An expression of relief flitted through Mike's eyes. "Be right back."

Vivian noticed several other people sitting alone, reading the Sunday paper. She suspected Eryn Goddard's article was featured in the entertainment section and hoped nobody recognized her. In her official role as *prima donna assoluta*, with impeccable makeup and an awe-inspiring hairdo, she made an unforgettable impact on most people. She dressed to enhance her position as one of the most beautiful mezzo-sopranos working. A full spread in *Vanity* had claimed that none of the new talents could compare, despite their youth. *If they saw me now or, worse, early in the morning, they wouldn't argue this so-called fact any longer.* Vivian hid a smile at the mere thought.

Opera reviewers around the world unanimously agreed her voice was at its best these days, when maturity and life had put its mark on her vocal cords and her soul. Vivian knew they were right, but they didn't know many things, which made her worry about the charity event four weeks from now.

A Sunday paper was tucked into the narrow basket beneath each table, but Vivian didn't attempt to pick one up.

"Here we go." Mike placed a tray between them and sat down. "Oh, God, you have no idea how long my feet have screamed at me to sit down." Vivian heard her kick off her shoes under the table. "There, better!" She eyed the tray. "Now, here's your latte and baguette. I spiced it up for you with some new mixed herbs that go really well with tomatoes...Vivian?"

Vivian tore her eyes from Mike's enthusiastic face and regarded the steaming mug of coffee and the large baguette. "It looks delicious. Thank you."

"You're welcome. You seem a bit tired. Is being on your home turf catching up with you?"

Vivian sipped her latte and felt the caffeine hit her system almost instantly. "In a way, yes."

Mike stirred her drink, fished out a dark tea bag, and squeezed it against the inside of the mug with her spoon. Blowing on the tea she looked thoughtfully at Vivian. "Something bothering you? Can I help?"

"Thank you, but I don't think so. As I said, this will be my last performance for quite a while." *Most likely ever.* The thought hurt, and Vivian steeled herself against it, pushing it to the back of her mind. "The media is focusing a lot on my part of the concert...and I guess I'm nervous. I have rehearsals all month, but still..." She shrugged. "I'm probably just overanxious."

"I think it's wonderful." Mike leaned forward and placed her mug back on the table. "Was it your idea?"

"No, it wasn't." Vivian sipped her coffee. "Manon Belmont approached me several months ago, asking if I could fit this event into my schedule. I was booked for another year abroad, but my circumstances changed, so I could agree to Manon's request." Vivian bit into the baguette, managing not to drop the tomato. "I'm not the only one performing. A local concert pianist will be playing, and Madame Verdi's ballet group will dance."

"Madame Verdi! Oh, I remember when my fondest daydream

was to dance. A girl in my class, I think it was second grade, took her classes. I desperately wanted to be a ballerina, but I sprouted into a gangly tomboy faster than you can say 'beanpole.'"

Vivian could easily picture Mike as a child. The tousled black hair, skinny knees beneath denim shorts, and those dark blue eyes studying the world in much the same way Mike was looking at her now, with undivided, but guarded, interest. "So what did you end up doing?"

"Oh, nothing much." Mike's eyes grew impossibly dark. She shrugged and cradled her chin with her palm. "Survived, mostly. I grew up with just my father and had to be responsible for myself early on."

"Sounds familiar. I grew up with both my parents, though. They worked shifts at the cotton mill—long days and sometimes nights. I was home alone a lot."

"You're an only child too?"

"Yes. I remember wishing for siblings. How about you?"

Mike shook her head, her knuckles whitening as her hands clutched the mug. "No, I didn't. Not ever."

Vivian remembered what Mike had told her about knowing someone who drank too much. *Her father perhaps?* She knew better than to pry, especially in a public place. Still, she couldn't help but respond to Mike's obvious distress. Barely missing the tea mug, she placed her hand on Mike's wrist. "Life can be tough on kids."

"Understatement." Mike's voice didn't waver. "Say, can't you discuss your stage fright…or whatever…with Manon Belmont? From what I know, she's a neat lady, really classy, and on TV the two of you looked like good friends. I think everyone in town admires her. Well, perhaps except Reba Ronaldo. She wrote a nasty column a while back in the *New Quay Chronicle,* which she had to apologize for, and *that* must've stung."

"Who on earth is Reba Renaldo, and what did she write?"

"She implied that Manon Belmont goes from one man to the next like wildfire. You know, chews 'em up, spits 'em out. That sort of thing."

"What a terrible thing to say, about anyone. It's nothing but lies. I'm amazed she wasn't fired. I mean, a local paper, which relies on local adverts?"

"Ah, believe it or not, Reba has her fans. When a large number of *them* wrote to the paper, complaining, she and the chief editor finally thought she ought to apologize. On the front page, no less. Only time that woman's made the front page, and she has to eat humble pie."

Mike snickered, a sound Vivian found surprisingly charming. She could easily picture Manon's haughty expression as she read this Reba person's column. She'd certainly seen it many times in the past. "The Belmonts have earned a lot of respect and loyalty in the community."

"Yeah, I guess." Mike grimaced. "They've had their share of bad luck, more than their share. Seems like they've been sort of cursed. I think a lot of people feel bad for Ms. Belmont because of that." Mike's voice was low, almost hollow. "She's the last one. That's got to be awfully lonely. Who could blame her for looking for company?"

"I agree." Vivian wondered why Mike sounded so pained. She leaned her chin into her palm. "I guess I could talk to Manon about my stage fright. On the other hand…"

"What?"

"I don't think it's really stage fright—I've done this too many times for that. However, I suppose I could talk to Manon about this strange uneasiness. It's not like me. She's my friend, but…and perhaps this is my pride speaking here, I don't want the press to get wind of this. You have no idea how the media can blow things out of proportion." Vivian's eyes hardened. "They file everything you say or do and store it for future reference. No matter what, they always get the last word."

"Oh, trust me, I have some idea." Mike made a wry face and twisted her napkin into a ball. "But is the local paper that bad when it comes to the charity event? Surely you thought Eryn Goddard's piece was fair?"

"The Belmont Foundation arranged for the press conference. They need the publicity." Vivian willed her shoulders to relax and shook her head. "Since I'd already agreed to do it, there was no way out. They need to sell every single one of the tickets. And I really don't have an opinion about the *New Quay Chronicle*. If I remember correctly, Ms. Goddard appeared intelligent and pleasant. At least I think it was her, sitting in front. I'm sure she did a good job."

"Haven't you read it yet?" Mike reached for the newspaper. "I glanced at it earlier and think it's actually well written. Granted, I'm more used to bookkeeping and dealing with business management, but it seemed to do you justice."

Vivian felt herself grow cold and shook her head again. "No, I haven't read it."

"Here." Mike unfolded the entertainment section and offered it, but appeared slightly puzzled when Vivian waved it away.

"I'd rather not." Vivian knew she sounded short and smiled weakly. "Why don't you read some of it to me?"

A few seconds ticked by before Mike dropped her gaze toward the article. "All right. No problem." In a low, clear voice, she read the beginning of Eryn's text.

As she took in the words, Vivian began to relax. She liked how Eryn had written the article. The straightforward text wasn't full of the ingratiating adjectives that inundated some of the articles written about her in Europe. More importantly, it was neither disrespectful nor malicious. Instead it focused on Vivian's link to East Quay and her work in general over the years. Eryn had appeared to be confident and friendly. Her questions had indicated that she'd done her homework, but…she was a reporter, and the media always made Vivian feel on guard.

"She's done a good job," Vivian said with a quiet sigh of relief when Mike stopped. "Thank you for reading it to me. I…I haven't subscribed to the *Chronicle* yet."

"My pleasure." Mike folded the paper and put it back into the basket. "Got to get back to work."

"Can you bring me the check? I need to go walk the dogs."

"Do you think you'll be back, Vivian?" Mike asked tentatively.

Mystified, Vivian nodded. "Yes, of course. Why do you ask?"

"If you leave your name, address, and phone number on a slip by the cash register, you can keep a running tab. We do that for our regulars."

To Vivian's surprise, a faint blush crept up Mike's neck and colored her cheeks.

"That sounds perfect. You know where I live, after all." She smiled and rose from her chair. "And don't forget to visit. You did promise."

After a brief silence Mike grinned and said, "I did, didn't I? Well then, since I never break my promises, I'll come by later in the week and check on your stage fright."

Not bothering to notice if any of the patrons were watching, Vivian slid her hand up along Mike's bare upper arm. "Good. See you soon, *cara*."

❖

"We'll be off then, Michaela," Martha said just after closing time at ten, tucking her hand under her husband's arm. "See you tomorrow morning."

"Night. Have a good one." Mike walked them to the door and locked it after them, waving through the window before returning to the counter. She emptied the cash register, counted the money, and added up the credit card slips. As she went through her normal routine, part of her mind was elsewhere.

She hadn't been able to stop thinking about Vivian all day. She'd smiled at her customers and provided the best service possible, all the while mulling over her earlier conversation with Vivian. Vivian fascinated her. She was a world-famous celebrity, and yet she was kind and warm and approachable. She was obviously wealthy, but she didn't seem bothered that she and Mike came from different sides of the track. She had offered friendship, with no strings attached, and Mike felt her defenses were weakening, whether she liked it or not.

As she sorted the paperwork, she returned to her thoughts of Vivian and her heart sped up.

She'd watched Vivian during lunch, memorizing her image for future reference. With her hair pulled back and no makeup, Vivian looked fresh and naturally beautiful. She'd seemed intently focused on Mike, her eyes sometimes clouded with emotions Mike couldn't read. Unaccustomed to such exclusive attention from anyone, Mike still felt the weight of her gaze. And to think she was afraid of faltering during her first performance ever in her hometown. Her, with all her talent and experience.

Mike gave a short bark of a laugh. Until a decade ago, failure had been her specialty. She would have to tell Vivian how the Belmont Foundation had helped her turn her own life around. It wasn't something she talked of easily, but something in the way Vivian listened to her made her want to. With that thought in mind, Mike placed the money in the safe and switched off the lights.

Edward jokingly called her basement apartment "Mike's bunker," which wasn't far from the truth. The stairs took her down to a narrow hallway, which in turn led into a large room where she spent her precious little free time.

The room boasted a twin bed, an entertainment center holding her wide-screen television and stereo, and a leather couch with a driftwood coffee table. In the far corner stood a small, elevated stage where her prized possession reigned in solitude. She'd dreamed of owning a drum set ever since she'd played in high school. Being able to buy the latest state-of-the-art Yamaha digital drums had healed yet another of her wounds.

Too tired to play that evening, Mike went into the bathroom and showered quickly. The hot water soothed the shoulder that always ached after carrying trays all day. After drying slowly, she dropped the towel to the floor.

Unusually aware of her own nakedness, Mike wondered for the briefest of moments if Vivian could ever find her attractive. Hell, she didn't even know if Vivian was into women. She glanced over at the stack of newspapers that she'd bought earlier that day in hopes of finding out more about her new friend. She couldn't remember reading anything about Vivian's private affairs. There was no mention that Vivian had ever married.

Mike shuddered from the cool air against her damp skin as she pulled on a pair of gray flannel shorts and a tank top. After quickly brushing her teeth, she climbed into bed, grateful to tug up the covers for warmth. She grabbed one of the many pillows and buried her face in the crisp cotton fabric. Out of long habit, she began to hum an old lullaby. "Twinkle, twinkle little star, how I wonder where you are..." It was one of the few things that always helped settle her.

Unprepared for the image of Vivian that appeared behind her closed eyelids, Mike stopped humming and drew a deep breath, uncertain what to think. The memory of how Vivian had focused on her made her heart race. She hugged the pillow to her chest and let Vivian's image fill her mind as sleep overcame her.

## CHAPTER FIVE

G ood morning, Ms. Belmont," her assistant, a blond, thin man with a receding hairline, said. "The press conference went well."

"Glad you approve, Dennis," Manon said absently and put her briefcase down next to her computer. With dark cherry hardwood floors and an enormous rolltop desk from the early 1900s, her office held a lot of Belmont history. It was located in a building constructed in 1796 and protected for many years by the National Historical Registry.

Manon sat down behind her desk and welcomed the familiar surge of comfort. This was home, so much more so than her penthouse condo. Here she did what she was meant to do and interacted with the people who helped her make it happen. Her staff had been with her a long time, a couple of them having even worked for her grandfather. They were as loyal as family members and nearly as dedicated to the foundation as she was.

"Are those my messages?" Manon pointed at Dennis's hand.

"Yes. They require your personal attention."

"Thanks. Coffee?"

"I'll make some."

As Dennis left the room Manon booted her computer and glanced through her phone messages, two of which were from the woman coordinating the charity event. Concerned, Manon dialed the phone number at the bottom of the notes. Someone answered after only one ring. "Belmont Foundation. Kay Masters."

"Kay, Manon here. I got your messages. What's the problem?"

"Our leading lady."

"Vivian?" Manon frowned. "What's wrong?"

"I can't put my finger on it—but something seems off and it's making me nervous."

Manon knew how Kay could get when every single detail wasn't ironed out. "All right. Can you at least give me a hint?" *Please, not yet, Vivian. Hold on.*

"I don't know. It's how she's dealing with the staff at the concert hall. I know she's *the* prima donna whatever, but she's always had a reputation for treating her crew properly."

"She's mistreating the stagehands?"

"Heavens no! But she's acting…weird. She doesn't seem to want to be around anyone—or have anyone near her. I've even seen her literally stumble backward when any of the crew comes near. If I didn't know any better, I'd say she's paranoid."

"Sounds odd. Want me to drop by later? I've got some time just before lunch." She checked her watch. The concert hall was just two blocks down the street. "If rehearsals have started by then."

"Yes, that'd be a good idea. Maybe she needs to talk to you. You know, friend to friend."

"Maybe so," Manon said noncommittally before she hung up.

She logged into her e-mail and browsed through the urgent messages, responding to the most critical ones and then starting on the others.

She'd been at it for several hours when the intercom buzzed. "Yes, Dennis?"

"A Ms. Goddard from the *New Quay Chronicle* on line one. Do you want it or should I take a message?"

Manon flinched. The call was unexpected and, considering last night's guilty pleasure, somewhat disturbing. "Thank you. I'll take it." Manon switched lines. "Ms. Goddard…Eryn. Manon Belmont here."

"Ms. Belmont. Am I interrupting anything important?"

"Call me Manon, please. And no. I'm just about finished." Manon rolled a fountain pen between her fingers, her mouth dry. "What can I do for you?"

"Since you arranged the press conference for Ms. Harding, I'm curious what you think of my article."

Eryn sounded enthusiastic but cautious. She also sounded as if Manon's opinion mattered.

"I thought you did a very good job. The townspeople will know a lot more about our most famous performer." Manon fiddled with the up and down arrows on the laptop keyboard. "So, is there—"

"I was wondering—I have to go to a photo shoot near your office this afternoon. Are you free for lunch?"

Manon glanced at the calendar sitting next to her computer, surprised by Eryn's directness. *Say no to her!* "Yes, I think so. Let me check." Her calendar was clear. *Why didn't I just say no?*

"Great! How about meeting me at the Lobster House, on the corner of your block?"

"Would it be on or off the record?"

"Neither. Just lunch between neighbors. I just want to try the chowder. Nothing to do with work and no inquisitive questions, I promise."

"Their chowder is superior." Her cheeks warming, Manon relented. I can be there at 12:30. Should I ask my assistant to reserve a table?" She heard papers being shuffled.

"Perfect. See you there!"

Eryn hung up before Manon had a chance to say good-bye. Manon slowly put the receiver down and considered the unexpected invitation. Despite her reservations, she was looking forward to seeing her persistent, and very attractive, neighbor again.

Eryn turned to her computer and tucked another pencil into her hair, just where the loose braid began. She was having lunch with Manon Belmont! Her boldness didn't surprise her—she was normally spontaneous—but she *had* been pretty daring.

She'd been at her desk since seven o'clock, working on her current assignment. The school board misappropriation of funds appeared to reach as high as the principal himself. And the whistle blower who had made the situation public was none other than Manon Belmont.

Manon was definitely mysterious and exciting, even if her less than positive attitude toward the press still pushed Eryn's buttons. She thought of all the hours she spent doing her job in a way she could be proud of, and her ire flared again.

She Googled the Belmont Foundation in search of more info

about the family. She scrolled down one page after another, certain that there was more to Manon Belmont than the woman Manon allowed the world to see.

The first several hits showed clippings from different newspapers' society columns. It didn't take her long to conclude that Manon had never married and attended functions with a different man on her arm each time.

Looking regal, Manon posed for photos at charity events, elegantly turned out in designer dresses and expensive jewelry. The men by her side beamed at the cameras more than Manon did, and Eryn wondered if she was imagining it or if the measured smile on Manon's lips was just for show.

Her interest piqued, Eryn moved on to the archives of both the *New Quay Chronicle* and the *New York Times*. It didn't take her long to assemble a rough timeline of events in Manon's early life, and the resentment she'd harbored for her new neighbor's standoffish approach evaporated. Eryn squeezed the mouse hard as she read about Manon's twin being killed when they were thirteen.

Because the articles became fewer, Eryn deduced that the Belmonts withdrew from the spotlight after the tragedy. From what she could determine, Eryn pieced together that Manon grew up living with her father, who never remarried after his wife left him, and her grandparents. She graduated from Harvard with a double major in social science and business management, which suggested to Eryn that Manon had always been as driven and goal oriented as she seemed now.

"Hey, kid." Her boss's harsh voice broke Eryn's concentration. "How much more do you need to print the school board scandal story?"

"Hello, Harold." Eryn sighed, irritated by his favorite nickname for her. "*Kid.*" *Presumptuous asshole.* "It won't take me long. I just have to interview a few more people to verify where the money actually went. So far, all we know is that it didn't end up where it was supposed to and that it may cost some teachers their jobs."

"Write the story ASAP. I've got some other assignments after that, kid. There's the horse show, and the Maxim Circus is coming to town."

"I need more time." Eryn frowned and tossed her braid back over her shoulder. "We can't print what we have now or jump to conclusions about who's culpable. Everyone respects these people. Besides wanting to get at the truth, I don't want to have someone suing us for slander. Someone's got their hand in the till, but for now—"

"As I said, get it done ASAP. Horses and clowns await your review."

Eryn bit back an acerbic comment. *Oh, joy. Just the reason I became a reporter. I'm sure the hot stories in East Quay will get me the freakin' Pulitzer Prize.* "I'll get the story for you, Harold. Don't worry."

She clenched her teeth. She'd worked at the *New Quay Chronicle* since graduation. The excellent articles she'd produced on subjects ranging from high school reunions to a series of local bank robberies had prompted several larger newspapers and news stations to offer her a job. But she declined them all because she wanted to stay in East Quay. Frank, her mentor and the previous editor-in-chief, had lived and worked here. Unfortunately, Frank had retired early due to health problems and Harold, who lacked both skill and tact, took over.

On days like today, when she wanted to choke her overbearing boss, she regretted her decision. The general consensus at the news desk was that Harold Mills was a twenty-four-karat bastard.

"I'll hold you to it, kid." Harold stalked toward his office and glared at his assistant, who cowered behind her computer.

Eryn checked her watch. Time for the photo shoot uptown. She looked forward to meeting Manon in a more relaxed environment. As she leaned down to grab her purse, she was startled when three pencils dislodged from her hair and fell to the floor.

❖

The resonant voice of the woman standing center stage surpassed even the powerful sound of the orchestra. Her hair glowed in the light as the sound reverberated, weaving its magic.

As Vivian reached new heights and incredibly rich tones, Manon stood at the back, listening intently to a new, special quality. Not only had Manon attended a multitude of Vivian's performances, but she also owned most of her recordings. She had listened to this particular aria many times, and when the music reached its crescendo, Vivian's voice rose with it, both chasing and leading it. When the aria "Printemps qui commence" from *Samson et Delilah* ended with only a whisper, Manon held her breath and furtively wiped away tears from her eyelashes. *If she sings like that at the charity concert, she'll go out with a bang. Oh, God, Vivian...*

She watched a stagehand approach Vivian and frowned when the singer backed away from him as he gestured toward where Manon stood in the aisle. Vivian then nodded briefly and edged toward the steps leading down from the stage, descending them slowly.

Now she walked toward Manon with longer, more confident strides and let her hands slide along the backrests of the chairs closest to the aisle. "Manon," she exclaimed and extended a hand. She wore a flowing blue caftan over black slacks, black pearls glimmering around her neck and dangling from her earlobes. An ebony comb secured her hair in an intricate twist.

"I thought I'd stop by and enjoy some of your performance, Vivian." Pretty sure the prima-donna act was intended for the benefit of the stagehands and the rest of the staff, she took Vivian's hand. Manon admired her poise and larger-than-life energy. "We're honored to have you here, you know that. Is everything okay?"

"Everything's perfect." Vivian gave a dazzling smile. "I'm very impressed with the musicians. They would be welcome in any concert hall in Europe."

"I'm glad you think so. We're proud of our orchestra. I've come to see if you've decided on a final program yet. Is singing four arias in a row too much for you?" Manon added the last question in a low voice, out of earshot.

Vivian shook her head slowly. "I sing three or four times that during an opera, Manon. Four arias is nothing. Not even now."

The sadness in Vivian's voice made Manon's heart ache. She seemed confident enough, but Manon wondered if she wasn't asking too much of herself—under the circumstances. She tried not to sound too concerned. "I realize that, but I also know you haven't had much time to rehearse, and you've also come straight from a strenuous tour. The rehearsals must be wearing. You seem nervous, to tell the truth. Feeling a little jumpy around people?"

"No, no, I'm fine. Still a bit jet-lagged, I suppose." Vivian spoke quickly, too hasty for her words to ring quite true. "Guess that kind of thing gets worse with age."

Manon wondered why Vivian was downplaying the subject. They were good friends, if not extremely close, since they were both busy women with demanding careers. Still, the fact that Vivian seemed to be stalling worried her. *Why do I get the feeling that I can't probe further?* "You sure?"

"Positive. I'll be fine once I adjust." Vivian smiled brightly. "You know us old divas. We're used to performing more or less under any circumstances. It'll take more than a little jet lag to stop this concert. Trust me."

"You know best, I'm sure." Manon suspected that if she pushed, Vivian would only recoil further behind her onstage persona. "All right. I won't keep you any longer. Just so you know you can talk to me if you need anything. Anything." Manon reached for her black leather briefcase.

"Thank you," Vivian said. "I'll keep that in mind."

Not convinced, Manon said good-bye but remained standing in the aisle while Vivian slowly made her way back to the stage, then stopped and hesitated before she resumed her position by the microphone.

While exiting the building Manon pulled her cell phone from her jacket pocket. "Kay? Manon here. I just visited the concert hall and spoke with Ms. Harding."

"And?"

"I've just heard her, and if she sings like that at the benefit, and I don't see why she shouldn't, we'll be more than fine."

"I'd hoped I was imagining things."

"Just keep an eye out and get back to me…once a week from now on, unless there's something urgent, all right?"

"Fine. We'll keep our fingers crossed."

Manon walked to her car, where Ben opened the door to the backseat. "Where to, ma'am?"

"Back to the office." She checked her watch and frowned. "No, make that Dante's, on the corner of Hammers and Lloyd, please. I'll be a while, so you can take your break then."

"Very good, ma'am."

Manon sighed, fondly exasperated by Ben's refusal to relinquish the manners that were more fitting for her father's day. But she couldn't break him of the habit.

She leaned against the leather backrest and thought about the woman she was about to meet. Still uncertain why Eryn Goddard wanted to join her for lunch, and chastising herself for being overly suspicious, Manon decided to keep an open mind and a watchful eye.

## CHAPTER SIX

Eryn wasn't surprised to find Manon seated at the best table in the room. As Eryn approached Manon, who clearly studied her every step, she felt oddly self-conscious, as if she was destined to trip on the carpet any second and make a fool of herself. Manon, on the other hand, in a black business suit, crisp white cotton blouse, and her deceptively simple jewelry, projected a professional, self-assured image of a woman who could handle anything. Not pleased with her rare lack of confidence, Eryn lengthened her stride and smiled self-assuredly.

"Hi. How late am I?" Eryn pulled her long braid free from the shoulder strap of her purse. "There was a lot of traffic."

"Don't worry about it. I just got here." Manon looked at her over the menu and pointed at the tall glasses. "Is mineral water okay?"

"Thanks." Eryn grabbed the glass and drank thirstily. She felt heat creep up her cheeks as she put the almost-empty glass back on the white tablecloth. "Yes, I know. Don't tell me. No manners."

"You drink when you're thirsty. Should I mind?" Manon raised her eyebrows while sipping her own water.

Eryn resisted the urge to smooth her corduroy jacket. It was a few years old and supposed to look wrinkly, but she was afraid she looked sloppy compared to the vision of perfection across the table. She wondered if there was anything she could say or do to keep Manon smiling forever. Eryn's chest heaved as she drew a deep breath and grabbed the menu to quickly find her favorite dish. She thought it best to go with what she knew. "I'll have clam chowder. And iced tea. I have a busy afternoon."

To Eryn's surprise, Manon ordered the same. "Seems our tastes are similar," Manon acknowledged with a faint smile before she continued. "You know, I don't remember seeing you in the apartment building before now. Your aunt didn't appear to have many visitors, though I do remember someone on a motorcycle visiting her once or twice a week."

"That was me." Eryn laughed. "I normally ride my Yamaha Wildstar, weather permitting. And Amanda was my mother's aunt. My great-aunt. My mother…just didn't have time to visit her." Eryn heard how critical she sounded and hastily added, "Mother has a lot of commitments. She volunteers for our church several times a week… and…I was brought up Baptist. It made things kind of hard further down the line."

"I'm sorry for your loss," Manon said quietly, suddenly subdued. "I didn't mean to sound insensitive."

"That's all right. Amanda's been gone six months now, and I'm coming to terms with her death. In fact, living in her apartment, surrounded by her things, helps. All I had to do was paint the living room and the bedroom, and other than that, the place is just like when she lived there." Eryn wanted to tell Manon more, to share, since she didn't like secrets. *Secrets backfire.* She looked up at Manon. "She accepted me as I was, with all my faults and fears."

"I'm glad. She was a nice lady. We visited some when we had meetings regarding the house. She was chairman for several years."

Eryn thought fondly of her low-key great-aunt, who could turn quickly into a frightening disciplinarian when Eryn was little. Amanda Ritter had been patient up to a point, though Eryn and her two younger sisters had tested her limits several times. *Still, it was Amanda who took me in when Mother began her ridiculous ultimatums.* Eryn suppressed another shudder. She didn't want to explore the subject of her mother.

"I finally realized that I'd read more of your articles in the *Chronicle,*" Manon said and pulled Eryn out of her reverie. "When I saw your byline, it dawned on me that you cover most of our local news. I can be absent-minded sometimes."

"Or maybe it's the picture of me in the byline that shows me as a seasick person who's just lost a tall-ship race."

"No, no." Manon laughed. "You look fine. Perhaps a tad more"—

she raised her hands in a helpless gesture that Eryn found both endearing and sexy—"neat?"

"A tad?" Eryn snorted. "I think I had glue in my hair spray that day. The photographer demanded that I look respectable, 'not like a wild-looking mermaid.'"

"So far I haven't seen you look anything but quite presentable." Manon relaxed visibly, her hands loosely folded together on the table.

"I appreciate that. I do try." Eryn winked and enjoyed seeing Manon's cheek's color a faint pink.

"Your piece on the benefit was excellent. Surely that's what matters," Manon said, and sounded sincere.

"Thanks. I worked hard on that piece, especially since I just had one day. The press conference was really a breath of fresh air. Interesting things don't happen very often in East Quay. I wonder if Ms. Harding realizes what a legend she is, not only in this town but worldwide."

"I believe she does, to a degree. She has her fair share of paparazzi. Actually, I saw her just now, during rehearsals, and I'm glad she insisted on pretty strict security, because the stairs leading up to the concert hall were filled with fans and reporters. I had to use the side entrance."

"The price of fame," Eryn mused. "Some of my less tactful colleagues can be a pain, but I suppose there's a story there…and anything regarding Vivian Harding is good copy. How did rehearsals go? Will she have a program for us soon?"

"Yes, she should. She was excellent. Of course, she's so flamboyant. That, plus her great stage presence, helps make her so popular."

"Yes, she makes opera appealing—though I admit it's not the first CD I'd buy." Eryn stirred her cooling chowder. "I play the guitar, so I listen to a lot of instrumental stuff. You know, like Clapton, Malmsteen, and Morse."

"Eric Clapton I know," Manon admitted. "The other two, well…"

"Guitar gods. But the goddesses are my thing. Bonnie Raitt and Juliana Hatfield do so much more for me."

"Never heard of either of them." Manon blinked, seeming totally out of her element. "They play the guitar?"

"Yes. Mean, howling electric guitars." Manon was obviously trying to show interest, which Eryn appreciated.

"What do you like to play?"

"I have an old black Fender Stratocaster. I saw one in the window of Harmony Instruments when I was fifteen, and it took me three years of landscaping to save up for it. I own a vintage Gibson too, but I love my Stratocaster. Probably because I saved so long for it."

"Couldn't your parents have chipped in at least half?" Manon had finished her meal and was now leaning her chin in the palm of one hand, picking at the tablecloth with the other.

"I suppose. But they didn't." *But Mom made sure they supported Kelly's ballet classes, even if she cut half of them. And they bribed Sandy to do her homework all through high school.*

Manon studied her in silence. "You were brave to follow your dream and buy the guitar on your own."

"That's not how my mom would've put it," Eryn muttered. *She wouldn't let me practice in the house and said it was just another way of showing my "unfortunate disposition."*

"But you kept your guitar."

"Yes." Eryn shrugged. "What I wouldn't give for a cup of Mike's coffee right now."

"Who's Mike?" Manon carefully placed her spoon in her empty bowl.

"Michaela Stone. She owns the Sea Stone Café, in the old marina. Haven't you been there? Mike's café latte is the best I've ever tasted."

"She a friend of yours?" Manon smiled and leaned forward on her elbows.

"We've known each other for a quite a while. Mike's very private and doesn't exactly invite people to share her life story, but she's happy to serve them the best coffee imaginable. I got to know her through a story I did about enterprising young women when I was new at the *Chronicle*. She stood out because she's so driven and street smart. And now her business is booming."

"Since I'm a coffee addict, it's odd I haven't heard of her place. Especially since we moor the family yacht there during the season."

"It's on the waterfront, near the pier. Mike's done a great job restoring it. It took her at least a year, since she did most of it with her own two hands."

"Michaela Stone. It rings a bell—"

"I can introduce you. She's succeeded where most people wouldn't stand a chance. I think you'd appreciate her."

"She sounds quite remarkable."

"Want to get together at the café tomorrow after work?" Eryn held her breath, unable to believe what she'd just asked. "I'd like to see you again. Like this. In private." *Shut up, Goddard. You're making a fool of yourself.*

Manon slowly removed the napkin from her lap with measured movements and placed it next to the bowl. She nodded toward their waiter and then focused on Eryn, a guarded expression in her dark green eyes. "So you think I'd like to meet this Mike Stone?"

*That's an elegant way of answering a question with another question, Belmont.* "I thought you might. You did say you love good java. Unless you're busy."

Manon didn't show any emotion, though Eryn could practically hear the wheels turning as she considered the invitation. The muted light picked up the highlights in her shiny hair, making it shimmer. Eryn loved trying to decipher her enigmatic expressions.

"You said earlier you work long hours." Manon's eyes were impenetrable beneath her thick lashes. "Do *you* have time?"

"Sure," Eryn answered readily, never one to dodge a direct question. "I'm working late tonight, but tomorrow I get off around six. I can be there in less than ten minutes." She grinned, as much from nerves as from the possibility of seeing Manon again. "I'll be the one in black leather."

"I beg your pardon?"

"Motorcycle outfit."

"Oh." A smile spread over Manon's features. "I see. Well, I'll be there. The old marina. Give me a call if something comes up, and I'll do the same, all right?"

"Sure." *Our plans, eh?* Eryn's breath caught as Manon's smile seemed to illuminate the entire room, pulling her in. With trembling fingers she reached into her purse for a business card and a pen. She scribbled down barely legible numbers. "Here's my cell number and my new home number."

"Thank you." Manon glanced at it before putting it into her briefcase.

When the waiter showed up and handed Manon the check, Eryn shook her head, a credit card already in her hand. "This one's on me."

Manon hesitated only a second before handing the leather folder across the table. "Thank you. Lunch was delicious."

Eryn was pleased that Manon didn't argue. Their financial

circumstances didn't compare, but in all fairness, she had asked Manon to lunch.

Out on the sidewalk, Manon stopped and turned to Eryn. "Can I give you a ride?" She motioned toward the limousine parked nearby.

"No, I'm fine. I'm off to a photo shoot just around the corner. Thanks anyway."

Manon squeezed Eryn's hand firmly. "See you tomorrow."

"Tomorrow," Eryn repeated. Her heart fluttered, and she recognized the weakness in her knees for what it meant. She was attracted to Manon Belmont.

❖

Something cold and wet nudged Vivian's cheek. Drowsy, she fumbled as she ruffled soft dog ears. "Hello, you. Good boy. Where's your brother?" she whispered. Squinting, she made out Mason's shape, but recognized him from the way he whimpered. He sat down and wagged his tail, thumping it on the hardwood floor. "Perry's sleeping, as usual?"

As Vivian started to get up, a sudden, yet familiar, pain stabbed the back of her eyes. She blinked against the light filtering through the half-closed shades but saw only unrecognizable shifting patterns. Reaching for her anesthetic eyedrops, she accidentally knocked the bottle off the bedside table.

"Blasted thing," she murmured, and sat up. "Mason, move. I have to…" She jerked the cord that pulled the blinds back completely and let the stinging sunlight in; tears began to stream down her cheeks. When she shifted carefully and tried to see where the small bottle had gone, the burning pain behind her eyeballs made her bite her lip to stifle a moan.

The phone rang, making her flinch. As she felt around for the receiver, she sent the sunglasses lying next to it to the floor with a clatter.

"Hello?"

"Vivian, this is Mike—"

"Mike. I really can't talk now. I have to…" She gave a muted moan. "I'm in the middle of something. Can I call you back?" *I sound like a perfect wimp!*

"What's wrong? You sound terrible."

"It's just…I need to use my medication and managed to knock it over." Vivian knew the pain was evident in her voice despite her best efforts to remain calm. She slid down on the floor next to the bed and felt around with her free hand. "*Merde,* I can't find it!"

"Don't worry. The lunch crowd's gone and I'll come right over. I'll be right there." With a distinct click Mike hung up.

As Vivian held her hands over her eyes and tried to block the painful light, Mason whimpered. Then Perry loped into the bedroom and yelped. He licked her cheek and sat down next to her.

"Oh, boys." She sighed. "I'm such a klutz. Where the hell is the stupid bottle?" She felt around with one hand. "Surely it didn't roll very far. Maybe it's under the bed." She bent down to half crawl under the bed, but lowering her head only made the pain worse. Cursing under her breath, Vivian sat back up and leaned against the side of the bed. The floor was cold and she began to shiver.

She tugged at the covers behind her and, with Mason's boisterous aid, pulled them down to wrap around her. She felt utterly vulnerable and silly where she sat, with her head tilted back, cheeks cold from her drying tears. "Mike said she was coming. She can help me look for the stupid bottle, isn't that right, boys?"

The dogs woofed in response, making Vivian feel marginally comforted as she waited for Mike.

It seemed like forever, but Mike arrived at the beach house in only eleven minutes. Gasping for air, she banged on the door. When nobody answered, she ran to the back of the house and tried again at the glass doors she figured led into the master bedroom. "Vivian?" She listened for a response through the loud barking inside.

"The door's locked and I can't move yet," a barely recognizable voice finally called. "There's a spare key…under the rocks to the left of the front door."

"Okay, I hear you." Mike rushed back around front and dug under a display of decorative rocks and plants. Eventually finding a blue key, she grabbed it and opened the door. One of the dogs, she thought it was Perry, greeted her with a wagging tail.

"Vivian?"

"In here." The overwrought voice led her to a disheveled bedroom. Vivian sat on the floor, huddled under some bedcovers.

"Are you hurt?" Mike said anxiously.

"No. I just…I just need my medication."

"First of all, let's get you off the floor. Here we go." Mike slid her arms around Vivian to help her up. When she felt Vivian tremble she pulled her close and stroked her back. "Here. Into bed now."

Once Vivian was comfortably settled against the pillows, Mike took in the pained expression on her face with alarm. Vivian's eyes were pressed shut and her cheeks tear stained. "Tell me what's going on. What do you need?"

"My medication is somewhere on the floor…but I can't find it," Vivian gasped, obviously trying to stay calm. "Maybe under the bed."

Mike knelt and looked underneath but couldn't see anything. Putting one cheek on the floor and peeking under the bedside table, she spotted a small white item. She sat up and pressed her shoulder against the sturdy table, moving it just enough to be able to reach the bottle. She handed it to Vivian. "You couldn't have reached it on your own. Your eyes are blurry, aren't they?"

"Yes," Vivian whispered. Her hands trembled as she gave the bottle back to Mike. "Can you help me? Normally I can do this on my own, but I'm in rather a lot of pain—"

"Of course." Mike unscrewed the top of the bottle and found an eyedropper. "How many drops?"

"Two in each eye." Vivian's voice was barely audible.

Mike leaned over Vivian. "Try to look up."

Vivian opened her eyes slowly, clearly wincing when the light and air hit her cornea. Quickly but carefully, Mike took the eyedropper and administered two drops in each eye. "Okay. You can shut your eyes again, I think."

After Mike sealed the bottle and placed it on the nightstand, she remained nearer than necessary, telling herself it was because Vivian was even paler now. Her long hair, usually so neatly contained in a twist, lay tangled around her shoulders, reaching almost below her breasts. "Better?"

"In a minute or two." Vivian sighed. "I want to rub my eyes, but that's strictly forbidden."

Mike thought she saw Vivian shiver. "Are you still cold?"

When Vivian nodded, Mike reached for a white comforter lying on the foot of the bed and wrapped it around her. "There you go."

"Oh, God, that feels a lot better." Vivian sighed again, her eyes still closed. "I guess I don't have to tell you that today is a particularly bad day."

"I can see that for myself."

"I left rehearsals early. Right after Manon Belmont paid a visit. I hate canceling rehearsals but I just couldn't go on." The dismay was obvious in Vivian's voice. A deep blue cashmere sweater hugged her above black slacks.

"What's wrong, Vivian? It's something with your eyes, right?"

"Yes. I won't go into any boring details, but I'm pretty dependent on my medication. When the eyedrops start to work, I'll have to take a battery of pills. Then I'm fine. I have to go back within the hour because I have to rehearse with a children's choir this afternoon." She opened her eyes slowly and blinked a few times before focusing on Mike. "Good Lord, you must have a million things to take care of at the café. And here you are looking after me. You should go back."

"Don't even think about it. I asked Martha and Edward to hold down the fort. I'll help them later." Mike hesitated, but couldn't resist pushing the hair back from Vivian's forehead. "Are you sure you're okay? You look exhausted."

Vivian sat up straighter and smiled with obvious effort. "I'll be fine."

Taking in Vivian's high cheekbones, her full lips, and the way her sweater clung to her form, Mike realized that Vivian Harding was probably the most beautiful woman she had ever seen. Something forbidden, at least for her, constricted her throat and made it difficult to swallow.

Shaken, Mike recoiled. Her mind whirled in response to her body's red alert.

*It's the way she looks. Fragile and helpless right now. I can't forget that these things tend to change, and fast. The fragile become the furious.* As she rose she willed herself not to reveal her apprehension.

"Can I do anything else, Vivian? Make you some coffee or a snack?" She was backtracking while she spoke, eventually standing in the doorway, and felt her cheeks burn as Vivian shook her head.

"No, thank you, *cara*."

The term of endearment hung between them, testing the last straw of Mike's resolve. She took two more quick steps backward. "All right. I'll be off, then. See you at the café later today? We serve great pies for the after-work crowd." Mike knew she was babbling. She wanted to see Vivian later, but in a more…secure setting. This gorgeous woman's bedroom wasn't a safe place.

When Vivian swung her legs over the edge of the bed and stood up, slightly wobbly, Mike resisted the urge to rush to her side.

"I'll be there after rehearsal. Around five thirty or six." Walking up to Mike, Vivian smiled. "I can't thank you enough. May I impose on you by asking you to promise me something?"

Mike nodded, already guessing. "You want me to keep your eye problems a secret."

"Mind reader. That's exactly it. I won't be able to hide anything much longer, but for now, before the concert, I need to keep my condition confidential. Thank you for understanding."

Mike clasped her restless hands behind her back, though all she really wanted was to hug Vivian. *I'm never this mushy. What's the matter with me?* "I never gossip," she said, knowing she sounded short.

"Somehow I'm not surprised to hear that."

"I'll let myself out." As Mike walked toward the door, a cold nose against the back of her knee made her jump. "Hey, Perry, or Mason, cut it out." She smiled as the two dogs followed her to the door. "See you later, guys. Keep an eye on her, okay?"

The low woofs sounded enthusiastic but did little to alleviate Mike's concern.

## Chapter Seven

Manon parked her British racing green Lotus Elite at the far end of the nearly full parking lot.

Donning her sunglasses, she glanced around the marina at the people readying their boats for winter. She walked to the pier and saw an unpainted wooden building, its cast-iron sign swinging in the breeze. "Sea Stone Café," Manon murmured, half smiling at her old habit of talking to herself. "Appropriate."

"Manon!" Eryn's eager, slightly out-of-breath voice made Manon whirl. Dressed in black leather, the outfit hugging every curve, Eryn approached in long, energetic strides, her braid, deep red in the setting sun, swinging behind her. She carried a red helmet under her arm, and the strap across her chest led down to her by now trademark leather bag.

"I saw you drive up. What a car!" She grinned. "You travel in style, Belmont."

Manon returned the infectious smile. "I'm a sports-car aficionado."

"Me too, but I still drive an old Volvo when it's too cold to ride the Yamaha." Eryn scowled.

"Nothing wrong with that."

"Only if the Volvo's a 1982 station wagon."

"Oh, a vintage car."

"Try a dying car." Eryn sighed. "I doubt it'll last another winter." Peeking through the café windows, she waved for Manon to follow. "The place is packed. I was afraid of that, so I called ahead. Let's see if Mike managed to save us a table."

Inside, Manon was struck by the warm ambience. Traditional red-and-white plaid tablecloths covered rustic tables, and a roaring fire cast a cozy glow, creating patterns on the dark paneled walls. A bar outlined the entire length of the inner wall, and the counter shone.

"Eryn, good to see you." A dark-haired woman appeared, carrying a tray of sparkling glasses. "It's been too long. How are you doing?"

"Fine, thanks. This is my friend and neighbor, Manon. Manon, this is the owner, Michaela, or Mike."

"Nice to meet you, Manon." Mike put the tray down on the counter, wiped her hands on a towel hanging from her black apron, and smiled cautiously. "Your table's over there." Mike pointed toward the corner where two walls of windows met. "It's got a great view of the marina."

"Mike. It's a pleasure." As they shook hands, Manon began to realize where she'd encountered Mike Stone, but she merely said, "Thank you for saving us a table."

"Awesome." Eryn grinned. "Thanks for the VIP treatment."

"Don't mention it." Mike's dark eyes lit up. "Come with me."

Mike led them among the tables, and Manon noticed that she moved with the grace and control of an athlete. Though she attracted the attention of more than a few men, she didn't even glance in their direction.

When they reached the corner table, Mike removed the Reserved sign and pulled out the chairs. "There you go, ladies. What can I get you to drink?"

"Since I've heard great things about your coffee, I'll have a latte, please." Manon felt her stomach growl and reached for a menu.

"Same here." Eryn opened one as well.

"Two lattes, then. Take your time. I'll be right back."

Manon watched Mike hurry away. "Nice woman, and rather different." She turned her attention back to Eryn.

"Yes. She stands out in a crowd. Kinda dark and edgy, if you know what I mean."

"Dark and edgy? Is she Goth?"

Eryn's eyebrows flew up. "I don't think so. How would someone like you know about Goth people?"

"What do you mean, someone like me?" Manon frowned.

"Well, you must admit, you travel in slightly different circles."

"A lot of different people come by the foundation office. I usually find them interesting. Talking with them is a welcome change from the rigid, formal functions I have to attend on a regular basis."

"I didn't mean to suggest—"

"I know you didn't." Without thinking, Manon placed her hand on top of Eryn's to reassure her. *God. Pull your hand back. Now.*

Eryn leaned forward, turned her hand palm up under Manon's, and squeezed it. "Do you get that a lot?"

"What?" Manon felt her fingers tingle from Eryn's firm touch. *Pull back.*

"The poor-little-rich-girl-she-knows-very-little-about-life-in-the-real-world routine from people." She grimaced. "That's how I sounded. I'm sorry."

"I used to get that," Manon said, and managed to slowly pull her hand free. Pleased with Eryn's intuition, she grabbed the menu and opened it just to occupy her hands. "It's a rather sore spot."

"Your lattes, ladies." Mike interrupted the awkward moment. "Have you decided on anything to eat?"

"What do you recommend?" Manon looked up.

"The ham and tomato quiche. And it comes with a salad."

"Then I'll have that and some mineral water."

"I'll have the spinach crepes," Eryn said. "And water too."

"Sure. Until then, enjoy the coffee."

Manon sipped and then sighed in pleasure. It tasted as wonderful as it smelled.

"That good, huh?" Eryn grinned. "I told you." She sampled hers.

"Very, very good."

She had a dreamy expression on her face, and for a moment Manon could easily envision her as a character out of a Shakespeare play. *A female Puck perhaps, or… Quit that. Say something.*

"I've been coffee deprived all day." Nervous, Manon drank too quickly, and hot coffee flooded her throat. She coughed, reached for her napkin, and pressed it to her mouth as she tried not to wheeze.

"Are you all right?" Eryn was halfway out of her chair. "Do you need anything?"

"No, no," Manon croaked. "I'm fine." Finally catching her breath, she wiped annoying tears from the corner of her eyes. "I just swallowed wrong."

Eryn gave her a doubtful look but didn't persist. Her eyes lit up as she glanced around the room. "Hey, look over there! Your good friend and our favorite mezzo-soprano just walked in."

"Vivian's here too?" Manon turned around. "This must be the place to go." This time sipping her coffee with great care, she asked, "Unless she's meeting someone, would you mind if she joined us?"

"Not at all. I'd like to get to know her better."

Manon waved Vivian over and thought she detected a relieved expression on her friend's face.

"Manon, so nice to run into you."

"Why don't you join us? It's crowded tonight."

"I just popped in for some coffee at the bar, but if you don't mind, I'd rather sit here."

"You've met Eryn Goddard." Manon gestured, not quite liking how her voice became deeper and more intense when she spoke Eryn's name.

"Yes. The press conference. Thank you for writing such a lovely piece in the Sunday paper, Ms. Goddard," Vivian said as she sat down. "It was so much better than what that impertinent woman from the *Boston Phoenix* did. I honestly couldn't tell if the two of you were at the same press conference."

Manon noticed Eryn's cheeks turn pink, enhancing her freckles. She looked cute fiddling with her utensils to cover up her discomfort. *Not only capable but modest. That's a refreshing change from most reporters.*

"Thank you," Eryn murmured, sounding more pleased than embarrassed. "I'm glad you liked it. What's really important, though, is that I convinced my editor to run an ad on the first page every day for the next few weeks, telling people where to send their money for the hospital wing."

Manon's heart warmed, shattering a few old icicles. As she and Eryn gazed at each other, she felt an instant of silent communication. It was unexpectedly welcome. She only looked away when Mike approached the table.

"Hello, Vivian. I see you've found some company," Mike said. "How about a latte and some of that salad you like?"

Manon thought it was unusual for her friend to let Mike in so quickly. Vivian was a private woman. *She must feel lonely.*

"Yes, I found some special people, *cara*. Can you join us?"

"I'm sorry." Mike shook her head. "We're packed to the brim. I have to keep serving the pies as soon as Martha finishes baking them. Something to eat, Vivian?"

"No, thank you. I'm not very hungry."

"All right." Mike's incredible eyes shifted to violet. "Let me know if you change your mind, okay?"

"I will."

After Mike moved lithely between the tables, a slightly awkward silence filled the air.

·Finally, Eryn cleared her throat. "So, you're settling in, in your old hometown, Ms. Harding? It must've changed a lot over the years."

"Please call me Vivian," she requested, after tearing her eyes from the disappearing Mike. "Ms. Harding is my stage personality. This," she gestured, "is just me. A woman from East Quay. And yes, the town has grown and become...something else. Something I'm happy to explore, now that I've returned."

Manon was stunned. Vivian had never mentioned anything about East Quay or her life there before she became famous. It was as if her first sixteen years had been erased, and Manon knew she wasn't the only one who wondered why.

"I'll be honored to call you Vivian. And I'm just Eryn. And as I've told your friend here, things are always off the record unless I say otherwise."

"Fair enough. If Manon trusts you," Vivian smiled at her friend, "so do I."

❖

As they ate, making casual conversation, Eryn studied her two companions. They contrasted in style and personality, but both were clearly women of the world. However, she refused to feel outclassed. Besides, Manon at least found people from all walks of life interesting. *I wonder if she'd still find me a suitable lunch date if she knew I was a lesbian. She gives out such mixed signals.* Eryn could have sworn Manon trembled when their hands briefly touched earlier. Then she'd detected something close to panic in Manon's eyes before she withdrew her hand.

Eryn put down her fork, content to listen to Manon and Vivian.

"I wish I had more time to work on the Rossini aria," Vivian said, sounding a little tired. "I haven't played Rosina in ages, and though I know *The Barber of Seville* well…I'm not pleased. This is my last performance, at least for a while. I want it to be perfect."

Manon frowned and leaned back in her chair. "Aren't you rehearsing almost every day with the orchestra?"

"Yes, but I miss Sherry, my regular accompanist. She's touring with *Othello*. She couldn't put her career on hold just because I decided to take a leave." Vivian looked uncomfortable. "And to tell the truth, I don't want to make it known that I'm uncertain…or perhaps intimidated by the fact this is my last concert. With Sherry, I knew I was in safe hands, musically and personally."

From her research about Vivian, Eryn knew Sherry Millard was one of the most sought-after accompanists in the opera world. She wondered if Vivian had cut off all ties to her career.

Manon placed her napkin next to her plate. "If you're not too picky and really need extra rehearsals, I could accompany you. I play the piano."

Eryn stared at Manon.

"I'm not a virtuoso like Ms. Millard, but I'm not entirely bad."

"You know *The Barber of Seville*?" Vivian asked. "I'd love to fine-tune my intonation and phrasing. Do you have time tomorrow evening?" She gestured, obviously imitating herself on stage. "I need to *be* Rosina, not just sing the aria." With an overly dramatic motion of her chin, she mimicked a stereotypical opera singer. Then she laughed so resoundingly that several people turned their heads toward her.

"I have a baby grand, and my tall ceiling makes for decent acoustics. Why don't you come over after rehearsals Friday?" Manon asked. "Then it doesn't matter if it gets late."

"That's a great idea," Eryn managed, and tried her best to sound convincing. She looked down at her hands squeezing the napkin into a ball and wondered what was erupting in her chest. *This is ridiculous. I can't be jealous, for heaven's sake.* "I had no idea you were musical too. You're a woman of many talents, Manon."

"Thank you. I'm good, but not great. I enjoy playing." After scribbling something on the back of a business card, she handed it to Vivian. "Here's my address. You already have my phone number. I'll be home after six. We can order some takeout if you're hungry."

"What a wonderful solution." Vivian closed her hand around the card. "I'm so grateful."

Much to Eryn's relief, Mike joined them. "Everything all right, ladies?"

"Everything's fine." Vivian's expression mellowed as she looked at Mike. "Manon's going to rehearse with me Friday, which leaves one less thing to worry about."

Eryn wondered what else Vivian worried about. Ever since the press conference she'd sensed that Vivian had a hidden agenda, and she was also curious about the electricity between Vivian and Mike. Quite the odd couple, she thought while finishing her coffee, almost choking on the last sip. *Couple? Nah.*

"That's awesome," Mike said and placed a hand on Vivian's shoulder. "Let me know if I can walk Perry and Mason."

"Oh, you're right!" Vivian threw her hand into the air. "How could I forget the boys? Could you possibly let them out late Friday afternoon?"

"Why don't you bring them over here when you leave for rehearsals? They can stay in my backyard, and I'll be able to walk them several times."

"Are you sure? You know how big they are. I'd have to bring you some of their food."

Eryn's eyebrows had just about reached her hairline. "I suppose we're talking about dogs?"

Vivian laughed. "Yes, two Great Danes."

Manon joined in. "Oh, my…I'd forgotten about them. Perry and Mason."

"They'll love being spoiled by you," Vivian said quietly. "I'll pick them up when I'm done." She bit her lower lip. "But I don't know how late I'll be, Mike."

"No problem. I'll wait up."

The words, uttered with certainty, relaxed Vivian's expression again, and her voice sank to a gentle purr. "Thank you, *cara.* Put this on my tab?"

Mike nodded, her face mirroring Vivian's and gentler than Eryn had ever seen it.

Vivian looked as if she was about to say more but then glanced at Manon and Eryn. "I need to go home now, no matter how lovely this has been."

Manon rose. "See you tomorrow, Vivian."

Vivian turned to Eryn. "Will I see you at Manon's condo? Perhaps you'd like to listen in on the rehearsals."

"Yes, I'd love to." Eryn tried to sound confident, not sure why her stomach was still in a knot. Annoyed at herself, she pushed her chair back. "Time for me to leave too." She hated to sound so abrupt, but it was damn near impossible for her to figure out her mixed emotions. Why was she so jittery?

Vivian checked her watch. "Long overdue for me. The boys have been alone long enough to level the house."

They walked behind Mike to the counter where Manon insisted on picking up the entire check. "You can treat me next time," she said, apparently not about to give in. Eryn and Vivian surrendered, the latter claiming that she didn't have time to stand around and argue.

"Next one's on me!" Vivian called, and disappeared out the door.

As Eryn and Manon headed toward the parking lot, Eryn managed to sneak a look at Manon, her thoughts whirling. She knew how irrational her response earlier had been and was trying to make sense of it. But at the moment, she couldn't make sense out of anything.

❖

Manon turned the key in the ignition and listened to the low growl of the powerful engine, then backed out and started to leave. As she passed a red motorcycle, Manon glanced at Eryn's frustrated face and saw her slam her fist into the handlebars while she straddled the cycle's low, wide saddle.

Manon stopped next to the bike, rolled down her side window, and quirked an eyebrow. "Has it given up on you?"

"Looks like it." Eryn closed her eyes. "Damn it, I can't believe this. It's never done this before. And no, I didn't forget to fill up. It's probably an electrical malfunction." She gave her bike a gloomy look. "Traitor."

"Why don't you push it into Mike's backyard and have a garage pick it up tomorrow? I'm sure she won't mind. If you're on your way home, I can drive you. It's the neighborly thing to do." Manon groaned inwardly at her own comment. *How silly did that sound?*

Eryn hesitated a moment, then nodded. "Thanks. That would be great." She ran over to the café and ducked her head in for a second, then dashed back to her bike and pushed it behind the wide plank fence.

Returning with a large white and blue gym bag in her left hand, she tossed it behind the seats, then sank down next to Manon and closed the door. She sighed heavily, equally relieved and annoyed.

"Why the gym bag? Have you been working out?" Manon asked, as Eryn buckled up.

"Yeah, I go twice a week, not because I'm into sports, but because I sometimes sit for hours typing. It's murder on my back."

"I know what you mean. I should exercise more, but at least I programmed my computer to insist I take breaks and stretch every hour." As Manon maneuvered the Lotus smoothly along the streets leading into the city, they sat in silence. Finally Manon glanced at Eryn before speaking asking cautiously, "Is something bothering you?"

To Manon's surprise Eryn blushed. Just when Manon thought she wouldn't get an answer, the words tumbled over Eryn's lips.

"You're going to think I'm incredibly stupid, but when I saw you talking to Vivian, I felt…out of my league. You two have so much in common. You move in similar circles." Eryn clasped her hands and looked straight ahead. "I'm not even sure why this matters. I mean, we're neighbors. That's all."

Manon shivered at the unexpected words. Only her years of practiced self-control made it possible for her to speak at all. "Why this sudden bout of insecurity?" she asked gently, a bit out of breath.

Eryn leaned her head against the backrest, giving another deep sigh. "You tell me. I feel so silly."

"Vivian may seem worldly and privileged, that's true, but we both know that isn't so. When it comes to me…well, we're all just people, aren't we? Do I make you feel inferior? I'm sorry. I don't intend to."

"No, that's not it at all." Eryn tugged at her braid, inadvertently releasing more locks of hair.

"Then I don't understand…" Manon took one hand off the wheel and gestured in confusion. "Why would you feel out of your league?"

"This'll probably make you short-list me for your persona non grata award." Eryn clearly tried to keep her voice light, but it sounded strained and sank to a low murmur. "I don't play games, Manon. I'm attracted to you."

*What?* Manon braked reflexively and felt the Lotus shiver before she gathered herself and continued down Main Street. Stunned by Eryn's declaration, as well as her candor, Manon kept driving, relieved to see their condo unit appear at the far end of the street. She changed lanes twice and pulled into the garage on the other side of the alley near the landmark building. After parking in her designated spot, she turned off the ignition and waited a few seconds to collect her thoughts.

"Eryn—"

"I know, I know. You don't have to say anything." Eryn grimaced and wound her braid around two fingertips. "I never should have said anything either. I do that all the time. Speak before I think." And now she looked as if she wanted to bite her tongue to stay silent, despite the brave smile.

*And do you tell other people...other women...what you told me? Just like that?* As they still sat in the parked car, Manon shifted to face Eryn. "Some would call that honesty."

"Yes, well, honesty's overrated sometimes. It tends to get me in trouble." She peeked at Manon. "Would you call me honest or am I in trouble?"

Despite the facetious tone of voice, Manon sensed that Eryn had braced herself for the reply. And when she realized she might lose a rare friendship if she said the wrong thing, Manon curbed her initial impulse to withdraw.

"I see you as honest. Why would you be in trouble?" she asked gently. "I'm not sure why and how you're attracted to me, but I'm flattered." *Yes, that's it. Keep it light. Friendly. Defuse it.*

"You really have no idea, do you? You're intriguing and stunning, and... But I'll stop now before I dig this hole any deeper." Eryn unclasped her fingers and instead laced them loosely together on her lap.

Manon's heart was beating rapidly. The idea that this exciting, beautiful woman found her attractive amazed her. *Damage control. That's what it's about.*

"Why don't you join Vivian and me after work tomorrow?" she blurted. "If you'd like to, that is?" *Was that damage control? God almighty.*

"Really? You sure?"

"Yes."

"Okay. I don't know when I'll be back after my assignment, but if it's not too late, I'll pop up and see how the rehearsal's going." Eryn's attempt to sound casual failed miserably since she couldn't help but grin.

Manon returned the smile, torn between the giddiness she felt at the sight of Eryn's sparkling eyes and the dread filling her. They walked through the glassed-in pathway one floor up from street level and reached their lobby.

"Allow me." Eryn pressed the button for her floor and the one for the penthouse. When they reached her stop, Eryn gave a salute with two fingers and stepped off. "Night, Belmont. Appreciate the lift."

Leaning back against the wall as the elevator proceeded up, Manon smiled at the charmingly irreverent use of her last name. No one ever treated her so casually, but then Eryn was constantly surprising her. She rather liked that. She wasn't sure how she was going to deal with Eryn's unexpected admission or even how she felt about it. That was more than she wanted to think about now. She was really only certain of one thing. She'd never met anyone remotely like Eryn Goddard.

## CHAPTER EIGHT

Fucking idiot!"
Chaos erupted at East Quay High School when a tall, middle-aged man shoved from inside the building through the glass doors straight into a large crowd that thronged the school grounds. Eryn felt caught in the middle and stood aside when the irate speaker continued to curse and barged forward past her. "You can't do this! My kids deserve more!"

Principal Archibald Rex froze. He and the school board had just decided, in a closed emergency meeting, to cut the staff by four teachers and consolidate the eight classes into six. This would increase each group of students by eight and consequently decrease the time the teachers could devote to each student.

Eryn had followed the escalating debate over the last few weeks, and now, doing a follow-up, she and her photographer Don found themselves in the middle of an outraged group of parents.

"We need a comment from Rex, Don. Damn it! Now he's heading back into the school. He's not going to deal with the parents. What a coward. Think he'll use the west entrance?" Eryn yanked Don's sleeve. "Let's go!"

They hurried away from the crowd and ran around the corner. As they approached the side door they saw a crowd of teachers gathering there. "Damn," she muttered. "This could get ugly." *This is about as action packed as it gets in East Quay.* Eryn didn't know whether to be concerned or amused.

"Mr. Rex, Eryn Goddard, *New Quay Chronicle.*" She pressed down the record button on her tape recorder and extended it as Rex stepped outside. "What's your response to the concerns of the parents? Aren't the kids going to be the ones to suffer from these cutbacks?"

Rex gave her an annoyed glance. "No comment."

"Isn't your decision going to diminish the quality of education for East Quay's children?"

"The quality will *not* diminish."

"Then the citizens of East Quay have a right to know how you plan to ensure the same level of education with fewer staff and larger classes." Eryn cocked her head and moved closer to the tall, bulky man. "After all, it's their children and their tax money."

Rex stopped in midstride, his face suffused with anger. "I'll address this issue at the next PTA meeting, not here on the sidewalk."

"Sir, we have to get going," a woman behind Rex said. "We have another appointment."

"I have nothing more to say," the principal said, turning away. "You heard that, Ms. Goddard. Good-bye."

"Just one more thing, Mr. Rex. I hear you've decided on these cutbacks because of problems with last year's budget. Is it true you overspent on technology? Surely you want to comment on that accusation?"

Rex's mouth hardened into a thin line. "What part of 'no comment' don't you understand, Ms. Goddard?"

"Here comes the rest of the gang," Don murmured next to her, and raised his camera to film the now-enraged Principal Rex.

Eryn heard the noise of the angry parents. In front of her, Rex tried to circle the smaller crowd of teachers, and Don turned with the camera to keep him in view.

Clearly annoyed, Rex swung at the camera, and though Don managed to duck in time, Eryn wasn't as lucky. A fist slammed into her temple. Her tape recorder hit the sidewalk, and after two stumbling steps backward, she followed.

She landed on her left shoulder before her head connected with something hard. Her vision wavered and she blinked at the sharp flashes of light that danced against a curtain of blackness. With effort, she willed herself to stay conscious, then groaned and felt around the back of her head for blood.

"What the hell are you doing, man?" Don was by her side instantly. "God, Eryn." He slid an arm behind her back and carefully helped her sit up. "You okay?"

"Damn, I hurt my shoulder," she managed, tears of pain streaming down her cheeks. The sound of screeching tires and the shouting voices didn't help her headache either. "Godalmighty. Is he crazy?"

"He must be. Jesus." Don scanned the gathering crowd. "Fuck. He's gone." Don helped her lean against one of the columns that flanked the door. "Don't move. I'll call the police and an ambulance."

"No…well, I do want to report this, but no ambulance. I can walk to the car."

Holding his arm, she stood on wobbly legs and let Don escort her to his car across the street.

Several people called out in unison. "We saw what happened, lady! We'll testify to it!"

After Don helped her into the passenger seat, he handed her his cell phone. "Here. Call the police while we're on the way to East Quay Memorial so they can get some statements. That bastard won't get away with this."

Every movement hurt, and Eryn couldn't hide a quiet whimper while she punched 911. When a dispatcher answered, Eryn kept her voice steady when she reported the details of the assault and their destination, but she still trembled from pain. "Oh yes, I can identify him. And I have a witness."

❖

Manon checked the clock next to her grand piano again as Vivian's voice reverberated throughout her living room and filled it with the magic of her famous sound. After they had practiced the entire aria several times and stopped to work on certain parts, it was well past eight o'clock, and Manon suggested a supper break.

"Didn't you say Eryn was supposed to join us?" Vivian asked as she followed Manon into the kitchen.

"Yes. I suppose something must have come up. She doesn't work from just nine to five."

"Nor do we." Vivian rubbed her neck. "All four of us work far more than normal eight-hour days."

"All four? Oh, you mean Mike too? Yes, being your own boss means working twice as much."

"Can I help?" Vivian asked as Manon pulled a tray from the refrigerator.

"No, I—" The doorbell rang. "That must be Eryn." Relieved, Manon hurried to the door, opened it, and stared. "Eryn! My God! What happened?"

Eryn managed a grin despite the blue sling on her arm, the white bandage on her left temple, and the red bruise on her right cheekbone. "Would you believe I won?"

"I'll try, but…" Manon guided her inside with a hand on her uninjured arm, shaken by the sight. "You're hurt. Don't make light, please."

"I'm okay," Eryn said, touched by Manon's concern. "I had a run-in on the job with somebody bigger than me. I just finished giving a statement to the police at the hospital." She sighed. "The doctor and my photographer insisted I shouldn't be alone. Sorry to barge in so late."

"Don't be ridiculous," Manon said sharply, her worry making her impatient. "Of course you should have come." Mellowing, she slid her arm gently around Eryn's waist. "Who did this?"

"I'll tell you all about it later, I promise. I just need to catch my breath." Eryn began to shake her head, but stopped with a grimace. "Ow. Bad move."

"Have you eaten? Can I get you anything?"

"Come to think of it, I *haven't* eaten since breakfast." Eryn didn't really want Manon to move her arm. It felt very good on her waist. Very. The worry in her eyes was kind of nice too. But if they stood there much longer, this close, Manon was going to feel her tremble at just how damn good it felt. Reluctantly, she said, "Maybe just a sandwich or something?"

"Of course. Vivian and I were just about to eat."

Eryn smiled. "I didn't miss her after all? Great."

When Vivian saw them, her smile of welcome changed to a look of horror. "Eryn! For heaven's sake, sit down. What happened?"

"She'll fill us in after we fill her stomach," Manon explained, placing the chicken salad her housekeeper had prepared earlier on the kitchen table. "Eryn, would you rather sit here or on the couch?"

"I'm fine. Let's eat." Eryn grabbed her fork. "This is just what the doctor ordered. Literally."

After quickly finishing her meal, Eryn explained. "I spent two hours in the ER—X-rays, doctors, the police…it's been a long day."

"Why didn't they keep you for observation?" Manon frowned. "You hit your head, after all. You may have a concussion."

"They discussed it, but since I never lost consciousness and the neurological exam cleared me, they just told me to take it easy this weekend."

"What about your arm?" Vivian looked at the sling. "Is it fractured?"

"No, just some badly sprained ligaments around the shoulder joint. I have to keep it immobilized for a while. Thank God I'm right-handed."

Manon stared down at her untouched salad and stabbed a tomato. The thought of Eryn being hurt upset her deeply, and she had to chew for a long time before she could swallow.

"So, did the police pick up the guy?" Vivian asked.

"Yes, since Don had taken pictures and handed his compact flash card over to the police as evidence. The next school board meeting should be even more interesting than the last, Manon, considering it was Principal Rex who—"

"Archibald Rex?" Manon was stunned. "I knew I should have gone to that emergency meeting. I could have stopped him. What a coward—"

"An incompetent coward, it turns out." Eryn grimaced. "Believe me, there was quite an uproar. At least two hundred parents and the entire faculty were at the high school. When I got to the hospital I talked to one of the nurses, whose sister teaches English at the school. She knew all about it, so I called the story in from there. It'll be in tomorrow's paper."

"I can't believe you managed to do all that while injured," Manon said. She couldn't fathom anybody being unaffected by such an ordeal.

Eryn shrugged as well as she could in a sling. "It's my job. I wasn't about to miss filing a great story."

When Manon murmured, "I'm impressed," Eryn flushed with pride. Then she glanced at Vivian.

"Sorry I missed your rehearsal. I was looking forward to it."

"I was going to run through the aria once more before I head home," Vivian said. "If you're up to it, Eryn, you can be our audience."

"Sounds like a plan to me." As Eryn rose she swayed toward Manon. "Damn. I feel almost drunk."

"Did they give you something for pain?" Manon circled her arm around Eryn's waist again.

"Percodan. I guess I'm pretty stoned."

"They let you go home with a head injury and a drug like that in your system? Come on. Let's get you on the couch." Manon guided Eryn to the living room, feeling more protective than she could ever remember when she realized Eryn was shaking. Her scent, fruity, with a tinge of vanilla, was mixed with antiseptics. "There. Sit down and put your feet up." When she noticed the vulnerability in Eryn's eyes, now dazed and dulled by the medication, she could hardly breathe. She tucked a blanket around Eryn and tried to cover her own turmoil with a smile. "Comfortable?"

"Yes. Go play for Vivian."

With an effort, Manon tore her eyes away from Eryn and went to the baby grand. She stared blindly at the music for a second, then gathered her control and hit the first chord. "All right, Vivian. From the top?"

❖

The music filled the room and, with relief, Eryn rested her injured head against the velvet cushions; the plush couch hugged her body, soothed it. Her shoulder ached also, a dull throbbing sensation, mellowed by the painkillers. The doctor had insisted she fill a prescription for more before she left the hospital, so Don took care of that detail while she signed her statement for the police. She had spoken to her boss before they left the ER, and surprisingly, Harold grumbled something about her resting up and Don making sure the *Chronicle* had the photos of the events ready to print ASAP.

As Vivian's amazing voice soared, Eryn felt tears escaping. She closed her eyes and wiped them away with her sleeve, welcoming the warmth of the music and the comfort of Manon's care. Despite her casual attitude earlier, it was good to be here, safe.

When the music stopped, she opened her eyes drowsily and tried to smile. "If my arm wasn't in a sling and I wasn't so out of it, I'd join you guys with my guitar."

Vivian regarded her with interest. "You play the guitar?"

"Electric guitar. I used to be in a band in college." Eryn's tongue felt swollen. "Schorry, ladies." She could hear herself slur. "I'm so tired."

Worriedly, Manon took Eryn's hand. "You're not feeling strange, are you? Tell me what day it is."

"Friday. October seventh." Eryn winked. "I'm tired. Not concussed."

"Sometimes these things don't show up right away." Manon still looked uncertain. "You should stay here tonight, though. In case you need something."

"Thanks. If it's not too much trouble that would be great." Eryn sighed and shifted on the couch. It was a relief not to have to move.

"It would be more trouble if Manon were up here worrying about you." Vivian looked closely at her watch. "It's late. I'll call a cab and go pick up my dogs." She collected her coat and purse and leaned over Eryn. "Take it easy the next few days, all right? Listen to Manon."

"All right," Eryn whispered, already half asleep. "I promise."

The next thing Eryn knew, she felt a gentle touch on her uninjured shoulder and heard Manon say, "Let's get you a little more comfortable."

"I'm comfortable here."

"I don't think so. You're still wearing your jacket and boots."

"I have my boots on, on your couch?" Appalled, Eryn tried to sit up. "I'm so sch-sorry, I…oh, man…" Her head pounded from moving too quickly.

"Shh. Don't worry about it. No harm done. Come. Let me show you to the guest room—"

"Please. Can't I stay on your couch? I'm really comfortable." Eryn tried again to sit up and frowned when her legs wouldn't obey her. "I can just take my boots off."

"All right. But I'll bring something better for you to sleep in, though. Be right back."

Eryn moved slowly, finally sitting up. She was sorer than she'd expected. Her shoulder burned like fire. *Time for more pills.* After pulling a small bottle from her pocket and trying to flip the lid open with her thumb, she glared at it. "Childproof. Of course. Damn it."

"What?" Manon arrived carrying a long white button-down flannel shirt. "Oh, want me to open that?"

"Please."

Manon opened the bottle, handed it to Eryn, and went for a bottle of water. "Here. For the medicine."

"Thanks." After taking her pills, Eryn felt cross-eyed as she looked down at her boots. "I think you're going to have to help me with those. Sorry."

"Of course." Manon knelt before Eryn and removed each boot. Then she rose and sat down next to the Eryn, gently tugging at her jacket. "Here. Let's take this off. It's only half on as it is." She carefully removed the jacket, folded it, and placed it on the backrest. "Want to try for the flannel shirt?"

Eryn looked at the garment in Manon's hands. Suddenly self-conscious, she nodded briskly and winced when the movement set off another stab of pain. "All right. It looks comfy."

❖

Manon reached for the buttons on Eryn's sleeveless denim shirt. Her fingers trembled when she undid them, skimming over pale, freckled skin. She examined the sling. Fortunately it had practical fastening devices to hold Eryn's arm stable while she removed the shirt. Bare to the waist except for her creamy lace bra, Eryn looked vulnerable, the bruises on her left side emphasizing her frailty.

Manon shuddered at the sight of the injuries, as well as the feel of Eryn's satin skin. She slipped the short-sleeved flannel shirt over the sling and refastened the clasps. "There, always start with the injured side." Then she held the other sleeve for Eryn. As she buttoned the shirt, Manon felt her fingers brush Eryn's skin. She had to bite her lip when the brief touch made Eryn shiver.

"Can you stand up a minute?"

"I'll try." Eryn held on to Manon as she helped her rise.

Manon willed her hands not to give away what touching Eryn this way was doing to her. As she undid Eryn's slacks, she noticed the torn fabric around the left knee for the first time. *I could kill the bastard.* As she helped Eryn step out of the trousers, she clenched her teeth and harnessed her outrage. "Much better. Lie down again."

Eryn looked grateful and dazed as she sat down. Manon scooped her legs up and tucked the blanket around her again, then settled carefully on the edge of the sofa beside her. "Much better."

"Thank you."

"You're so welcome." Manon's voice was gentle. "Just go to sleep. I have to read some papers, and then I'll check on you."

"Manon? Could you undo my braid? It hurts my head."

Manon's fingertips tingled as she reached for the end of the long braid and removed the ribbon. Slowly she ran her fingers through Eryn's hair, amazed at its texture and the scent of citrus and flowers emanating from it as she freed the tresses. Despite its curls, Eryn's hair was silky smooth, and Manon combed through it several times, reluctant to let go. Only when Eryn's eyes slid open and gazed at her with unspoken questions did she jump up and smooth her slacks down to keep her hands busy. *Careful.*

Eryn's eyes closed again and Manon remained for a few more seconds, watching her sleep. Deep red hair pooled around her pale face. Reddish-brown eyelashes formed dark half circles above high cheekbones. Though her vivacious smile was absent, her finely sculpted lips made her look almost angelic.

Manon couldn't recall ever seeing such beauty.

As her cab drove away, Vivian inwardly cursed whoever was supposed to light the marina for not doing a good job. She tapped on the door to the closed café.

"Vivian, come inside. It's freezing out here." Mike's low voice startled her.

"Yes, it's not summer anymore, that's for sure." She noticed Mike had changed into low-cut jeans and a dark shirt. She liked the way the casual clothes emphasized her lean, graceful build. The fact that she noticed surprised her. "Did the boys behave?"

"They've been great. They're sneaky, though. I saw Martha slip them some treats at least three times."

Vivian walked into the café, lit only by a few lamps. "I'm sure she spoiled them rotten. They can look at you as if they haven't eaten in three weeks."

"They're downstairs." Mike took Vivian's hand. "Just hold on."

Vivian allowed Mike to guide her and was met with enthusiastic woofs and licks. "Hello, boys, did you miss me? I didn't think so. Mike's treated you like princes." She grinned when the dogs lay back down on the rug by the TV. "I see they've made themselves at home."

As Perry and Mason yawned and rested their big heads on crossed paws, Vivian glanced around the large room and said, "This is a remarkable room, Mike. Honestly, I'd expected it to feel claustrophobic and closed in…but it feels like a safe haven."

"That's exactly what it is to me." Mike looked surprised and happy at Vivian's comment as she settled on the couch and motioned for Vivian to join her. "Long day, huh?"

"*And* night. We had quite an evening." Vivian sat down next to Mike. "Eryn was attacked while on assignment."

"What? Is she all right?"

"She'll be okay," Vivian said quickly. "She hurt her head and her shoulder."

"Where is she? Is she in the hospital?"

"No, at Manon's. She's spending the night there."

"That's terrible." Mike regarded Vivian with concern. "You and Manon must have been pretty upset too."

"We certainly were, but it helped that Eryn's such a trooper." Vivian laughed with apparent kindness. "All she could think about was her story."

"You admire her."

"I do. She's bright and insightful, with a gift for writing."

"Like you." Mike cupped Vivian's cheek. "But your gift is the music."

The touch on her face was tender, but disturbing too. Vivian's pulse quickened. "Mike?"

"Yes?"

Vivian swallowed hard, not taking her eyes off Mike. Her eyes, black in the muted light, studied Vivian intently. "What are you thinking? I have to—"

"How I worried about you today and thought about you after the other morning and…hoped you were feeling better." Mike lowered her hand to Vivian's shoulder.

"You're so sweet," Vivian whispered. "Somehow I think you're not used to opening up like you do to me. Am I right?"

"Yes. More than you know." Mike blinked, as if surprised at her own candor. "You make it easy, somehow. To…share things that matter to me. It's just that life is short and…I guess I found that out the hard way. And I'm not trying to be mysterious. Life's also too short for riddles." Mike shrugged and her expression hardened. "This life is all I have, and these days, I'm proud of what I've achieved. It wasn't always that way."

Vivian heard more hurt and depth behind the words than Mike might have realized. "I like what I see, Mike. And I mean *you*, not just what you've accomplished."

"And I see Vivian. Not the famous diva adored by millions of opera fans. I look at you and I see…you."

Vivian refused to shed the tears that Mike's gentle admission stirred. Silently, she nodded.

Mike brushed a thumb across Vivian's forehead. "Don't frown. You're safe."

"I…what do you mean?" It was hard to breathe.

"Yes. It's just me."

There was nothing "just" about how Mike looked at her. Prompted by the trust and caring in Mike's eyes, Vivian put her arms around her. "I know. I'm glad." In that instant. Vivian couldn't explain how, but something in Mike's eyes prompted her to act. She surprised herself when she reached out and pulled Mike into a firm hug.

A muted whimper escaped Mike. Vivian felt it against her cheek and turned her head to whisper a word of comfort.

"Don't…talk," Mike said. Her lips were close enough for Vivian to feel them move against her skin.

"You're trembling," Vivian murmured after a moment of silence. "Why is that?"

Mike tensed in her arms. "You know why. Surely you must know?"

"I think so." Vivian tightened her embrace at the naked darkness in Mike's voice. "Are you attracted to me, Mike?"

"Oh, yes." Mike buried her face in Vivian's neck.

"There's no hurry. I don't have to go anywhere. Oddly calm, Vivian leaned back, her arms still around Mike. "We can just stay like this."

Mike rested her head on Vivian's shoulder. "Thank you."

Vivian laughed. "My pleasure." She placed two fingers underneath Mike's chin and tipped her head back. Mike's eyes shimmered with restrained emotions. "What is it, Mike?"

Vivian was unprepared for the intensity when Mike's mouth closed gently over hers. The tenderness of the kiss spoke more to Vivian than if Mike had actually deepened it, demanded more. Vivian kept her arms around Mike, somehow knowing that the fragile bond between them would shatter if she let go.

## CHAPTER NINE

Mike's heart thrashed like a trapped animal. Vivian still held her close, their lips pressed together in a caress that stole her breath. She trembled as Vivian stroked her back in languid movements.

She simply wasn't used to this. It had been ages, years, since anyone touched her this way. She'd fallen for Brenda's caresses too, and gotten so scorched by life she ought to be smoking around the edges. Until now, she'd kept her distance. But this was different. This was Vivian. And all she could think was this amazing woman was returning her kiss and, more than that, holding her so tenderly.

*This amazing, supposedly* straight *woman...* Mike stiffened. It hurt to break contact, but she was already steeling her resistance, rationalizing as she retreated. *She's just being kind and understanding. She's grateful and perhaps lonely. Or even worse, she pities me.*

"Mike?" Vivian murmured, reaching for Mike, who quickly pulled back even more.

"I...I should apologize."

Vivian regarded her silently for a long moment. "Why?"

Taken aback by the simple question, Mike tried to think of what to say. Vivian had been nothing but kind to her. "Friends should never cross some boundaries."

Another pause. "Do you regret kissing me?"

"No! I mean, no, not from my perspective. But it wasn't right." Mike tugged a small pillow close and dug her fingertips into the dark brown velvet. "It won't happen again." She hated how desolate her words sounded.

Vivian angled her body sideways and stretched out her arm, but never averted her eyes. "Why did you kiss me?"

Mike flinched. *Nothing like going in for the kill right away.* "I think I lost my head."

Vivian smiled. Not the condescending, taunting smile that Brenda had flashed at her when Mike had tried to voice her thoughts. Instead, Vivian's smile was encouraging, lacking any malice. How could it disturb her more than anything Brenda had ever said or done?

"I think I did too." Vivian didn't reach for Mike again. Instead she leaned her head against her palm, briefly closing her eyes. "I've never kissed another woman."

"I said I was sor—"

"I didn't mean it like that." Vivian shook her head. "Quite a few men *and* women have propositioned me during my career. I'm not inexperienced. My affairs with men were short bursts of…some type of theatrical passion. The women never interested me, at least not the ones I met at the time, and I've always been more committed to my work than to any special person. Singing, to me, is more than a profession. Singing is what I am."

The clear blue eyes clouded over, and Mike forgot her own bewilderment and grasped Vivian's free hand.

"Or what I *was*," Vivian continued in a matter-of-fact voice. Mike guessed her comment was meant to cover a deep hurt, but for her, Vivian's pain was obvious.

"Are you really retiring?"

"God, Mike. I…I don't know." Vivian shuddered. "I haven't been able to say it. I've hardly dared think about it. I've always been booked years in advance, always known exactly what I was doing and when. But this upcoming concert is the last I have planned for a long time." She closed her eyes. "I feel lost."

Mike suddenly knew. Tenderly, she asked, "It's your eye condition, isn't it, Vivian?"

Vivian dragged an unsteady hand through her hair, disheveling it thoroughly. Mike held her breath when the golden locks tumbled around Vivian's shoulders, glowing in the muted light of her living room.

"Yes." Vivian's voice was strangled.

Mike couldn't stand the pain in Vivian's face. She pulled Vivian close and, thankfully, Vivian let her hold her, her curves melded with Mike's leaner frame.

"How bad?"

"Bad." Vivian sighed against Mike's skin. "*Cara*, I'm going blind."

❖

Manon tugged at the belt of her terry cloth robe as she left her elaborate bathroom. When the building was restored, Manon had fought the National Historical Registry about only this concession, convinced that a Jacuzzi wouldn't destroy the protected structure.

She tiptoed over to the couch to check on Eryn. The bruise on her face was darker now, and Manon was ready to string Rex up for what he'd done, even if it was an accident. If it wasn't, then she imagined a direr fate.

"No."

Manon jerked when Eryn muttered in her sleep and shifted restlessly. She leaned over and barely touched her uninjured arm. "Eryn?"

"Not fair."

Eryn was obviously dreaming, and from the sound of her voice, even if she didn't thrash around, Manon guessed the dream was unpleasant. Her lips quivered, and tears formed at the outer corners of her closed eyes, darkening her eyelashes.

"Eryn. You're dreaming." Manon knelt next to the couch. "Wake up! Come on—"

"No, no." Eryn's eyes opened slowly, unfocused and wary. "What—"

"Just a dream. You're fine."

"Dream. Yes." Eryn was obviously not quite awake.

"Here. Roll over on your right side so I can rub your back." Immediately regretting her spontaneous suggestion, Manon waited a few seconds. "If you want."

"Mmm, yeah. Thanks." Eryn struggled to turn, but only when Manon helped her did she manage to move. "God, I feel helpless," she whispered. "How long have I been asleep?"

"Two hours. I was just on my way to bed." Manon slid up to sit next to Eryn and placed her arm around her back. She stroked her back gently, up and down, outside the large nightshirt. "How's that?"

"Wonderful. My shoulder's throbbing, but it's probably too early to take any more of those dynamite pills."

"Yes. You should wait at least another four hours."

Eryn frowned and Manon stopped, keeping her hand at the small of Eryn's back. "Did I hurt you?"

"No, I…the dream just flashed by. How strange. I rarely remember dreams."

"Want to talk about it?" Manon resumed her massage. "You don't have to."

"It was weird. I kept seeing faces. Mom, Dad, my sisters. They were shouting at me and then ignoring me, and then shouting again. Nothing I said mattered."

Eryn's voice was raw, and deep with emotions.

"No wonder you were upset." Manon instinctively moved closer. She slowed her caresses, trying to make her movements more soothing.

"Just plain silly, huh?"

"Nothing silly about it at all." Manon shook her head. *I know what nightmares can do to a person. I also know how crying through sleepless nights can eat away at your soul.* Nights of tearstained pillowcases were over for her, but the thought of Eryn suffering alone through forgotten nightmares bothered her.

"Manon. Can I ask you something?"

"Sure." *Or maybe not?*

"How do you do it? Be so poised and together all the time?"

"What?" Manon stared at Eryn and forgot to move her hand. Obviously Eryn wasn't kidding. "Well, it takes a bit of training, which I've had plenty of. My grandfather and father sent me to a boarding school in Vermont when I was fourteen. You learn how to take care of yourself when you're on your own."

"They sent you away?" Eryn rolled over on her back, trapping Manon's hand. "Why?"

Manon felt heat flood her cheeks. Her close proximity to Eryn was making her dizzy, and all she could see were Eryn's sensuous lips curving as she spoke. Manon's breath caught in her chest, and she had to clear her throat twice before she could slowly free her arm and answer.

"They didn't send me away, exactly. My family thought I'd be better off, but I just stayed for three semesters, until I persuaded Granddad that my place was at Belmont Manor with him and Father."

"Did they agree?" Eryn asked with concern.

"Yes. I studied with tutors over the next two years until I graduated from high school."

"Homeschooled, huh? Wasn't that lonely?"

Manon considered her reply and tried to control her reactions. "Not really," she said, and was rather surprised at how true her response was. "I went with my granddad to the foundation office almost every day and did my schoolwork in one of the conference rooms. My tutors joined me there. I not only studied but learned about the company from the inside out. I became friends with some of the younger office staff, at least in the beginning."

"And you never missed going to regular school?"

"I took physics and chemistry at a private school and participated in a few sports. I also played in the school orchestra." However, Manon cringed at some of the memories her words produced. "I was happiest when I was at the foundation, though."

"Sounds like you were more comfortable around adults."

"That's true. I had to grow up quickly when my parents divorced and Jack…" Manon regretted her choice of words immediately, aghast that she could even mention Jack this casually. What was it about Eryn, a *reporter,* for heaven's sake, that made her lower her guard like this? "Anyway," she stumbled, "a lot changed in my teens that made life very different."

"I read about your brother," Eryn said, placing a hand over Manon's. "You must miss him."

The simple words cut through pain and anger—anger mostly directed at herself for being too softhearted and weak at this moment—and left Manon astonished. *I never let anyone talk to me about Jack. No one.*

"Yes, I do." The confession was even more staggering. Normally she immediately let people know, beyond any doubt, that Jack was off topic. "I loved him."

"You still do. And he knows it, wherever he is."

Simple words, and yet they warmed her heart, breaking through the ice that usually formed instantly when the topic of her brother's death came up. "Thank you, Eryn." *And bless you for not prying.*

"I have two sisters," Eryn said. "One older, one younger. My parents adore them."

Pain, different from Manon's, but nearly tangible, permeated Eryn's voice. Manon held on more firmly to the warm hand in hers. "And you?"

"No."

Manon waited, unwilling to inquire further, since Eryn hadn't.

"I'm a disappointment and have been since I was sixteen."

Eryn's face paled, but her eyes were bright in the dim light. A shimmer of tears? Manon said gently, "I can't imagine that."

"I don't fit their mold of a good daughter. Well, I guess my father could've come around if he wasn't so intimidated by my mother."

"And your sisters?"

"They're not like my parents. They detest being favorites, and my younger sister drives my mother half insane by bringing up 'the issue' at least once a week, bless her heart."

"The issue?" Slightly bewildered, Manon had to ask.

"The fact that I'm a lesbian."

"Oh." Silence hung between them. Manon wasn't surprised, exactly, but to have Eryn's sexual preference out in the open galvanized all her own fears. She knew she sounded rigid, unyielding, but her inner alarm system wouldn't allow her to relax.

Eryn studied her intently for a few seconds, then pulled back her hand, her eyes tired. "I see," she said quietly, with a tone of finality. "You too."

❖

*Oh, God, no!* Mike wanted to cry in frustration. Instead, she pressed her lips against the top of Vivian's head and muffled her sobs. Vivian needed reassurance and support, not an emotional weakling who needed comfort herself.

"I'm sorry to hear that, Vivian," Mike managed, hugging her closer. "How long have you known?"

"Two months." Vivian spoke in a dull voice, as if trying to stay detached from the horror. "In that time, my sight has slowly deteriorated.

Days like last Monday are quite bad, and every day like that makes me lose more of my vision."

"And have the doctors told you how long…" Mike didn't want to sound too clinical, but really wanted to know.

"Within a year, perhaps much faster. It all depends on my individual version of this disease." She sighed against Mike's neck. "I'm sorry to unburden on you. You have enough on your plate with the café."

"No, no. I don't mind. Feel free to tell me anything." Mike hated to think Vivian would be all alone to deal with such a loss. Then she had a new thought. "Unless you already have someone to confide in."

Vivian tipped her head back, smiling with sorrow. "You're the third person I've told, after Malcolm and Manon."

"You need to talk to someone. A friend." Mike felt her cheeks grow warm, and she stumbled over her words. "I…I hope you think of me as a friend." *At least.*

"I know a lot of people, but I have very few friends," Vivian murmured and scrutinized her.

Mike wondered if her illness distorted the way Vivian saw her.

"You're special to me, *cara.*"

*Special? What does that mean?* Mike wanted to ask but was afraid to push too hard. Her hands were tingling from holding Vivian in her arms, and it was difficult to breathe. She stroked Vivian's back, trying to comfort her, and felt an undeniable guilty pleasure at the touch.

"I'm glad," Mike murmured. "I know we've known each other for only a week, but…I want to be here. For you." Annoyed with herself for almost stuttering, Mike spontaneously kissed Vivian's forehead. Her skin was smooth and the fragrance from Vivian's hair pleasing. "I don't mean to overstep any boundaries—"

"Shh." Vivian cupped the back of Mike's head. "Kisses don't hurt. I would never want to hurt you, Mike."

"I believe you. I do." Mike swallowed against impending tears and felt tender. She couldn't just switch from hiding her heart in a foxhole to trusting implicitly, but she had to reward Vivian's faith in her. She couldn't hold back human contact, physical or emotional. *But, damn, I haven't been this close to having my heart broken again in years.* Keeping her distance from people worked well most of the time, except when the person in front of her was hurting. *What's a broken heart compared to becoming blind?*

Vivian squinted and laced her fingers through Mike's hair. "I know you don't quite trust me, and one of these days you're going to have to share your reason."

Startled, Mike stiffened. "There's really nothing very interesting to say—"

"Didn't you hear me, *cara*? Not tonight. We're fine, for tonight." Vivian leaned her head to the side and rested it against Mike's upper arm. "Now I have something entirely different to ask you."

"Yes?"

"You took me by surprise. The way you kissed me, the way it felt." Vivian blushed faintly. "I'd like to try again. A little more prepared."

Oxygen. None. Mike forced air into her lungs. "Vivian!" Vivian's eyes filled Mike's entire field of vision—beautiful, glittering, and unwavering.

"Yes."

Mike lowered her gaze to Vivian's full mouth, slightly parted as a smile played at its corners. Filled with equal parts desire and dread, Mike leaned forward and hovered above Vivian for a breathless moment, afraid she might unleash all her built-up passion.

Vivian closed the last bit of distance, pulled Mike's head closer, and raised her own. And she initiated the trembling embrace. Brushing her lips along Mike's, she nibbled at them. Mike whimpered helplessly when pleasure blossomed in the pit of her stomach and flew down between her thighs.

"Vivi…"

"Mmm," Vivian murmured against her mouth. Mike felt the tip of Vivian's tongue explore the outline of her lips. *She's not gay! She's not. How can she kiss me like this?*

Convinced she was going to self-combust, Mike gasped.

Vivian could barely hear Mike's sharp intake of air over the thunder of her own heart. Mike's mouth was over hers, Mike lying half on top of her. And still it was Vivian who instigated the kiss.

Vivian could never have prepared for those incredible, soft, soft lips that parted readily. *Forgive me. I have to.* She slid her tongue inside and tasted a woman's, Mike's, mouth for the first time. She'd kissed the air next to other women's well-made-up faces a million times and allowed quite a few men to devour her lips with more or less skill, but…this? This was entirely different.

When Mike's tongue met hers and pushed, caressed, tentatively, but with increasing passion, Vivian could no longer remain careful. Her emotions ran high, and she invested much more in this kiss than she'd ever thought possible.

She pulled Mike closer and leaned back against the armrest. Lying with Mike on top of her, she tilted her head to allow for more ardent kisses.

Mike followed her easily, exploring Vivian's mouth with equal parts fervor and tenderness. "Vivi," she murmured, "I didn't count on this. I just wanted to be…your friend."

"You are." Vivian could hardly believe her own body's reactions. Sweat beaded on her temples and between her breasts. Her thighs shook and she squirmed beneath Mike's legs, fighting the urge to part them and engulf her. "You…are." She kissed Mike again and groaned in the back of her throat when Mike slid a knee between hers.

Mike broke free and straightened her arms. The sudden distance between them made Vivian feel cold, and she stared up through her dishevel hair, trying to gauge Mike's expression.

"We have to slow down," Mike panted. "Please, Vivian."

"I know."

"Too fast."

"Yes. I agree. Just let me hold you a little longer." The thought of losing the connection was unbearable.

Mike hesitated, looking down at Vivian with smoldering eyes. "We're playing with fire."

"I won't burn you, *cara*."

"What if I end up hurting you?"

"You won't."

"How can you be so sure?" Mike asked, still on rigid arms above Vivian.

"Instincts, intuition…come here." Vivian pulled at Mike, who slowly gave in, lowering herself to the couch. "There."

It was a blessing to just lie there, with human touch, *Mike's* touch, instead of her cold and lonely bed where only Perry and Mason noticed if she took her next breath. Shaken by her ominous thoughts, Vivian held Mike closer, again hiding her face against her neck.

Mike stroked Vivian's arm in slow, languid motions, as if trying to lull her to sleep.

"Pain is part of life," Vivian murmured.

"But I would never deliberately hurt you. I promise."

Vivian knew then that Mike had suffered more emotional agony than most. She kissed Mike on the neck and vowed to never add to those wounds.

❖

Eryn's head pounded and she wished she could take some pills right away, instead of in four hours. Most of all, she wished she could take back her last words. She glanced down at her blunt, short nails and let her index finger trace the pattern on the blue blanket.

"Eryn. Look at me."

Reluctantly, Eryn raised her eyes and prepared for the all-too-familiar expression, the one her mother assumed as soon as she walked into her childhood home. Instead she saw regret and something else, something unreadable, on Manon's face.

"I'd already guessed. It wasn't that hard, after what you told me in the car the other day." Manon blushed faintly but reached out and took Eryn's restless hand in hers. "I'm not like your parents. I don't consider sexual preference when it comes to friendship."

Eryn didn't believe her. She'd noticed something, a shudder as if someone had walked across Manon's grave, when Eryn told her the truth. "It's all right," she said, recoiling. "It really doesn't matter, does it? I'm just an unexpected guest on your couch, right?"

"No, please. You're not merely any guest, Eryn. I've never met anyone like you, so give me a chance to get to know you better." Manon's words came out in the same measured, collected way she always spoke, and yet she sounded almost frantic.

"Perhaps it would be better if I went down to my own place and—"

"No, you can't. It's not safe. You've hit your head. Eryn..." Manon leaned forward, her hand placed firmly against Eryn's uninjured shoulder.

Eryn wondered if Manon was backtracking, insisting she stay because of political correctness, since, after all, Eryn was a reporter for the local paper. *It wouldn't do to let anyone assume the head of the Belmont Foundation was a bit of a homophobe, would it?* Eryn immediately regretted her ungrateful thoughts. *I'm no better. Didn't I give her the poor-little-rich-girl remark just the other day? Loosen up.*

"Okay, okay. I'll stay. Your couch is more comfy than my bed, actually." Eryn gave a self-deprecating grin. "I'm so damn sore."

"Your shoulder?" Manon seemed relieved, most likely because they were moving away from the hot topic of Eryn's sexuality.

"Yeah. It burns like hell."

"Here. Let me rub it." Manon moved closer. "No wonder it aches. You're black and blue. And the sling has twisted. There." She gingerly moved the sling around and unwound it. "Better?"

"Thank you...yes." Relief and fatigue flooded Eryn and made her less careful about what she said. "I want to get to know you too. I'm just so tired of criticism about something I'd never change even if I could."

"I'd never criticize you for anything like that." Manon moved her hand in small circles around Eryn's aching shoulder. "Whether you believe it or not, that's not who I am or what I'm about."

"Who are you? What are you about, exactly?" Eryn managed to open her eyes and look up at the austere woman next to her.

Manon appeared at a loss for words. She kept her hands on Eryn's shoulder and stroked it as her face became pensive. "I'll be damned if I know."

## CHAPTER TEN

Y ou look like hell, kiddo!" Harold belted from across the room. "That pompous ass really got you good."

*Geez, why don't we just put a freakin' ad in the paper and announce it to all of East Quay, you idiot.* "I'm okay, Harold. Where's Don?"

"Out with Hernandez, covering the extra PTA meeting. The parents and the teachers at East Quay High School are joining forces."

"That was my story!" Eryn was furious. "I want to finish it."

"Rex sees red when he hears your name, Goddard. Hernandez is on it."

"This isn't fair—"

"Get used to it. Nothing's fair. You pressed charges against him. Don't get me wrong, he deserved it, but I don't want you in his face just yet."

Fuming, Eryn laid her bag on the chair by her cluttered desk. "And what am I supposed to do instead? Lick stamps?"

"Watch it, kiddo." Harold's plump features darkened, and when he slowly licked his lips Eryn recognized the signs of an impending storm. "In fact, I want you to do an article about the Dodd woman."

"Who?"

"The closest thing we have to royalty in this town. The old bat has a hundredth birthday coming up in three days. She and her family go way back. You know, the one that owns almost all of New England's fishing industry."

"Marjorie Dodd Endicott?"

"Yeah."

"They don't just own most of the fishing industry, but also half the town, along with the Belmonts. I didn't know she was *that* old."

"It'll sell papers and ads if we run a this-is-your-life story on her. The Harding piece you did put you on the map. I want you to do something similar with the Dodd broad."

*Dodd broad?* Harold was a moron, and his lack of respect about other people never ceased to amaze her. *Why don't I just say "screw you" and get out?* She bit her lower lip and reached for her bag. *Out where?*

"I need you to cover her birthday arrangements. Supposed to be an all-day hoopla."

"Sure. When?" Eryn wondered if he detected her tone of resignation.

"Oh, in about," Harold checked the large clock on the wall, "thirty minutes."

"Thirty! God, that barely gives me time to grab my stuff and get the car." *That darn Volvo better not give me attitude.* Switching from resigned back to furious in a second, Eryn tugged the shoulder strap back over her head and made sure she had her computer, new tape recorder, and a notepad. She pulled on a baseball cap and hoped it would disguise the worst of her bruises. "Where is this 'hoopla' taking place?" She knew her not-so-subtle sarcasm was wasted on Harold.

"At the old lady's mansion behind the marina. You know, just after the pier."

"Got it. Want me to take photos too?" *That'll cost you.*

"Probably won't be anything worth taking except maybe the old bat and whoever she shakes hands with. Be good to know who's taking care of her stuff once she croaks. You never know, any dirt we can dig up on her might bring in more ads. That's what pays our salaries."

"I'm off." Eryn didn't wait to listen to the well-known litany.

In the parking lot, she stared gloomily at her old Volvo. She still hadn't collected her Yamaha from the Sea Stone Café. She'd called Mike to let her know she'd be by after work and try to fix the problem herself, instead of calling AAA. Eryn was used to working on her bike and wasn't afraid to get her hands dirty. In fact, she enjoyed tinkering with engines, when she found time.

It was hard to find time for her favorite hobby, but the hours she spent in the garage with her bike were worth gold. She drove past the marina, thinking it would be easy to swing by Mike's later. *Always something.*

She recapitulated the Dodd family history as she approached the house. As famous as the Kennedys, the Dodds had affected American history directly both politically and economically for more than three centuries. Marjorie, the head of the Dodd clan, still resided in East Quay where her dynasty had started out generations ago.

Marjorie Dodd Endicott had been a widow for more than forty years, having lost her husband in a boating accident. As far as Eryn knew, she had never remarried or been seen with a man since.

Cars overflowed the large circle in front of the Dodd mansion. Its beautifully aged cedar shingles and black slate roof had never yielded to a storm during its almost hundred years, and neither had its owner.

Eryn navigated her Volvo between a BMW and a Bentley and chuckled as she got out. "Be on your best behavior now, dear car. Looks like you're out of your element here." Shaking her head, she hurried toward the main entrance where livery-clad men stood guard.

"Eryn Goddard, *New Quay Chronicle.* Member of the press," she announced, holding up her press card.

A guard scrutinized it thoroughly. "Do you have a copy of the invitation faxed to your newspaper's office?"

"What? No. I don't know anything about an invitation. My boss…" *Damn that idiot!* "Surely you must realize since I'm with the *Chronicle*—"

"I cannot let you in without an invitation, ma'am." The man clearly wasn't going to budge.

"Wait. Hang tight." Eryn chewed her lower lip for a few seconds, then checked her watch. She still had time.

Picking up her cell phone she dialed the reception desk at the office. "Amanda? Hi. Eryn here. Do you see a fax about an invitation to a press conference at the Dodd Mansion? You do? Excellent. Now, can you fax it to my cell phone number in two minutes? Thanks. I'll bring you some of that godawful tea you love so much."

Eryn hung up and sat down on the wide staircase leading into the mansion. Her fingers flew as she placed her phone next to her PC tablet and allowed the Bluetooth to connect. Two minutes later the phone rang the special three-tone signal alerting her that a fax was coming in. Eryn let it download into the computer and then unplugged the phone.

Rising with the computer in her hands, she shoved it under the guard's nose. "Here's my invitation. Can I pass now?"

The guard looked impressed, and with a half smile he nodded. "Yes. Welcome to the press conference, Ms. Goddard."

"Better late than never." Pleased with herself for solving the problem, Eryn flashed him a smile and jogged up the stairs, the computer under her arm. "And only three minutes late. I deserve a medal."

Inside, the cedar-shingle house appeared unchanged by time and very well kept. Eryn knew the Dodd family had lived here for at least four generations, and the current Mrs. Dodd Endicott was the last of her line. Eryn thought it was sad that Mrs. Dodd Endicott had lived so many years without any close family members.

A Welcome sign directed Eryn toward a large sitting room where at least fifteen other reporters had gathered in a small circle around a frail woman on a cobalt blue silk sofa. Eryn stopped in the doorway when she saw who sat next to her.

Dressed entirely in red, Manon looked perfectly at ease. The sight of her long legs disappearing up the above-the-knee-length skirt took Eryn's breath away. Manon's hair was swept up in a loose twist tucked into the nape of her neck. She looked relaxed, her elegant hands lay idle on top of each other on her lap, and the memory of how they had massaged her three nights ago rushed back.

Eryn's own hands trembled as she flipped the top of her laptop to engage the tablet mode. She gripped the stylus with sweaty fingertips and tried to blend with the wall as she sat down behind the other the reporters.

*Another press conference. And who's here to support the center of interest? Of course, she is.* It wasn't enough for Manon to invade her thoughts constantly, causing Eryn to daydream. She had to show up every time she turned around.

"Welcome to this press conference," Manon began, and her voice created goose bumps along Eryn's arms. "Mrs. Dodd Endicott appreciates your interest in her upcoming birthday, which coincides with the 150th anniversary of Dodd's Fishing, Inc. Founded by Mrs. Dodd's grandfather, it was one of the few companies that didn't go under when the fishing industry was struck hard two decades ago. I could keep talking for hours about how I admire the way Mrs. Dodd diversifies her business, but I won't." Manon smiled and gestured toward the woman next to her. "Instead, I'll let Mrs. Dodd Endicott answer a few of your questions."

"Call me Marjorie." The wrinkled face was faded like an aging rose, yet still delicately beautiful. Her voice was low, but she spoke with force and command.

*I don't suppose you live to be a hundred and remain at the helm of your ship without being tough and determined.* Eryn glanced at Manon. *Is this your future? Rich, powerful—and alone?*

The reporters asked the usual questions: how it felt to turn a hundred, what her life had been like since she retired only a few years earlier, and if Marjorie had any special plans for her 101st year.

Marjorie answered every question politely, all the time maintaining a certain distance. Clearly Marjorie Dodd had dealt with the press before.

Eryn raised her hand. "Eryn Goddard, *New Quay Chronicle*. How long have you and Ms. Belmont been good friends?"

Marjorie tilted her head for a few seconds, peering between two other reporters. "Ms. Belmont began to visit me regularly when she was a child. We quickly became friends despite our age difference."

"Do you and Ms. Belmont really own most of the buildings and real estate in East Quay?"

"Yes, I believe so."

"Such power must entail tremendous responsibility. How do you handle it?"

"You're right." Marjorie seemed to consider the question. "It *is* a huge responsibility, and not all landlords take it seriously. The people and companies that inhabit the structures I own—as well as the ones Ms. Belmont owns—will testify to our care and maintenance."

Reluctantly charmed by Marjorie's candor, Eryn asked another question. "You can't reach such a venerable age without gaining wisdom. What have you learned that is worth sharing with our readers?"

Marjorie laughed and shook her head. "Dear one, your assumptions aren't very well based. Some people live a long time and don't learn a damn thing. Yet some children are born with wisdom sprouting out their ears. Life has taught me lessons, but they may be valuable only to me." She glanced at Manon. "But if you still want me to say something, there's always the subject of following your heart."

Eryn held her breath. Why did Marjorie look at Manon like that? Eryn noticed something resembling caution flicker over Manon's face.

"Sounds like a cliché," Eryn pointed out, putting a smile in her voice so she didn't sound offensive.

"Certain clichés came into being for a good reason." Marjorie sounded unfazed. "I defied convention when I insisted on going to college and on to university. When I started working my way up through the family business, my peers disapproved. I went against the wishes of my parents when I married my husband, a scholar uninterested in money or profit. I certainly rubbed people in my circles the wrong way when I kept working after getting married. We were never blessed with children, and I suppose work…was what I wanted and needed."

Marjorie suddenly looked fragile, and Manon rose from the couch. "That's it for today. As you know, we're having a huge celebration at the city hall on Friday, and if you give your name and the name of your publication to the guards outside, you'll receive an invitation. Thank you for coming."

Everyone began to leave the room, and Eryn typed a few more notes on her computer before sliding it into her bag.

"I would like to speak to Ms. Goddard in private."

❖

Manon watched Eryn's head snap up. Marjorie didn't sound at all frail anymore, and Eryn stepped closer, cautious. "Yes?"

"Not like this, in here," Marjorie said. "Why don't we go into my study? The leather couch there is much more comfortable. Marie can bring us something to drink."

Manon had to admire Eryn's poise as they walked into a dark wood-paneled room. A fire crackled in the fireplace, and Manon helped Marjorie into the chair closest to its warmth.

"May I ask what this is about?" Eryn took a seat across from Marjorie.

"Certainly, dear. Let's just give Marie a ring. Would you, Manon?"

"Of course." Manon pulled a brocade rope by the fireplace. Marjorie's determination to keep the house in its original state amused her. All the modern conveniences were available but well hidden behind an eighteenth-century façade.

"Now, Ms. Goddard. May I call you Eryn?"

"Sure."

"Eryn, I asked you in here for a reason."

"What can I do for you then?"

"You get straight to the point. I like that." Marjorie turned her head as the door opened and a middle-aged woman stepped inside. "Ah, Marie. Please bring my guests a hot drink and some of your scones. I'll have Darjeeling tea."

Both Manon and Eryn opted for black coffee, and Manon returned her attention to Marjorie, who focused on Eryn.

"Do you work on commission?"

"Excuse me?"

"Do you work, I mean write, on commission?"

"I haven't so far. I'm employed by the *Chronicle*. Why do you ask?"

"Let me put it this way. Do you find the history of East Quay worth telling?"

"Of course. Being one of the earliest settlements in New England makes it special. I'm proud to be from here."

"Did you know that my ancestor, William Dodd, helped found this town in 1699?"

"Yes. The library and the park are both named after him."

"Well, I'm not so interested in William's accomplishments—they've been well documented." Marjorie nodded at the woman who returned with a large tray. "Thank you, Marie. But I need a talented author to write about the female Dodds, their endeavors and achievements. They did a lot of good for this town, but you wouldn't know it from the way history's been written." Marjorie's voice hardened. "Nine generations of Dodd women."

"What makes you think I can pull that off?"

"You come highly recommended." Marjorie shot an unmistakable glance of appreciation at Manon.

Eryn's eyes narrowed. "I'm flattered, Marjorie, but I already have a job that takes up all my time."

Manon wanted to groan. *Don't let this opportunity slip by, Eryn. You're worth so much more than writing about council meetings and dog shows.*

"I know, but surely you can take a leave of absence. How could they refuse? You've worked there for, what is it, fifteen years?"

"Yes. But you don't know my boss. He can't even spell 'leave of absence,' let alone give me one. And he doesn't care much about

East Quay's history. He's not from here." Eryn grimaced. "Actually, sometimes I think he's an alien."

Marjorie slumped against the sofa back, her teacup clattering against the saucer. "I'd never ask you to resign."

*I would.* Manon thought vehemently. *It's a dead end.*

Eryn sipped her coffee, then reached for her long red braid, twisting it around her hand. Manon gazed at the long fingers, able to almost feel them against her own, like she had at the restaurant. *Say yes, Eryn.*

Eryn suddenly glanced up at Manon, catching her off guard. "The 'highly recommended' part?"

Feeling naked, as if Eryn could see the surge of desire that now raced through her veins, Manon recoiled. "When Marjorie asked if I knew of a local writer she could trust with this commission, I thought of you."

"Why? You have to know a million people. Surely some of them are better, more famous writers than I could ever hope to be?"

Manon had to smile at the exaggeration. "I know a couple of other writers. None of them are local, and the way you wrote about Vivian Harding proved that you might just be who Marjorie is looking for."

"Do you think so little of your own skill, Eryn?" Marjorie asked.

"What do you mean? I'm just realistic. For a small-town local reporter to make it big in the publishing world is…not very rational. Having a job that pays the bills is, however."

"Nothing wrong with being able to pay your bills," Marjorie concurred. "But this job would easily cover your bills for a couple of years. I don't have to tell you that there are a lot of journalists out there who'd sell their grandmother for a deal like this. My family is still prey for the media, and nobody's ever written about them like this before."

Eryn reached for a cup of coffee and took a large gulp. Swallowing repeatedly, she never took her eyes off Manon. "So, just for argument's sake, is this an offer or a suggestion? I mean, would I have to prove myself further?"

"No, you've proved yourself enough. You just have to decide if you want the commission."

Manon wondered what was going through Eryn's mind. They hadn't talked since the Saturday morning when Eryn had woken up on Manon's couch.

"It's beginning to sink in," Eryn said. "How long do I have to decide? How much would you pay me? Would I be able to support myself? It's an extensive project…"

Marjorie gestured for Manon to hand her a briefcase that sat next to the couch. Pulling out a bunch of papers, she handed Eryn a contract. "As you can see, you'd make enough to set aside money for two years after you finish the project. And, my dear, if you can't take a leave of absence, and instead quit your job now, you won't have any problems finding a new one. Especially since this book might be your ticket to the nonfiction best-seller lists." She briefly smiled. "The women in my family were as illustrious and interesting as the Kennedys, so, they have never been written about, and you'd have plenty of information."

"I'm sure I would." Eryn looked at Manon. "How did you know that Harold would send me here instead of Hernandez?"

"We asked him." Manon struggled to sound casual. *I bet her boss is dying to know what's going on, but it'll be up to Eryn to tell him. If she tells him.*

Eryn didn't comment. She put down her coffee cup, reached for another one of her bags, and pulled out a camera. "I need a few shots for the *Chronicle*. Is that all right? My photographer is on another assignment."

"Certainly," Marjorie agreed. "Go ahead. Make sure Manon is in the picture."

Manon didn't like to have her picture taken, but didn't want to disappoint Marjorie. She watched Eryn snap several shots of Marjorie. As Eryn moved around the room, Manon gazed into a floor-to-ceiling mirror where she secretly devoured every angle of Eryn. She noticed how Eryn's slacks enhanced her narrow waist and nicely shaped hips, embarrassed by her guilty pleasure. The thick braid danced across Eryn's back, and Manon remembered how those silky red masses had looked when spread across the pillow on her couch.

"Manon?" Eryn motioned for her to move in closer, so she hid her discomfort and managed a smile for Marjorie's benefit as Eryn kept clicking.

Eryn took three more photos, then put her camera away. "Thank you, ladies. When will you need my final decision?"

"I'd like to announce it during the festivities Friday," Marjorie said.

"Then I'll let you know by Thursday."

"That's cutting it a bit close." Manon got up as well. "It's Monday. Could you notify us—"

"On Thursday." Eryn's eyes reminded Manon of the green ice she'd once seen during a cruise in the Arctic Ocean. "I don't like being manipulated."

*Oh, this is going well.* "All right. Thursday."

"Thank you for the coffee, Marjorie. Manon." Eryn nodded stiffly and pulled the shoulder strap of her leather bag over her head, securing it on her hip. "I'll see myself out."

A stunned silence followed, then Marjorie turned to Manon, a frown on her thin face. "Not quite the enthusiasm I'd hoped for."

"I did warn you that she might be cautious."

"Yes, but I detected something else. She seemed more apprehensive about you, my dear, than me. Shouldn't it be the other way around since she's your neighbor?"

"Perhaps." Manon felt her cheeks warm. "We got off to a rocky start. And being assaulted by Archibald Rex last week has probably made her distrust everyone more."

"But you trust her?" Marjorie tilted her head.

"Yes. I do." Manon shrugged. "Despite everything else, Eryn shows a lot of integrity."

"Everything else?" Marjorie held up her hands. "Strike that. None of my business. I do hope she'll say yes. All my instincts, and you know they've always served me well, tell me she'd be perfect for the job."

"I'd never doubt the famous Dodd instincts." Manon smiled.

"And a few of them insist there's more than meets the eye between the two of you." Marjorie gave a regal nod. "But as I said, none of my business."

Only Manon's impeccable manners prevented her from rolling her eyes. *Sneaky.* "There's no business either to examine or to leave alone."

Marjorie gave a surprisingly resounding laugh. She didn't look at all convinced.

# CHAPTER ELEVEN

Mike flinched as the bell on the café door chimed. She half hoped it was Vivian and half dreaded seeing her. The three days of silence after their heated kisses on her couch made her feel as if cold fingers were digging holes in her heart.

Instead she watched Eryn enter the almost-empty café, rain dripping from her leather coat. "Hi, there. God, it's pouring."

"Hello. Latte?"

"Please. I just had some awful coffee at the Dodd Mansion."

Surprised, Mike glanced over at Eryn, who sat at the bar. "Dodd Mansion? You're moving up in the world."

"Not likely." Eryn grinned. "Purely business. Marjorie Dodd turns a century old Friday."

"Wow, that's not bad. She's still going strong, isn't she?"

"Very strong. Very convincing too, if you ask me."

"What do you mean?"

"They offered me a job."

"They?"

"Manon Belmont was there too. Turns out they're good friends."

"No surprise there." Mike began steaming the milk. After the noise quieted, she said, "They're bound to move in the same circles."

"I suppose. Thanks." Eryn reached for the steaming glass. "It was just so sudden, you know. What if it's not right for me?"

"But you hate your boss. Would Mrs. Dodd be worse?"

"No way." Eryn squirmed. "But you know, I have to pay my bills, and this commission would just last two years—"

"Two years?" Mike couldn't understand why Eryn hesitated.

"That's not bad. A lot of people don't know what they'll be doing in two *days*."

Eryn's cheeks turned pink. "I'm having a rather luxurious problem, I know."

"Sorry, Eryn." Mike wanted to take her words back. She knew how important Eryn's independence was to her. With a mother like Eryn's, she had to support herself. Mike had never met the woman, and she didn't particularly want to. In fact, Mike hated to think what she would say if she ever saw how Mrs. Goddard treated her daughter. "I didn't mean to sound holier-than-thou."

"You didn't. Don't worry about it."

Mike studied Eryn. She looked pale, which emphasized her bruises. "Sure you're okay?"

"Yeah. Well. No, not really." Eryn sighed and sipped her latte. "I may be in trouble."

"What?" Mike grabbed the stool she kept behind the counter and sat down. "Surely a job offer isn't—"

"I'm not talking about that. It's something else. Something a lot more likely to screw up my life." She rested her chin against her palm. "God, my head hurts."

"I've got aspirin."

"Thanks, but my stomach won't tolerate it. I better get some Tylenol on the way home. I can't keep taking the pills the doctor gave me. They make me act weird."

"Really?"

"Yeah." Eryn met Mike's gaze. "Too loose-lipped. I told Manon that I found her attractive even before I hit my head. After I started taking medication, it got worse."

"What did she say? What did *you* say?"

"She was the perfect lady. She took me in when I was hurt and took care of me."

"But no…response?"

"No, not really." Eryn pulled her eyebrows together. "But something about her, something I couldn't put my finger on, made me wonder…I don't mean to gossip. It's just that thinking about her is driving me crazy. And now she's recommended me to Marjorie Dodd to write a book!"

For a minute, Mike's own worries felt manageable. "So?"

"It's an exciting project, and normally I'd give my eyeteeth for it."

"But?"

"But…I don't know." Eryn's eyes glimmered with unshed tears. "Damn, just look at me! I don't know what to do, and I have this stupid headache and…"

Mike knew Eryn was never weepy. She rounded the desk and put a protective arm around her, making sure the few customers couldn't see Eryn's distress. "You don't have to decide on any of it right now. Just breathe." She gently tightened her grip. "Why don't you come behind the counter? I keep a comfy chair and a computer behind this curtain. You can put your feet up and…I may have some Tylenol. Come on."

Eryn followed Mike. "Thanks. You're being so thoughtful."

"Hey, what are friends for? You wrote that piece about the Sea Stone Café and didn't drag up my sordid past." Mike deliberately exaggerated her relief. In fact, just thinking about her first publicity campaign for the café made her stomach churn.

"You don't have a sordid past. You did the best with what you had. Nothing to be ashamed of."

*You still don't know all of it. You don't know how much I've hidden.* Mike forced a smile and reached for the medicine cabinet underneath the counter. Pulling out an unopened box of Tylenol, she waved it in the air. "We're in luck."

"Thanks again." Eryn accepted two capsules and a bottle of water.

Two large gulps later, Eryn sat down in the "office" behind the curtain. Mike took care of two new customers in the meantime, but kept a close watch on Eryn to make sure she didn't look any worse off. When she finished, she dragged a stool up next to Eryn, making sure she could still check on the café.

"I've never met anyone like her." Eryn spoke in a low voice.

Mike didn't have to ask who Eryn was talking about. "She's quite the mystery, isn't she? Contradictory."

"Yes, isn't she?" Eryn nodded emphatically. "So collected, with her official image usually in place. But so…caring, with a strange sort of passion showing through, which I don't think she realizes."

Mike sat waiting for her friend to choose to confide in her—or not.

"She was so good to me last Friday night. She rubbed my back and acted like I mattered. And then she goes right back to being strict and stern...acting like freakin' nobility!"

"And you think that's a problem?" It wasn't like Eryn to be this upset. Mike wondered just how vulnerable she'd become.

"I'm so stupid." Eryn clenched the mug. "I have no clue if she's into women. God knows she's had enough men to fill two soccer teams. All hunks, from the look of them."

"You researched her?" Mike raised an eyebrow and tried not to sound judgmental, even if she was surprised.

"Yeah." Eryn's cheeks finally colored when a faint blush crept up from her neck. "I went through some files. There were pictures from the social events she goes to. You know, fund-raisers, openings, that sort of thing."

"Not everything's the way it seems."

"Some things are. Most, even."

"Don't judge her too quickly. I know what some people still say about me after all these years." Mike swallowed. "I'd hoped they'd invite me to the East Quay Chamber of Commerce dinner this year. Someone, somewhere, put a stop to that. And the Sea Stone Café is one of the fastest-growing new businesses in East Quay." She knew she sounded angry and hurt, but that was how she felt, and it was a relief to finally tell someone.

"Damn, Mike, they're idiots."

"Yeah, but they have the power. You know, Mr. Ludlow, the banker, is chairman and he decides if I do or die. I thought I'd proved myself, and after the article you wrote, I actually thought someone like me could enter their realm. But I guess not."

Feeling defeated, Mike slumped against the wall. *And then there's Vivian. Have I pushed her away for good? It felt so right to kiss her. How could that be a mistake?*

"You could appeal their decision." Eryn turned and looked at Mike. "They've got standards for membership. You fulfill those standards and ought to be voted in. It's that simple."

"It's not simple at all. I'm persona non grata."

"That's the most ridiculous thing I've ever heard. Who says that?"

A famous voice interrupted and Mike twirled. "Vivian!"

"Hello, Mike. First of all, I need a double espresso. Your best."

"You got it." Happy to have something distract her rampaging emotions, Mike turned to the espresso machine and pressed finely ground coffee beans into the mallet. She had to force herself not to use too much strength with the tamper, not to destroy the beans.

She inhaled and exhaled three times, slowly and deliberately. Holding Vivian's espresso in a tall cup, she made sure she was smiling politely. *If it's possible to smile with such stiff lips.* Mike was sure she looked like an idiot, grinning from ear to ear in pure nervousness.

"Thanks." Vivian sighed and sipped her coffee. "I needed this. All of it." She gestured around the room. "I had to meet with a New York conductor, an old friend, but he kept trying to persuade me to do three concerts at Carnegie Hall in six months. I had to tell him twice that I'm not doing any concerts after my farewell performance here." Vivian sounded strong and certain of her decision, but Mike saw the hurt in her eyes, the beautiful eyes that were going blind.

"I'm looking forward to hearing you sing and take your hometown by storm," Eryn said.

"Thank you, but I'm not so sure these days. I…have a lot on my mind, and it affects my voice."

"Then we just have to make sure your mind is where it should be." Mike grabbed a cloth and began wiping off the spotless counter. She'd rather put her arms around Vivian and hold her tight, to comfort her. She rubbed more vigorously.

"Time to call it a day," Eryn said, and rose. "I feel better now. I'll call AAA after all and have them come pick up the bike. I'm too tired to fiddle with it myself."

"I put a plastic cover over it."

"Great. Thanks." Eryn lit up. She felt around in her pocket, flipped open her cell phone, and walked away from them to place her call.

Vivian looked at Mike with a question in her eyes. "Are you all right, Mike? You seem…muted."

"I'm fine. The after-work crowd should be here soon, and business is great." Mike knew she was stalling, but Vivian's steady gaze didn't let her off the hook. Annoyed and feeling cornered, she reached for a crate of oranges and began stacking them next to the juice press.

"Have I done something to upset you?" Vivian's voice, tinged with sudden sorrow, stung.

*Upset doesn't even begin to describe it. I kissed you, for heaven's sake! I more or less attacked you on the couch and forced a kiss on you...* "No. Yes. I mean, it was my fault." She sent the customers at the other end of the room a worried look. "Let's don't talk about it here."

"Fine. Where then?"

"I don't know. I'm busy now." Goose bumps rose all over Mike's arms and legs. *Can't you see I'm dying, Vivian? Stop pushing.*

"Can you come over tonight? We could walk the dogs and have a late-night snack."

Mike wanted to decline. More than anything she wanted to hide from Vivian, who had pierced her shields with strange effortlessness. *But I did promise to be there for her.* "All right. I close at ten. I can ask Martha and Edward to cover for me the last half hour."

"I'd like that. A lot." Vivian slumped back a little on her stool.

"I'm off, then. Thank you, Mike," Erin said.

"Go home and rest. You're still pale."

Eryn frowned. "I'll try."

She left, and Vivian also rose from the stool and finished the last of her espresso. "Delicious, as always, *cara*. See you later."

Mike nodded, reached for the cup at the same time as Vivian, and their hands met. Vivian, who apparently hadn't seen Mike's hand, grasped it. "Mike. Don't shut me out," she whispered. "Please."

The touch almost did Mike in. She squeezed Vivian's hand and held on for a few seconds too long. "I'll be there."

❖

"Hold the elevator, please!"

Eryn, about to press the button for the third floor, opened the outer gate while Manon hurried through it, holding at least eight shopping bags from different boutiques and carrying her briefcase under her left arm. "Eryn. Great. Could you save my computer? I overestimated my strength."

"Got it." Eryn grabbed the briefcase and tried to hold back the gasp that escaped her when she inadvertently stroked the outside of Manon's breast. "Sorry."

Manon put down her bags and reached for the briefcase. "Thank you," she said. "That could have been a disaster."

"Here you go." Eryn handed it over and motioned toward the bags, happy to have something else to focus on. "You've been busy."

"Yes. I have so many functions coming up, not to mention the fund-raiser concert in a few weeks. I had to restock my wardrobe. I realized just how busy I'd be when Marjorie and I tried to find a time to go over the research material with you—should you choose to accept."

"You sound like *Mission Impossible.*" Eryn smiled. "'Should you choose...'"

Manon hesitated, then chuckled. "I did, didn't I?" Manon seemed more at ease and younger as she leaned against the elevator wall. Only when it stopped with a sudden jerk did she square her shoulders again. "You *will* give it serious thought, won't you, Eryn?"

"Yes. I said I would." *Please, don't try to weasel a decision out of me just yet.* Eryn opened the inner gate.

"I know. I know." Manon held up her hands, palms toward Eryn.

Eryn pushed the outer gate open and regretted her terse reply. *They might be offering me the chance of a lifetime, and I'm acting like I'm being stalked.* "Hey. Want a cup of coffee?"

Manon looked at her for several seconds, and Eryn had no idea what might be going through her head. "Coffee would be lovely. Thank you."

"I don't have Mike's flair for making espresso, but I make good regular black coffee."

"I'd take instant after trying on seventeen cocktail dresses at Genevieve's."

Genevieve's Boutique & Shoes was one of the fancy clothing stores on Main Street that carried shoes costing half a month of Eryn's salary. "Seventeen? You're kidding."

Eryn took mercy on the briefcase again, and Manon gathered her purchases. "No. All gorgeous, which made it almost impossible to choose."

They walked into Eryn's condo and into the kitchen. "Please, sit down. I'll have some real coffee—not instant—brewing in a minute."

"Sounds heavenly."

Eryn busied herself with the coffee machine, pouring ground coffee beans into the filter and measuring water. Manon's discreet scent permeated the kitchen, and Eryn hoped it would linger after she left. "You like it strong, don't you?"

"Yes, please. Nothing's worse than weak coffee."

*God, that voice of hers.* Its velvet, throaty qualities rippled along Eryn's spine and sent dark shivers through her abdomen. *How can a voice cause physical reactions?* Eryn had never experienced such a blatant response. Sure, her former lover Jenny had been hot, sizzling, even, but it had taken obvious overtures and hands-on caresses for Eryn to react the way she now responded to Manon's voice. *Say something more. Please.*

"I like the way you've arranged the copper pieces."

*That's it. A topic.* "They were my aunt's, and she kept them in a cabinet."

Eryn glanced up at the collection, everything from copper coffeepots to cookie cutters that she'd polished and now displayed on the window sill. She wasn't going to tell Manon how, while polishing the smallest toy-size kettle, she'd begun to cry.

Amanda never spoke ill of Harriet Goddard to Eryn's face, but Eryn had once overheard her great-aunt talk to one of her friends. "The child needs love. It's as simple as that. If Harriet can't see past her own prejudice to meet her daughter's needs, then I will. She praises Eryn's sisters for tying their shoes, and this child...she brings home top-grade essays to show her mother, and...Harriet's a fool. A blind, misguided fool."

The conversation had stuck in the seventeen-year-old Eryn's memory all these years, and Amanda's condo had been the only place she'd been able to relax and be herself.

Not now, though. She felt jittery and as if she were running a temperature, merely because Manon was sitting on one of her kitchen chairs.

"Your kitchen is so cozy. Perhaps I should go for something less... strict. My interior decorator talked me into an austere-looking...well, you've seen it."

Manon's kitchen was white, gray, and brushed steel, very modern. "Yes. It's beautiful, but not very homey."

"I know."

There was an uncomfortable silence as Eryn finished setting up the coffee machine. She turned and reached for mugs from the cabinet, moaning when she accidentally raised her left arm too high.

"Let me help." Manon was immediately by Eryn's side and placed an arm around her waist. "You've been carrying that bag of yours all day. It may have made your shoulder worse."

"No, I'm okay. It's only when I try to raise my arm above my head—"

"Listen to me. Sit. I'll pour the coffee when it's ready."

"All right." Eryn knew when to give in. Manon's voice, as sexy as it could be, sometimes sounded relentless. "You take it black, right?"

"Yes."

"Me too."

"I downloaded the pictures I took at the Dodd Mansion." Eryn sat down, reached into her bag, and pulled out her computer. "Want to see?" *Anything to get away from feeling so darn jittery.*

"I'd love to." Manon rose and pulled out two ceramic mugs from the open cabinet before walking over to stand behind Eryn. "Marjorie's still striking, don't you think?"

"Yes, you can tell she was gorgeous. She doesn't look her age at all."

Eryn pulled up the image folder and made sure only the pictures she wanted to show Manon were highlighted, then clicked the button that launched the preview.

Manon leaned closer and steadied herself against the kitchen table. "You're a good photographer," she said as the first few images rolled by. "Marjorie looks really great and…what…"

Eryn stared at her computer in horror. Frozen, she watched as the slideshow kept going and displayed the five close-ups she'd taken of Manon.

*Shit! What the hell…how could this happen? I selected only the pictures of Marjorie.* The silence was overwhelming, and Eryn wanted to crawl down under the table and hide.

"When did you intend to use these?" Manon straightened up and walked over to the counter. She poured coffee into two mugs and slowly, deliberately turned around. Her slate gray eyes were cold. Darker than usual, they bored into Eryn and demanded an answer.

"Never." Eryn clasped her hands tight in her lap.

"Never? I find that hard to believe. You were there as a reporter, and you made sure I thought you were taking pictures of only Marjorie or the two of us together."

"I was. I mean, I was there for the *Chronicle*. These…" Eryn gestured toward the computer screen with a queasy feeling in her stomach. "These were…for me. It was still wrong of me. I…You looked so photogenic, but that's no excuse." *Damn, I really screwed up. She doesn't trust me as it is. And now…I'm such an idiot!*

"For you? What do you mean?"

"For my personal viewing pleasure." Eryn knew her attempt at irony was futile. "I'll erase them right away." She placed her index finger on the touch pad.

"No! Wait. Let me look at them." Manon walked closer and handed a mug to Eryn, her eyes on the screen as she sipped her coffee. "They're not bad. I don't like being the center of attention for pictures, so you actually took some good ones…because I didn't know I was your target."

Eryn's throat constricted at Manon's choice of words. *Target*. It made her sound like paparazzi or, worse, a stalker. She merely held on to her mug, not sure what to say.

"And you won't use these for the *Chronicle* or sell them to anyone else?"

"I can burn them on a CD for you, then erase them from my hard drive."

"You could already have e-mailed them to your office."

"I haven't! I shouldn't have taken the pictures, but, damn it, I'm not a freakin' liar!"

"All right." Manon bit into her lower lip. "Don't erase them. Just give me your word that you won't share them with anyone without asking."

"I promise." Eryn had to put her mug down on the table since her hands were shaking so badly. "Are you very angry?"

"I was for a moment." Manon leaned closer and examined one of the pictures. "What am I looking at? I'm so focused on something behind you. Oh."

Eryn turned her head and found that Manon was closer than she realized. She accidentally bumped her nose into Manon's cheek, making her jump.

Manon held on to the backrest of Eryn's chair. "I should get upstairs. It's late."

"Manon, please. We keep tiptoeing around each other." The words flowed out of Eryn, tumultuous and scattered. "Ever since I told you I'm attracted to you and…and I have no idea if you ever have or could imagine…I mean I have the feeling you're not indifferent to me, but…"

Manon inhaled deeply and drank some coffee, perhaps to buy time. "Eryn, don't."

"I *have* to say this. I don't want to waste time beating around the bush. I look at you and go weak at the knees. Literally," Eryn insisted, and stood up. "And at times you look at me with this strange expression of…I don't know what! Am I that scary?" Another joke fell flat to the ground and incinerated on impact.

"You have no idea," Manon quipped, her eyes sooty black.

"That's what I said! I have no idea how you feel and it's driving me insane. You set up this great working opportunity for me and make it very hard for me to refuse, and then you act as if we're casual acquaintances. Where do you stand, Manon? And most important—are you gay or not?"

# Chapter Twelve

Manon tried frantically to think of a plausible excuse to run out of Eryn's kitchen. Instead, her mind went blank, and all she could do was to stare at Eryn for several agonizing seconds. Her tone turned from chilly to ice age. "That's a very personal question. What do you expect me to say?"

"How about the truth?" Eryn said kindly. "How about quitting this I-don't-know-if-she-knows-that-I-know game? I've been an out lesbian since I was fifteen. My mother hates me for it, but the rest of my family range from very supportive to 'fine, live your life, but let's not talk about it.' I've fought hard to remain out."

"It must've been difficult." Manon tried to refocus the attention back to Eryn's life.

"For me, it would've been harder to stay closeted." Eryn pulled out the chair next to her. "Please. Sit down. I think you know quite a bit about being in the closet."

"You assume too much." Manon's chest constricted. Reluctantly she sat down, ramrod straight, on the very edge of the chair, at a ninety-degree angle from Eryn.

"Do I?" Eryn said gently. "My gaydar is rarely off."

"Your what?" Manon had no idea what Eryn was talking about.

"Gaydar. Inner radar that says if the other person is gay."

"There's no such thing."

"I disagree, but okay—ever heard the saying 'it takes one to know one'?" Eryn leaned forward and grasped Manon's arm.

"Yes, I have," Manon managed. The touch burned through her shirt. She looked at the pale hand, adorned with pink, blunt nails and occasional freckles. It was small yet unmistakably strong. "But it's still a personal matter that—"

"We've shared lots of personal things. Especially last Friday night. What's your worst fear? That I'll jump your bones if you admit you find women attractive? Or that I'll out you?"

Manon heard a faint trace of resentment in Eryn's voice, but also something else. *She's laughing at me. She's openly gay and proud of it. I must seem pathetic, but she has no way of knowing...* Manon looked down at Eryn's hand. "No. I don't think that at all," she said quietly. *I think you must see me as the most pitiful person you've ever met.*

Eryn squeezed her arm and moved to caress her elbow. "Damn, Manon, I'm sorry. I'm being an ass."

Manon could barely make herself look at Eryn. Her heart was pounding, and nothing in her upbringing had prepared her for this situation. Normally she skidded in and out of conversational traps with the ease of an Olympic slalom skier, but now her fear and conflicting emotions immobilized her. "You're right," she whispered. Her throat hurt.

"What?" Eryn sat as if frozen, her hand still around Manon's elbow. "About being an ass. Yeah—"

"No. You're right about me being afraid. Afraid of the repercussions. I have my work and my responsibilities. I don't have the time or the energy for any type of relationship. Don't you see? The legacy, my family's dedication to everything I also hold sacred...it all matters more than—"

"Than what? Your own happiness? Your life? Your future?"

"The foundation *is* my happiness and future! I've spent my life in that office." Tears of frustration rose in Manon's eyes. "It's what I've lived for all these years. Ever since I was thirteen, the foundation has been my pride and joy, my everything." She wanted to move her arm out of Eryn's reach, but her touch was strangely comforting.

Eryn sat still, watching Manon with sad eyes. "That's normally how people talk about their family or their children."

"My existence might seem pitiful to you, but I don't lack anything!" Manon forced her tears back, blinking repeatedly. "My foundation means a lot to a great many people, and the reward I get from helping people create better lives for themselves is more than enough."

"How about companionship? How about human touch?" Eryn's voice rose as she began to rub Manon's arm. "How about *this*?"

Eryn sounded so passionate that Manon expected her touch to be equally forceful. Instead Eryn rose and pulled Manon with her into a careful embrace. Manon didn't struggle. She stood passive, determined to prove Eryn wrong. She couldn't surrender to the secret feelings she'd kept from everyone for so long.

"How about this?" Eryn whispered, now in a low purr. "I can feel your heart beat, faster and faster." She placed her hands on either side of Manon's chest, and her thumbs, hot through the fabric, reached just below her breasts. "I'm not forcing you. You want this." She sounded so certain.

"You won't achieve anything with this demonstration." Manon used her most haughty tone of voice. "Why are you doing this, Eryn?"

"Because you're trying to fool yourself and everybody else. And because I'm at my wits' end how to act around you. You're so exciting and so hot. And you look at me with such confusion and desire. That in itself is damn sexy."

She stepped even closer and pressed her breasts against Manon. "I saw how you checked me out when I took the pictures of Marjorie. Don't you think I know what such glances imply?" She reached under Manon's chin and tipped her head back. "And the way you look at me now…down that aristocratic nose. You try to keep me at a distance, and it must annoy you that it doesn't work."

As she tried to avoid Eryn's touch, Manon found their lips only a whisper apart. Mesmerized, she stared into Eryn's eyes and leaned in closer, unable to resist. "Eryn, please…"

After Eryn brushed her lips against Manon's, parting them with gentle insistence, she deepened the kiss, and Manon forgot to breathe. The incredible tenderness, the small nibbles—it all flooded her senses with arousal and panic.

"Manon," Eryn whispered against her mouth. "I've longed for this. Your lips. Kiss me back."

Manon clenched her fists at her side, where she stood stiff and shaking within Eryn's embrace. She wasn't in control of her body or her mind, and couldn't think of anything except how Eryn's arms felt around her.

"Relax, honey. Relax." Eryn's breath was hot against Manon's lower lip. Manon could feel her resistance crumble. Her body ached, and even worse, her soul was in agony, demanding she give in. Eventually, Manon gave a tormented whimper, raised her arms, and slid them up along Eryn's sides. She wrapped them around Eryn's neck and held on as she parted her lips.

"Ah…" Eryn pulled her closer and cupped Manon's neck. Manon felt the tender fingers in her hair, massaging, pressing her closer into the embrace.

Nothing could have prepared her for how Eryn's mouth would feel or taste. All those years when she struggled alone with her feelings, she'd never known this, never expected…this.

Eryn's tongue, gentle and passionate, explored her mouth, nudged at Manon's tongue and teased it. Manon held back sobs of dread and allowed herself to reciprocate. She kissed Eryn with startling abandon and cupped Eryn's cheeks as she angled her own head for better access. She reveled in the feeling of Eryn's tongue against hers, wrestling, as if fighting for domination. The caresses sent surges of blood to her breasts and the delta between her legs.

Blatant desire welled up and blinded Manon for a few precious seconds before panic took over and she broke free. She held up her hands, palms outward, and backed away from Eryn, only to stagger when she bumped into the kitchen table. "No…I can't. I'm sorry."

"Hey, calm down," Eryn said, flushed. "It's all right, Manon." She reached out.

"No. Don't. Just don't *touch* me."

"I won't." Eryn's face twitched with an expression of pain that passed so quickly, Manon wasn't sure it had ever existed. She lowered her hand. "I promise."

Manon breathed heavily and made sure the corner of the table was between them. "This was a mistake."

"Yes. I realize that."

Manon didn't know if she had imagined the luminescence of Eryn's eyes. Anyway, they were now a dark, dull forest green.

"I should go."

"I'm not stopping you." Eryn also took a step back.

Despite her words, Manon remained where she was, her mouth dry. "You understand, don't you? Why this can't happen?"

"I understand that we kissed and it was wonderful. You panicked and I'm sorry if I scared you. Most of all, I'm sorry it wasn't wonderful for you."

Manon flinched. "Nothing you did scared me." *I scared the hell out of myself.* "As I said, I should go."

"Then leave."

"Very well." Manon began gathering her purchases, but the bags' handles slipped through her fingers and the contents spilled out of one of them. "Great. Perfect." She wasn't in control of anything in this situation, and she hated the feeling.

"Here. Let me help you." As Eryn bent down and picked up the silky material of the extravagant nightgown she'd let Genevieve persuade her to buy. The crimson silk ran through Eryn's fingers like blood when she placed it back into the bag. "Pretty."

Manon took a deep breath, feeling ridiculous. *She's right. I'm panicking. I'm acting like a damn cliché of an old maid. How silly is this?* She stopped what she was doing. "Eryn."

Eryn knelt next to her and now looked up with trepidation. "Yes?"

"Can we start over?"

"What?" Confusion replaced the apprehension. "How do you mean?"

"Whatever my reaction just now suggests, I'm not a coward." Manon was glad her voice was steady, although barely more than a whisper. "And I don't tell deliberate lies, even if I'm usually not very forthcoming."

"I never thought you were either a coward or a liar," Eryn said, and she raised her hand, palm up. "Just afraid."

"You're right." Manon tilted her head, examining the concept. A strange sort of calm settled in her chest. "I've been afraid for a very long time."

"What can I say or do to reassure you? I shouldn't have kissed you like that." Eryn blushed. "God knows I was dying to taste your lips, but I was still wrong."

"Perhaps. You were my first."

"First woman to kiss you? For real?"

"Yes." *And that's not all.*

"So you've only been with men up till now?"

"Three, to be exact. One when I was in college. One twelve years ago. Very nice, both of them, but I let them slip through my fingers."

"And the third?"

"Two years ago." Manon shuddered. "Let's just say that he didn't adhere to the arrangement."

Eryn looked like she wanted to ask follow-up questions.

"I may tell you about that another day," Manon added, to forestall questions she wasn't prepared to answer—yet.

"All right." Eryn sat down on the floor again and pushed the bags aside. "It makes sense, though. You're a lesbian. Of course you had to let them go."

Manon swallowed repeatedly and slumped into a sitting position with her back against a leg of the kitchen table. It didn't occur to her until later how absurd it was for her to sit on a kitchen floor. She couldn't even remember the last time she'd sat on any floor. Unable to avoid Eryn's statement, she leaned her head back. "Yes. Yes, I am." Cold shivers launched icicles throughout her body. *I don't talk about this. With anyone. I don't want to. And here she is, gazing at me with those hypnotic green eyes. Damn her to hell. Why do I let her? Why can't I say no?*

"Reba Renaldo was way off base there, wasn't she?"

"Who? Oh, the columnist." Manon shook her head. "Way off."

"And you're obviously not only closeted, but you have a serious problem with your sexual preference."

"Are these questions?" Manon sighed. "It doesn't matter what I am or not. I'm single. I live alone and like it that way."

"But what about love?" Eryn's eyes grew wider, and she covered her forehead with her hand. "You make it sound as if you've decided to never give love a chance. Do you have any idea what you're missing with someone of your own gender?" Green eyes flashed a whole range of emotions as Eryn scooted closer. "You're a wonderful woman. Any person, male or female, would count themselves lucky to be with you."

"I don't think so. In fact," she added, again uncharacteristically forthcoming, "I have a very modest libido." Manon tried to explain and cringed at how she exposed herself. "I have no…particular urges. That doesn't bother me much."

"Hey. There was nothing wrong with your libido just now." Eryn looked at Manon cautiously before she spoke. Eryn's gaze raked up and down as if gauging Manon's potential reaction before she spoke. "You were furious, and you may have resented me for kissing you, but you can't deny that you clung to me and kissed me back. You melted into me, and your kiss was passionate. I'd call that having urges!"

*Oh, God, she's right. It was as if I discovered…something.* In fact, Manon could still feel the physical traces of her body's reactions.

Eryn's shimmering eyes didn't let her off the hook, and she wanted to grab her briefcase and hold it up as a shield. "Fine. Urges." She pressed her lips together for a moment. "That's not normal for me."

"So, shouldn't that tell you something? When you kiss a woman for the first time, or rather, another woman kisses you, and you feel more than usual, it should." Eryn's eyes blazed. "And, damn it, it was such a wonderful kiss, you would've had to be dead not respond to it!"

"You may be confusing anger with passion…" Manon stopped talking and placed a slow hand over her mouth. "What?"

"When you feel more than usual in a woman's arms—"

"No. Not that." Manon spoke past a painful lump in her throat that made her voice darker.

"Oh." Eryn smiled carefully. "You meant the part about the kiss being wonderful?"

"Yes."

"It was. Breathtaking, arousing…and it grabbed me solidly by the heart." Eryn hugged her arms around her bent legs and placed her chin on top of her knees. "I'm not exaggerating. It did."

Manon knew this was no time to play the slalom skier. Eryn deserved the truth, even if Manon had to back off afterward. "Then I should level with you. It wasn't just my first kiss with another woman. It was my first kiss—ever."

❖

Vivian glanced up as Perry and Mason escorted Mike into the living room with its panoramic view of the Atlantic. She had arranged a tray with cheese, crackers, and fruit and put it and an open bottle of red wine on the coffee table. Now she leaned against the armrest of the couch and smiled at Mike.

She felt nervous again. Their conversation at the café earlier had almost disheartened her. Mike had acted offended, or hurt, and Vivian wondered what she might have done wrong. She was afraid to ask but had promised herself not to waste any time ever again. Time was not her friend these days, and Mike's companionship was becoming increasingly important.

"Welcome. I see the boys let you in." Vivian motioned for Mike to sit down.

"They more than let me in. Mason nudged me from behind, and Perry took my wrist in his mouth and pulled me along."

"Smart fellows. They can sense you like them." *And me?* Mike remained standing a little longer, then sat in the armchair. "That looks good. May I?"

"Of course. Could you pour us some wine? My eyes are a bit blurry tonight. It's been a long day."

Mike immediately turned and looked at Vivian with concern. "Are you in pain?"

"Only a bit. It's not bad."

"Maybe you need to go to bed. I can let myself out." Mike was halfway up from her chair and looked ready to bolt. "We can do this some other time."

"Stop it, Mike. Listen to me. I'm fine. I've been looking forward to talking with you." Vivian held her breath. "Please don't go."

Mike still rose, but only to pour the wine and hand her a glass. She sat down next to Vivian on the couch and pulled the coffee table closer. "There. Now we can reach everything. Some cheese?"

"Not yet." Vivian felt sheer relief that Mike had decided to stay. "What do you think of the wine? It's a South African Graham Beck that the conductor of my last performance in Milano gave me after closing night."

"But that's a special bottle! A gift." Mike stared into her glass. "Don't you want to share this with someone special?"

"I am," she said quietly. "At least I'd like to think we're special together, *cara.*"

Even if Vivian had to squint to make out Mike's features, she could still see how Mike's eyes darkened. *Pale skin, black eyes. I wonder… what's the color of your heart, Mike?*

"Then I propose a toast," Mike replied evenly. "To today."

"Today?" Vivian raised her glass, though she had no idea what Mike was talking about.

"It's an important day. It's all we have." Mike sipped her wine. "Oh. This is great."

Vivian followed suit, her brain still trying to wrap itself around Mike's toast. "Yes, it is. It's one of my favorites." She took another sip, which soothed her throat. "Glad you like it."

Mike closed her eyes, and Vivian could observe her unabashedly. Dressed in a navy blue shirt over black jeans, she was a study of shadows in the firelight. Her short hair glimmered with a bluish tint, and a new scent, a mix of coffee, vanilla, and cinnamon, wafted toward Vivian. When Mike looked up at her again, Vivian saw an ocean of unspoken questions. *Why do I get the feeling that she may never ask them, unless I start first? So withdrawn. So...scared.*

Mike held on to her glass of wine and took small sips every now and then, staring wordlessly into the fire. It had taken Vivian quite some time to get it started. She had no problems entertaining the world's leading classical musicians, but she wasn't sure she could make a room cozy and inviting to a friend. *A friend that I've kissed. A friend who doesn't feel like merely a friend anymore.*

❖

Mike's skin tingled from being in Vivian's presence. The wine warmed her stomach and lulled her body to a more peaceful state. Normally she was very careful around alcohol, but a luxurious bottle of wine like this one was meant to be savored. The smell of hard liquor and beer turned her stomach. She had never tasted any of it, though she had certainly smelled it on her father's breath when he yelled in her face. She turned her attention to Vivian, who looked at her with a pensive expression.

"You're beautiful," Vivian whispered. "And there's something about you, something utterly natural. You're like a wild animal, and the way you look at me… You steal my breath away."

Mike didn't know what to think. Was Vivian saying that she was unpolished, or even feral? Was it a compliment? Or was it something Vivian resented her for? For all she knew, Vivian might be reluctantly attracted to her, and how could that be a good thing. "I'm sorry," she managed, and immediately wanted to bite her tongue. *So* lame.

Vivian missed a beat, but smiled after a moment. "You're sorry? Oh, Mike. I'm the one who should apologize for making you uncomfortable. But you bring out new and extraordinary feelings in me that I don't know how to deal with."

"What do you mean?" Mike wasn't sure where the conversation was going, though Vivian's intensity warmed her.

"When you kissed me, I felt something I'd never expected. Certainly not with a woman."

"How did you feel?"

"Tender, passionate, sexy, arousing." Vivian averted her eyes. "But there's a lot going on and I'm not sure this is right."

"You regret the kisses," Mike murmured. She placed her glass on the coffee table and leaned back, crossing her arms over her chest.

"No. I don't." Vivian apparently hated the abyss that was opening between them as much as Mike did. "But I'm twenty years older than you, with deteriorating eyesight. I'm not sure I had the right to kiss you back, but I couldn't resist. The kisses were wonderful."

Mike's pulse boomed louder in her ears, and she was sure she must've misheard the last word. Vivian blushed faintly and fiddled with the hem of her shirt. *She's nervous. Perhaps as nervous as I am.* She placed a hand on Vivian's knee and hesitated. "I was sure you pitied me. I thought you had regrets. Serious regrets." The words actually stung her throat.

"God, no!" Shock colored Vivian's widening eyes. "Pity never entered into it. I was perhaps stunned…but pity. Never."

Mike wanted to trust her. More than anything she wanted to feel the warmth of Vivian's embrace, but wanting to trust wasn't enough. The same voice that had cautioned her so many times in the past, saved her life even, drowned out most of her ability to believe Vivian. "As long as you give me sympathy kisses," she tried to joke. Instead it sounded as pathetic as she feared.

"No sympathy. Well, at least when it comes to kisses." Vivian held out her glass. "Can you put that down for me?"

"Sure."

"I'm too old and too sick to get involved with anyone," Vivian insisted. "But I don't want you to think that I…that I don't find you attractive. I do." She groaned and rubbed her face with both hands. "Oh, God, I do."

The room went quiet as Mike absorbed the startling words. Perhaps Vivian had other reasons for her three-day silence than lack of interest in their friendship. Mike hated for Vivian to deny herself things as kisses because of her illness. *She might think I'm not that interested in her, that I'd let her down…turn away from her because of what she's going through. Twenty years' age difference as well as a health problem—who can blame her? And…I'm not exactly a catch.*

Angry at herself for the self-deprecating thoughts, she straightened her shoulders. She had her own life with her own projects. She certainly didn't have time to experiment with every woman who came along.

"So, in what capacity do you want me?" Mike asked, immediately regretting the ambiguity of her question.

"Honestly?" Vivian smiled, a sad irony in her voice.

"Yes."

"Even if I'm being extremely selfish?"

"Yes."

"A temporary lover." Vivian extended a hand. "Someone who can back off from the sexual relationship when I need her to, without regrets. And perhaps remain a friend, though I know that's too much to ask."

White-edged pain shot through Mike, and she knew it was too late for her. She'd fought through the years to protect her body and her soul, but her success had also created her solitude. Now, when she'd lowered her guard for the first time in ten years, the result was worse than any of her fears. Her stomach lurched, but then she looked up at Vivian and saw her agony reflected in porcelain blue eyes. "Why would you want a lover that way, instead of a friend?"

"Because of how you make me feel. Alive. Vibrant. Desirable." Vivian lowered her hands slowly to her lap. "I'm selfish, and I know it. I'm about to lose everything. Everything I worked for and my life as I've known it for the past thirty-eight years. When you hold me, I can forget everything. My blurred vision doesn't matter then."

Mike remained still for a few moments and then moved slowly, almost as slow as in her nightmares when she tried to outrun the demons that chased her through narrow alleys, and finally knelt next to Vivian. "I will. I'll be the lover you need. But, and this is your choice, Vivian, once you don't want me anymore, I can never go back to being merely your friend. Is this still what you want?"

## CHAPTER THIRTEEN

Vivian watched Mike come closer and eventually kneel next to her. She tipped her head back and tried to make out Mike's expression in the flickering light from the fireplace. With blurred vision and dry eyes, it was impossible to gauge Mike's feelings. Her words had made them pretty clear, though.

"I may live to regret this," Vivian managed, and she could hear how strangled she sounded. Her voice coach would have her head if she heard her straining her vocal cords that way. "But, damn it, I can't resist you."

Vivian knew, as soon as the words passed her lips, that she'd taken yet another step toward utter darkness. *Mike will be mine—for a moment. One precious moment in time.* Vivian realized she could have no regrets, yet she was filled with remorse when she heard the hunger in Mike's voice.

"How long?" Mike leaned closer. "Do you have a rough estimate?"

"What do you mean?" *Yes, I'm stalling.*

"How long before you decide you don't need me anymore?"

Vivian's heart hurt as it constricted in her chest. "I...I can't imagine how..." Her voice broke. *I always want to feel the way you make me feel. You take my pain away.* She cursed at herself for being so single-minded and selfish as she reached up and cupped Mike's chin. "*Cara.*"

"You know the price," Mike said, her eyes narrowing. "I promised I'd be there for you, and I will. I just can't lie or let false pride stand in my way. The way you affect me…I have no defense against it." She moved closer, and Vivian's hand slid up the length of her neck, ending in Mike's hair.

"You mesmerize me." That Mike found her attractive amazed her. "I don't know how long it'll be…but I will cherish every moment."

"So will I." The words sounded pained as Mike lowered herself to half lie down next to Vivian. "I never thought I'd chance this again and certainly not…like this."

Vivian let her hand remain around the back of Mike's head and laced her fingers through her hair. Mike's scent engulfed her and her own breasts felt heavier. Small flutters startled her as they appeared along the insides of her thighs. She had never felt this vulnerable and open, or frightened.

Vivian didn't really think this relationship was possible. Mike was young and beautiful, with a bright future. She wasn't going to grieve over Vivian. Her throat constricted again and she pulled Mike into her arms. The thought of losing this new feeling, so right, so exciting, was unbearable. A deep sob escaped, and Vivian felt Mike's arms tighten around her.

"Vivian. Don't cry. I'm not going anywhere. Not until you tell me to." Mike pressed her lips to Vivian's temple. "Just let me hold you." Maneuvering until she was stretched out next to Vivian, she raised her hands and smoothed Vivian's hair.

"I can still see you well enough to see how beautiful you are," Vivian breathed. "I'll never know what you see in me."

"You will, in time." Mike wrapped her arms tighter.

"Perhaps." Vivian turned her face up. "Kiss me?"

Mike didn't move at first. Vivian held her breath as she waited for Mike to help her create the magic that made her forget everything else. Tenderly, Mike brushed her lips against Vivian's, over and over, until the moment was all that mattered.

Vivian parted her lips and placed both hands around Mike's cheeks, to caress and, possibly, to hold her in place. She waited for Mike's tongue to enter her mouth and then buried her hands again in her hair.

Mike, in turn, ran a hand down Vivian's side, and the touch ignited a series of small bonfires along her nerve endings. Her satin shirt didn't diminish the sensation of Mike's touch, and Vivian could feel her breasts tighten. She gasped into Mike's mouth as her head spun.

"What are you doing to me?" she managed, tearing her lips from Mike's.

"Showing you."

Vivian tried to focus through the haze. "Showing me what?"

"What you'll give up, once you let me go. This." She placed a trail of moist open kisses down along Vivian's neck. "And this." She leaned down, and Vivian felt small nibbles along her mouth and opened it with a moan of surrender.

"Oh…" She arched her back and captured Mike's lips. Vivian pulled the woman in her arms closer and deepened the kiss. Mike tasted fresh, new, and young, like an elixir. Half aware she was losing control, Vivian caressed Mike's back and whimpered into the kisses.

❖

Mike ached, and yet it was impossible to stop the kisses. Vivian's supple body cushioned her toned frame. Full breasts pressed into her, and she had to force herself not to reach in between their bodies and touch them. Instead she reached for Vivian's left hand and placed it on her hip. "Hold on to me," she whispered against Vivian's lips. "I need you to hold on to me."

Vivian obeyed and grasped Mike.

Mike felt how Vivian shivered against her. "Are you cold?" Mike teased.

"Hot."

"Yeah, very hot. Vivi…" Mike's voice lowered into a growl. "Blistering." Unable to resist the more intimate touches anymore, Mike wedged a hand in between them and placed it on one of Vivian's breasts. The hardening nipple pushed at her palm through the fabric, and Mike shuddered as this sensation sent new surges of arousal through her. The ache between her legs was only surpassed by the pain in her chest as she gasped out loud.

Vivian froze. Her eyes opened, and she stared at Mike for long seconds without saying anything.

Mike became still as well. She thought she saw an echo of her own excitement in Vivian's eyes, but an inner voice nagged her. *Perhaps this is more than she bargained for. She may have wanted only a few romantic kisses and nothing more. A straight woman. I should've known better.*

"Mike—"

"I'm sorry." Mike sat up, her entire body aching from the loss of connection. "I shouldn't have done that."

"Why?"

Mike didn't know what to say. She didn't see any fear in Vivian's eyes. "It was too soon, and I don't know if it should've happened at all."

"I don't know what you're talking about," Vivian said. Her eyes darkened with obvious pain. "Unless you weren't ready for how a body older than your own feels."

"No!" Dismayed, Mike shook her head. "That's not what I meant. I was trying to remember that you haven't been touched like that by a woman before. I was trying to be—"

"Considerate?" Vivian pushed up on her elbow and reached for Mike. "I see. Why not lie down here with me and just relax? We both need to calm down...for now."

Mike was confused. Vivian was handling the situation much better than she was. Slowly she relaxed, slid down next to Vivian again, and they shifted into a comfortable position. Mike pushed an arm underneath Vivian's neck and tucked her into the crook of her arm. The enticing feminine curves sent tingles along her skin and created goose bumps along her arms and legs.

"Better?"

"Yes. Better." Mike forced herself to relax, and to her surprise her breathing quickly slowed down and her heart stopped pounding. She was still turned on, but the flame had mellowed and Vivian's body felt more familiar. Now her protective side reasserted itself. With her free hand she smoothed down Vivian's wrinkled shirt. "We're moving too fast."

"I agree. I just don't know how to slow down. Or if I want to." Vivian paused and kissed the top of Mike's head. "*Cara*, I don't know if I should."

"Be with me?" Mike flinched.

"No. Slow down."

"Oh."

"I don't have a lot of time."

"In other words, you're going to leave once you decide where to and when."

"There will come a time for us to part, yes," she said in a low voice. Vivian's arms tightened around Mike. "I can't say exactly when, but it might be sooner than we imagine. I don't want to lose any time alone with you. I don't want any regrets."

"You sure you won't regret being physical with me?" Mike forced her voice to sound casual, even if her heart ached with every painful beat. "You've lived a straight existence up till now."

"I'm sure. And I'm equally sure that I'll regret if I'm *not* with you, in any way possible, before…" Vivian quieted and pressed her lips against Mike's temple.

"All right." Mike pulled Vivian closer and returned the embrace by placing a kiss in the opening of her collar. "Then, I'm yours. For now."

Vivian's voice sounded slightly hollow. "For now."

❖

*First kiss? Ever?* Eryn stared at Manon's reddening cheeks and her gray eyes that radiated so many unspoken feelings. "First ever?"

"Yes." Manon looked ready to bail.

"But you've been with men. You said so."

"Yes, I have."

"I see." Slowly the truth dawned on Eryn, and her respect for Manon grew. "You didn't want to share the intimacy of a kiss with a man, did you?"

"Exactly," Manon murmured. "I had sex with them and tried to find pleasure in the way they…touched me. Don't get me wrong, it was enjoyable enough with the two young men I dated at Harvard—"

"What about the third man?" Eryn wasn't ashamed of asking.

Manon recoiled. "He…it was all right."

Eryn narrowed her eyes and scrutinized Manon. "You're not telling the truth."

"I don't want to talk about Garrison."

The name rang a bell and Eryn wracked her brain to remember why. "Garrison, as in Garrison Hollingsworth?" The image of the unfathomably wealthy playboy appeared in her mind. He was New England's most eligible bachelor before he married and moved to Seattle a year earlier. "You were with him?"

"For a while." Manon sounded far beyond cold, and Eryn watched as she scooted sideways to reach for her briefcase.

"He was rumored to have a glass or two too many," Eryn said. "Was that what you meant when you said he 'didn't adhere to the arrangement'?"

"Whoever started those stories wasn't wrong. And yes, that's what I meant."

Eryn knew she had to tread lightly. "Did he become unpleasant when he drank?"

"A little embarrassing, perhaps, but I could handle that."

"Then what was it?"

Manon dragged a hand through her hair. "He drove while under the influence."

It took Eryn a few seconds to see the connection. "And you lost your brother to a drunk driver."

"Yes." Manon rose to her feet in one fluid motion and held the briefcase in both arms in front of her. "I have to go now. Thank you for the coffee."

"Manon, don't run off. Not like this. We haven't had time to…" Eryn got up as well. Her knees oddly weak, she steadied herself against the counter.

"I really have to go." Manon's features hardened. "I have a bunch of case files to read, and it's getting late."

"Please, stay." Eryn knew if they didn't clear the air, Manon would continue to dodge her and Eryn wouldn't get a second chance. "Read your files here. Just don't leave like this."

A brief hesitation. "You seem adamant."

"I am." Eryn swallowed, her throat dry. "I don't want you to leave here in anger or regret. And I have an apple pie that my sister made for me sitting in the fridge. I can pop it into the oven…"

Manon took a step toward the doorway, then hesitated. "Can we at least sit on something a little more comfortable than your kitchen floor?" she said. "I have papers to browse through, and if you insist I stay awhile—"

"The couch should do it. You can pull the coffee table closer. Look." Eryn felt her cheeks warm at her eager tone and pointed in the direction of her living room. "It's an old couch, but it was my aunt's and it's very comfortable." *Damn, I sound like a freakin' idiot. Babbling on like this.*

Manon held on to her briefcase and sat down. "Very comfy." She nodded. "Oh, I forgot my mug."

"I'll get it for you." *I need to get a grip here. It's only her. Manon. Only? Nothing "only" about her. I'm in so much trouble here, but I can't let her know.* Eryn turned on the oven and picked up their mugs. After she placed them on the coffee table and took a step back, her chest constricted at what she saw.

Manon had opened her briefcase and taken out two thick folders. She now reached up behind her and pulled out her hairpins. Her shiny hair fell in waves around her shoulders, and Eryn wanted to fill her hands with the rich softness of the fragrant strands and bury her face in it. Manon smelled of something sweet, slightly musky, with a tinge of chocolate. As Eryn inhaled the scent soundlessly, she remembered how it felt to hold Manon close. *She's perfect for me. And perfectly able to break my heart.*

Unable to merely relax, Eryn walked over to the small den next to her bedroom and picked up her guitar and a mother-of-pearl plectrum. Bringing them back to the living room, she sat in an armchair in front of the unlit fireplace. She didn't plug the guitar into its amplifier; instead she began to pick out the chords to one of her favorite Faith Hill songs.

As always, the music wrapped itself around her, like armor against the world, and she forgot the stress she'd felt lately. She didn't hum the lyrics like she usually did, but she put every emotion into the muted sound of the guitar. After a while she looked up, feeling much calmer, and saw Manon sitting slumped back on the couch, her documents still in their folders on her lap. Eryn stopped playing. "I didn't mean to disturb you. I just—"

"You didn't. It was beautiful. Is that your Fender Stratocaster?"

Eryn had to smile. *She remembers what I tell her.* "No, this is my vintage Gibson Les Paul. 1970," Eryn said with pride. She basked in the surprised appreciation in Manon's eyes as she continued. "And I've played both my guitars practically every day since I bought them. Well, except last weekend when I was still sore."

"What song was that?"

"'There You'll Be.' It's one of my favorites."

"I've heard it before, but I mostly play classical pieces. Some more, please?" Manon gestured toward the amplifier sitting next to the open fireplace. "But this time, plug it in?"

"All right." Seduced by the request, Eryn could never have denied Manon, no matter what. She hooked up the system to the Les Paul. "Do you enjoy jazz? Like Billie Holiday?"

"Oh, yes."

Eryn adjusted the volume and let the first chord ring through the system. Manon's eyes grew thoughtful as Eryn began to play "God Bless the Child." She had come up with a new arrangement, slower, more haunted, and she loved how the guitar climbed toward an inevitable crescendo. She didn't take her eyes off Manon as she worked the strings with the plectrum. Manon, in turn, had put down her folders and was sitting on the worn couch with her legs pulled up beneath her. Her eyes were that familiar dark thunder gray, as if stormy emotions fought for dominance.

Manon's response inspired Eryn, and she put all her feelings into the music, her breath quickening with each tone. When the song was over, her fingers continued on their own, entwining the well-known chords with new ones, her own, meshing them until the Les Paul sounded as tormented as Eryn felt inside. She slammed down the last chord and let it ring until it faded out. Gasping for air, she was taken aback by how emotional she had become.

"My God." Manon's breathless voice reached her as if from a distance.

Eryn slowly took in the familiar surroundings. Everything was different somehow, and she wondered if it was because Manon sat on her couch and aimed her full attention at her.

"Where did that come from?" Manon sounded baffled.

"I have no clue. I jam when I'm on my own, sometimes, but it's never sounded like this. Never." *It was magical. She sat there and never took her eyes off me, and I couldn't have stopped playing, not even for a million dollars.*

"It was amazing. A sound that I've never heard before. Like a voice. It spoke to me."

"What do you mean?" Afraid that her guitar might have given her away, Eryn held it closer.

"It told me of pain and of happiness at the same time. I don't know how you did it, but if you can do it again, you'd be able to reach a lot of people."

"I've never thought I was good enough to play for a paying audience."

"Oh, you are. Surely other people have told you so."

"My sisters, but they don't count." Eryn studied the pattern of her rug.

"May I see the guitar?"

Eryn unhooked it and walked over to the couch. She sat down next to Manon, feeling self-conscious for a moment until Manon reached out for the guitar with a smile.

"Oh, look at that. I never learned to play, but I know a few basic chords." She placed her fingers in the correct position for a D chord with her left hand and let her free hand gently strum the strings. When the guitar gave a clean, muted sound, she turned her head and smiled again. "Hear? That wasn't too bad. At least it wasn't false!"

"It wasn't false at all," Eryn said, reciprocating Manon's irresistible smile, which had altered her usual austere expression completely. "Maybe I can bring my guitar to your place one day, and we can jam."

"I've never jammed in my life. I wouldn't know what to do."

"Neither did I, before I started playing like this. Why not give it a try?" Eryn smiled again. "We could ask Mike to join us. She plays the drums like there's no tomorrow."

Manon shook her head. "It sounds fun, but as you said, we're both busy women, and my schedule is booked solid for years to come."

"Years? You have to be kidding." Eryn couldn't imagine being that organized. "You already know what you're going to do a year from now?"

"Yes. Well, almost. Though my weekends are usually sacred unless there's a function I can't get out of."

Eryn was stunned, but Manon's busy schedule helped explain what governed her life. *The foundation. She lives, breathes, and damn near eats it. She didn't exaggerate when she said it was her everything.*

"So if I can track you down during a weekend before you have to put on one of the stunning dresses you bought at… Wait a minute. You haven't showed them to me."

"What are you talking about?" Manon looked around. "Oh, the dresses I bought today." She sounded as if she'd completely forgotten her errands.

"Yes, I'd love to see them."

"Help yourself." Manon motioned at the bags sitting next to the couch. She shook her head. "And you don't have to track me down. I live upstairs, remember."

❖

Manon watched Eryn open one of the shopping bags and pull out an emerald green sleeveless dress. *There's simply no way to predict what she's going to say or do. Who is she, really? She looks like a mythical forest creature, yet she's much more modern than I am.* Eryn's braid had become half unfastened during their embrace in the kitchen, and now strands of it curled in all directions across her back. *Silky.* The forbidden thoughts came uninvited, and Manon struggled to focus on what Eryn was saying.

"This is great." She held up the green dress. "I love the fabric. It's almost golden green. What is it? Silk?"

"Yes, raw silk. I believe it's imported from the Brahmaputra Valley in India by a local seamstress who works on commission for Genevieve."

"Sounds fascinating, but I'd rather see it on you. Model for me?" Eryn winked and held up the dress.

Manon gaped for a second before finding her equilibrium. "I don't think that getting undressed right now would be smart," she blurted. As soon as she spoke, she felt a hot wave creep up her neck and cheeks.

Eryn almost dropped the dress. "What?"

Not sure whether to backtrack or act innocent, Manon opened and closed her mouth without a sound.

"Manon? You okay?" Eryn got on her knees.

*No! I'm not okay. I'm pathetic and certainly far from okay. Please, God, allow a large hole to open up and swallow me.*

Eryn stared at her for another ten seconds, obviously waiting for a reply, and when she didn't get one, her face contorted for a brief moment before she gave a resounding laugh. "God, Manon. I was joking!"

Manon cringed and had no idea how to handle Eryn's mirth. Eventually, the contagious sound pierced her embarrassment, and she couldn't hold back a low chuckle.

"Oh, that's rich. You honestly believed I expected you to model the dresses for me, huh?" Eryn shook her head. "That would have been a sight."

"Yes, that's truer than you know. If you'd seen me behaving so uncharacteristically, I'd have had to kill you."

Another fit of laughter from Eryn, combined with a surprised happiness in her eyes, made Manon smile at her own joke.

"So, in the interest of my own continued good health, I should let you just do your thing?" Eryn motioned toward the folders lying on the coffee table.

"Exactly." Manon relaxed against the couch again. "However, I wouldn't mind if you played some more. Unless you have something else you need to—"

"No. I don't. Go ahead and work. I'll play."

Despite Eryn's distracting presence, when the first tones of "Nature Boy" flowed from Eryn's fingertips onto the strings of the Les Paul and out through the speakers, Manon opened the next folder and found it surprisingly easy to focus.

## CHAPTER FOURTEEN

Eryn entered the study at the Dodd Mansion, where Marjorie Dodd sat behind a large walnut desk. The floor-to-ceiling bookcases were filled with books and folders, some appearing very old and some brand-new, suggesting this room had been Marjorie's workplace for many years.

"Eryn. So glad you could make it." Marjorie put her pen down on a thick folder.

"I've come to let you know my decision."

Marjorie motioned toward a leather chair across from her. "Please, have a seat. I hope it's good news."

"Yes, I've decided to accept."

"That's wonderful." Marjorie laced her fingers in front of her and rested her hands on the desk. Eryn didn't know if she imagined it, but Marjorie looked smaller in only a week. Her voice wavered slightly, unlike her previous commanding tone.

"This is a chance of a lifetime. Now I just have to convince my boss to give me a leave of absence." Eryn shook her head. "I'm afraid he'll refuse."

"What will you do then?"

"Resign. Not that I want to sound conceited, but I've outgrown the local paper. I want to write longer pieces, like this history."

"And I know you'll do a good job. My assistant will show you where you can find all the research material we keep here. There's more on microfilm at the city hall and the East Quay library."

"Thanks. Will I have a chance to interview you?"

"Of course. Just make an appointment. You can have all the time you want." Marjorie leaned forward, seeming to see right through her, down to her unruly emotions stirring just below the surface. Handing her a business card, she said, "I don't want to leave anything about this project to chance, now that I've finally found you."

"I understand." Eryn checked her notes. "I have a few comments already, about format and my system, if that's all right?"

"By all means." Marjorie said, "Here. If you run into problems that my assistant can't solve, you can always reach me on my private line."

"Whose handwritten numbers are those?"

"Manon's private numbers, both home and her cell phone. Also the direct line to her office. You might already have some of them, but you need them all in the same place."

"Good thinking," Eryn murmured, and hoped that her cheeks hadn't turned bright red at the mention of Manon's name. She hadn't seen her since two evenings earlier, when Manon had worked on her couch.

Eryn had pulled double shifts after that, since two of her colleagues were ill. *It just didn't seem right to pop up to the penthouse and say, "Hey there, let's continue where we left off, honey."* Truthfully, Eryn was afraid to jinx everything since they'd parted on such good terms, despite the almost disastrous turn of events.

"Anything else, Eryn?" Marjorie asked, interrupting her thoughts.

"No, I don't think so. I have this," she waved the business card, "and if I survive telling my boss I need time off, I'll start tomorrow morning." Eryn felt jittery and realized she was excited about work for the first time in years. The thought of writing about these no doubt colorful women appealed to her immensely.

"Then I'll expect a weekly progress report. Agreed?" Marjorie rose, and Eryn noticed how hard she had to grip the desk to move with any semblance of ease.

"Yes, that sounds fine. I'll probably inundate you with details in the beginning." Eryn grinned. "Let me know if it gets too boring."

"I don't think this topic could ever bore me." Marjorie raised a hand. "Wait. I have one more question."

"Yes?" Marjorie's serious tone brought chills to the back of Eryn's neck.

"When I offered you this commission, you acted reluctant, even upset. What made you change your mind?"

*When you talk to a woman who's a century old, who's seen more than most people, you don't try to pull a fast one on her.* Eryn sighed inwardly. "I felt manipulated. You know, 'I'll make you an offer you can't refuse' and all that. This was a dream job offered on a silver platter. Too easy."

"You deserve the silver platter. Manon talked to some of your colleagues, so I know you've put in more hours than most reporters at the local paper, with very little thanks. I've read clippings from several years back, and you've always done a superb job, even if you must've been bored to tears at times. You've proven yourself."

"Yes, I realize that now, but when you and Manon were sitting there, sprinkling fairy dust over me...you seemed to assume I'd be tremendously grateful and jump at the opportunity without considering it." *And now I'm sounding like an ungrateful prick.*

Marjorie was momentarily silent. "So, did you question *her* motives more than mine, since you and I are strangers?"

"Yes. I don't want to be one of her charities."

"I can't blame you." Marjorie nodded. "We all have our pride, and you're independent, obviously capable of taking care of yourself. However, I'm glad you saw through your own misgivings. Did you talk about this with Manon?"

"Well, yes, and no, not exactly. We talked about some other things, and that's when I realized what I was supposed to do. I know that doesn't make sense—"

"Oh, but it does, dear one. Manon is amazing, just like you, and she works just as hard. Sometimes she forgets herself in the process, and having you as a neighbor should be good for her. She certainly admires and appreciates you."

"Really?" A small flame burned inside Eryn's stomach at the unexpected praise.

"Yes. Which reminds me. Manon and I wanted you to have this." Marjorie lifted the leather desk cover and pulled out a small envelope. "Here are ten tickets to the charity concert. Take your family and friends."

"But that's too much..." Eryn felt her face heat up. "They're worth a fortune!"

"And so is your work going to be—priceless, in fact. Now enjoy the tickets and the performances in good health."

"Thank you. Thank you very much." Eryn fingered the envelope while she tried to find her equilibrium. "I'll try to portray your family with heart and accuracy—in that order. Can we talk at the same time next week?"

"That should be fine, but check with my assistant."

"I will. And again, thanks for this offer. By the way, I'm looking forward to seeing you tomorrow at the party."

Marjorie grimaced in a way that Eryn interpreted as either exasperation or sheer fatigue. "I'm sure I'll see you, and half of East Quay."

"You don't sound too keen on the huge party idea."

"I'm flattered, but let's face it. I'm old. I've never been a party sort of person, and all the preparations and the money that have gone into this…well, let's just say I'm a bit ambivalent."

"I understand. Manon will be beside you, and you can call on me if you need reinforcements."

Marjorie laughed deep in her throat. "I will, dear one."

Eryn took Marjorie's frail, cold fingers with care. "See you then."

❖

"Ms. Belmont! Manon!" The frantic voice behind her in the corridor made Manon flinch. She turned around to greet the former principal of East Quay High School.

"Mr. Rex," she barely grunted.

"Manon, how many times do I have to tell you to call me Archie?" He sighed as he caught up with her. "I need your support."

"With what?" Manon glanced around for help. Several people rushed by, but avoided her. *Traitors.*

"You're on the City Hall education committee, and people in the community respect your opinion. I need you to help me clear up this misunderstanding."

"Which misunderstanding? The one where your budget crashed and burned, halfway through this semester? Or the one where you assaulted a reporter outside the school a week ago?"

"The budget can be repaired. I've talked to a private financial institute in Providence and—"

"That sounds dicey…and it's not your choice. The school board decides what to do, and as far as I can tell, they're going to fire you."

"That's where you come in, Manon!"

"Ms. Belmont to you, Mr. Rex. You lost your first-name privilege when you injured Ms. Goddard."

"What the hell…" Rex stared at her. "She's a friend of yours?"

"She's my neighbor and, yes, a friend. You caused her a lot of pain, and she had a right to press charges."

"She's dragging my good name in the dirt!"

"You're in this predicament because you swung at her and sent *her* flying into the dirt." Manon took a deep breath. "Listen, Rex. You can still save your good name. Take responsibility for your actions, both at the school and injuring Ms. Goddard. From what I heard, it was more or less an accident. You can't lord it over others and then expect them to be loyal. You're dealing with good people and excellent teachers who care about the children. They'd back you if you stood up and admitted you were wrong."

"What the hell are you talking about?"

Manon sighed. It was like talking to a lump of clay, but she truly believed every human being contained something salvageable, even a stubborn, egocentric bully like Archibald Rex.

"Apologize publicly to Ms. Goddard, the pupils, and their parents. That's your only chance of keeping your job. Invite Leo Schwartz from the financial department at City Hall and discuss a new budget with him. Present it to the school board, and I'll be there to make sure you get a fair response." *Be a man. Or be human, for once. Get off your high horse and lose the macho attitude that got you into trouble in the first place.*

It was difficult for Manon to disregard Eryn's injuries right now. Deep down she wanted to throttle the man for the pain he caused the woman she… Manon's breath caught in her throat. *Who am I to tell Rex to come clean and confess? I can't even be truthful to myself!* She thought about the injured Eryn lying on her couch…dark red hair flowing down a smooth back, sleek muscles playing under pale skin, and her scent. Fruity, light, with a barely traceable vanilla base.

"You'd stand by me?"

"I wouldn't go that far. It depends on how you perform." Manon forced herself to focus on Rex. "If your apologies are sincere and you have a good enough plan to get the school back on track financially, I may be able to persuade the school board to offer you a contract for another semester."

Looking smaller, Rex took two steps back and leaned his left shoulder against the wall. He was pale, with beads of sweat on his tall forehead, and dragged a trembling hand over his face. "I can't even show myself in the street without someone cursing me."

"You may have to live with that for a while. It's understandable that people are angry. Once you make things right, the people of East Quay will come around."

"Very well," Rex said doubtfully. I'll call Leo this afternoon. I can't live like this."

"Good. I'm glad you realize that." Manon hesitated. "And don't forget Eryn Goddard. She'll see through any falsity, so do it right."

"Okay." Rex extended a hand, slowly, as if he almost regretted it. Manon squeezed it. "Good luck. Just do it, Archie."

His massive chest heaved as he sighed. "Thank you, Manon. I won't forget this."

Manon hoped he wouldn't. It had taken all her strength not to call him every name in the book, and she was proud to have reached him on a totally new level. They had butted heads at many meetings, and this was the first time she had really been able to talk to him. *Perhaps Eryn's directness is rubbing off on me.*

Her first reaction was to laugh at the thought, but the next second she understood that it was true. Eryn's candid nature obviously affected her profoundly.

❖

The crowd in the café produced a lively hum as they drank lattes, cappuccinos, and chai.

As Vivian stepped inside the door, the warm air steamed up her new glasses. It was hard to get used to wearing them, but they did help some. Right now, though, they were of little use so she removed them, blinked a few times, and, unable to get rid of the blur, remained just inside the door, uncertain where to go.

"Ms. Harding! Great to see you," a vaguely familiar short, round figure to her left said. "I'm Martha Ivers. My husband Edward and I work for Mike."

Relieved that one of the patrons hadn't recognized her, Vivian smiled. "Hello, Martha. I've heard so much about you. Mike obviously regards you and your husband highly."

"Ah, she's a sweetheart. We think of her as family."

*Words of warning, perhaps?* Vivian kept her smile in place. "Is Mike here? I don't have a reservation, but—"

"Mike isn't working until tonight, but I'm sure I can find you a good spot. I assume you'd like some privacy?"

Was there a forced tone in Martha's voice? Vivian thought so, but wasn't sure.

"The counter will be fine, thank you. I just wanted some of Mike's latte."

"Well, fortunately she's taught me her secrets, so I won't disappoint you there, at least."

"Do you know when she'll be back?" Vivian asked as she followed Martha. She sat down on the stool with great care and took off her blue scarf, damp from the slight mist outside.

"Oh, Mike isn't out. She's in her apartment."

"Is she ill?" Vivian knew she sounded more concerned than a casual friend would but couldn't help it.

Martha paused before answering. "No, she's fine. She was feeling under the weather this morning and just needed some rest." She lowered her voice. "She's been a little stressed and tired lately."

"Are you gossiping again, love?"

"Hey, don't give me that, Edward." Martha gave an exaggerated sigh. "This is Vivian, a friend of Mike's. It's not gossip to let her know Mike's not up to par."

"If you say so." Edward Ivers was a tall, bulky man with thinning gray hair. He extended a hand. "Nice to meet you."

"Nice to finally meet you as well," Vivian said, and shook his hand. "I can't help but worry about Mike. I thought she never missed a day."

"She seldom does," Martha said. "But on rare occasions, like today, she takes an afternoon off. She works every day of the week otherwise, so I can't say I blame her."

Vivian knew there might be more to Mike's absence this time than Martha realized. *I can't very well tell them this might be because of me. They'd want to know why.*

She watched the blurred outline of Martha rummage around by the espresso machine, and soon a steaming glass of latte stood in front of her. "Thank you." The aroma hit her nostrils and Vivian inhaled the seductive scent of the hot drink. Carefully wrapping her hands around the glass, she warmed her cold fingers against it before sipping. A sudden voice to her left almost made her choke in surprise.

"Hello, Vivian, we meet again."

Vivian coughed to avoid inhaling the coffee and looked sideways. "Eryn," she said, still hoarse. "Hello."

"Oh, damn, I'm sorry. Didn't mean to startle you. Are you okay?"

"Fine." Vivian coughed again.

"I think Eryn's trying to kill our prima donna and jeopardize the entire charity event," another, more familiar, voice said. Manon showed up at Eryn's side. "She's dangerous to herself and others, as you can tell."

"Funny, Belmont," Eryn huffed. "Just because I have one small run-in with the principal doesn't mean I'm self-destructive…or destructive in any way."

"Not so sure about that." Manon laughed deep in her throat. "Look at poor Vivian."

"Poor Vivian" had finally cleared her windpipe long enough to speak for herself. "Please, join me for a cup of coffee," she said. "I'd love some company." *Now that Mike isn't here.*

"Great," Eryn said, and lowered a large case that she'd carried on her back. "I managed to persuade Manon to come with me, since I wanted to show her Mike's drums." Eryn sat next to her, and Manon moved to the stool on Vivian's far left.

Vivian's curiosity stirred. "Mike's drums?" She let her hand rest on the neck of the guitar case between them. "Are you going to play together?"

"I've been thinking about how we're all into music, one way or another. I mean, you're the only pro, but the rest of us aren't half bad."

"At least we can play without making fools of ourselves," Manon said, and Vivian thought she detected a trace of tenderness.

"You know, you're right." Vivian leaned her elbow against the counter so she could make eye contact with both of them. "Drums, guitar, piano, and voice."

"And you should hear Mike play the drums…" Eryn frowned. "Speaking of drums, isn't that what she's doing now? Can you guys hear that?"

Vivian tried to listen through the buzz of the crowd and soon made out a rhythmic beat with a curiously unsettling frenzy. "I hear it," she murmured. Why was Mike playing her drums like that? *Is it because of me? Or am I just being self-centered?*

Concerned, and with a strong urge to see Mike right away, she turned to Martha, who had just appeared behind the desk. "Is it all right if we go downstairs and visit Mike?" She wasn't sure why she asked Mike's employee, but she trusted her instinct.

Martha stepped closer and wiped her hands on a towel attached to her black apron. "Normally I wouldn't suggest anybody disturbing her when she's in one of her moods," she answered slowly, "but in this case, I think…yes, why not. If she doesn't want company, she'll tell you."

"Join me?" Vivian asked Eryn and Manon over her shoulder.

"Sure," Eryn said, and grabbed her guitar case.

Martha beckoned them behind the counter and through a black curtain leading to the narrow staircase Vivian had descended once before. She felt along the wall for the handrail, the dim light making it nearly impossible for her to see.

"Are you okay, Vivian?" Manon asked. "Want me to go first?"

"No, I'm fine. Be careful, though. This is a very old building and the steps are uneven."

"Tell me about it," Eryn muttered. "They're sloping."

At the bottom of the stairs, Vivian stopped in front of an oak door. The sound of drums was louder now. She hesitated only briefly before knocking, but soon realized Mike couldn't hear her. Feeling around for a bell, she found nothing but a doorknob.

"We'll have to just go in and call her," she told the others.

"Okay." Manon nodded. "Let's hope she doesn't think we're completely invading her privacy."

Vivian grabbed the doorknob, turned it halfway, and heard a resounding click. The door moved a fraction of an inch, then she pushed it open enough to poke her head in. The tiny hallway was dark, but a faint light came from the living room. "Mike? It's Vivian! Can you hear me?" She tried to drown out the drums. "Mike? It's me, *cara!*" She noticed Eryn and Manon exchange glances at her affectionate wording. *Perhaps they'll eventually guess that Mike and I are more than friends. I really don't care. I just hope Mike hasn't changed her mind. The way she's beating those drums...It sounds as if she has a lot of pent-up energy.*

Mike stopped, and the sudden silence was as deafening as the skilled drumming, making Vivian's ears ring.

"Who's there? Martha? Is there a problem?" Vivian had never heard Mike sound this stern and impatient.

"It's me, Mike. Vivian. Eryn and Manon are with me. We just wanted to drop by and...say hello," Vivian finished, and grimaced at how tentative she sounded. She glanced apologetically at the others.

"Vivi?" After a rustling of clothes, Mike appeared in the hallway dressed entirely in black—black jeans, black button-down shirt, and black boots. She moved with the same feline grace that Vivian had seen several times before, and her mouth went dry.

"Yes. Are you all right? Would you care for some company?"

Mike didn't speak for a few seconds. Instead her eyes darkened to a blue-black flame and studied them intensely. "Sure. Come on in."

# CHAPTER FIFTEEN

Mike watched the three women step inside and glance around her living room. Though she expected signs of disapproval or condescension, she saw neither.

Instead Manon, whom she suspected of having impeccable taste, looked around smiling. "You've done wonders with this room, Mike. I never knew a basement apartment could be so cozy."

"I know," Vivian said. "If you ever get tired of the coffeehouse business you could have an entirely new career as an interior decorator."

Mike wondered if they were being patronizing, but their smiles and comments dispelled her suspicions. When Eryn put an arm around her waist, she began, slowly, to relax.

"You okay, Mike?" she asked quietly. "I worry when you lock yourself in here and beat the living daylights out of your precious drum set."

Embarrassed, Mike glanced at Manon and Vivian, but saw only concerned kindness in their eyes. "I had a bad morning," she murmured. "You know, some days you just reach a point where…" She shrugged. It was hard to explain.

"Some days you just need your friends to help you beat the drums," Vivian said. "And here we are."

*Friends?* Eryn was one of her few friends, after Martha and Edward. She barely knew Manon, and Vivian…Vivian was far more than a friend.

"Yes, and I appreciate it." Though Mike was hesitant, she meant it. When she withdrew, like today, she felt very antisocial. But to her surprise she didn't feel invaded now, though their presence made her apartment seem smaller.

"Eryn and Vivian, you've been here before, but Manon, feel free to look around. It's just this room and a bathroom and kitchen. Not much to write home about." Mike remained standing next to her couch. "Can I get you anything to drink?" she asked, when she finally remembered her manners.

"Not for me, thanks, I'm fine. Which reminds me, I haven't seen your kitchen," Vivian remarked, and moved carefully toward the doorway at the far end. "Over here?"

"Yes." Mike watched Vivian step inside the small kitchen and flip the light switch.

"Ah, there's an espresso machine here if I change my mind. That's my girl!"

Mike self-consciously felt her cheeks warm. Why wasn't Vivian more careful with how she chose her words? Or was she simply being facetious?

"I really like how you've mixed old and new things," Eryn said. "I've been here a lot of times and still notice new things each visit. Like that one." She pointed at a dark wood figurine. "That's beautiful. Where did you find it?"

"I've had it for over a year, Eryn," Mike said. "I bought it at Before, the antique store on Main Street."

"Oh, yes, I know it well." Manon walked up to Mike. "I saw a twin to your figurine not long ago, if you're interested."

"I am, actually." The small talk was making Mike nervous, and she didn't know what to do with her hands. Usually, her image as an educated, street-smart woman helped her out of most situations, but nothing was remotely normal today.

She had worked up a sweat playing her drums and had released all the negative energy that had mounted the last few days. But to be interrupted before she felt ready had thrown her for a loop, and she was balancing on a tightrope with no safety net.

"Mike, I want to tell you something," Manon said, as she took Mike's hand between hers and moved her out of earshot. "You hardly know me, but I'm very proud of you."

"What?" she asked, stalling. Mike knew exactly what Manon was talking about.

"You were one of the Belmont Foundation's first applicants for a grant from the City Youth Center. You've turned it into a remarkable success story."

"You remember," Mike whispered with stiff lips. "Yes, I'm one of your charity cases."

"You're nothing of the kind. You required a modest grant to finish high school, but then you worked and put yourself through college."

"I needed more charity to make it through the university."

"Only because you became ill."

"Ill?" Mike laughed, and she didn't like how she sounded. From the corner of her eye she saw Vivian and Eryn walk over to the small dais where she kept her drum set. Vivian glanced at her but kept listening to Eryn.

"That's one way of putting it." Mike gave a short, joyless laugh. *Yeah, ill is a very safe way to put it. Politically correct, no doubt.* Mike didn't want to listen to the inner voice that told her Manon was only trying to be considerate and polite.

"Anyway," Manon continued, "it's comparable to taking a student loan or accepting a basketball grant. Not many succeed with their studies the way you did. I was so proud of you for graduating *summa cum laude* at Providence State University."

"You kept track of me." The words ached in the back of Mike's throat. "Why?"

"Yes." Manon's voice didn't falter. "I remembered your application and the circumstances you lived under at the time. When I came to the café with Eryn the first time, I didn't know you were the Michaela I'd heard of a long time ago. You were so very familiar so I checked my records and was surprised when I realized it was indeed you. You've done so well." Manon became misty-eyed for a moment, which baffled Mike completely. "I also know that you repaid the foundation by submitting monthly payments over the last three years."

Mike couldn't believe her ears. "That was supposed to be anonymous."

"It would've been, if one of our assistants hadn't overheard you arranging the transactions at the bank." Manon brushed invisible lint from the sleeve of her Armani jacket and smiled.

Mike was annoyed, though she preferred that feeling to the irrational feelings of dread she'd battled all day. It was better to be irritated than wallow around in painful confusion. "I intend to repay you completely." *I owe you the money...and more. God, Manon, if you only knew.*

"I realize that," Manon answered kindly. "Since you don't have to, we consider your contribution 'extra money' that we intend to spend wisely."

"Really? How?"

"We're going to need toys, books, TV sets, et cetera for the children in the new hospital wing, so my assistant and I thought that your contribution would be a great start. What do you think?"

"I...I think that's terrific." Mike couldn't imagine her money, the repayments she'd struggled with ever since the café began to show a decent profit, could be better used. "I like it." She felt the tension in her shoulders gradually lessen. *There might be atonement after all.*

"Good."

"Hey, Mike, show me how this works." Eryn called out, interrupting them. "Something like this?" She banged on the drums in a series of ear-damaging thuds.

"Stop! Stop!" Mike called out, half laughing as she hurried toward the drums. "Not like that. The ceiling might cave in."

She replaced Eryn and let her sticks run over every instrument, ending with a resonant boom from the bass drum as she used the pedal. She loved the powerful sound of her digital drum set.

"That's more like it," Manon agreed. "You need to stick to your guitars, Eryn."

Eryn didn't seem at all rebuked. "If you say so, Belmont." She walked over and took her guitar out of the case. "I should be able to hook into your amplifier, shouldn't I?"

"Yeah, try that one." Mike pointed at a box behind her. "I can hook up four other instruments too."

"Do you still have your keyboard?" Eryn asked, and then peeked at Manon, who raised an eyebrow. "You had a Yamaha set up when I was here a while ago."

Mike pulled aside a curtain next to the drums. "I traded it for this digital piano. Better sound quality." She caressed the keys. It had taken her a year to save up for it. She'd hoped to have time to learn how to play, but the café took most of it, and her heart was still with her drums.

"A Roland!" Manon exclaimed, and there was very little of the cool socialite in the way she approached the Roland MP60. "May I try?"

"Of course. I think that's what Eryn has in mind."

Eryn glared at her in a friendly way and shook her head. "Don't make me look like a calculating mastermind." She paused and made a production of looking around as she contemplated her words. "Well, come to think of it, mastermind is pretty accurate." Eryn grinned.

"We'd all testify to the calculating part. You're not exactly subtle." Vivian winked and sat down on the chair next to her.

Mike immediately walked over and placed a hand on Vivian's shoulder. "Are you all right?"

"I'm fine. Just a little tired. I had lunch with Mayor de Witt and her husband. What a couple. The husband's a bit of a windbag, though, but a nice one." She wrinkled her nose. "I think they wanted to make sure I'd attend the celebration for Mrs. Dodd Endicott tomorrow evening."

"Are you?"

"Yes. He asked if I would honor her with a song too, but I declined. I'm not singing anywhere but the charity event." Her voice sank into a raspy whisper. "That's…it."

"Don't let them push you into something you don't want to do."

"I won't."

A chord from Eryn's guitar interrupted them. "Mike, grab your sticks and get over here." She motioned toward Manon. "Give me an E, please."

Manon complied, and Mike had no idea what they were up to but obediently sat behind the drums. "What are we playing?"

"I thought we'd jam," Eryn suggested as she quickly tuned her Stratocaster.

"Jam?" Manon said. "I'm not very good at improvising."

"All right, I'll show you. Pick three chords you think go well together. Any chords."

Manon looked down at the keys, as if she contemplated the myriad of possible chords to choose from. After she slowly raised her hands and let them land gently on the keys, shimmering tones filled the room, and Mike held her breath. She wasn't about to join in yet; instead she waited for Eryn to do something. She didn't have to wait long. When Manon had played her three chords twice, Eryn's guitar came to life.

Sharp as a knife, the first tones hung in the air before the Stratocaster plunged deeply into a roar and met the piano perfectly. In only a few seconds Mike's arms rose almost of their own volition and expressed the rhythm she could hear among the other women's tones. The bass drum set the pace, and her hands worked the sticks over the snare and toms, but without the need to beat out her usual inner turmoil.

Mike heard the other two instruments play against each other, with each other, and it took her almost a full minute to realize how well they had incorporated her into the mix. They never excluded or ignored her, and when she tried a new pattern, a new rhythm, they caught on and followed it, teased it, and helped her sustain it.

She saw Manon lean over the digital piano and caress life into the keys. The aristocratic woman looked striking and, in some strange way, more approachable.

Mike's eyes slid over to Eryn, and she noted how Eryn's unraveling braid made curls surround her rosy cheeks, and her eyes glimmered under half-closed lids.

A rich tone—unexpected and beautiful—resonated through the room. The three women kept playing and exchanged mystified glances. There were no words, only tones, but Mike had never heard anything like it. Then Vivian got up and approached them, and her voice merged with the instruments. It rose and sank in perfect harmony.

Manon appeared to find new inspiration, and her hands rushed to the lower octaves of the keyboard. To match Manon's move, Eryn's guitar roared, and Mike let the hi-hat and the snare drive the bass drum, to encourage Vivian to keep going.

Vivian moved both hands out in front of her, as if she embraced a lover or greeted an invisible audience, and her voice, still wordless, carried the full tones all the way home.

After another minute of chasing and dancing with each other's instruments, Mike felt the surge of energy ebb away and the music fade to an end.

She sat with her sticks resting on her thighs, breathless, and waited for the others to find their bearings. Eryn's face glowed with enthusiasm, and Manon remained silent, as if at a loss for words. Vivian sat down again, her expression indecipherable. *What's she thinking? Did she like it? Surely she must've sensed the magic.*

"What did we just do?" Eryn asked, and rested her guitar against the wall. Then she raised her hands in a gesture of incomprehension as she answered herself. "I'll be damned if I know…but I do know that it sounded like nothing I've ever heard before."

"It was an inspired moment," Manon said. "I had no idea such tones could just appear. Out of nowhere."

"Not out of nowhere," Vivian stated. Her hair reflected the muted light, and she looked directly at Mike when she spoke. "We all carried them somewhere inside."

*Do the others realize she can hardly see us?* Mike ached, both for the beauty that they'd all given life to just now and also for Vivian. Her pain grew when she remembered she was destined to lose Vivian, perhaps before she got to know her. "Still, isn't it amazing how new it sounded?" she asked, determined to not allow the agony to take over. "That's so unusual. It's almost impossible to create a new sound."

"Too true," Eryn agreed. "I've played since I was a kid and gone from punk rock to Eric Clapton and back again. I've listened to just about every genre involving electric guitars and have never heard anything remotely like that."

"But can we repeat it?" Manon asked. "Can we do it again?"

"Are we supposed to repeat it?" Mike countered. "Perhaps we're meant to explore further."

"That's brilliant, Mike!" Eryn exclaimed. "I think you hit the nail right on its freakin' little head."

"What do you mean?" Manon twisted on the small stool in front of the piano. "Just keep jamming?"

"Why not?" Eryn grinned. "We had a hell of a session, and it was our first. Can you imagine what we could find if we were completely unleashed?"

It was an almost frightening thought. Mike wondered if they'd find more of the same or risk losing it altogether. "I'm willing to try again," she heard herself say.

"If Mike's in, so am I," said Vivian. "I can use the vocal exercise if nothing else."

Manon looked back and forth at the other three, raising a trembling hand and smoothing her hair back over her bun. "I haven't played with anyone else in years. It was fun to accompany Vivian the other day, and this…was amazing." She glanced at Eryn and shook her head as if she couldn't believe it. "I want to find those tones again. I don't usually exaggerate and I'm not doing it now. It was magical."

Mike's hands moved again. The hi-hat began to whisper, and soon the bass drum picked up a lazy rhythm, the toms finding a muted, echoing beat.

Eryn grabbed her guitar and hung it over her shoulder. The mother-of-pearl plectrum glittered between her fingers as they hovered above the strings. When the fingers of her other hand fell in intricate patterns down the neck of the guitar, the plectrum moved so quickly across the strings it became invisible.

Mike kept the hi-hat whispering but allowed the snare and the toms to dance, challenging their pattern with the insistent bass drum.

Vivian remained seated, but her voice still carried easily across the room. It wept; it cheered and howled, only to fall into a well of despair before Manon began climbing up, octave by octave, on the piano. She pulled Vivian with her, created a new atmosphere where Vivian's voice reached new heights. The high voice found joy as it followed the piano, and when Eryn's fingers climbed up also, chased by the hi-hat and the snare under Mike's hands, Vivian let go of the last sorrow, and her voice became as clear as a spring well.

The sound washed over them, and Mike couldn't hold back her tears. She wept because of her traumatic day, and because it broke her heart to watch Vivian sing in a way an audience might never hear. Still, as Mike hushed the hi-hat and let the bass drum slow down and become the last instrument to grow quiet, she knew Vivian had never counted on creating such music. *I wonder what she's feeling and thinking.*

They remained silent for at least fifteen seconds. Eryn stood with her guitar in her hands, her eyes on Manon. "Beautiful is too imprecise a word," she murmured finally, breaking the silence. "I don't even know what to call this."

"Music." Mike cleared her throat, embarrassed.

"Yes, music," Vivian said. "The very essence of it. I'm not being conceited, but to me, this was naked, unshielded music."

"I reached the core of something," Manon said. "I don't know, but all those hours I practiced scales when I was a child finally made sense, and I certainly wasn't thinking of music lessons or my teachers…I put my fingers on the keys…and played."

"My guitar came to life. I moved my fingers where it told me to go. That's all I can say. My shoulder still hurts, but when I was playing, I didn't feel the pain." Eryn shrugged and rolled her injured shoulder.

Mike watched her face but saw no sign of discomfort.

"Neither did I," Vivian added. "My voice soared, and for the first time in quite a while, it was sheer joy to sing. I sang without inhibitions, without rules."

*And it made you relax enough not to feel the pain.* Mike wanted to take Vivian in her arms and just hold her.

As if Vivian had read her mind, she rose and walked over to Mike. Placing her hands on her shoulders, she leaned down and gently kissed Mike's forehead, twice. "Are you all right, *cara*? You look stunned."

Vivian was worried about *her*. Mike had no idea why, but when she rose to assure Vivian she was fine, she felt light-headed and wondered if she was as pale as she suspected. *I haven't eaten all day.* "I need a glass of juice. Can I get you anything, Vivian? Manon? Eryn?"

"It's time for me to go home, actually," Manon said, leaving the piano. "This was…amazing, though."

"We should do this again. Soon." Eryn slid out of the shoulder strap and placed the Stratocaster into its case. "Why not meet Saturday afternoon when we've rested after Mrs. Dodd Endicott's party." She looked questioningly at the others. "If you have time, Mike?"

"A few hours on Saturday? Sure, as long as it's after the lunch crowd, I'm in. Vivian?"

"Certainly."

They all looked at Manon, who in turn raised both hands with a half smile. "I surrender. Of course I want to play together again. This was fun."

"Fun? It was amazing!" Eryn laughed. "If this continues, we'll have to think of a name for our band."

"Need a ride home?" Manon asked Eryn. "Guitar and all?"

"Yes, please, neighbor dear. I'd never miss an opportunity to ride in that beauty of yours."

"Let's go, then." Manon walked up to Mike. "Thank you for letting us visit you. It was so nice to see how you live." She leaned forward. "And to see that you're doing okay."

"You're welcome. See you Saturday. Two thirty?"

"Sounds good."

After Eryn and Manon left, Vivian said, "Go get that glass of juice, *cara*. You look pale and you're trembling."

"Okay. Can I get you anything?"

"Actually, I'll go with you and you can teach me to make that wonderful espresso."

Mike was relieved that Vivian wasn't leaving yet. "All right."

They moved into the kitchen where Mike instructed Vivian. "Never open the top if it's hot. You press water through the finely ground beans with at least a fifteen-millibar pressure. If you open this you can burn yourself." Mike pointed at the top lid she had just screwed tight.

Vivian nodded, and Mike continued to demonstrate how to let enough water press through the beans and how to steam milk to perfect foam. Then she handed Vivian a café latte and watched with amusement as she savored it, eyes closed.

❖

Vivian opened her eyes and let the taste of the coffee blend with the sight of Mike's dark eyes. "Your juice."

After looking at her a few seconds longer, Mike pulled out a carton of orange juice and poured herself some. Vivian, unable to take her eyes off Mike as she drank in large gulps, could barely make out a drop of juice that escaped the corner of her mouth and ran down the side of her neck.

Vivian didn't think. She put her latte down and slid her arms around Mike, licking the trail of orange juice from Mike's neck and holding her close. "Oh, *cara*. Did you isolate yourself down here today because of me? Do you regret—"

"No!" Mike buried her face in Vivian's hair. "No."

"I was afraid. I had to see you, and Martha said you weren't working. I thought it was because of me…us."

Mike moved and Vivian found the small of her back pressed against the counter. Mike's quick fingers moved in her hair, and one after another, her hairpins ended up in a small bowl.

Slippery masses tumbled down, and Vivian groaned with pleasure when Mike laced her fingers through it, combing the tresses and arranging them around Vivian's shoulders.

"You sang so beautifully," Mike whispered. "I've never heard anyone sound like that. It was hard to focus on my drums. I just wanted to close my eyes and let your voice move closer, surround me… command me."

"Command you?" Vivian felt a twitch within, and her voice turned into a husky murmur. "How do you mean?"

"The way you sang was hypnotic." Mike's eyes turned impossibly darker, filled with emotions and dreams. "I wanted to surrender. Just give in."

"To what, *cara*?" Vivian caressed Mike's cheek. "You can tell me. You can show me how you felt."

Mike leaned forward and slid a hand around Vivian's waist. "Can I? What if I shock you? What if you say, 'No more of this'?"

Vivian knew Mike's fear was talking. "I won't."

She felt Mike's body press into hers and it stole her breath, made her inhale deeply several times. "Please, Mike, don't hold back. Show me everything. Show me how." *Show me yourself. Show me all those things I'll never see again once you're gone.*

Mike caressed Vivian's sides and her scalp. Mike balled her hands into fists full of hair, and Vivian tipped her head back to try and see at least something of Mike. Dark shadows outlined Mike's features and created a mysterious puzzle of her face.

"Kiss me, Vivian."

"Oh, yes." Vivian raised her hands and framed Mike's face. She angled her face and pressed her lips against Mike's, vibrating with desire. As she parted Mike's lips with her tongue and deepened the kiss, she tasted orange juice and something entirely Mike. Vivian whimpered into the kiss and felt Mike shiver as they clung together to keep from falling. The kiss erased all thoughts from Vivian's mind except those of passion and lust, and a need so deep it frightened her.

"*Cara*," she breathed into Mike. "Let me touch you. I need…to touch you."

Mike drew a deep breath and reached for one of Vivian's hands. "Here," she whispered. "Here, Vivi."

She ripped open her shirt with the other hand and pushed Vivian's hand inside. Vivian held her breath as she filled her palm with Mike's breast. The hard nipple tickled her, and Vivian instinctively closed her hand on the soft roundness and rolled the nipple between her thumb and index finger.

Mike gave a muted cry. "Vivi, please…"

And Vivian knew it was too late to stop now. Much too late.

# CHAPTER SIXTEEN

The evening was pleasant, with an unusual calm, despite East Quay's reputation for being beyond windy. "Watch out for the wind, girl. It'll take your head off," her father used to joke when Eryn left for school in the mornings. He wasn't wrong. The exaggeration held some merit, since the wind had actually blown her off her bike and into a garden, crushing Mrs. Jenison's award-winning rhododendron when she was twelve.

Now, Eryn stood outside Manon's car after she'd closed the door and didn't feel the faintest breeze. She blamed her vivid imagination for her fancy that perhaps nature was holding its breath for her sake. Eryn just wanted to level with Manon, to tell her how she felt up front and get it over and done with. But still, she tiptoed around Manon, afraid to unsettle her, to drive her away. The situation was driving her crazy.

"Beautiful night, isn't it?" Manon walked around the car she'd parked by the curb outside their building.

"Yes, it is." The street was practically abandoned, as if she and Manon were the last two people on Earth. "But it's a little eerie too. So desolate. I mean, it's only eight o'clock."

"Yes. I'm going inside."

"Right behind you." Eryn followed Manon to the elevator. They had driven back in silence, and Eryn was still engrossed in the strange—amazing, but strange—event that had taken place. At first, she had found it almost too much to talk about. "That wasn't half bad, was it?"

Manon pressed the button for the elevator, turned around, and leaned against the wall. "It was amazing." Her low voice created goose bumps on Eryn's arms and thighs.

"We've stumbled on something unique." Eryn pressed the buttons for floors three and four. "It's worth exploring, Manon. And did you see how Vivian related to Mike? They've grown very close these last few weeks."

"They seem to have become good friends, yes."

Eryn had to laugh at Manon's proper reply. *She* really *has no gaydar.* "There was nothing *friendly* in the way Mike looked at Vivian, babe." The sassiness was over Eryn's lips before she had time to think.

Manon blinked but didn't avert her eyes. "No?"

"No."

"How did she look at her?"

The elevator stopped at Eryn's floor, and she pushed the gate open to keep it from moving farther. "Pretty much the same way I look at you," she said, her voice low. "With admiration...but also desire."

Moving closer to Manon she placed a hand on the wall next to her head. "I know the feelings well." Eryn leaned in and kissed Manon's closed lips. She didn't deepen the kiss; instead she slid her other hand inside Manon's tweed jacket and let it rest against Manon's waist while she kept her prisoner with her lips.

"I know exactly what Mike wants to do to Vivian," Eryn whispered against Manon's mouth. "I just didn't know that Vivian's gay."

"Neither did I. Is she?" Manon closed her eyes briefly and sounded dazed.

"I don't know. I wonder if Vivian herself knows." Eryn nibbled along Manon's cheek, down her neck. Her hand did a little traveling on its own and ended up just below the curve of Manon's breast.

They both stopped breathing at the same time. "Eryn," Manon whispered.

"Vivian would have to be made of stone to resist Mike." Eryn placed her lips to Manon's ear. "I hope she can see into Mike's heart and be careful, however she responds. Mike's been burned. Several times."

"Haven't we all, at one point or another?" Manon placed her hand on Eryn's shoulder.

Eryn wasn't sure if the gesture was meant to keep her at bay or draw her closer. "Yes, we have. But you don't gain anything from hiding. You may think you're safe if you don't rock the boat, but it's not true."

Manon shivered and squeezed Eryn's shoulder harder. "Eryn. This scares me."

Eryn realized that Manon didn't volunteer this comment easily. "I've got you." She pressed her mouth to Manon's again, and at the same time, she moved her hand an inch upward and cupped the underside of Manon's breast. Briefly slipping her tongue inside Manon's mouth, she found its counterpart there, unexpectedly eager. The kiss lasted only a few seconds longer, while Eryn cradled Manon's breast fully. She felt Manon shudder and gently pinched the raspberry-sized nipple underneath the bra, which made Manon gasp.

Eryn finally stepped back and reached for her guitar before pushing the outer door of the elevator open. She wanted nothing more than to take Manon back into her apartment and show her just how good they could be together, but all she did was smile and push the gates closed. "See you at the Dodd party tomorrow. Night."

Eryn looked at Manon just before the gates closed completely. Her eyes were the same dark gray that they'd been in Eryn's apartment the night she first played for her. And the conflicting emotions obvious on Manon's face were even more intense than they'd been that night.

Eryn knew she'd taken a big risk, again, with Manon. But her gut told her that if she gave Manon too much space, she'd begin to rationalize, eventually find a perfectly sensible reason for her own reaction, and pull back. *I have to keep her off balance as much as possible.*

Eryn turned the key in her door lock, hauled her guitar inside, and placed it carefully against the wall. *We created music today! And Manon was part of it, and just as taken as everybody else.* Eryn knew their shared creation might work in her favor. If Manon was as moved with the musical experience as Eryn was, she'd want to repeat it.

Eryn usually disliked dressing up for formal functions, but this time she looked forward to it. *I have to find time tomorrow to go to Genevieve's, no matter if I max out my Visa card. I need a dress.*

❖

As Mike slid her fingers inside Vivian's button-down shirt and created small, fiery patterns on her stomach, Vivian went from warm to sizzling in seconds. She'd never responded this quickly, or this hotly, before.

"You smell so good," Vivian murmured. Her right hand still on Mike's naked breast, she circled Mike's waist to hold her closer.

Mike tugged gently at Vivian's hair and coaxed her to raise her head. Their lips met again, and this time Vivian plunged her tongue into Mike's mouth, devouring her with a sob. Vivian's legs trembled, and a heavy feeling between them emphasized the increasing wetness there.

She couldn't stop undulating as she moved against Mike, spreading her legs and tasting soft lips. Her hand, still pressed against a woman's, *Mike's* breast, tingled. The firm mound with its rigid nipple felt both delicate and supple. Vivian massaged it gently, afraid to accidentally do something wrong, but Mike pressed into the caresses and moaned aloud.

Mike broke free from the kiss but remained close enough for Vivian to feel her hot breath on her face. "Vivi, yes, touch me. I've dreamed about this. I need it."

"Like this?" Vivian let her fingertips slide in an outward motion along the pebbled nipple. "Does this feel good, *cara*?"

"Wonderful. More than good. Don't...stop."

"I won't." Vivian's heart sped, and drops of sweat ran between her breasts and along the back of her neck. "I need to take my shirt off," she managed. "It's too hot in here."

"Yes. Too hot." Mike tossed her shirt on the floor and left her breasts naked and exposed. As she pulled Vivian toward her and made short history of her shirt also, Vivian became aware of her own silk camisole and white, not very sexy bra. Counteracting gravity, it was designed to hide the fact that she wasn't seventeen anymore and was carrying a few extra pounds. Shy and self-conscious, she felt utterly foolish.

She wasn't usually physically shy. For many years, before her *prima donna assoluta* status was confirmed, she'd had to share dressing rooms with many other women, sometimes in very cramped places. And she wasn't very shy, period. She rarely blushed.

"What's wrong?" Mike asked, and took her by the shoulders.

"You'll think I'm a pathetic fool."

"I'm sure I won't. In fact, I can promise I won't."

"I...I haven't been undressed in the same room as anyone, except my dresser, for years. I'm not a young woman, Michaela."

Mike's eyes softened until they were almost violet. "You don't have to apologize, and you don't have to get undressed either. There are no 'musts' at all."

"I know that. And I guess I'm being insecure for no reason."

"Nothing is for no reason." Mike smiled crookedly and shrugged. "I'm twenty years younger than you are. You think I expect your body to look as if you were my age or younger?" She cupped Vivian's cheek with one hand and put Vivian's hand back on her breast with the other. "But don't you see? This feels good because it's *you* touching me. Just as you'll feel good for me to touch, because it's *your* body. I happen to think you're gorgeous, but if you weren't, you'd still make me want you, just for being you."

"Gorgeous, *cara?*" Vivian tried to take in what Mike had just said. Of course the words were reassuring, but a part of her still doubted that Mike knew what she was talking about. Her legs were trembling now, and she had to lean back against the counter for support.

"Am I hurting you?" Mike backed away.

"No. Don't." Vivian reached for Mike again. "Stay with me."

Mike nodded and reached for the hem of Vivian's camisole. As she pulled it up and over her head and then placed it on the countertop, Vivian suppressed her urge to cover herself up. She shivered where she stood, undressed down to her bra.

"Beautiful," Mike whispered. Her eyes shone a radiant black-violet and were getting darker every second. As she reached out and pushed the bra straps down Vivian's arms, Vivian moaned at the faint touch.

"May I?" Mike said confidently.

"Yes." Vivian couldn't hesitate. Or be afraid. And yet her mouth went dry, and she held her breath as Mike edged her hands around her back and unhooked the bra.

Naked to the waist, very aware of the fullness of her breasts and her painfully stiff nipples, Vivian gathered her courage and looked at Mike.

"Oh, God," Mike whispered, barely audible, and reached out. She cupped Vivian's left breast and weighed it gently. "You feel wonderful, Vivi."

"Thank you." *Damn, what a silly thing to say.* Vivian tried to moisten her lips.

Then Mike took the other breast in her free hand. With a gently massaging touch, she explored both of them thoroughly and left Vivian blissful, all her insecurities quieted.

"Let's get more comfortable," Mike suggested. "Come on." Taking Vivian by the hand she led her to the black leather couch. "Here. Lie down. You're shivering."

Vivian fell back against the pillows by the armrest and closed her eyes, but opened them immediately, afraid of missing what little she could see of Mike's expression. *A time will come, soon, too soon, when I won't be able to make out any details at all. I won't be able to see her face, her eyes. How will I go on without being able to see her beauty...without her at all?* Vivian moaned as Mike tweaked her nipples carefully. She had never known her breasts could be this sensitive. Small tremors began traveling from where Mike touched her, through her stomach, and new moisture pooled between her legs.

*She's bound to notice...* But there was no time for embarrassment. Vivian couldn't help but close her eyes and groan when Mike kissed her again. Her breasts were on fire, and Mike's tongue in her mouth fueled it further.

"Vivian," Mike sobbed, apparently as moved by the intimacy as Vivian was, "oh, God, Vivian. Hold me."

As Vivian raised her heavy arms and pulled Mike on top of her, Mike lost hold of Vivian's breast, but another, completely new sensation flooded her when their breasts rubbed together. Short stabs of pleasure pierced Vivian's nipples, which puckered into two throbbing bullets that raced toward her wet sex. Vivian instinctively raised her legs again and wrapped them loosely around Mike. "*Cara*," she whimpered. "You make me...I've never..."

"Me either. Not like this." Mike's voice was small and almost fearful. "Never."

The pain over their impossible situation and comfort in their mutual touch were just as strong as the lust between them, and Vivian cradled Mike as her lover rubbed against her. *Lover? Yes. Of course. Mike is my lover now. From this moment on.* The seams of Mike's jeans ground into Vivian, and she almost lost control. She was shivering all over, and hot and cold flashes seared her, leaving her breathless and teary-eyed. "Mike?" Did it come out as a whisper or a cry? She had no idea.

"Vivian. I know. Just let it happen. It's okay."

*Is it?* Was it okay for her to orgasm, here on the couch, with this wonderful woman in her arms? Vivian tried to restrain herself, but the sight of Mike destroyed her determination. Mike's eyes shone of something resembling love, and even if Vivian knew that was wishful thinking, her body latched on to the emotion and sent her flying.

"You're fine. Give it to me." Mike moved with gentle insistence against Vivian. "Come!"

With a husky cry, Vivian came, over and over, while Mike kept rocking against her. Trembling, sweat running from her temples, chased by the tears that streamed from her eyes, Vivian felt the convulsions surge and fade. "Mike!" *Impossible. Oh, God, I can't believe it!* Vivian arched and closed her eyes. The tremors reverberated within her for a few seconds more, and then she slumped back on the armrest, pulling Mike with her. "*Cara...*"

"I'm here." Vivian welcomed Mike's weight on her, despite her heat within and the warmth from the fireplace. "I have you."

"Yes. You do. You really do." Vivian felt incoherent and licked her dry lips. She couldn't remember ever coming like that, and definitely not from being fondled in this particular way. Mike felt wonderful against her, soothing where Vivian had ached so badly just moments earlier, and smelling divine. "Don't let go," she repeated. "I feel dizzy."

"You need water." Mike sat up despite Vivian's words. "I'll go get some."

The living room felt desolate when Mike left. Vivian was still trembling inside, and she moved awkwardly when she felt the soaked panties between her legs. Reaching for a blanket, she wrapped it around herself with unsteady hands. Being naked in the throes of passion was one thing, but greeting Mike in the same state now was unthinkable. *God, what will she think of me? What if she sees me as a pathetic fool... half blind and in such dire need of human contact that I climax at the drop of a hat?*

How could she explain to Mike that she had come like she did because of her? Only Mike's presence, her touch and her voice, could explain why Vivian had launched into orbit and soared so high from the mere rubbing of Mike's hips into her own.

When Mike returned with the water and their clothes, Vivian took the glass, grateful Mike didn't try to help her drink it. *At least she doesn't treat me like an invalid.* Vivian's stomach lurched, and she took another large gulp of water. *So far, that is. What if I do become dependent on other people for my very existence? What if I need help with much more than drinking a glass of water?* Vivian put the glass down on the coffee table and placed her tremulous hands on her thighs.

Her eyes radiating unspoken questions, Mike watched her intently. Unlike Vivian, she was clearly oblivious to her seminaked state and did nothing to cover herself up.

"You never drank much juice," Vivian heard herself point out and wanted to groan. *Merde! I'm such an idiot. That was probably the least romantic, and the most lame, thing I could have said.*

"I was busy taking care of you." Mike's voice was noncommittal, but she didn't avert her eyes.

"Yes." Vivian smiled quickly and allowed caution to guide her. "And it was...lovely."

Mike smiled guardedly. "It was."

"But you didn't come—"

"It wasn't important right now. I wanted to be close. I was happy that you came, and next time, it'll be my turn, okay?"

Vivian grabbed her glass quickly and nearly choked on the next sip of water. *She wants to repeat this embarrassment?* "Next time?"

Mike recoiled visibly. "You don't want to." It wasn't a question.

Vivian cringed since she didn't mean that at all. "I thought, I mean, was sure, that you found this something of a disappointment. I'm not used to...feeling this strongly. And when you touched me...I just never...expected..."

Somehow Vivian's fragmented speech hit home with Mike. "You're no disappointment," she murmured and smiled shyly. "You're beautiful, and bringing you to orgasm like this was one of the most exhilarating moments I've ever experienced."

"Thank you." Vivian was stunned. "Can you take a few hours off tomorrow night?" she asked spontaneously, not prepared for her own words. "I'm invited to a big bash at the city hall, and I'd really like for you to come with me." *She's going to say no.*

Mike's expression shifted from shock to delight and then to horror. "City hall?"

"But would you come with me?" Vivian's eyes filled with unshed tears. Mike's reply was so important. She knew she sounded pleading. *Again. Pathetic.*

"Of course. Just tell me what the dress code is, so I don't make a fool of myself."

"Tuxedos for the men and evening dresses for the women. And you'd never make a fool of yourself."

Mike shrugged. "All right. What time?"

"Eight o'clock."

"Why don't I pick you up at seven thirty, then? I have a small car that I seldom use, but it's reliable."

Vivian exhaled, relieved. "Sounds perfect." She paused and reached for Mike's hand. Taking it in hers, she rubbed her thumb over the back of it. "I take it you're on your way upstairs to work?"

"Yes. I think you need your rest for the big bash tomorrow. Why don't you relax on the couch, and I'll call a cab when you're ready?"

Vivian had to smile at how formal Mike sounded. "Thank you."

"I'll see you later." Mike leaned in for a quick kiss, then began to get up.

"*Cara.*" Sudden panic at the thought of Mike leaving before she had a chance to say what she really wanted to say made Vivian scoot closer. She reached up and cupped Mike's chin. "You know how special this was, don't you? How incredible you made me feel?"

Mike's features softened, and she nodded slowly. "Yes. I think so."

"I guess you'll have to be patient with me, and more than anything, teach me how to…please you." Vivian nearly lost her breath at her own words.

"I promise. Soon." Mike wrapped her arms around Vivian and hugged her.

They sat in the silent embrace for a moment and then parted, which left Vivian feeling emptier than before. *Oh, Mike.*

"See you upstairs, then." Mike rose and then hesitated. "Will you be okay with the stairs?"

"Yes. See you later."

She sat still for long moments after Mike left and pulled the blanket closer. The basement was lit by many small lamps, carefully placed throughout the rooms, which made Mike's apartment very cozy. Yet, without its owner present, it was what it was—a dark basement, cleverly decorated. Vivian shuddered and closed her eyes.

❖

Manon sat by the piano, staring at the keys. Her head was still filled with the tones of their musical experience. *Jam session*, she corrected herself. But as much as that astounded her, the events in the elevator played havoc with her heart and her body. She could still feel Eryn's hand on her breast and the relentless lips against her own. Manon let her fingers strike a chord and grimaced at the sound. It was clear and not false, but definitely in a minor key. The sorrowful tone rang through her living room, and Manon wondered if Eryn had heard it below.

She tugged the terry cloth robe closer around her naked body and pushed her damp hair out of her face. Another attempt to recall the feeling in Mike's basement resulted in a similar solemn chord. Manon impatiently flipped the lid down over the piano keys. She rose and padded into her bedroom, and for once she didn't bother meticulously drying her hair.

Manon closed the curtains and slipped out of her robe. She glanced down at herself and frowned at her own flushed appearance, the blush stretching from her chest upward. *So much for taking a tranquil bath and relaxing at the piano. It used to work.* She turned down the bed and climbed in, shivering slightly as the cool, crisp cotton yielded to her body. As she fell back against the pillows with a sigh, images of Eryn flashed through her mind, the way her hair had loosened as she harnessed that wild guitar of hers, and how she'd kissed her with such confidence. *And heat. She shimmers and yet she's so...real. She feels real.*

Manon moved her hands along her body, trying to calm it, or satisfy it, but she couldn't focus or relax enough to really feel them. As she tossed feverishly from one side of the bed to the other, her thighs ached from the need between them. She rubbed herself haphazardly, wanting this torment over and done with quickly. *She's weaseled her way into my mind and she's driving me crazy.* "No!" *Not now. Not with her face plastered all over my thoughts. Her hair. Her long, long legs... and her small, pert breasts. Just a handful...No!*

She entered herself and emitted one muted, tormented whimper after another. She was so close to coming, and every time she thought she would achieve some relief, it eluded her. Over and over she hovered near temporary satisfaction, but eventually her arms tired and the sweat chilled her body. Instead of feeling her initial heat, she shivered. Angry tears welled up and, on the verge of screaming in frustration, Manon finally gave up. She buried her face in her pillow, hugged the bedcovers close, and after struggling with residual images of Eryn, finally fell asleep.

# CHAPTER SEVENTEEN

As Eryn browsed through the rack of dresses, she sighed. They were beautiful, but nothing that would suit her. She was too tall and lanky, and her skin too pale. She gazed around Genevieve's, ready to call it quits. But this was the best boutique in town, and if she didn't find anything here, she wouldn't find it anywhere else.

"Ma'am? May I help you?"

It was the shop owner herself. "Yes, please. I need a dress for tonight."

"For the Dodd Endicott party?"

"Yes. And none of these feel quite right."

"I see." Genevieve scrutinized her. "What about a vintage dress?"

"Vintage? Sure, why not? This year's pastel colors are a disaster with my hair. I'm Eryn, by the way."

"Genevieve. Over here's a rack of vintage designer clothes, several in suitable colors. They're all like new, and some even collectors' items."

"Really?" Eryn usually wasn't very interested in fashion, but occasionally she'd spend lavishly on jackets and boots. The rack stood behind a curtain, which Genevieve pushed to one side, and Eryn immediately saw much more potential in these dresses.

"The dresses are arranged in chronological order, by decade. Browse and see what you like, and if you need help just call."

"Thanks." Eryn hoisted her shoulder bag farther up. The colors from the sixties and seventies were much more flattering, she decided.

When she finally selected two dresses and headed toward the fitting rooms, the dresses hanging over her arm, someone stepped in front of her, and she almost tripped. Strong arms grabbed her and steadied her.

"I'm so sorry...Eryn?"

Mike looked surprised.

"You're shopping for tonight too?"

"Mike! Yes. I was about to give up before I found these." She waved her arms.

"Can I watch you try them on? They might inspire me. I've looked at three or four dresses and...I'm going nuts."

Eryn tried to remember if she'd ever seen Mike in a dress. Or a skirt, even. She didn't think so. "Yes, come help me. It's one of these or my corduroy jacket and chinos." Mike followed her to the large fitting room area, where she tried on a long, bottle green, velvet dress with raglan sleeves. She modeled it for Mike. Eryn stepped outside where Mike sat waiting for her. "This one?"

"Looks great. I didn't know you were that stacked."

"Yes, it does bring out some curves. That's good." She pinched the wide skirt beneath the narrow waist. "All right. Good. Next one."

Then she changed into a short, deep blue dress that hugged her body in another way. Although it left her legs naked up to her mid thigh, she wasn't prepared for Mike's reaction.

"Oh, my God, Eryn. If you show up in that one... You look gorgeous!"

"I don't even look like me." She tugged at the hem, feeling a little naked.

"Actually, we have the perfect stockings and original-looking boots to go with that dress," Genevieve said as she entered the fitting room area. "Let me get them." She returned in a minute with tight knee-high leather boots, very thin and pliable. "I figured you for a 9."

"You figured right." Eryn smiled and pulled them on. She didn't dare check the price tag, but the sight that met her in the full-length mirror said it all.

Stepping behind her, Genevieve folded her braid up, quickly creating an up-do and securing it with a few hairpins that she magically produced. "There. If you buy the dress, I'll add some amazing custom jewelry."

"You drive a hard bargain, lady," Eryn murmured, but kept

watching her image as she twisted and turned in front of the mirror. "Are you sure this is okay for the party? It's rather short."

"Yes, but not too short. You have the legs for it, Eryn, and the dress covers what it needs to cover."

Mike got up. "You have to buy this dress, Eryn. You'll knock 'em dead."

"Really. Well...I'm not sure—"

"I'll let you have the boots at a 65 percent discount." Genevieve smiled.

"Aw, you're going to kill me. Okay. Show me some of the jewelry, and if it fits, I'll take it."

"Just be a second." Genevieve disappeared through a door.

Mike pinched the fabric. "What is it?"

"Some sort of silk underneath and muslin on top. We have to ask."

Returning with an assortment of custom jewelry, Genevieve said, "Here. These are all in the same price range. I'll throw in a necklace and a set of earrings. Do you have pierced ears? Oh, good. Then sit down and look. Take your time."

Eryn took the tray and listened to Mike and Genevieve talk as she browsed through the colorful items.

"And what can I do for you, ma'am? I saw you earlier but was on the phone. I'm sorry. Do you need a dress too?"

"No. Yes. I mean. I looked at the dresses, but they aren't for me. They're fine, don't get me wrong, but I'm not a dress kind of woman."

"You're right. Normally I'd say there's no such creature, but I have something else you'll look stunning in." Genevieve turned to a small door. "I keep these for special requests," she said, as she pulled out a hanger with what looked like a black suit. "You'll still fulfill the dress code."

Curious, Eryn glanced up. "A tux! What a great idea."

Mike stared at the clothes. "You sure this is possible?"

"As possible as this dress is. Try it on, Mike."

"Yes, do," Genevieve said. She had new warmth in her eyes, and Eryn wondered if she wanted to see Mike in the tuxedo for more than business reasons.

"All right," Mike said, clearly hesitant. "Is this my size?"

"It should be. You're already wearing a white shirt, so you can see how it works out."

Mike disappeared into a booth, and when she returned after a few minutes, Eryn almost did a double take. Mike looked taller, darker, and heartbreakingly handsome. "Oh, yes. You've got to buy it, Mike. You look awesome."

Mike walked over to the mirror. Her expression was hard to read at first, but when Eryn leaned forward and made a circle with her index finger and thumb, a smile gradually formed on Mike's lips. "Yes, I look kind of cool, don't I?"

"Beyond cool. Vivian's going to swoon."

Mike's eyes darkened and the smile disappeared.

*What the hell's going on between those two? Clearly something.* "Why don't we get in debt over these things and then head to the Sea Stone for some coffee?" Perhaps Mike would confide in her.

"Okay. Good idea." Mike glanced at the jewelry on Eryn's lap. "Find anything you like?"

"Yes, these." Eryn held up a necklace and two earrings, blue cameos of a delicate female face.

"Beautiful," Mike commented before she went to change. "Be ready in a second."

Eryn walked into the booth next to Mike's. "So, now we're dressed fit to kill, I wonder if we'll get lucky tonight."

"What?"

"Never mind. I'll tell you later, over a latte."

❖

Mike poured steamed milk over their espressos and created lattes for herself and Eryn. After making sure Martha had everything in the café under control, she sat down on a stool behind the counter. "Okay. Spill the beans."

"About getting lucky, I suppose." Eryn sipped her latte after licking the tall spoon. "Well, since I'm so curious about you and Vivian that I could self-combust, I'll share first. I'm hoping to woo Manon with my sexy dress tonight."

Mike smiled, but other, darker, feelings stirred in her heart, which felt as hot as her latte. "So you've got it bad for the beautiful heiress," she teased. "I don't blame you. She has everything you could want: brains, looks, heart, money."

"Money isn't a factor."

"I know that. I just said she has it."

"She also has a very large closet where she's taken up permanent residence."

Mike placed her chin in her palm. "Damn." So, they were in the same boat, almost. *How strange, really.*

"My thoughts exactly."

"So what's your plan?"

"I don't have one, other than try and try again." Eryn shrugged. "She's good at thinking of a million reasons why we should be just friends." She laced her fingers tightly. "I couldn't do the 'just friends' part, Mike."

"I know. Neither could I." Mike murmured her words into the tall glass.

"You're attracted to Vivian."

"Very." *I'm crazy about her. I dream and breathe her.*

"And what about her? I saw how she looked at you yesterday."

Mike placed the glass back on the counter and let her finger follow the rim, over and over. "I know she likes me. I also know she's attracted to me, despite everything."

"What do you mean, despite everything?"

"Despite my background, my age, my gender." Mike's voice hardened. "Despite everything."

"You're a gorgeous, self-made woman. You've come a long way."

"A long way since the streets of Providence, you mean? Yes, I know. But Vivian deserves someone in her own league. And she's only in East Quay for a while. She'll move on, once she's...done."

Eryn placed a hand on Mike's. "Are you sure about that? I mean, the way she looks at you...those are strong feelings."

"She's an artist, a performer. Strong feelings are her thing." Mike knew she sounded bitter, but couldn't stop herself. "She can identify with roles, with different characters. And right now she needs me, for some unfathomable reason. She's made it pretty clear that she'll leave once she's...over things."

"Things? You mean, you?"

"Partially." Mike didn't want to betray Vivian's confidence about her medical condition.

"That doesn't strike me as something she'd say. She seems so straightforward. Even more so than most regular people." Eryn smiled. "A typical New Englander, if you ask me."

"Perhaps." Mike's stomach lurched for what seemed the thousandth time lately. "I wish I could back out, but I can't."

Eryn studied her closely. "You've got it bad, haven't you?"

"Really bad."

"What a pair of fools we are. Falling for difficult, hell, damn near impossible women. One straight and the other closeted. Ridiculous, when you think about it."

"Yes. We're so silly." Mike raised her glass and clinked Eryn's. "Here's to endangered hearts."

"Endangered hearts," Eryn echoed and sipped her latte. "You said it."

As they sat in silence, Mike knew Eryn had quickly gone from a good friend to a close one today. "Thank you for understanding."

Eryn looked up, her eyes warm beneath the now-fading bruise on her forehead. "Thank *you*. Anytime, Mike. I mean it."

Comforted, Mike knew she'd probably need Eryn's understanding and friendship even more very soon, when Vivian left East Quay.

❖

Manon distantly acknowledged her image. She wore the pale yellow cocktail dress she'd bought at Genevieve's, with a white lace bolero jacket sprinkled with rhinestone crystals. Diamond studs glimmered in her earlobes, and she wore her hair in an intricate low twist kept together by her grandmother's diamond hairpins. They were priceless, not only because of the stones, but because they belonged to the only woman in her life after the age of fourteen.

Clarisse Beloc had been a strong, almost hard, woman, forged by her experiences in France and London during World War II. She hadn't been easy to approach, since she prized formality, which made her very reserved. Only after Manon's mother left her father did Clarisse melt a little. She made sure Manon learned what she called "*le devoir une femme d'avoir l'air d'une reine*," the duty of a woman to look like a queen. She gave Manon lessons in etiquette and other social graces, interrupted only when Manon's father sent her to boarding school. When she returned home her grandmother kept instructing her, and along the way Manon and Clarisse found a mutual interest in classical music, which allowed them to become close, in part thanks to Marjorie, to whom Clarisse introduced Manon. Marjorie helped Manon understand Clarisse. Eventually it was their mutual love and adoration for J.B., Manon's grandfather that welded their relationship solid.

Manon checked her stockings and slid into her gold high-heeled sandals, which added another two inches to her height. After one last look in the mirror, she wrapped the fake fur stole around her shoulders and grabbed her small matching bag.

Downstairs, Benjamin saluted her, and she wrinkled her nose a bit, since she knew full well he did it in jest.

"And now, ma'am?" he asked, as he took his place at the wheel.

"We're picking up my date at the Thatcher Victorian Inn." Manon checked her gold watch.

"Very well." Benjamin pulled out into traffic.

Feeling cold, Manon pulled the stole closer. *Eryn. She'll be there. She'll know why we can't pursue this. No matter how much—* Interrupting her own thoughts, she adjusted the air-conditioning vent for more warmth.

"We're here, ma'am." Benjamin pulled in along the sidewalk and stepped outside.

The door opened to Manon's left and a handsome man in his late thirties climbed in, flashing a smile. "Manon. Wonderful to see you again."

"Dustin." Manon smiled politely. "You look dashing, of course."

"Of course. Nothing but the best for you, love."

Manon had used Dustin Pender twice before, over a year ago. "Good. You know where we're going and why?"

"Yes. Pearl gave me all the details."

"Very well." Manon looked out the window. "It's showtime."

Dustin Pender stepped outside first and then offered Manon his hand as she followed him. She tucked one hand into the bend of his arm and held her purse in the other. As they walked through a large crowd, Manon realized the press must have gotten wind of Vivian's presence at the party, since several media vans were parked farther up the street. *Our world-famous, and lost, daughter returns to celebrate our Grand Old Lady, as well as to perform for free. Of course the vultures are here.* She blanched. If Marjorie hadn't given Eryn a special invitation, she would've been one of the "vultures." *No, never!*

As they entered the enormous marble hall that led into the huge auditorium, also used occasionally as a ballroom, Marjorie stood just inside, resting her hand on an ebony cane.

"Manon, precious one. Welcome," Marjorie said, and leaned forward to kiss Manon's cheek. Unlike so many others in their circle, she actually kissed Manon's skin.

"Happy birthday, Marjorie. I had your present delivered earlier today. I hope it made it."

"I'm sure it did, and I'm very curious. Now, speaking of curious, who's this handsome young man?"

"This is Dustin, Marjorie. You met him once before, in Newport at the yacht club."

"So I did." Marjorie extended her hand, and Manon was pleased when Dustin kissed it lightly.

"You look most youthful, ma'am, if I may say so."

"Oh, of course you may." Marjorie smiled. "As long as you say nice things like that, you are more than welcome."

"She enjoys flattery," Manon theater-whispered to Dustin, which made Marjorie laugh aloud.

"Go on, children." Marjorie winked. "Go mingle and find out where you're seated. I need a break, but I'll be back when it's time for dinner."

When Manon and Dustin strolled over to the seating charts, Manon accidentally nudged a tall woman in a deep blue dress. "Oh, I'm sorry, I...Eryn..."

It was indeed the woman who'd kissed her in the elevator yesterday, but she was nearly unrecognizable. The dress made Eryn look taller than usual. Tight, high-heeled boots, surely the same kind her mother had worn when Manon was little, hugged Eryn's feet. Manon gazed up the long legs, along the surprisingly curvaceous body, until she rested on an expertly made-up face and blood-red hair pulled back in a perfect French twist. "You're stunning," Manon breathed. Something blue flickered in Eryn's earlobes, and Manon could only shake her head. *Breathtaking.*

"Manon," Eryn greeted politely, sending Dustin a confused look. "Don't you want to introduce me to your friend?"

*Friend?* Manon struggled to find her bearings. "Yes. Of course. Dustin, this is Eryn Goddard, my neighbor. Eryn, this is Dustin Pender, my date for tonight."

As soon as she spoke, Manon wished she could have taken her words back. Eryn's green eyes lost all color, and her face grew pale.

"Your date?" Eryn's voice sounded normal, but without its usual energy. "Of course. Nice to meet you, Dustin."

"Likewise, Eryn," Dustin replied, and Manon knew he was checking Eryn out, discreetly. "You look beautiful."

"Thank you." Eryn glanced away, and then she turned quickly toward the chart. "I better find my place. Oh, right there." She pointed toward a table in the middle. "But there must be some mistake."

"Why?" Manon leaned closer and Eryn's perfume, a scent of light vanilla and citrus mixed in a seductive blend, wafted past her.

"It's the head table!"

"So it is. It's quite a large table too," Manon observed, trying to keep her voice noncommittal. "You're there, right next to…oh, my God."

"Right next to Rex." Eryn stepped back. "That's it. I can't—"

"Of course you can't," Manon said, and clutched Eryn's arm without thinking.

Eryn took yet another step and Manon's arm fell down, apparently unwanted. "I'll take care of it. Rex was probably invited long before last week's events. The person in charge of the seating arrangements obviously hasn't followed the local news very well these last few days."

"And you're seated right across from me." Eryn's voice had lost its lilt and now sounded tired and disappointed. "Five minutes ago that would've made my day." Dustin had walked a little to the side to let a larger party of guests pass. Eryn sent him an empty look and lowered her voice further. "Now, it really doesn't matter, does it?"

Manon's heart nearly shattered at Eryn's defeated look. She wanted to tell her the truth, but suddenly she wasn't so sure what the truth really was. She could've canceled the escort service if she'd wanted to. Hadn't she brought Dustin as a message to Eryn? A cruel, definite message that whatever existed between them was doomed to fail. And now…Manon was calm on the outside, but inside, her stomach was in a knot, her heart beating hard and fast. She was sure it was visible on the front of her dress.

"Let's find our seats," Manon suggested, half expecting Eryn to refuse. "I'll find Marjorie's assistant and fix the problem."

"Fix it? *All* of it?" Eryn's eyes were now like green polar ice.

"That's impossible." She glared at Dustin, and raised her voice. "You're being rather obvious. I know he's a fake, but he'll help confirm your status as a man- eater."

*Trust Eryn to be nothing but blunt and honest, even in this setting. I'm glad we're among the first ones here. No one within earshot.* "Please, Eryn. Not here."

"Of course not." Eryn smoothed the dress down over her hips, then looked up and smiled. "Let's play the keeping-up-appearances game all the way through." She walked closer to whisper her next words, her face blank. "But just so you know. If you think bringing Mr. Stud Number 375 here will help keep you safe, you're fooling yourself. One of these days people are going to figure out what's going on. Instead of being proud of who you are, with all it entails, you'll have your big secret revealed whether you want to or not. And you'll face it alone, since you chose to push me away."

Eryn's eyes became shinier. "I knew we were invited separately. This wasn't a date. But...I thought...you'd at least come alone. I can't believe you did this."

"But, Eryn—"

"Don't worry, Ms. Belmont. I'll keep up appearances for tonight, but to do that...I need a drink." She turned and stalked toward one of the bars in the far corner of the ballroom.

Manon stood frozen, wondering if she'd ever feel warm again.

## CHAPTER EIGHTEEN

Vivian replaced the cap on the bottle that held her painkillers and put it in her pearl-embroidered evening bag. She had deliberately waited to take them so she would be pain free during the most important hours. She knew a lot of eyes would be on her, even if this was Marjorie Dodd Endicott's birthday party. Just the rumor that the town's most elusive celebrity would attend was bound to attract the media.

The woman from the day spa had just left. When Vivian had called earlier in the day, desperate since she couldn't see well enough to put on makeup or do her own hair, a young woman had promised to arrive in plenty of time to help her get ready.

Vivian had asked the hairdresser to describe the result, and according to her, Vivian's hair was piled up in a loose bun, with long, curling tresses framing her face. "Like a Greek goddess, ma'am," she'd enthused. "And I used light pastels for your makeup to fit the pale pink dress and shawl. You look beautiful, ma'am." Tears nearly destroyed Vivian's makeup when the hairdresser also offered to walk Perry and Mason.

Now Vivian reached for her shawl and wrapped it around her. Narrowing her eyes, she looked at her reflection in the mirror. She could make out only the pink color of her dress and the light spot that was her hair. She'd have to trust the hairdresser regarding her appearance.

The doorbell chimed and Vivian flinched, startled. Since neither of the dogs barked, she figured it was Mike. "Coming," she called and, holding on to her shawl and purse with one hand, she fumbled for the doorknob.

After a brief silence Vivian heard Mike murmur, "Oh, God, you're beautiful, Vivian."

"Thank you, Mike. Come in for a second." Vivian wanted to force her eyes to let her see Mike this evening. She could faintly smell sandalwood and something else. *Soap?* "Let me look at you." She could make out a lean, dark form and the oval, pale shape of Mike's face. "Let me guess." She smiled and ran her hand down Mike's side. "A tuxedo? How perfect."

"You have to guess?" Mike sounded choked. "Oh, Vivi. That bad?" She cupped Vivian's cheeks. "Are you sure you'll be able to go?"

"Very sure. You'll be there with me. Right?"

"Right."

"Then let's be off. I know you drove here in your little car, but I figured we'd arrive in style."

"Oh, yeah?" It was clear that Mike intended to help keep the good mood going.

"Yes, I've ordered a stretch limo. There might be a bit of a crowd, and I thought—why disappoint them. They expect a person like me to arrive appropriately."

"That's great. I'll sit back and enjoy it. This'll be my first ride in a limo, stretch or otherwise."

"Really?" Vivian raised an eyebrow. "And your prom?"

"I didn't go to the prom." Her voice gave nothing away, but Vivian knew something heartbreaking lurked behind the matter-of-fact answer.

"Neither did I," she said without too much inflection. "I was already in New York by then, under the care of Malcolm and his wife. I actually never graduated from high school. They put me to work learning other things, such as singing and piano lessons, music history, et cetera." She reached for Mike and hugged her close. "And if you want to tell me, I'll ask again, another day, why you didn't go to the prom."

"Okay."

Another knock on the door announced the limo driver, who guided them to a long white car and held open the door.

Mike sat quietly next to Vivian in the backseat as the driver maneuvered through the dunes toward the main road leading into the center of East Quay.

Vivian closed her eyes and reached for Mike's hand. "This is going to be difficult. I don't want anyone to realize I can't make out their faces. Fortunately, I haven't met anyone, except you, Eryn, and Manon, since I got back. I mean, in person. If I run into an old acquaintance, they'll simply figure I don't recognize them because it's been so long. Don't you think?"

"Yes. And I'll be your escort, so don't let go of my arm too long."

"I won't." Vivian hesitated. "You realize showing up with me like this, especially dressed the way you are, will create quite the buzz."

"I know."

Vivian couldn't judge from Mike's calm tone what she was thinking. "It might have a greater impact than we expect, *cara*."

"It doesn't matter." Mike's voice changed from noncommittal to stubborn. "You can never affect public opinion. People create their own image of you, no matter what. And if they have opinions about us, they'll think about you more than me. You're the celebrity. Perhaps you're the one who should think twice about arriving with me. It's pretty obvious that I'm your date."

Vivian squeezed Mike's hand. "You are. And if anyone has a problem with that, so be it. I don't care." She really didn't. Her professional life lay in its death throes, as far as she was concerned.

Showing up on the arm of a gorgeous young woman in a tuxedo was like going out with a bang. *Just my style.* Vivian gave a wry smile. *That'll give the paparazzi something to chew on.* But her spiteful thoughts left as quickly as they came. She needed Mike with her for many, very personal reasons. Her palm became sweaty and she shuddered.

Mike released her hand but didn't let go completely. Instead she wiped Vivian's palm on her pants leg and held it again. "You'll be fine. I'll be close all evening. Don't worry."

It was amazing to feel a flood of relief drown out the worries, at least for now. Vivian leaned her head on Mike's shoulder for a few seconds, then straightened up. "You're my strength. I'll be all right."

The limousine drove up to the semicircular path in front of the city hall. "We're here," Mike said. "Look at that huge crowd. Damn, and at least four media vans."

"Don't let it bother you. We walk in together, heads high." Vivian was determined to pass this ordeal with her chin up. "Let them stare. Wave to the crowd and ignore the press for now."

Mike pressed her lips quickly against Vivian's cheek. "Okay."

After the driver opened the door, Mike stepped out first. Vivian reached for Mike's hand and followed her. Effortlessly, she slipped into her prima donna role and exited the car.

❖

Mike took her cue from Vivian, who'd had years of publicity and was oblivious to the limelight. Managing to smile and offer Vivian her arm, she knew she looked handsome in the tux. She had put on some neutral makeup and even used a little blush so she wouldn't look so pale. Combing her unruly hair back with a wet-look gel, she had fashioned a short, tight ponytail, tucked into the nape of her neck. She had been surprised to see that the look brought out her face in a new, revealing way that, at first, made her feel exposed and quite naked. Still, it was the only hairdo that went well with the tux.

Vivian's hand rested in the bend of Mike's arm, and with the other she waved to the crowd that was chanting her name. *You'd think she was a rock star returning to her roots.* Mike wanted to scoff, but truthfully she was utterly proud of Vivian and thought she deserved the positive attention.

A reporter pushed his upper body over the railing put up by the police. "Ms. Harding! Who's your date? This your new love?"

Mike went rigid but kept walking.

"She's my friend, thank you," Vivian called back as they made their way up the red carpet.

*Friend. Yeah, that's it. That's where we're heading eventually. But there was nothing friendly in how she responded to me yesterday.*

They strolled among the photo flashes and waving people. Finally they reached the tall double doors and made it through the entry rituals.

"That went well," Vivian whispered as they made their way through the crowd in the hallway. "Let's go find out where we're supposed to sit."

"Okay." Mike half expected Vivian to let go of her arm now, but instead she walked closer and held on harder. "I have you." Mike shivered at her own words and remembered when she'd uttered them yesterday. Then, a sweat-soaked Vivian had embraced her, trembled in

Mike's arms after coming so hard it nearly drove Mike to a rare orgasm as well.

"Yes, thank heavens, you do." Vivian took a step closer, and Mike knew no one would believe she wasn't merely a friendly companion, but Vivian's date.

When they stopped at the seating chart, displayed on a painter's easel, Mike scanned it and found Vivian's name. To her relief, someone had written "guest" on the seat next to her. Mike guessed Manon or Marjorie had pulled some strings. Glancing at the other names, she noticed both Manon and Eryn were at the head table as well.

Inside the room filled with small groups of people chatting quietly, Mike noticed Eryn and Manon farther in. Glad to spot them, she patted Vivian's hand. "Want to go over and talk to Manon and Eryn?"

"Yes, let's do that. Manon should be at the head table also."

"She is. And Eryn too, right across from her."

Mike guided Vivian carefully among the round tables. Almost there, Mike saw the expressions on Manon's and Eryn's faces. "They don't look too happy," she murmured to Vivian. "In fact, they look furious. And there's a man there, next to Manon."

"What's happened now?" Vivian squeezed Mike's arm as they halted.

"Hello, there," Mike said, and two heads snapped in her direction.

"Mike! You look...stunning!"

"Thank you. You look wonderful. What a lovely dress." Mike had a chance to study the other couple while Manon and Vivian exchanged pleasantries. Eryn looked pale, with an unusual darkness in the way she looked at them.

"This is Dustin, my date for tonight."

*For tonight? Does she mean that literally, or is he her current lover? Either way, that gossip columnist will have a field day if she's here.* Mike shook hands with Dustin, who looked like a nice man, and then stepped closer and lowered her voice. "You okay, Eryn?"

Eryn sipped from her glass of champagne. "Yes." The clipped tone suggested otherwise. "Damn, this pink stuff is too sweet, but it was this or something nonalcoholic. I'd hoped for a beer, but they don't serve that till after dinner."

"I can tell something's wrong, but we can't talk about it here."

Mike tried to convey her sympathy. "If you haven't eaten recently you shouldn't down that champagne too fast."

"Yes. I know. I'll be careful." Despite her words she sipped the champagne again. "We can talk later. Too late, maybe."

That's when Mike knew Eryn was on the verge of tears. *I bet this has everything to do with Manon.* Eryn was clinging to a drink, and Manon was animated and nodding with a brilliant smile to people in passing. *Something went down just before we came. Something really bad.*

"I see we're at the same table," Vivian said. "Mrs. Dodd Endicott is so kind to include Mike and me."

"Of course, you're a guest of honor. We truly appreciate your contribution to our fund-raiser. The hospital wing is one of Marjorie's pet projects, and she knows how much your participation will mean."

"Then I'm honored." Vivian reached out to Mike. "And glad she let me bring a guest too. I know this is East Quay's biggest event of the year."

"I'm not so sure," Manon said. "The foundation's event may be the most talked about." She gestured toward Vivian. "Because of you, of course."

Mike couldn't judge if Manon's eyes were darker than usual. Manon wore her official persona like a layer of cellophane, impenetrable and almost invisible. This woman was light years from the one who'd played the keyboard in her basement only yesterday.

"All right," Vivian conceded. "But where's Mrs. Dodd Endicott? Does she plan to make a spectacular entrance once we're seated?"

This remark elicited a giggle from Eryn. "Like joining us on a trapeze swinging down from the rafters, huh? I wouldn't put that past her. She's got more energy than all of us put together."

Manon gave Eryn a worried look and stepped closer. In response, Eryn walked to Vivian's other side and placed her hand on her arm. "I really have no idea, but I can't imagine the poor woman standing by the door shaking everyone's hand. At least a hundred and fifty people are invited."

Mike noticed a flame ignite in Manon's eyes at Eryn's obvious display. "More. Almost two hundred," Manon said through clenched teeth. "It's time to sit down. I'll just go have a word with the organizers first. Dustin, will you go with me?"

"Of course." The man sounded relieved to get out of a potentially explosive situation.

"Now, then." Vivian turned toward Eryn. "What's up?"

"Not now," Eryn replied, and paled again.

"Not in detail, no," Vivian insisted. "But when you left Mike's yesterday with Manon, everything was fine. Today you can cut the atmosphere with a knife." She placed her hand on Eryn's arm with the barest hint of fumbling. "Did you argue?"

Eryn swallowed hard, and Mike ached for her friend when she saw how hard Eryn clutched her champagne glass. "You saw," she managed. "Him."

"Her escort." Vivian nodded. "Yes. That's her front. She usually brings an escort to large functions like these. She's done that for years. It took me a while to figure out that they were pretend."

Mike stared at Vivian, who was talking so casually about Manon's current lover. *Pretend?* "What do you mean?"

"Dustin is a nice, polite young man." Vivian lowered her voice to an almost inaudible murmur. "Manon always uses a professional, aboveboard escort service."

Mike felt floored. She'd heard of such a service but assumed it had to do with sex; yet somehow she knew no sex was involved in Manon's case. Mike made sure nobody was within earshot before speaking. "So Dustin's for hire? Then," she turned to Eryn, "you don't have to be jealous."

"I'm not jealous." Eryn shook her head slowly. "I know she doesn't want him that way. That's not it. At all." She choked on her words and had to swallow in between them. "Let's not talk about it anymore now. Maybe tomorrow, if we're still meeting in Mike's basement?"

"We are." Vivian's voice was absolute. "Now we need it more than ever."

*We do.* Mike wanted to hug Eryn. For the first time ever, her friend looked fragile, as if the smallest gust of wind could shatter her. With all her feistiness gone, her openhearted core was exposed to the elements. Mike cursed under her breath and felt Vivian gently squeeze her arm.

"Ladies and gentlemen, dinner is served!" The speaker's voice broke the mood, and they moved toward the head table. As Mike sat down next to Vivian, she watched Eryn find her seat, five chairs away.

Tonight would test their relationships. Mike hoped they'd come out unharmed, but she doubted it.

❖

Eryn honestly didn't care about Dustin Pender's person. She did, however, care greatly about what he represented. Manon's lies, hiding, denial—it all upset her, and she felt nauseous when she thought about how she'd struggled to be proud of her identity since she was fifteen. *I paid for it, the hard way, just to be me. I suffered the consequences and saw it through. You hide, Manon. You hide and you're going to pay eventually. Damn, you just don't get it, do you?*

Eryn watched Manon converse skillfully with her neighbors at the table and reluctantly had to smile when she saw Mike. The coordinator of the birthday bash had obviously assumed Vivian would attend with a male escort, so Mike had messed up the seating arrangement. Archibald Rex now sat at the other end of the long table. Keeping ten people between them was enough for Eryn, and she made a point of not looking in his direction.

"I hear you're commissioned to write the Dodd biography," a young man named Gordy, who sat next to Eryn, said. After a brief conversation about the project and his background with the Belmont Foundation, he remarked, "The woman in the tuxedo. Michaela Stone. She was quite the poster girl for the foundation. That success story inspired a lot of people to actually open their wallets. She came to the Youth Center in Providence several times a week and told us her story, talked about how she'd beaten the odds. And look now. She's here."

"And so are you."

"Well, yes, but mostly because my parents are invited." Gordy grinned. "Marjorie has been kind and always taken a special interest in me, since I was her first 'case.'"

As Gordy talked, Eryn took mental notes on the things she wanted to explore further about Marjorie herself. All the time, she thought about this new piece of information about Mike. *You talk about your past sometimes, Mike. But you never talk about all the things you've done to compensate for it. Damn.*

The lights dimmed, and a spotlight focused on Marjorie Dodd, who stood up from her chair. Dressed in a long silvery dress with white and gray embroidered ribbons, she looked regal. "Ladies and gentlemen, friends, coworkers, employees…all of you, family." She smiled when her voice wavered. "And I promised myself to not become emotional."

Marjorie collected herself. "Thank you, everyone, for helping me celebrate my century birthday, as one of my gardener's children called it. Manon Belmont, I especially want to thank you for setting a good example in many ways. Your foundation assists numerous people, and your social conscience shames us all. You've taken your grandfather's ideas and transformed them into a well-oiled charity organization that helps people help themselves."

Marjorie waited while spontaneous applause resonated throughout the auditorium, then continued to list a few more people. "Finally, I'm honored to have a small part in bringing East Quay's most famous and celebrated daughter home. Just when we need her most, she returns to offer us her greatest gift, her beautiful voice. Thank you for being here, Vivian Harding!"

Applause echoed through the room, and Eryn watched Vivian blush. *She didn't expect that. Way to go, Vivian. You deserve it.* She glanced at Manon, still applauding like the others and warmly gazing at Vivian. All at once Eryn knew it was Manon who had persuaded Vivian to come home. *And Manon and Marjorie are very good friends. In a way they're like leading ladies, a queen and a crown princess of this New England town.* Eryn felt the distance between Manon and her grow to oceanic proportions.

*Doomed to fail before we even started. Damn.* She clenched her fists, unable to clap for Vivian anymore since her hands were trembling so much.

Damn.

## CHAPTER NINETEEN

Vivian sat at one of the tables near the dance floor with Mike by her side. "I like this band," she said, and motioned toward the twelve-man big band that played a potpourri of standards. "They're good."

"Yes," Mike said. They had been talking to different people all evening, with no problems. She had rarely left Vivian's side and didn't think anyone had picked up on Vivian's condition. But it was almost time to leave; she saw lines of fatigue frame Vivian's eyes. "Are you ready to call it quits?"

"Yes, in a second. It's just..." Vivian turned on her chair and it was as if she was able to look into Mike's eyes. "I was just thinking how long it's been since I danced."

"Danced?" *Oh, God, Vivi.*

"Yes. And they're playing 'Night and Day,' one of my favorites."

"Are you trying to tell me you want to dance with me?" She wasn't sure what she wanted Vivian to say.

"Yes. Would you mind?" Vivian's hopeful expression made Mike feel sad.

"But all these people. We've talked to half of them, at least, and they're bound to notice."

"Are you about to chicken out?" Vivian was obviously teasing her.

"I'm thinking of you."

"And I want to dance."

Mike sighed and hoped nobody would pay attention to them.

Some were more than a little drunk, and perhaps afterward they'd think they'd imagined it. "Okay. I'll lead."

"Please do."

Mike took Vivian's hand as they walked toward the dance floor. Then she encircled Vivian's waist protectively and clasped her hand in the other. "Just follow me." As she took two gliding steps backward, Vivian, safely within the circle of her arms, moved effortlessly with her, making it easy to change direction and lose herself in the dance. As Mike pulled Vivian closer and leaned her cheek against her temple, she smelled flowers and musk.

People danced around them, and for a moment, Mike wondered if she was imagining things or if the dance floor was twice as crowded as when they began. "People are joining us."

"Let them." Vivian moved her head against Mike's cheek in a little caress. "Just don't let anyone cut in." She sighed and sank deeper into Mike's arms. "I don't want to dance with anybody else."

"Not even the mayor's husband? He's looking our way."

"Heavens no. He's nice, but a bit of a pompous ass."

Mike laughed at Vivian's uncharacteristic comment. "Oh, then we'd better move to the other end of the dance floor. Hang on." Mike guided them away from the band and the bright stage lights. "Better?"

"Much. It's darker here."

Mike pressed her lips together for a moment before she spoke. "Too dark?"

"No. Just dark. I have you to hold on to. I'm fine." Vivian sounded calm and content, and Mike prayed this feeling would last for a long time.

She dreaded the hour when Vivian ended their relationship, but all she could do about it right now was to keep her promise. She would be there for Vivian, to dance, to do anything, until Vivian said she didn't want her any longer. To return to mere friendship after having kissed, caressed, and held Vivian was impossible. *She needs me. I fill a purpose. The story of my life. Am I ever going to meet anyone who merely wants me?*

It was nice to be needed. Brenda had needed her—for a while— but when the need became a rationalization for abuse, with accusations, blame, and finally, rejection… Mike cringed. How had Brenda materialized while she was holding Vivian so close?

Vivian was nothing like Brenda and never would be. Vivian was honest and warm, with a loving nature. Brenda couldn't even spell the word "loving." *I was useful for a while and lost four years of my life because I was young and foolish. Haven't I learned anything? Haven't I grown beyond this?* Mike turned her head and kissed Vivian's forehead. *I have. This is different. It has to be.*

❖

Manon danced past Vivian and Mike, and the sight of the two women together, oblivious—or indifferent—to what people might think made her anxious. She gripped Dustin's shoulder tightly, and only when he groaned and tugged at his hand did she realize how hard she'd squeezed his fingers.

"Wow, Manon, you're strong," Dustin said, and teased her by wiggling his fingers and grimacing. "Lift weights?"

"Actually, I do." Manon had to smile. "But my strong fingers…my piano exercises caused them. I'm sorry."

"I bet." Dustin looked up and saw Mike and Vivian. "Hey, cool. Your friends are dancing. That's turning a few heads. Way to go."

"Yes." Manon's stomach churned. *Where's Eryn?* She hadn't seen Eryn leave, but considering her state of mind, it was entirely possible that she had, without bothering to say good-bye. *Can't she understand that I needed to show up in style? I booked Dustin more than four months ago. Should I have just canceled him because she was coming?*

Manon tried to muster more indignation, but she should have known how Eryn would react. The way Eryn looked at her, touched her, and the way they connected on every level when they were together… *But she has no right to demand anything of me! I haven't made her any promises. In fact the opposite. I've told her over and over why we can't even try. She can only blame herself for building castles in the sand.*

Manon tried to see Eryn's side. *I responded to her kisses. I never stopped her advances. She probably thinks I was playing hard to get, and now I'm giving her the cold shoulder just because it suits me.*

Dustin swung by Vivian and Mike. "Ladies." He grinned after winking at Manon, though she had no idea what he had in mind. "May I just dance around the floor with Ms. Harding?" he asked. "I promise to take good care of you, ma'am."

Manon stiffened and was about to stop Dustin, and Mike began to move away while shaking her head when Vivian interrupted. "I'd be delighted, Dustin."

Manon felt trapped, since she'd never make a scene in public, something that had probably not escaped Dustin, because he smiled at her and winked again and whispered, "Hey, Manon, live a little. Let East Quay see that Manon Belmont is a modern, tolerant woman." Then he took Vivian in his arms, moving in smooth, short steps along the outskirts of the dance floor.

Uneasily, Mike said, "Manon?"

"Let's dance, then, Mike." Manon shivered but took a deep breath. To her surprise it was even easier to follow Mike than Dustin, and she knew that her new friend was the better dancer, which was no small thing, since Dustin was quite the expert. "Where did you learn to dance so well?"

"A woman I knew at the Providence Youth Center, Josie Quinn, loved to dance. She taught me all the classic dances." Mike sounded wistful. "I haven't seen her in a long time."

"I remember that name. Wasn't she one of the driving forces behind the youth center?"

"Yes. She encouraged me to apply for a scholarship from the Belmont Foundation."

Manon forgot about feeling self-conscious for a moment. Something in Mike's eyes, and in her voice, demanded all of her attention. "And that changed your life."

"It changed everything. I was pretty broken when Josie reeled me in. She was the reason I stayed at the center."

"Like a surrogate mom. Or sister? She must be in her sixties now, right?"

"Yes, I think so. Last I heard, she was sick and on medical leave. I went to see her, but she'd moved and left no forwarding address. The center won't give out their employees' home addresses." Mike sighed, pulled Manon closer, and turned. Still the couple behind them accidentally nudged Manon's back, and Mike tugged her a little closer.

"I could have my staff look into it. The youth division is in constant touch with all the youth centers in this area. Someone may know what happened and where she is."

"Would you? I'd really like to know…unless…" Mike swallowed and fumbled for words. "Unless she's dead."

"Let's don't believe the worst. I'll get my people on it first thing Monday morning. Both for you and because this Josie sounds like a good candidate for one of our awards. Was she ever recognized for what she did for you?"

"I don't think she wanted any attention. Josie was a bit of a mystery," Mike murmured. "She never shared much, she was more hands-on. Teaching us to dance, to cook, and to laugh again."

"Important things, all of them."

"Then why do you look so sad?" Mike asked gently. "And where's Eryn?"

Manon became rigid and pulled back a fraction of an inch. "I don't know. Perhaps she went home."

"She was pretty upset. You know that, don't you?"

So it was more obvious than she realized, what had happened between her and Eryn. "Yes."

"She has it bad for you," Mike said in a low voice, close to Manon's ear. She held on a little tighter, as if she feared Manon would break free and run to avoid her words. "If you'd seen how she glowed when we tried on our outfits at Genevieve's. She bought that dress hoping you'd find her beautiful."

Manon went hot and cold. "She bought that dress today?"

"Yes. When she found it, she was radiant. Surely you saw that?"

Manon couldn't speak. *I saw nothing of the sort. All I saw was a disgruntled, rude woman who made a scene in public and embarrassed me.* Manon had to confess to herself that Eryn hadn't raised her voice once. Nobody, not even Dustin, had overheard a word. *And all I could think of was my right to bring whom I wanted to the party, and how I have to keep up appearances, at any cost.* But now Eryn was hurt, no matter the reason, and this was not just Manon any longer.

"May I have my date back?" Vivian interrupted Manon's self-accusing thoughts. "Mike?"

"Here, Vivi." Mike stepped close to Vivian and wrapped her arm around her waist. "I think it's time to go home. I'm tired."

"*You're* tired." Vivian sighed. "I'm completely wiped out. Thank you for the lovely dance, Dustin. I wish you well and the best of luck in show business."

Dustin sounded utterly starstruck and was about to start dancing with Manon again when she held up a hand. "I'm tired too. It's time to leave."

Dustin nodded as if he wasn't very surprised. "I had a great time, Manon. I'm always available for you."

"I know. Let's go." Manon never used the same face twice in a row and probably wouldn't ask for Dustin for another two years. And right now she was leery of professional escorts.

Benjamin soon pulled out into traffic and drove to Dustin's hotel. After they dropped him off, Manon pressed the intercom button.

"Drive down to the beach, please." She couldn't breathe.

"Very well, ma'am. The one at the old marina?"

"Yes. That one."

Benjamin turned the limousine around. As he parked not far from the boardwalk, he asked, "Are you sure this is safe?" motioning toward the waves crashing onto the sand and the cliffs.

"Yes. I'll be fine. I just need some air."

"All right. Just checking, ma'am." Benjamin opened the door for her.

"I'll be right back." Manon walked on the path between the dunes, but eventually she took off her high heels and carried them. The air was crisp and stars crowded the sky. Her grandfather had taught her the names of the most common constellations, but her grandmother had given them a touch of mystery by telling her about astrology. She was a Capricorn, which was hardly surprising, she thought. A Capricorn's most common characteristics included ambition, adherence to duty, and being utterly methodical, loyal, and objective.

Manon sighed. So much of that was true for her, but it wasn't all that she was about. So many sides of her had almost withered away, and she was afraid she couldn't resurrect them. Perhaps in her youth she could've been persuaded that being gay was totally all right. Instead, the Capricorn in her put a lid on these feelings. She'd buried her head in the sand and pretended her life was complete.

*Sand.* The cool sand chilled her feet, which ached from wearing the sandals, and Manon stopped to savor the sensation.

"Are you freakin' psychic?" a tired voice asked, startling Manon to gasp aloud. "I came here to be alone."

❖

Vivian stepped out of the limousine and took Mike's hand when she felt it against her shoulder. They strolled up the path to the house as the driver turned the limo and drove away. The night was clear, and the moon cast ink-black shadows among the dunes. Vivian was grateful for the motion detector that turned on the patio lights as they approached the house.

"Mike," she began, and stumbled a little on her words. She fumbled in her purse and pulled out a key. "You don't have to go home yet, do you? Stay awhile?"

Mike took the key out of Vivian's hand and unlocked the door before she replied. "Sure. I don't have to be back at the café until six to accept tomorrow's deliveries."

Vivian greeted the euphoric dogs. "Hi, boys. We're back." Then she turned to Mike. "Would you stay the night?"

"If you want me to." Mike closed the door behind them and helped Vivian remove her stole, then hung it on a chair in the hallway.

Something heavy, dark, and sweet filled Vivian's stomach and moved slowly downward, into her thighs. "Yes. Oh, yes, I want you."

Mike stopped and took Vivian by the shoulders. "You sure?"

"Very sure." Vivian couldn't make out anything but Mike's outline, and part of her mourned that she'd probably never be able to see Mike's face again. *Stay positive. Live in the moment, for this.* "Would you let the dogs out really quick? They're used to doing their thing on their own at this hour. They won't stray."

"Sure. Be right back."

Mike left Vivian to her thoughts. *She's staying with me. She's not leaving me just yet.*

Mike returned momentarily and Vivian heard her order the dogs to go lie down. She returned to Vivian, who was still standing by the bay window in the hallway.

"Help me out of my dress, please," Vivian requested.

"Come on." Mike led her through the bedroom and into the adjoining bathroom.

The light in the bathroom made it possible for Vivian to actually see the two dark spots that were Mike's eyes in the pale oval of her face. Vivian trembled and reached for the pins in her hair.

"Let me." Mike's hands were there before Vivian had time to reply. "You have such beautiful hair. Like silk."

"Not now," Vivian objected. "It's full of hair spray."

"I can brush it out. That'll get rid of it."

Vivian's breathing stopped. She reached out and touched Mike's hair, stroking her ponytail. "Yes."

"I might want to shower right away, though. My hair's sticky from the gel." Mike tugged gently at Vivian's dress. "Can you manage?"

"If you unzip me." Vivian turned her back toward Mike and felt soft fingertips pull the zipper down all the way to her waist. The thin fabric immediately fell off her body, and she caught the dress just before it ended up on the floor. Stepping out of it, she held it out to Mike. "Is there a hanger somewhere?"

"Yes. Here." Mike hung up the dress, then moved behind Vivian and began to remove the hairpins holding the elaborate hairdo in place. One by one, heavy strands fell on Vivian's naked shoulders.

Mike reached for something, and then Vivian felt a brush run through her hair, removing the hair spray. Soon it felt like a silken mist around her shoulders, and Mike leaned forward and buried her face in it.

"You smell so good," Mike murmured. "I'll take a quick shower now. Why don't you go lie down?"

Vivian turned around and hugged Mike, not bothered that she wore only her bra and lace panties. "All right," she whispered. "I'll be waiting for you." She paused, uncertain. "You're okay about spending the night with me, aren't you?"

"Of course. Don't worry. As long as you want me here—"

"Oh, God, yes, I want you to." Vivian groaned and nuzzled Mike's neck. "Hurry." Reluctantly, Vivian let go and completed her nightly ritual. After she removed her bra, she discarded her panties and silk stockings and slipped into bed naked, her heart pounding. She heard the shower run and then stop, and a moment later, the hairdryer buzzed.

Eventually she saw the shadow of Mike approach the bed. "I borrowed a toothbrush from the package in the drawer."

"Good."

As Mike sat down on the bed Vivian reached out. She could smell the fragrance of her own soap, which made Mike seem even more familiar. *Safer. More mine? God.* She ran her fingers over the top of the towel Mike had wrapped around herself and tugged gently at it. "Come," she whispered. "Be with me."

A muted whimper later, Mike slid down into the bed next to Vivian. "No regrets?"

"None. Never." Vivian placed her hand on Mike's shoulder and let it run down along her side. Mike felt wonderful to touch, her softness and feminine curves enticing her so much more than an angular male body ever had. Vivian mustered more courage and reached up and cupped a small, pert breast. She flicked her thumb over the taut nipple and was rewarded by a gasp from Mike. With more courage, she rolled the nipple between her fingers, grazing her blunt nails over it.

"Vivi..." Mike inhaled deeply. "Taste me, please."

Eager and nervous, Vivian leaned on her elbow as she bent over Mike's chest. She cupped Mike's breast, raised it to her lips, and took the nipple into her mouth without hesitation. She'd never expected the sensation of it all. She sucked at the nipple and gently bit it several times, rewarded by Mike's quiet whimpers.

Mike arched her back, as if she wanted to prolong and intensify the feelings, telling Vivian she was doing it right. She kissed a moist trail over to the other breast and repeated her actions there. Mike shivered and held on to Vivian's head, burying her fingers in the thick hair.

"That's it. You feel so wonderful," Mike whispered, her voice choked. "Yes, bite me like that. God, you make me..."

Vivian alternated between the breasts, cupping them both and licking in long, sensual movements. Mike held her the entire time, and eventually she turned Vivian over on her back and hovered above her.

❖

Mike had never seen Vivian look this beautiful. The blond masses covered most of the pillow, and her full-figured body glowed beneath Mike's. Vivian was all deep valleys and high hills, and her skin was smooth and flawless. Mike examined Vivian, taking in the details and mentally storing them for the future.

Vivian was a true blonde, Mike noticed, and the sight of the thin patch of blond hair at the apex of Vivian's thighs made Mike's mouth go dry. Instead she turned her attention to the large, full breasts and lowered her head. She blew teasingly at the closest nipple and watched it pebble even further. She licked it slowly and Vivian groaned, raising her hips off the bed. "*Cara*...oh, yes." Her voice was deep and husky, urging Mike on. She sucked the nipple deep in the wet cavity of her mouth and licked it rapidly while she gently used her teeth to elicit more groans from Vivian.

Mike moved her hand down Vivian's slightly rounded stomach and let it rest, motionless, on top of her pubic hair. When Vivian opened her eyes and looked into Mike's, Mike knew she couldn't see her, at least she didn't think so, and yet she returned the look as she pressed harder against Vivian. "Spread your legs for me, Vivi," she murmured, gazing at her. "That's right. And look at me. I want to see what you're feeling."

As Vivian slowly spread her legs and pulled one knee up, Mike shivered at the trusting gesture. Vivian's swollen sex was now at her mercy, and Mike knew she had to act quickly but also gently. Positioning herself between Vivian's legs, she pushed them apart and lay down on top of Vivian, careful not to put too much of her weight on her. Vivian moaned again and wrapped her legs around Mike.

Mike felt engulfed by hot velvet, and she sank farther into the embrace. Vivian's lips found hers and they kissed deeply for long moments before Mike pushed away a few inches. "I have to touch you." It had been so long since she'd trusted anyone enough to be this close, this intimate.

"Touch me, then," Vivian urged huskily. "Touch me any way you want."

Mike slid a hand down between them until it rested between her sex and Vivian's. The feeling of their hot wetness on either side of her hand was almost too much. She buried her face in Vivian's neck. "Are we going too fast? I wanted this to be romantic and wonderful for you," she whispered as she tried to control her raging lust.

"You're doing fine. Your touch is driving me crazy," Vivian replied in a strained voice. "It didn't take much for me last time, remember."

*But I want it to last. I don't want you to become sated too soon and lose interest. Please, make it last.* Mike curled her fingers between Vivian's folds and for the first time, she touched Vivian's clitoris, if only briefly. Swollen and wet, Vivian undulated against Mike's fingertips.

"Mike, *cara*, I need more. Please."

Mike sobbed at the plea and moved to have better access. She was shivering at the realization that she was about to make Vivian hers. *Mine. If only for a moment.* She parted Vivian's swollen folds completely and found the source of her wetness. Without hesitation, she slid two fingers inside and curled them slightly to reach the spot that would create more enjoyment for Vivian. Moving her thumb to the clitoris again, she could tell by Vivian's sharp intake of breath that she was doing this right.

Mike pushed all the way inside, marveling at the tightness around her fingers. Vivian was now moaning, and she pulled her knees up farther, exposing herself entirely. Mike kept her hand in place, absorbed in giving Vivian pleasure as she moved again to kneel between Vivian's legs. She stared at the sight of her fingers plunging deeply into Vivian and pulling back, covered with her juices.

Eventually the sensations became too much and Mike couldn't hold back any longer. She leaned forward, doubling over, and pressed her tongue to Vivian's swollen clitoris. The sweet wetness was even more arousing than Mike had dreamed. She treated the clitoris with tenderness until she realized Vivian was pressing harder and harder against her, apparently seeking a firmer caress.

Vivian went rigid and hooked her legs around Mike again, whimpering and moaning out loud as convulsions began and increased with every lick from Mike. When Mike took her clitoris into her mouth and sucked at it, Vivian gave a sharp cry, clipped short when she trembled all over.

Vivian's orgasm made Mike's own sex overflow with moisture, and Mike crawled up Vivian's body and straddled her thigh. "Raise your leg, Vivi," she instructed in a husky voice. "That's it. Keep it there. I have to…" She slid up and down Vivian's thigh, coating it with her slick wetness. "Yes. Yes!" She rode the leg unabashedly, undulating and pushing toward the orgasm that always eluded her. The harder she pushed, the further away the orgasm seemed to escape. Mike shivered and tears stung behind her eyelids.

"Here, *cara*, let me help you. Let me do this for you," Vivian whispered, and nudged Mike off of her leg. She pushed Mike onto her back and unceremoniously took an aching nipple into her mouth, while she thrust her hand between Mike's legs. "This part I know," she murmured around the nipple.

Long fingers entered Mike and filled her completely. Mike could hardly breathe anymore. She clung to the sheet with closed fists and forced herself to lie still, to merely feel what Vivian was doing to her. *I can allow her. I can let her give me pleasure. I can.* Mike waited for the moment when the feelings would diminish and eventually fade away, prepared to do what she'd always done before. She hated it, but she didn't want to annoy or disappoint Vivian. After all, she was the expert. Brenda certainly never suspected that she faked every orgasm for four years.

Mike listened to her body and counted the seconds as the burning sensation between her legs became more and more agonizing. She didn't understand how it could keep increasing like that without setting her aflame.

"Let it go. You're so close," Vivian whispered, before she moved up and kissed Mike tenderly. She slid her tongue into Mike's mouth and kissed her without pressure. "There," she murmured against Mike's lips. "Come on, *cara*. You're okay."

"I…oh, God. Oh, oh." Mike gasped for air and small fires erupted in her clit, gathered more energy inside her, and then shot in different directions—into her legs, her stomach, over and over. Stunned, Mike realized that Vivian had coaxed her into having an orgasm. "Vivian!"

"Give it to me. Share it." Vivian aligned her body with Mike's, her fingers still buried inside her.

Mike flung an arm around Vivian and pressed her face into the long hair, sobbing violently. "Oh, God. Vivi."

"I'm here. It's okay to cry. There, *cara*." She held on to Mike and rocked her gently, and Mike's heart broke again when she realized all the more what she was about to lose when Vivian decided she'd had enough of this novelty. If it was hard enough before, it was pure anguish now.

"You all right?" Vivian whispered in Mike's ear.

"Yes. Yes."

"You were amazing."

*Me?* Mike wanted to tell Vivian about her unexpected orgasm, her first in the arms of someone else, but knew it would only put yet another strain on their relationship. The last thing Mike wanted was to create more guilt for Vivian. "You made me come so hard." She couldn't help the wonder in her voice.

"Only because you inspired me." Vivian pulled at the covers. "Here, this'll keep us warm." She curled up next to Mike. "I've dreamed of us lying together like this."

Mike's heart was slowly calming, but now it stopped for a few moments before racing again. *You have?* Vivian wasn't in this relationship for the long haul, but she had a special gift for being loving and caring in the present. Determined to take everything she was offered, to collect it for cold, lonely nights, Mike greedily absorbed each touch, each word.

## CHAPTER TWENTY

Eryn stared at the shoeless, shivering Manon with more surprise than anger. After staring at the crashing waves for a long time, she knew her anger was primarily directed toward herself.

*I'm a fool. I knew she'd never be able to reciprocate and still I allowed myself to...* Eryn briefly touched her aching temple where the bruises had faded enough to be covered with makeup.

"Eryn." Manon, shoes dangling from her right hand, grasped Eryn's shoulder. "Can I give you a ride home?"

"You drove all the way to the beach to ask me that?" Eryn sneered and immediately regretted her reaction when Manon flinched.

"No. I didn't know you were here. I thought you'd already gone home." Manon gazed at the sea and hugged herself against the cold wind. "I...I needed some time alone, that's all."

"Where's your date?" Eryn glanced over Manon's shoulder, fully expecting Dustin to trot over the dunes any second.

"At an inn. He lives in Boston and is driving back tomorrow."

*Oh.* Eryn looked mesmerized how Manon's hair broke free and now launched one hairpin after another into the strong wind. Despite her best efforts not to, she removed a strand that had wrapped itself across Manon's eyes. The silky feel enticed her, and an aching, almost furious tenderness overwhelmed her.

"So, what do you say? Are you coming?"

"Didn't you want to be alone?"

Manon grimaced and looked down at her sandy feet. "It's a little too cold for a walk on the beach in this outfit." She glanced back up. "And besides, we need to talk."

Eryn jerked. "Yeah, I know. Why not? I'm tired, so let's go."

They trudged back to the limousine, and Benjamin held the door for them. After Manon climbed in and sat in the far corner, she opened the bar and smiled as she spotted a steaming pot. "Ben, you haven't?"

"I have for the last twenty years, so why not this time?"

"Thank you, again. Eryn, would you like some coffee?" Manon poured a tall mug full.

"Not that much, just a small cup."

"Here you go." Manon sat down next to her with the enormous mug in her hands, smelling the hot drink with obvious delight before taking a sip.

"I acted like a fool. I'm sorry I embarrassed you." The words left Eryn's mouth before she could formulate them better. *Perhaps just saying it out loud was better anyway.*

Manon sipped her coffee and leaned back. "I'm sorry I didn't have the courage to go by myself. Marjorie would have thought nothing of it. I should have canceled Dustin."

"No. You have to do a lot for appearance's sake, but I could never live like that."

Manon paled. "Never?"

"No. I've fought all my life for the right to be me, with all that it entails, and practically alienated my mother in the process. We argue constantly. We can't exist in the same room for more than half an hour without arguing. I've sacrificed a lot to remain out, for almost twenty years."

"And I have no choice?"

"Excuse me, Manon, but do you want a choice? Are you interested in me to that degree?"

Manon went from pale to a rosy blush in seconds. "I…I suppose. I don't know!"

"Damn. It's as if we're sitting on two different swings and spend most of the time moving in opposite directions. The short, wonderful moments when we're at the same place…aren't enough. In fact, they're frustrating!" Eryn clung to the hot cup, warming her fingertips.

"Agreed." Manon sighed. "You scared me tonight."

"What?"

"I thought I'd offended or hurt you so bad you'd want revenge. I was afraid you'd out me right then and there."

"I'd never do that!"

"I wasn't sure." Manon sipped more coffee. "It scared me. It always scares me to not be in control, I suppose."

"Then you must be afraid a lot. Nobody's in control all the time."

"Do you think I don't know that?" Manon flung a hand in the air and almost spilled her coffee.

"Hey, careful there." Eryn took the mug out of Manon's hand. "You're okay. I'd never do anything to hurt you or your reputation. Tonight's performance will never happen again."

"I believe you. And I've never lied to you."

Eryn frowned, not quite sure where Manon was going with this change of topic. "I'm glad to hear that."

"That doesn't mean that I've told you everything either. Not telling isn't the same as lying."

"I agree, up to a point."

"I *am* attracted to you. You know that." Manon laced her fingers and tugged at them, obviously battling a bad case of nerves. "But I've made it pretty clear what kind of existence I've chosen for myself."

*Yeah, the existence of a prisoner in that closet of yours!* Eryn fought to stay quiet and let Manon continue.

"I can't be selfish and ignore all the people who need the foundation's help. They have so much less than I do, we could be from different planets." She looked expectantly at Eryn, as if waiting for her to agree.

"But nobody, certainly not the people you help, demands that you live a lie. You just don't believe that you deserve to be happy. You think you have to be perfect and that lesbians aren't perfect."

"That's not true!"

"Yes, it is. Why can't you come out? Who would mind? Your rich contributors who can deduct every cent and sleep well for sharing with the less fortunate? Don't you think they'd prefer the wealthy French-descended aristocrat to be a lesbian instead of a man-eater, if they knew you truly loved a woman with all your heart, instead of acting like a man-eater?"

"A man-eater? How dare you?"

Realizing she was getting too loud, Eryn tried to calm down. "If you come out, sure, you'll run into bigots, and some will withdraw, but the best ones will stick by you. The wealthy gay people might open their wallets even more for your charities if you stopped living a lie."

Manon shook her head. "You don't understand—"

"Oh, but I do, Manon." Eryn's heart softened and so did her voice. "Better than you think. You started out in a picture-perfect family—a father, a mother, and a twin brother—and lost both your twin and your mother within a couple of years. Suddenly you were *it*."

Manon nodded slowly.

"You personified the future for your father and grandfather and learned, from experience and from assumption, what was expected of you. And somewhere along the line, you decided that because you survived, you needed to sacrifice your own happiness completely to be worthy. You lived when your brother died. You couldn't ask for unconventional happiness as well, could you?"

Tears ran down Manon's cheeks. "Stop. Stop it."

"I know I can't tell you how to live your life. But you're going to crack one of these days. You'll stress yourself into an ulcer or a stroke."

Eryn put her coffee cup down and took both of Manon's hands in hers. "You don't have to be alone. Let me show you what you're missing. I'm not being conceited. You may not be meant to spend your life with me, but you *are* meant to be with *someone* like me. A woman."

❖

Manon felt overwhelmed and clung to Eryn's hands as she struggled against the burning sensation in her chest and behind her eyelids. Finally, she gasped, "Do you really...think you're saying anything I haven't told myself a thousand times?"

"You may have," Eryn said gently, "but have you ever *listened* to yourself? To the voices inside that suggest you should be who you are?"

Was Eryn right? Did she listen to the stern, forbidding voices only? Manon was about to answer when Benjamin lowered the privacy window. "Ma'am, there's a problem up ahead."

Immediately, Manon slipped into her perfect self-control, pulled free of Eryn's hands and scooted closer to Benjamin. "What's wrong?"

"An accident on the bridge, and it's total gridlock ahead. I can't turn the limo at this narrow part of the bridge so we're going to have to wait until they clear a lane."

"Oh, no. Is anyone hurt?"

"I don't think so, but several cars have their fenders locked."

"Let's hope it doesn't take too long." Manon leaned back as Benjamin closed the dividing window.

"So we're stuck here. Well, that might be dangerous." Eryn shrugged with a lopsided grin.

"What do you mean?"

"I was afraid you'd throttle me earlier. I hope I live long enough to see the next sunrise."

Manon had to smile. "Very funny."

"That's me. Funny and amusing."

Something was amiss, and Manon studied the face that she already knew so well. It haunted her at night and appeared at every waking moment. "You're that and so much more. I'm sorry if my attitude toward you has made you doubt yourself."

"I don't doubt myself. At least not that way. I'm just…" Eryn shrugged. "I'm just more afraid of getting my heart torn to pieces than losing face."

"The attraction you've talked about all along…goes beyond mere sex?"

"Of course it goes beyond sex! Do you really think I'd be tormenting both of us if this was just about getting laid?" Eryn sighed. "And there's nothing 'mere' about sex. Or at least there shouldn't be."

Manon stared at Eryn, and Eryn covered her mouth with her hand. Then Manon felt her lips twitch. At the same time, Eryn's eyes started twinkling, and they both burst out laughing. When Manon looked up and saw Eryn clutching her injured arm, she laughed again until she wiped at the tears finally streaming down her face. "Oh, good Lord."

"Calling on deities will only get you so far," Eryn snorted. "And since I'm involved, the good Lord must be screening his calls."

A new bout of laughter hit, and this time Benjamin lowered the window again. "Is everything okay?"

"We're fine, Ben," Eryn said. "Just a bit tired, I suppose."

"Very well, ma'am." Benjamin sounded perfectly unfazed.

Slowly regaining some composure, Manon reached for her coffee and smiled carefully. "That felt sort of good."

"It felt great. We needed a release, and if I couldn't persuade you to make love to me in the back of this fine vehicle…"

Manon paused, then raised an eyebrow. "Since we're stuck here, maybe it's not too late."

"Manon!"

It was worth pulling a fast one to see the expression on Eryn's face.

"I'll get you for that!" Eryn leaned forward and buried her fingertips just under Manon's ribs, tickling her.

"No, no, no! Please!" Manon tried to pull away. "I hate being tickled!"

"Good," Eryn panted, but relented. "Good to know for future reference, because I can be ruthless." She smoothed Manon's hair. "You look a lot better. Color back in your cheeks and the wonderful sparkle in your eyes. I love your smile."

Manon felt as if she were swaying. "You're beautiful, like a forest creature from a fairy tale. Ethereal. Even if you're very strong and determined."

"Whatever gave me away?" Eryn smiled. "Ethereal? That's a first."

"I like that mix of traits in you. You're admirable in many ways. Brave, kind, annoying, persistent…the list is getting longer by the minute."

"For you too." Eryn scooted even closer and put an arm around Manon's shoulders. "Stubborn, selfless, shy, frustrating—"

"What do you mean, shy?"

"You have to take a breath or two before you talk to people, don't you? Even if you'd never let it show."

Manon closed her eyes for a second. "Yes. You're right."

"Nothing wrong with that. It's part of your complex, wonderful personality." Eryn leaned forward. "And I'm going to kiss you now, if that's okay. I won't make love to you in the limo, because that's a little too unromantic for a first time. I'll save that for a nice warm bed."

Manon held her breath, unable to object even if she'd wanted to. When Eryn brushed her lips along Manon's, Manon let Eryn's tongue in. The slow, deep kiss was sensual in a way she could never have anticipated. Eryn cupped both her cheeks and tilted Manon's head slightly, then examined every part of her mouth and kissed her senseless.

Manon parted her lips and gave as much as she was given, took as much as she was offered. Eryn's tongue caressed and teased Manon's tongue, coaxed it to play with hers. Eryn tasted of strawberries, or apples, which aroused Manon and left her breathless, moisture growing between her legs.

She moved restlessly in Eryn's arms and bit down gently on the greedy lips that kissed her. Eryn's gasp of pleasure into Manon's mouth only fueled her fire.

The car jerked forward. Eryn ended the kiss, and Manon let her head fall on Eryn's shoulder. Content to just sit there, they rode in silence all the way home. For now, this was enough.

Mike stirred in her sleep and woke up with her heart pounding fast and hard. "No!" she called out, uncertain where she was. "Please. No."

"*Cara*?" a sleepy voice next to her murmured, and then a naked arm pulled her back down. "Come here. Did you have a bad dream?"

"I...can't remember." But Mike knew exactly what the dream had been about. She'd had it before and it had been worse than ever.

"I think you can. Why not tell me?"

Mike really didn't want to. She didn't believe that everything you brought out into the daylight lost its power over you. Some things belonged in the shadows and should stay there.

"You said, 'No, please, no' and sounded like you were about to cry. You sounded, I don't know, very young." Vivian sounded more alert now.

"Perhaps."

"Were you a child in the dream?"

Surrendering to the tender voice and the loving embrace, Mike sighed and nodded against Vivian's neck. "Yes. I'm in a car and they're driving me away. They're taking me from my father and he's not"—the words stuck in Mike's throat—"he doesn't even try to stop them."

"Go on."

"It stops there. Sometimes I have the dream several times in one night until I give up and go running."

"How many times did this happen to you? Moving you from place to place?"

"I was in and out of nine foster homes, starting when I was eight. When I was fifteen I ran away."

"At fifteen? Where did you go?"

"To Providence. A lot of people don't want to admit we have homeless people and street kids in good old New England, but it's true. I lived in shelters, lying about my name and my age, for years."

"And then what happened? How did you go back to school and get a business degree?"

"I came out of a long, abusive relationship." Mike curled up in a small knot. "I lived with Brenda for more than three years, until I was twenty-one. She was hard to live with, but I thought she loved me, so I kept trying to adapt."

"And she used that."

"Yes. She said jump—I asked how high. "

A long silence became even longer as they both waited for the other one to speak. Eventually Vivian cleared her voice. "I'm sorry you're having such difficult nights sometimes. I hope being with me, right now, doesn't make it worse."

"Truthfully, it may, but I'm used to these dreams. They stop bothering me as soon as I wake up."

Vivian held on tighter to Mike and kissed the top of her head. "I'm not entirely convinced."

Mike felt Vivian's hand move slowly up and down her back. The touch soothed her, and her eyelids became heavy again. "You're here to comfort me," she murmured. "That counts for a lot."

"I hope so, darling." Vivian spoke with her lips against Mike's hair. "Just close your eyes and let me hold you. I'm sorry you had such a rough childhood. It breaks my heart to think you were all alone, with nobody to speak for you. But you're not alone now. If you have more nightmares, I'll be here." Vivian pressed her lips to Mike's temple.

*For how long? Until you've explored what I have to offer and decide you've had enough?* The dark thoughts frightened Mike, and she pushed them out of her head. Vivian wasn't the calculating type. She was warmhearted and fair. Protective, even. She'd never willingly put Mike's feelings on the line.

*I do that so well myself. I went from one impossible relationship to another, with almost a decade in between.* Mike drew a deep breath and pressed her forehead into Vivian's shoulder. She needed to say something, something that was so hard to utter, bile rose in her throat before she could swallow again. "Vivian?"

"Yes, *cara.*"

"Please, just don't leave me without some sort of sign first?" Mike was afraid that Vivian would pretend not to understand.

"I won't. My offer to remain a friend still stands. For now, I'm here, but we can't be lovers much longer because it's not fair to you. I'll always be your friend, I promise you that."

Unshed tears stung Mike's eyes. "You know I can't do that. We could have settled for friendship if we'd never started having sex."

"It was never just about sex." Vivian's voice had a catch in it, and Mike realized she wasn't as distant as she feared.

"Never," Mike agreed, and placed a kiss on Vivian's shoulder. *And for me, it never will be.*

Vivian placed a finger under Mike's chin and tipped her head back. "God, Mike, you wring my heart. I've made my decision, and you're making it hard to stick by it. Don't…please?"

*How she pleads with me. How she uses her beautiful voice to soothe me and be the one who calls the shots. It's your way or the highway, isn't it, Vivi?* Mike clenched her teeth so hard that a taste of iron permeated her mouth. "Don't worry," she replied in a hollow voice. "I won't." *And there I go again. Protecting her, from me.*

# CHAPTER TWENTY-ONE

Vivian stood among her friends in Mike's home, her eyes closed as they played their instruments, and let the shimmering tones flow through her. Eryn's guitar hit crystal-clear notes that sliced through the air and whirled around Vivian as if coaxing her to follow them.

She let her well-trained voice tell the story of her bewildered heart. Simultaneously, Manon's hands engaged the digital piano, thundering and vibrant, to help support Vivian. Liberated from the constraint of words, Vivian reached new heights and new depths. She shivered, amazed at her heartrending sound, almost too personal to bear.

Vivian slowly turned under the bright lights by the little podium where Mike kept her drum set. The warm light made it possible to distinguish the outline of Mike's face. Mike kept a suggestive low beat going, allowing Eryn and Vivian to compete. Vivian turned toward the guitarist, who to her dimmed vision looked like a wild fairy with her red hair loose around her shoulders. The light was also good enough for Vivian to see the rapid movements of Eryn's hands over the strings. Vivian operated purely by instinct, and as the music built toward a crescendo, she walked slowly over to Eryn and placed her hand on her right shoulder.

Eryn raised the neck of her guitar and leaned toward Vivian. Low notes teased, escalated, withdrew again, and then, finally, chased Vivian's voice over the precipice. The instruments all supported her as she tumbled down, and Vivian felt as if they were cradling her voice.

Slowly the music faded. Vivian was a little out of breath and remained with her hand on Eryn's shoulder in the complete silence, the music still ringing in her ears.

"Damn," Eryn sighed. "So, as I suspected, it wasn't a one-shot thing. Today was even better, don't you agree?"

"Yes," Manon said, as she rose and joined them. "I was afraid that we'd be really bad." She circled Vivian's waist and squeezed her gently. "I'm glad we weren't."

"Are you kidding?" Eryn laughed. "We're really on to something. Mike, I don't know how you beat that sound out of your drums, but it was brilliant."

"I'll be damned if I know. I listen to you guys and let my hands do the work. All I have to do is pay attention."

"Sounds like you've trained for years." Vivian was proud of the fact that Mike had developed a remarkable skill on the drums intended as an outlet for her turbulent feelings.

"Thank you. I just play."

"I know, *cara*." Vivian didn't care if Manon and Eryn saw, but leaned forward and kissed Mike's cheek carefully. She was really bad at judging distances now, and even if she was careful, walking Perry and Mason had become nearly impossible.

"You make a lovely couple," Eryn said, with joy in her voice. "You suit each other. What do you think, Manon?"

After a brief silence Manon answered. "I agree. It's pretty obvious how you feel. You complement each other well."

"I'm glad you think so. I'm happy as long as Mike will have me."

"Vivian." Mike sounded friendly but cautious.

"Mike is the faithful, dedicated kind," said Eryn. "She won't give up on you, whatever happens."

Vivian's lips became rigid. It was hard to talk about their situation, but she thought it was time to enlighten their friends. "She'll have to. I'm not in this for the long haul. I merely came to do the charity concert before I retire. You've guessed that my eyesight isn't what it's been? You're correct. I'm going blind, and at best I can look forward to distinguishing the difference between dark and light. Perhaps the outline of a figure."

"Vivian." Manon sighed. "I knew it was bad, but…I'm sorry." She put an arm around Vivian's back. "It doesn't have to affect your work, though. Your voice is intact and better than ever."

"I won't be performing after the charity event." Vivian shivered. *Can't they understand? No, perhaps not.* The mist around her became denser, and she pulled back from their touch.

"What you're going through is terrible, Vivian," Eryn said, "but there are other blind opera singers and other performers. Andrea Bocelli, Ray Charles, Stevie Wonder, and José Feliciano. Their audiences love them."

"There's a difference!" Vivian lashed out, her emotions surging. "You don't understand." With her quivering hands stretched out before her, she turned her back on the other three and walked toward Mike's kitchen.

"Vivi, wait." Mike caught up with her and took her gently by her elbow. "Make us understand. Please. We're your friends. Tell us."

It was almost impossible to resist Mike's low, pleading voice. The hold on her elbow felt loving, not constraining. "Let me go," Vivian demanded, but even she didn't think she sounded convincing.

"No. I don't *want* to. You set up those rules, but I never said I wouldn't fight them. You haven't figured me out yet, have you?" Mike sounded kind but also unyielding. "Unless you can tell me that I mean nothing to you and really mean it, or that our night together wasn't what you expected—"

"Stop it! I told you. You don't understand."

"Try me. Try *us.*"

"She's right." Eryn joined them. "Let's sit down."

Vivian walked over to the couch and sat down in the far corner, and she did indeed feel cornered. *I'm not prepared to dissect how I feel out loud.* "The progress of the condition I have, Leber's hereditary optic neuropathy, is rather gloomy. There's no cure. The pain will slowly go away, but…" At a loss for words, Vivian shrugged.

"Why couldn't you do concerts? Special television performances?" Manon asked as the others took their seats. "You're the most popular opera singer since Maria Callas among fans outside the opera world. Among the opera enthusiasts, I think it's a tie between you and Cecilia Bartoli."

"I've made up my mind." Vivian clung to her arguments. "It's hard enough to perform without having to stumble through, unable to read the music or see the conductor, the audience…anybody."

"I appreciate that this might pose a problem, but just look at our jam sessions," Eryn said. "You have incredible timing and, most likely, perfect pitch. That means you can eventually make reading the music redundant. And as for the audience—standing in the limelight, you don't *see* them anyway. You sense them."

Vivian tried to remember what she meant to say. Stressed by her friends' arguments, she clasped her hands on her lap. "You said it yourself. I was the best, I owned my audience, and they ate out of my hand. No way will I settle for a less than perfect performance just so I can stay in the limelight." She almost hissed the last sentence.

"No one would ask you to do that," Manon murmured, and leaned her head against Vivian's shoulder. "But there are other ways—"

"Not for me. I intend to make a quick, clean break."

"And that's how you plan to cut me off?"

Vivian faltered at Mike's words. Her eyes stung, she didn't know whether because of their discussion or her condition.

"This is how you reason, isn't it, Vivi?" Mike spoke almost inaudibly. "This is how you see our relationship, something of a last chance, a last try, before you isolate yourself because, in your own opinion, you're damaged!" Mike took hold of Vivian's upper arm and almost shook her. "Don't you see? We're all a little bit defective. We're not losing our sight, but other things in our lives make us less than perfect...nobody's perfect."

"You are." Vivian spoke the truth as she saw it.

"Manon, why don't we go make some coffee?" Eryn said quietly.

"Good idea. I could use a cup."

Vivian felt the two women get up from the couch and heard them leave the room. As if Manon and Eryn had provided a shelter from Mike's unleashed emotions, Vivian pressed harder against the backrest.

"I'm not even close to perfect," Mike replied. She moved closer and pressed her lips behind Vivian's ear and sobbed. "I'm more damaged than you can imagine. Damn it, I'm a pitiful excuse of a woman who can't fall asleep if I don't sing lullabies to myself! Maybe *that's* why you're breaking up before we really get started."

❖

Mike's heart pounded, and each contraction sent ice and hot blood in a strange mix through her veins. The pain was unbelievable and she blamed no one but herself. *I did this a second time. I had promised myself, and yet here I am...about to have my heart torn out and shredded.*

Vivian turned so quickly toward Mike that she accidentally bumped into her shoulder and arm. "I'm sorry. Did I hurt you? Stupid question. Of course I did." Vivian's face became as pale as her hair. "What can I say to make it better?"

"You can tell me that you're not leaving me just because you're battling a disability."

"You can't possibly want to stay with a blind, middle-aged woman."

"You tell me that like it's a fact of life! Damn it, Vivian. I can certainly decide who I want to be with. It's not your job to protect me!"

"I can't help it! We're heading for disaster if I encourage you to stay." Vivian gestured vaguely.

Mike considered Vivian's words. *She seems so tired.* And yet, for a moment during the jam session, Vivian had been invigorated and vibrant. Her voice had gone from angelic to earthy and raw. *You were marvelous.* "You don't paint a very flattering picture of me." She placed her hand on top of Vivian's. "If I were going blind or deaf, or became paralyzed...would you still want to be with me?"

"Of course, I would. That's different—"

"No, it isn't, prima donna!" Mike lowered her voice further, licking her lips. "Your attitude is so damn arrogant."

"How dare..." Vivian hastily flung her hands in the air, then slumped back, looking tired and empty. "Am I that horrible?"

"No, you're wonderful. Just afraid, I think." Mike coughed to clear her throat from threatening tears, afraid that she might have to live alone forever.

"But you're right. I am arrogant, in a way." Vivian folded her arms across her chest. "It's reality, though. You're not going blind. I am. You're young, with a future, and my future is..."

"...is different than you imagined it'd be, but it doesn't have to be a bad thing."

Something in Vivian's attitude told Mike she had only this one opportunity to try and convince her; otherwise she'd lose her. "You'll need help, that's true, but you'll be able to perform. You'll just have to sing in different settings. You have so much to offer, and it would be such a waste if you threw that away. Please,

Vivi, don't you understand? I *need* you." Her voice sank to a broken murmur. "I've never told anyone that before. Ever."

Vivian sat in silence for a moment, her beautiful blue eyes locked a fraction of an inch below Mike's. "Why?"

It was a question Mike had dreaded, and her insides knotted. No words would come. Desperate, Mike whimpered and hid her face in Vivian's neck. The satin skin, together with the fresh scent of citrus and sandalwood, comforted her. "I need you. You make me feel safe, sometimes. The way I feel about you scares me, but...I can't let you go. I can't."

"*Cara*—"

"Am I? Or is that a word you use for many other people?"

"No, no. You are my only dearest one." Vivian sounded different. "I never imagined I would feel like I do, since I've always kept people at a distance. You slipped in under my radar." She hugged Mike closer. "If I wasn't ill, or about to need help with so many things that I'd tie you down...when you deserve so much more, I'd reason differently."

"Tie me down? You haven't and you never will! Can't you see that you've set me free?" Mike whispered frantically. "You've given me so much. From day one you've treated me as an equal, a productive person who contributes like everybody else."

"Of course you—"

"To you, I'm not a misfit with a sorry excuse for a father. I'm not a charity case that society has had to fend for. With you...I thought, with all these feelings that just soar when we're together, I...you can't deny that they're there!" Mike was sobbing now and hated the tears that streamed down her cheeks.

The "mother" in her first foster home, who claimed that tears showed weakness and were a luxury for a foster child, had slapped her too often. "You'll cry your whole life if you start now." *I was a child.* And now as a grown woman, Mike still felt physical pain when tears trickled down her face. She swiped at them but more kept coming, as if she'd accidentally damaged whatever vessel inside her contained all her hurt feelings.

"Don't cry. Please, Mike. Please." Vivian held her and felt across Mike's face. She leaned forward and kissed the wet cheeks. "There. You're right. Of course you are. *Cara*, listen to me."

Slowly the sobs lessened, and Mike lay still in Vivian's arms. "Yes?"

"Of course you're right. I know you're right."

"Yes?"

Vivian kissed Mike's lips tenderly. "You're the most extraordinary woman I've met, and you deserve so much good in your life."

"Vivian, I—"

"Shh. Let me finish." Vivian placed a finger on Mike's lips. "I was certain that you need someone better, more appropriate for you, than me. But you have made it clear that you don't want me to leave, like I planned." Vivian's words were formal, but her tone of voice was not. Warm, like summer sand, it ran over Mike, tingling against her skin.

"So, you're not leaving right after the charity concert?"

Vivian raised her eyebrows. "No, no, that was never the plan. I'm going to retire, but that leaves me with an abundance of freedom. I intend to stay in East Quay since Boston isn't so far away, and they have excellent ophthalmologists."

"I thought…" Mike dragged a weary hand through her hair. "Hell, I thought you'd leave a week from now and I'd never see you again."

"I don't blame you for thinking that," Vivian murmured and leaned back, drawing a deep breath. "I haven't been very forthcoming, have I?" She cupped Mike's cheek and let her thumb quickly caress Mike's lower lip.

"Since you're staying, does that mean you're not going to push me away, like you planned?" Mike wondered where the courage to ask up front came from.

"I promise you two things." Vivian fumbled for Mike's hands and squeezed them for emphasis. "To not deliberately push you away and to not create a scene and make you stay if you change your mind."

"I won't change my mind." Mike didn't like the wording in the second promise. It suggested that deep down Vivian expected her to bail out sooner or later. "Just so you know."

"Very well."

They sat in silence until a cautious-sounding voice from behind made them both jump. "Hey. You okay out here? Manon and I drank three cups of coffee each, and frankly, I need a bathroom break before I go home." Eryn smiled crookedly. "And I'm glad I don't see a little mushroom cloud in here."

"We're fine," Vivian said.

"Mike?" Manon came up to the couch. "Are you all right?"

"Yes." And for the first time in a very long time, it was true. Mike knew she and Vivian had a long way to go before they would trust each other completely, and neither of them had mentioned the word "love." But for Vivian to take back her vow to bow out of their relationship was a huge step forward. *If I only could share how you make me feel, the magic we create and how it affects me. Can I ever dare ask you if you sense it as well?*

Mike knew how new and fragile such emotions were. She was willing to do almost anything for Vivian, and now she felt more confident that Vivian would never ask her to do anything uncomfortable. Brenda hadn't been as considerate, which had nearly destroyed Mike.

"Time to go. Mike has to get back upstairs and I have to write my resignation," Eryn said as she returned from the bathroom.

"Didn't your boss give you a leave of absence?" Manon sounded surprised.

"Nope. He tried to bluff me into staying, but I just said, 'I quit, Harold,' and walked out. I have enough vacation to cover the next few weeks. He probably won't give me very good references, but since I'll be busy for several years, I don't care. I'll be fine."

"Good for you." Mike smiled and got up. Only a few days earlier, Eryn had been worried and felt manipulated. Now she was eager to start. Mike dried her eyes, hugged both of her friends before they left, then turned back to Vivian. "Why don't you stay here until I take care of the afternoon crowd and can walk you home?"

"Sounds good. Will you come back to the beach house later tonight?"

"Yes."

Vivian beamed and extended her hand. "A kiss?"

Mike smiled at how breathless she became at Vivian's request. She kneeled on the couch and kissed her with all the tenderness she could muster. "Want to listen to the radio while I'm working?"

"No. I'll just sit here and remember our jam session. It was extraordinary, wasn't it?"

Mike let her eyes rake over Vivian, memorizing the beautiful features, and inhaled her distinctive scent of flowers and musk. "Extraordinary."

❖

Eryn sat up in bed, ramrod straight, uncertain what had woken her up. The phone on her nightstand rang, making her jump, and she fumbled for the receiver in the moonlit bedroom. "Hello?" She looked at the alarm clock, barely able to see it without her glasses. 4:23 a.m. *Who the hell...?*

"Eryn, this is Manon."

Wide-awake in an instant, Eryn clutched the phone. "What's wrong?"

"I just got a call from East Quay Memorial. It's Marjorie."

"What's happened?" Eryn's mind raced.

"She collapsed last night and the staff took her to the ER. She's asked for us."

"Us?" Eryn was already out of bed, mostly because she thought Manon needed her. "You sure?"

"Yes. How quickly can you be ready?"

Small, icy beads trickled down Eryn's spine. "How bad is it?"

"Bad."

"Give me five minutes."

"Okay. Five." Manon paused for a moment and then whispered, "Thank you."

Eryn rushed into the bathroom and pulled her hair back in a low ponytail. Grateful that she'd showered earlier, she pulled on khaki chinos and a green turtleneck. Instead of her favorite jacket, she grabbed a fleece one and her shoulder bag on her way to the front door. She was already outside in the staircase when the elevator stopped at her floor.

Manon gave a tired smile when she saw Eryn waiting for her. "You mean five when you say five. Good to know."

"It's not like I bother with makeup in the middle of the night. I just go for pale and interesting anyway."

Manon laughed, a short, surprised sound. "You do it very well. You're both tonight." The elevator stopped and they stepped outside. "We're taking the Lotus. I didn't see any reason to wake up Benjamin."

"Good decision."

They drove through the empty streets in silence, meeting only one cab during the short drive. Manon parked in a special part of the large parking lot behind the hospital.

Inside, a nurse directed them to Marjorie's room. In the big hospital bed, with a multitude of tubes and cords attached to her, Marjorie looked even smaller than before. She wore an oxygen mask that covered half of her face, and a nurse monitored her condition.

"Marjorie." Manon walked up to the bed and leaned down to kiss her forehead. "Can you hear me?"

Eryn approached the bed from the other side and watched how Marjorie's right, thin eyelid opened halfway. The left one remained closed, the left side of her mouth drooped, and a drop of saliva ran down her cheek. Eryn reached out and wiped it away with the back of her hand without thinking. *A stroke? Probably. Poor Marjorie.*

"Manon…" Marjorie whispered, and pulled the mask half off her face. "You came."

"Of course. And I brought Eryn. See?"

Marjorie managed to turn her head, even if it shook from the effort. "Yes, yes. Eryn. Listen. You will write the book. Everything…is taken care of. In my will."

Tears flooded Eryn's eyes and she took the immobilized hand. "I promise I'll do a good job." *She thinks this is it. Oh, God, maybe it is.* Eryn tried to connect the image of Marjorie in a hospital bed with her memory of the strong woman who gave unforgettable speeches such a short time ago.

"And Manon. Just so you know. The house. The manor…"

"What about it, Marjorie? You know it's in good hands when you're here—"

"No, the house!" Marjorie coughed. "The house goes to you, Manon." She replaced the mask and took labored breaths for a while.

Manon glanced up at Eryn. "What?" she murmured when she redirected her attention to Marjorie.

"One stipulation in the will," Marjorie said, a bit unclear in the mask as she breathed faster. "You can't live in solitude. Only with friends…or a loved one."

Manon's shoulders began to shake, and Eryn realized that she was crying but trying to hide her reaction. *Interesting terms! The whole Dodd Manor, if she doesn't live alone.*

"I understand, Marjorie," Manon managed. "But you can still get better."

"I have…lived my life long enough."

"Don't give up yet." Manon spoke in a low voice just beside Marjorie's ear. "We still need you."

"After an entire century…I need to rest."

"That's okay. You rest, and Eryn and I will deal with whatever needs taking care of." Manon glanced up at Eryn, the message in her eyes impossible to misunderstand.

"Yes," Eryn added, "you don't have to worry about a thing."

"Very good." Marjorie's words were almost inaudible and her paleness went beyond white. Drops of sweat beaded on her forehead, and she struggled for every breath.

The door opened and two women entered.

"I'm Dr. Goldberg," one began. "Mrs. Dodd Endicott's primary physician." She extended a hand.

"And I'm Vera Myles, the head nurse," said the other woman. "Should we step out into the corridor?"

"No," Marjorie interrupted from her bed, having removed the mask again. "I know the truth. You can talk in here."

Eryn had always admired Marjorie but never more than now.

A monitor beeped. "All right," Dr. Goldberg said, and walked up to the bed. "If you promise me to keep the mask on and breathe properly." She adjusted the monitor and frowned. "We can't have your oxygen level go below 93 percent. Deal, Mrs. Dodd? Good."

Dr. Goldberg motioned toward the corner of the room that held a few chairs. They all sat down, and Eryn made sure that nobody had their back toward Marjorie.

"Mrs. Dodd Endicott has signed a document rendering you next of kin, Ms. Belmont. She also told me that Ms. Goddard is writing about her life, and she wants you here as well." She stopped talking and looked intently at Manon and Eryn, as if to judge if they were following her. "Mrs. Dodd has suffered a stroke to her right cerebral hemisphere. She can't move the left side of her body and also suffers from a facial paralysis. We're treating this condition with a clot-busting drug called TPA, but with a person of Mrs. Dodd's age…the prognosis isn't very good."

Eryn, shaken by the doctor's cold, matter-of-fact words, glanced at Marjorie, who was smiling serenely.

"What can be done at this point?" Manon asked. Her hands were tight fists, and two small red spots on her cheeks emphasized her paleness.

"We've performed a CT, to establish where and how extensive the stroke is, and also scheduled Mrs. Dodd for a MRI tomorrow morning—"

An alarm from the monitors silenced the doctor, and she rushed to Marjorie's side, pushing up her eyelids and producing a small flashlight. Eryn and Manon rose and stood by the wall out of the way when more staff rushed into the room. "Damn, she's thrown another clot. Left pupil's fixed and dilated." Dr. Goldberg listened to Marjorie's lungs. "And in her left lung as well. What the hell's going on?"

"BP is 56/38, Doctor," a nurse's aide reported.

"Call a Code Blue." Dr. Goldberg listened to Marjorie's chest, and at the same time more monitors went off. "Asystole! Push vasopressin and adrenaline." She turned to Eryn and Manon. "Please wait outside."

Eryn cradled Manon's shoulders, and they let more of the staff into the room before they stepped out into the corridor.

Half an hour later, Dr. Goldberg joined them. "I'm sorry, but Mrs. Dodd Endicott died despite all our efforts. She threw several clots in her brain and lungs. I can't be sure at this point, but she seems to have developed a blood condition very rapidly. The autopsy, if there is going to be one, can tell us more."

Eryn began to cry quietly when she realized that the extraordinary woman she'd just begun to know had passed away. A glance at Manon showed how devastated she was. Manon was as pale as Eryn felt, and her lips were pressed into a thin, colorless line.

"No." Manon sounded mechanical in her response. "No autopsy."

"I'll make a note in her file, then. Please accept my condolences. Mrs. Dodd seems to have lived a long, healthy life. I know it's little comfort for you, but not everyone has the same good fortune."

"I know. Thank you."

"The nurses have made it somewhat more presentable in there, and they can come back later and take care of Mrs. Dodd. You can have a few moments to pay your respects. I'm sorry to have to rush you, but we have a shortage of beds. We need the room."

"We understand, Doctor."

Eryn was amazed at how collected Manon sounded until they were alone in the hospital room with Marjorie's body. The nurses had placed her hands by her sides and smoothed down the bedsheets. It was as if Manon shrank when she approached the bed and reached out to touch Marjorie's cheek. "Dearest, dearest Marge," she whispered. "You can rest now. I know Michael is there to greet you. Be safe and well, wherever you are…" Manon let go and walked over to the window, the glass reflecting her image as she hugged herself and began to cry.

Eryn crossed the room in three strides and wrapped her arms around Manon from behind. "Shh. I have you."

"She…she went so fast."

"I know. Good for her, though."

"Do you think she suffered?" Manon turned slightly in Eryn's arms and looked up at her with a vulnerability Eryn had never seen.

"I don't know, but she lost consciousness pretty quickly." Eryn hoped this was true.

"Yes, she did." It was as if Manon was eager to cling to Eryn's opinion. "She looked serene even when they worked on her." Manon buried her face in Eryn's neck and drew a deep breath. "I can't believe she's gone."

"It'll take a while for this to sink in. I didn't know her very long, but she was wonderful to me."

"She admired you very much." Manon apparently drew new strength from their closeness and hugged Eryn harder. "Marjorie was an excellent judge of character. She helped me so many times when I was at a loss."

"Were you ever at a loss about me?" Eryn asked, and felt a small tremor reverberate from Manon.

"From day one."

At a knock on the door, Manon pulled back, smoothing her already-perfect hair. She took one step farther to the side and glanced at Marjorie, her face softening, before she raised her voice. "Come in."

Two nurse's aides entered and apologized for having to take the room away so quickly.

The distance between them was back, but Eryn now knew more of the depth of Manon's emotions, so she didn't mind.

"We'll take care of all the arrangements once we've decided on which funeral parlor," Manon said.

Eryn felt, rather than heard, how Manon's voice trembled. She nodded to the nurses, placed a protective hand on the small of Manon's back, and guided her out of the room. "Let's go home and try to get some more sleep. We'll have time to deal with everything tomorrow."

When the elevator doors closed, Manon slumped back against Eryn's arm for a brief moment. "Yes," she murmured. "Tomorrow."

## CHAPTER TWENTY-TWO

Mike, wearing black leather slacks, white shirt, and a long, narrow, black coat, tucked Vivian's hand securely into the bend of her arm as they stepped out of the store. Mike's hair had grown a little longer and curled slightly above the collar. When Vivian had asked her to go to the optician with her, Mike arranged for part-time help.

Vivian had bought new sunglasses, prescribed by an ophthalmologist in Boston. They accented her hair, which she wore in a simple twist. Her red pants suit, however, accentuated by her snow white cashmere pashmina, spoke of elegance and money. Several passersby on Main Street turned their heads and gave Vivian admiring and curious glances.

"Do your new glasses help?"

"Yes, actually. I can make out more outlines of buildings and people than I could over the weekend." She turned toward Mike. "How do I look?"

"Beautiful." Mike smiled. "Very much the famous opera singer."

"Funny," Vivian muttered. "Is Arnold's Drugstore still located at the corner of Main and Graham? I need to fill my prescriptions."

"Yes, Arnold's is still there. Walgreen's tried to outmaneuver them, but for once, a giant chain had to surrender. Everybody in East Quay goes to Arnold's. His grandson is taking over now."

"Amazing. That's one of the things I've missed about this town," Vivian said. "The incredible way people can rally around the slightest thing sometimes."

"Yes. They can." *I know up close and personal just how they can join forces.*

"You sound like it's a bad thing." Vivian frowned.

"It can be, though not in Arnold's case." Mike brushed past the subject. "Here we are. Up two steps and then a self-opening door."

"Thank you."

They entered the drugstore and Mike guided Vivian toward the counter, where a young man smiled in welcome. "Ms. Harding. An honor."

"My pleasure, young man." Vivian beamed. "I'd like to fill these prescriptions."

"It'll be ten or fifteen minutes. You can sit over by the window while you wait and have some free coffee."

"Coffee? What do you say, Mike?"

"Why not?"

Mike chose a table a little out of the way. The closest ones were occupied, but most of the people sat with their backs turned. She made sure Vivian was seated comfortably, then returned with two steaming cups of black coffee. "It's not latte, but it smells good."

"Yes, I can tell." Vivian carefully tasted it. "Not like your java, but good."

"Why, if it isn't Mike Stone," someone behind them said. "You've certainly moved up in the world."

Mike clenched her teeth to keep them from clattering with dread. With deliberate slowness, she turned to face the woman who'd made her life a living hell. "Hello, Brenda."

"Ah, Mikey, always so cool and collected. Is that any way to greet an old friend?" Brenda Tilly had turned in her chair and now scrutinized Mike and Vivian unabashedly. "Aren't you going to introduce me?"

*I'd rather throttle you than embarrass Vivian with your intolerable presence.* "Sure. Brenda, this is Vivian Harding, a friend of mine. Vivian, this is Brenda Tilly. She's an…entrepreneur here in East Quay. We knew each other almost fifteen years ago."

"Ah, please, Mikey. We were more to each other than that." Brenda's eyes glittered with malice. "We lived together, you see, Vivian. We were inseparable."

"Nice to meet you, Ms. Tilly. Mike's obviously come a long way on her own since then, hasn't she?" Vivian's voice was polite, but Mike could hear the strength beneath it.

"Yes, but you know what they say. You can take the girl out of her habitat, but you can't take the habits out of the girl."

"Brenda. Not here." Mike glared at the woman who'd once been her world. Brenda had tied her to herself so closely, it had taken Mike more than a year to realize she had the power and the ability to make it on her own. Brenda's verbal abuse, her tantrums and demands for absolute obedience finally drove Mike away. *And I still feel ashamed. I look at her, and I'm embarrassed at how I let her run my life and how I bent over backward so many times to accommodate her. In every fucking way!*

Mike's ire was up, and it infuriated her that Brenda would try to cause trouble in her usual calculating way. She sometimes saw Brenda in town but made a point of ignoring her.

"I think old sayings like that are ridiculous and, most of the time, completely wrong. And I think Mike's success proves my point." Vivian still sounded polite, but her eyes, no matter how bad her vision, showed nothing but pure, blue-tinted steel.

Brenda, obviously taken aback, tried again. "You don't know Mike the way I do, so maybe you oughta wait before you judge," she said. "She used to be at my beck and call."

"You should stop now before you say something really stupid, Brenda," Mike growled. "The day I left was the first time I did something really good for myself. And after that, life only became better."

"Better? No matter how you like to pretend that you're playing with the big guns and the rich and famous in this town, everyone will always think of you as the daughter of the drunk child killer."

Mike grew cold.

"You have the man's genes, don't you, and you're cut from the same mold, pretty much." Brenda glowered at Mike. "You could follow in his footsteps."

"Stay away from me from now on." Mike's chest hurt. *Damn it. She talks about my worst fears like they're nothing. She has no right to say these things! No one has.* Mike leaned closer as her voice sank to a low, cold hiss. "I don't have anything else to say to you."

Mike returned her attention to Vivian and saw a faint smile play at the corners of her mouth. "Want to check on your prescription?"

"Yes, why don't we? It's nice outside, and I'll enjoy the walk back to the car. Good-bye, Ms. Tilly."

As if Brenda were air, Mike and Vivian walked over to the counter where Arnold's grandson was waiting with a small paper bag. "Here you go. All ready."

"Sorry 'bout that," Mike said as they left. It had felt good to finally tell Brenda off to her face, but now her stomach was quivering and she wondered what Vivian was thinking.

"Don't be. That's been brewing for a while, hasn't it?"

"Yes."

"Do you feel better for standing your ground?"

"Yes. But I feel awkward too. I wish you hadn't had to overhear the whole thing."

"*Cara*, it makes no difference to me." Vivian squeezed Mike's arm. "I think you're wonderful, and so strong, to have turned your life into what it is now after such a rocky start."

"Rocky is putting it very nicely. My father was a fisherman. He worked hard and partied hard. My mother died when I was about two years old, too little to remember her."

Mike guided Vivian into the William Dodd Park and up to a bench where an old oak provided some shade. "Want to sit down?"

"Yes. I want to hear what you have to say. This is important."

Warmed by Vivian's obvious interest, Mike sat next to her, still holding Vivian's hand. "Father had a lot of money when the fishing was good, and he used most of it to buy beer for himself and his friends at the pub. He would come home and I'd try to do what he wanted, take care of the house and do my homework. I even tried to cook, but I was only six or seven, so I failed a lot." She frowned.

"He didn't beat me very often, but it happened, and he yelled at me when I did something wrong. When I was almost eight, someone at school, a nurse or a teacher, reported him to the authorities, for child abuse. The child welfare services put me in a temporary foster home, but father regained custody only a few weeks later. I don't know how.

"Then one day, he didn't come home till late. And in the middle of the night, the police came to arrest him. They took me back to a foster home again, this time a different one, and that was the start of my treadmill." Mike sighed as the feeling of the years gone by flooded her senses and transported her through time.

"Many foster homes."

"I lived in nine before I ran away when I was fifteen."

"You couldn't take it anymore." Vivian didn't turn her words into a question.

"No. Not one day longer. I met Brenda a year later and she swept me off my feet. I had just come to terms with my sexuality, and there she was, a little older and so worldly and sure of herself. She was beautiful, and both men and women in our circles pursued her." Mike glanced at Vivian, feeling shy. "People going from shelter to shelter sometimes lucked out, and the social services helped them get an apartment. Brenda had a one-bedroom one behind the industrial area. The first weeks I stayed there were as close to heaven as I'd come."

"What happened?"

"Brenda...has her ways to get you to comply." Mike blushed. "She had a voracious sexual appetite and was very aggressive in bed. I tried to accommodate her, but soon the thrill and the feeling of being in love were gone. Instead, I was afraid of her. Afraid I wouldn't please her and make her angry. She could get really ugly, and her razor tongue lashed out at me in ways..." Mike clung to Vivian's hand. "I still dream about it."

"I don't blame you. I'm glad you decided to leave. Not everyone can find the strength to do that—certainly not without help."

"I didn't have any help then," Mike admitted, "but later, when I found shelter at the Youth Center in Providence, I met Josie Quinn. She worked as a volunteer counselor, and she was the first one I learned to trust."

Vivian's eyes turned a brighter blue, and she raised her hands to touch Mike's cheek. "I'm forever grateful to Josie."

"Manon's going to help me track her down. We could go visit her, if you like."

Vivian nodded. "That would be great, don't you think? She sounds like the type of person I admire immensely. Selfless and caring, like a kindred spirit to Manon."

"Yes."

Mike became silent when she thought of the afternoon's turn of events. *What a catharsis it was to run into that bitch. Who'd have known? Vivian took it well. She defended me. I knew she'd do that, though.*

"What did Brenda mean by those cryptic remarks about your genetic inheritance?" Vivian asked, interrupting Mike's thoughts. "And what happened to your father?"

Mike went cold. She'd hoped Vivian wouldn't remember to ask about that but realized that was a wasted hope. She pushed that thought so far out of her mind most of the time that she almost forgot it herself. "Oh, Vivi," she sighed, squaring her jaw yet shivering. "Can we drive back to the café? It's getting cold."

"Of course." They walked back to Mike's Honda Civic and drove back to the café in silence. Mike felt unsettled, and the topic they'd tapped into ate at her. After she parked behind the café, she helped Vivian to the back door, and Vivian managed the stairs on her own. Mike breathed in relief when they were finally within the walls of her basement. *Safe. Nothing can happen here. Nothing bad, right?*

"Ready to continue?" Vivian took off her cashmere coat, then sat down on the couch and kicked off her shoes. "We need to talk about this...whatever it is, if we stand a chance together."

*Are you talking about more of a future than you've allowed us before?* Mike was afraid the truth would divide them, but she realized Vivian had a point. Mike knew what it was to live a lie, to hide things from the world constantly.

She put her leather jacket on a chair and sat down next to Vivian. "It doesn't matter that I changed my name and tried to better myself. I'll always be Richard Collins's daughter. Fortunately, not many people knew he had a daughter, and if they do, they didn't know my name."

"Why is that fortunate?"

"Because he killed someone."

❖

"Belmont Foundation. Ms. Belmont's office, Dennis Altman speaking."

*Efficient fellow.* Eryn twisted a pencil between her fingers. "Hello, Dennis, this is Eryn Goddard. Is she in, please?"

"I'm sorry, Ms. Goddard, but Ms. Belmont isn't in and won't be back until Wednesday at the earliest. May I take a message?"

*What?* Eryn's heart dropped. "I'm a friend." *She didn't mention taking time off.* "Any way I can get in touch with her? I've left several messages on her cell phone."

"I'm sorry, ma'am, but Ms. Belmont hasn't checked in yet today. When, and if, she does, I'll give her your message."

*He's not sure she'll be in touch today? Manon, workaholism personified?* Puzzled, Eryn tapped the pencil on a notepad. "May I ask where she's gone?"

"Ms. Belmont is in Boston, ma'am."

*Boston!* Eryn dropped the pencil and caught it again. When they spoke early the day before, after returning from the hospital, Manon hadn't said a word about going to Boston. Granted, Manon didn't have to tell Eryn her every move, and things could have come up at the last minute, but it still…hurt. Perhaps it had something to do with Marjorie's will.

Manon had gone up to her penthouse, and Eryn hadn't seen or heard from her since, which was unsettling. She ached to see Manon, to hold her and reestablish their fragile bond. *I just need to see her. Period.*

Belmont Industries' headquarters were located in Boston, but Eryn had a gut feeling that *someone* rather than *something* had pulled Manon there on such short notice. "Thanks, Dennis. If she checks in, please ask her to call me. Here are my phone numbers, in case she lost them." As Eryn hung up she felt slightly nauseated and jittery.

She had begun her research of the Dodd dynasty and, encouraged by all she'd found already, had wanted to share it with Manon, hoping the subject might somehow console her. *And why did I bother to worry? She didn't worry for a second about me, certainly not enough to say she'd be gone for days.*

She returned her attention to the computer and saved a few more Web pages to her hard drive, hoping she could use a few of them. Elizabeth, the first "Dodd woman," to use Harold Mills's phrase, had come to the colonies from London in 1693 as wealthy landowner William Dodd's bride. He'd met her in England as a young man, married her after only two months, and they'd sailed for Newport a few weeks later.

Lizzy ran William's household with a determined hand. She cared for the sick and the elderly, and organized a group of her peers to do charitable work. Earlier Eryn had discovered Lizzy's oldest granddaughter's journal in Marjorie's private library and learned from it that Lizzy had died from pneumonia at age thirty-nine and her husband had never remarried.

Eryn leaned back and thought of the first Dodds in East Quay. Lizzy must have been a strong woman. She'd borne seven children, five of whom lived to form their own families. The country was hard to live in back then, and, she broodingly thought, it still was for a lot of people. *And those are the ones Manon burns for. She's all about helping the bleeding masses, and how can I compete with that? If she doesn't prioritize her own happiness, what chance do I stand?*

That was the nucleus of the enigma that was Manon. She had practically inherited her social conscience, and her grandfather, who had bled for the misfortunate and the displaced, had obviously molded her. But also Manon was apparently trying to make up for something. *Her lesbianism? The death of her brother?*

Eryn shook her head. She hoped Manon would call soon, just to make sure she was all right. She knew Manon missed Marjorie and wished she could help Manon feel less lonely. *She simply doesn't need you the way you hoped she would by now, you fool.*

Angry at her tendency to accept defeat in matters of the heart, Eryn focused on what she was good at and typed new search words into the Google search engine. "She'll call," she muttered. "She better."

❖

"I just don't know what to do." Manon was grateful that Faith, her longtime friend, took the time to listen.

Faith Dabrinsky was a tall, dark woman with an incredibly commanding presence. Manon knew you could hear a feather crash to the floor when Faith entered a boardroom. Preferring to dress in black or dark gray pants suits and crisp white shirts, today Faith wore a dark blue skirt suit which softened her otherwise austere appearance.

"You've really been through it over the last weeks, haven't you?" Faith asked with a trace of tenderness in her matter-of-fact voice. "You look worn out."

"I've lost my footing completely…everything I used to know; the truths I used to cling to…" Manon reached into her purse for a tissue and dabbed the corners of her eyes. "Am I going insane?"

"No, you're not. Actually, I think you've had your first real taste of what life can be like if you let yourself live it."

"What's that supposed to mean?" Stunned, Manon stared at Faith. "That I've been dormant for the last forty years?"

"No, of course not. You've done amazing things for years and can be more than proud of your contributions to society." Faith leaned back on her leather couch and stared into the fireplace where a log flamed with a cozy, crackling sound. "But for you, personally, you haven't done very much. Other than hide."

The honest reply stung, but Manon hid her pain and nodded briskly. "Go on."

"Oh, I know that look. Your Joan of Arc stance, remember? The bring-it-on look that intimidated more than one professor at Harvard." Faith reached out and patted Manon's knee. "You don't have to become all defensive. I only meant that you've done so much good for other people it's only fair that you look to your own happiness now. And trust me. You can only be happy if you acknowledge who and what you are."

"The foundation is more important—"

"Ah, but that's where you're wrong, partially, anyway. The foundation is important, vital even. But it doesn't need your complete sacrifice. In fact, the opposite. It needs your attention and love, which it will only get from a Manon who lives her life to the fullest. Don't you agree?"

Manon whispered as the restrained tears began to fall in earnest. "Her name is Eryn," she whispered. "Eryn Goddard. She's the most amazing person I've ever met. She's honest to a fault and has stolen my heart completely. I've never been more afraid in my life." She shivered against Faith.

"Oh, honey." Faith usually didn't use terms of endearment, but now she did as she slid closer and hugged Manon. "You're in love. Finally. Thank God."

"I'm not sure that's what I am…it could be mindless infatuation for all I know!" Manon withdrew from the hug; physical closeness was too much right now.

"You're talking nonsense and you know it." Faith's voice was mild but relentless. "You came here to ask me how to get out of this, didn't you?"

Manon's cheeks warmed. "Well, no, I wouldn't put it like that." She pulled her sweater closer around her. "I need your input how to… manage it."

"You don't need my help. You need to listen to your heart, not your head."

"What?"

"You already know. You have great instincts, for business, for charity. You know how to manipulate the big elephants to open their wallets and checkbooks, and do so smilingly." Faith cupped Manon's cheek and her brown eyes glittered with delight. "Are you telling me that you can't figure out a way to have your cake and eat it too? No pun intended, of course." She winked.

"Faith!" Manon gasped and then had to laugh. "You're just as impossible as you were twenty years ago!"

"I know," Faith replied, sounding pleased.

Manon sat in silence. Her thoughts whirled, and a strange sort of peace began to spread as part of her surrendered and her ever-analytical mind stirred into action.

"Tell me about her," Faith said, and reached for her mug of steaming black coffee. "I want to know everything about the woman who's managed to penetrate your defenses in a few short weeks."

"Describe her?" Manon hid behind her own large mug. "I wish I could do her justice. Honest and up-front. Loyal, friendly, brave. She's been an out lesbian for a long time."

"Gutsy. Go on."

"Red hair, green eyes, freckles. And she's all about giving hugs. She seems to thrive on them. She's good at comforting, and the way she looks at me when she listens, her head slightly tilted and her eyes narrowing...I could go on talking forever just to have her look at me that way..." Manon quieted and stared into her coffee mug.

After a while she slowly raised her head and peeked at Faith, who sipped her coffee and obviously waited for her to say something.

Manon nodded thoughtfully. "All right, Faith. All right. Now I know what to do."

# CHAPTER TWENTY-THREE

The doorbell rang and Eryn jumped up from her desk, hit her head on the desktop lamp, and cursed as she rushed to the door, rubbing her temple. *Manon! She's back.* She flung the door open with a smile.

"Hello. I was in the neighborhood and thought I'd drop by and pick up the toaster Sandy lent you. Now that she's moving to Newport, she's going to need it."

"Hello, Mom." Eryn sighed and let Harriet Goddard in. She hadn't seen her mother in over three months, which was pretty remarkable since they lived in the same town. "Sandy gave me the toaster as a housewarming present when I moved here." *Which is more than you did, Mother dear.* "I haven't changed the place much since Aunt Amanda lived here, but you're welcome to look around. I think I'll repaint the bathroom soon and install a shower."

"Sounds good," Harriet said, and hung up her coat. She fiddled with the hem of her blouse for a second. "I really didn't come about the toaster."

"I didn't think so. Want some coffee?" Eryn motioned toward the kitchen and refused to let the image of Manon sitting on her floor bother her.

"No, thank you, sweetheart. My doctor says I should stick to tea."

*Sweetheart? Doctor?* Eryn stopped and pivoted so quickly she almost knocked her mother over. "What? Are you sick?"

"Just a small ulcer, actually. Nothing to worry about. If you don't have tea, I'll just have a glass of water."

"No, no. I have tea. Several kinds. Take your pick." Eryn guided Harriet over to one of the cabinets where her mother examined the five boxes. "They're from Sea Stone Café, all of them," she remarked. "Isn't that run by a friend of yours? That tall, dark girl?"

"Yes, Mike Stone."

"That's right." Harriet pointed at the box in the middle. "Chai tea. That's what everybody raves about at the church meetings."

Eryn had to laugh. "They rave at the church meetings. Sounds like you have a lot of fun."

To her surprise, Harriet returned the laugh with a smile. "We have more fun there than you could imagine. Don't sell us short, Eryn."

"Okay, if you'll return the favor."

"I heard you quit your job at the paper. After having a steady job there for so many years…what possessed you?"

"A chance of a lifetime to do what I've dreamed of."

"Doing what?"

"You really have no idea what my dreams are, do you, Mom?" Eryn sighed unhappily. "You know that Sandy wanted to travel all over Asia and Kelly wanted to be a professional dancer."

"Neither of them has done any of that."

"That's not the point. You knew them so well but never took the time to ask me what I wanted."

"I knew you wanted to play that guitar of yours."

"You knew that only because I made so much noise rehearsing in the garage with my friends. But that wasn't my dream, not all of it, anyway."

Harriet took a deep breath and appeared to brace herself. "Then tell me now."

A childish part of her, immature and vengeful, wanted to refuse and say, "You snooze, you lose," but Eryn told herself to grow up. "I want to be a serious writer, a biographer, a novelist. I love words as much as I love music. I want to reach people with what I write, to touch their hearts. Same goes for my music."

"Oh, my." Harriet sighed and sank down on a kitchen chair.

Eryn made tea for both of them, and neither spoke until she sat down at the kitchen table, facing her mother. *On opposite sides as always. Yet she's different. She's here alone. When did that happen last? If ever?*

"It used to upset me that Sandy and Kelly got away with so many things when we were teenagers. I was the perfect child in every aspect but one, and I was always in the doghouse, no matter what." It was time for the truth, Eryn could feel it.

"You're right. You were."

Eryn's breath caught in her throat and she coughed before she drank her tea. "I'm glad you're not denying it," she managed. "We can't change the past."

"I thought it was a phase, something you'd grow out of. You were so young and easily the brightest of you girls. And when you told your father and me, I...I couldn't accept it." Sorrowfully Harriet shook her head. "You'll never give me grandchildren, a little girl or boy with your good looks and your sharp mind." Tears clung to Harriet's eyelashes.

"Is that it? Is that why you've never accepted that I'm gay? That can't possibly be it! What if I married a guy and was unable to have children because of a physical defect? That wouldn't have made you turn your back on me, would it?" Eryn tried to force herself to calm down.

"No, it wasn't just that. People at church were asking how and when your father and I were going to reel that wild girl of ours in. What you are goes against my faith, and my upbringing...and it's taken me until now to even be able to talk about it."

Honesty had replaced the cold shoulders and dismissal. Eryn reached out across the table, realizing maybe she had pushed her mother too fast. "I can understand where you're coming from, and I don't want you to go against your faith."

Harriet covered the hand with hers and squeezed it gently. "You don't?"

"No. I do want you to love me like a mother loves her child, no matter what. That way, I can learn to trust in your love, and perhaps Dad's, since he always follows in your steps. And maybe then I can live with the fact that you still have issues with homosexuality, but not with me. And as for grandchildren...with today's technology, it isn't out of the question. So perhaps. One day." *Would Manon want to have children?* Eryn closed her eyes. *Will Manon want to take a chance on me?*

"So you're telling me that you respect my faith?" Harriet now reached out and held onto Eryn as if she couldn't make herself let go.

*She loves me. Mom loves me, and she's hurt over her torn feelings all these years. She must've struggled with outrage and frustration, and I suffered because of it.* "You know, Mom, maybe the church will eventually be more lenient about gay people. We're all God's creatures, and he made a certain number of us gay. Doesn't that tell you something? I'm your daughter, Mom, not a product of the devil."

Harriet broke into tears again and Eryn silently cursed herself for coming on too strong, as usual. She rose and quickly rounded the table. "Mom, I'm sorry." Leaning down she hugged her mother for the first time in years.

"No, I'm sorry." Her mother turned her face into Eryn's sweatshirt. "I haven't been a good mother. I've committed more sins than you ever will."

"What are you talking about?" Eryn sank to her knees next to Harriet's chair, her arms still loosely around her.

"Pride. It's a powerful sin. And I've lied. I haven't fully loved my neighbor, which entails you, Eryn. But mostly, my pride has been speaking."

"And now?" Eryn hardly dared to ask; she felt as if she was walking on night-old ice.

"I don't want us to go on the way we have. Sandy and Kelly have tried to talk to me about you so many times, and I've refused. But when I read the *Chronicle* this morning and—"

"And saw what? I'm in the paper?"

"Yes. Your old photographer wrote some very nice things about you to thank you for all your years at the paper. There was also an article about the Dodd celebration and a eulogy about Ms. Dodd. The article about the party had pictures and you were there, sitting at the head table."

"Really? Wow." Eryn didn't know what else to say. "I had no idea anyone took pictures."

"And when I saw that…I wanted to take the clippings to our women's group at church and, well, brag about my daughter. And it hit me that I've had reason to brag about you many, many times, and I never have, because I resented…who…what you are." Harriet hiccupped and wiped her tears with a tissue.

"Mom." Eryn hugged Harriet again. "Maybe there's hope for us. Do you think so?"

"I do. I do, Eryn. I've found the daughter I was so proud of so many years ago, and I want to get to know her all over again."

Eryn returned to her chair. "This is really...something." As much as she loved words, they failed her now.

"Do you have a...girlfriend?" Harriet asked, and Eryn had to smile at her mother's attempt to sound casual.

"I'm not sure, Mom, but I've got my hopes up. I'll know when she gets back from Boston." Eryn's heart ached. "It's really scary, you know. If she decides to reject me..." She shrugged but knew her voice wavered and revealed her pain.

"If she does, whoever she is, then she's a fool." Harriet drank more tea.

Eryn laughed again, mostly to keep from crying. "Oh, you have no idea."

"Who is she? Anybody I've heard of? Someone from your old school?"

"No, not at all." *It's time for a leap of faith, but not quite yet.* "If she dares to take a chance on me, I'll be happy to introduce her, but I can't break her trust. She isn't out, you see."

"Out? Oh, you mean she's, how do you say, in the closet?"

"Very." Eryn felt drained, but some of the fatigue felt good.

"Well, since you're working from home now, I won't keep you any longer, this time. I'll come by later, perhaps next week?"

"Sure. And I can drop by the house too, you know. And...oh! Wait!" Eryn hurried into her study and rummaged around her desk. Finding what she was looking for, she returned to her mother, who now stood in the hallway, putting on her coat.

"Here, Mom. Two tickets to the Belmont Foundation Charity Concert on Saturday. You could never afford them, and neither could I, normally. I got them free. I thought I'd send one to Sandy and her boyfriend, and Kelly and Bob too. And Don and his wife, of course. That leaves one for me and one extra."

"But won't the charity lose out?" Harriet fingered the tickets. "That doesn't seem right."

"Oh, they're bought and paid for with honest money that's going directly to the hospital wing. And if it makes you feel better, you can donate what you can spare to the foundation. That's what I'll do."

"Ah, that will mean extra money for them. Good idea." Her mother nodded. "Your father will be pleased. He loves music."

"I know he does. Does he know you're here?"

"Yes."

"Bring him next time."

"Okay," Harriet said, almost shyly. "See you Saturday, maybe. And next week."

"Yes. We'll be sitting together. Very good seats, actually."

"Sounds wonderful." Harriet hastily kissed Eryn's cheeks. "Bye-bye."

"Bye."

Eryn listened until the sound of her mother's steps quieted. *Is this a sign that my life will change in more ways? I'm not sure I can handle any more surprises. Except one. Manon. Come back. This wait is killing me.*

❖

"He killed someone?" Vivian gasped and pulled Mike into a fierce embrace. "Oh, *cara*, my darling. How awful. For the person's family. For you."

"I didn't know about it for a long time. Father died in prison when I was fourteen, and that's when I learned the truth." Mike buried her face against Vivian's chest.

Mike's hair smelled clean and of her sandalwood perfume. Familiar by now. "Tell me about it."

Mike sobbed, a deep, painful sound. "According to the court papers, my father had left me home alone to go to the pub soon after I was released back into his care, to 'celebrate' with his friends. He drank quite a bit and then decided to drive home. It wasn't very late, and he took a shortcut from the pub, and…and hit a boy on the bicycle path."

"Oh, my God. And the boy was killed."

"Yes, on impact, apparently. My father, drunk and out of it, left the scene and drove home. So not only did he kill the poor boy, but he left him there, didn't even try to help. When the police came to arrest him, he insisted he didn't even know he'd hit someone. He was that far gone."

Something in Vivian's memory stirred, but she couldn't place her finger on it. "So he was sentenced to prison."

"Yes, since it was his third DUI, he got fifteen years. He died after six years in that place, from a heart attack."

Vivian tried to warm Mike through her denim shirt as she stroked her in long, languid movements. She'd stopped shivering and felt delightfully heavy against Vivian's breasts.

"And Brenda was trying to make you believe that you've inherited your father's genes," Vivian stated with a huff. "Granted, you can inherit the risk for alcoholism, but as for the rest of your father's actions? No. You have nothing of that."

Mike held on to Vivian. "Sometimes my past drives me nuts. I have the urge to hit something, sometimes," Mike whispered. "I beat the drums. I mean, really hard."

"That's my *point*." Vivian tipped Mike's head back. "You beat the drums. Not a living being of any kind. Lifeless things." She leaned down and kissed Mike. "There's nothing wrong with you, *cara*. You're amazing and have overcome hardships that most of us never even hear about. And you mean so much to me."

She kissed Mike again. This time she parted her lips and entered Mike's mouth with insistent softness. Mike answered the kiss, and Vivian hoped it washed away some of her fear, if not all.

Mike unbuttoned Vivian's shirt and snuck a hand inside, cupped one of her abundant breasts and caressed it.

Vivian moaned aloud. "Oh, *cara*, you do the strangest, most wonderful things to me." Then she kissed the top of Mike's head. "You make me feel things…things I never thought I'd ever experience. Especially not now…" *Now when everything else has fallen apart around me. You show me a new way. A new dream. Mike.*

"You're so beautiful. I want you, Vivian. I want to feel you against me."

"Then undress me, my darling." How easy it was to say. *Remarkable.* The affectionate word obviously wasn't lost on Mike. The pulse at her temples pounded so hard Vivian could see it.

"I want to watch you." Their closeness now obviously made Mike more daring too. "Every part of you, Vivi. You have such a sexy, wonderful body. I can't get enough of it."

Vivian jerked at Mike's unexpected and arousing words, feeling the warmth of a deep blush on her cheeks. "Mike, darling, do whatever you want," Vivian said breathlessly. "Let me just get undressed—"

"No, let me." Mike moved back to reach the buttons farther down. She opened Vivian's shirt completely, tugged it off her arms, and made it disappear. Vivian wore a lace bra that covered very little, which stole what little breath Mike still had. "I want to see everything," she insisted and removed the bra with unsteady fingers.

"God, Mike." Vivian arched into her touch when Mike took the nipples between her fingers and rolled them into firm peaks. "I want you so much it hurts. Don't stop." Desire, affection, nervousness, and an overshadowing tenderness toward Mike surged through her, leaving her shaking and determined to give Mike all the pleasure she deserved.

The thought of Brenda came uninvited, but Vivian immediately dismissed the comparison. She guessed that Brenda had wanted Mike to pleasure her in ways Mike wasn't comfortable with, and Vivian vowed to never demand Mike make such choices.

As Mike leaned in and took one of Vivian's nipples into her mouth, Vivian pressed against it. "Yes, just like that," she groaned. "You make me feel so good." Mike latched onto the nipple, tugging gently on it with her teeth, and Vivian gave a sharp cry before she sank deeper into the couch, pulling Mike with her. "Mike…*cara*…don't stop. I want out of these clothes, though. Hurry."

"No problem," Mike said. She unbuttoned and unzipped Vivian's slacks before pushing them off her raised hips, then tugged the panties and the nylon stockings down together at the same time.

"You too?" Vivian whispered, staring up at the outline of Mike's face.

"Yes."

Vivian felt Mike slowly undress, slowing their pace, and she touched her wherever she felt bare skin. Finally Mike sat naked in front of her. Vivian lost her breath and bit into her lower lip. "You feel wonderful." Vivian let her palms "see" Mike. "I'm so glad I was able to see you before my eyes blurred completely," she said. "I know you're satin smooth, with perfect olive skin." Her voice broke. "You know how I feel about you, don't you, *cara*?"

"I think you have to tell me. I am beyond guessing. I'm bound to get it wrong."

Vivian chuckled, nervous and exhilarated, as she drew Mike on top of her. "I know. It's not fair of me to ask." She quieted for a moment. No matter how she put this, it was going to sound either too formal or too mushy. "Sweetest Michaela, you've taken me by storm in every way possible. No matter what the future brings, I hope you'll be there with me…because I love you." *Merde, it sounds like I'm proposing or something…and perhaps I am, in a way.*

Mike became still. When Vivian placed a hand between her breasts, Mike's heartbeat felt erratic and powerful. Mike gasped for air several times and sounded as if she was about to cry. Vivian smiled wryly to herself. *I had hoped for a happier result when I confessed to love and meant it for the first time in my life.*

Mike then pressed Vivian's hand tighter to her chest. "I love you too. I love you, Vivian." Her voice was strained, but her words were clear. She pressed closer and hid her face in Vivian's hair. "I've loved you from the first day you came into the café."

Vivian wrapped her legs around Mike and held her even closer, unable to hold back her excitement or her arousal. "You make me so happy."

"Let me feel you."

As Mike pushed a hand down between them, Vivian parted her legs farther and bent them around Mike's waist. "Yes, yes. Touch me."

"God, Vivi, you're so wet." Mike whimpered. "So incredibly soft and drenched."

"Yes. Only for you, darling. I want you. Now."

Vivian knew her staccato words conveyed her deep need, and if Mike didn't do something soon, she wasn't above begging. *She's going to make me hers. And if she wants to, I'll show her just how I can claim her.*

Mike raised her hips a few inches and slid two fingers inside Vivian's copious moisture. Vivian's inner walls contracted around Mike's fingers, and as the wet heat pulsated it felt as if Mike searched for something.

Whatever it was, Vivian knew exactly when Mike found it. She gave a hoarse, loud cry when Mike curled her fingers up and sent thrills of pleasure shimmering through her thighs and stomach.

"Vivian…touch me too. I'm burning for you."

Vivian cupped Mike's buttocks with both hands and pulled her tight. She kissed Mike's lips, nibbled them with sharp teeth while she massaged her breasts. When she extended her fingers, she actually managed to dip into the wetness a few times.

Her actions obviously added to Mike's fire, but she squirmed so restlessly, Vivian understood Mike needed more. More of Vivian, more touches, and more love.

"Roll onto your side," Vivian murmured. "I can't reach you like this."

Vivian held on as Mike rolled off her and ended up just an inch from falling to the floor. "You better not let me go," Mike said with a smile in her voice.

"Never," Vivian replied with total sincerity. She still held on to Mike with one arm around her neck, the other searching the black curls between Mike's legs. The wetness urged her on and she knew what to do. "Spread you legs for me, *cara*."

Mike gasped and began moving her hand still buried between Vivian's legs, then lifted her right leg and hooked it loosely around Vivian's hip. Vivian immediately rolled Mike's clitoris between her fingers. It swelled, and Vivian kept circling it with her thumb when she entered Mike with first one finger and then two.

"I can't believe how wonderful you feel," Vivian breathed. "You're like fire against me and you're going to make me come...very soon." She rolled her hips against Mike's hand.

Mike pressed her damp forehead against Vivian's and their breaths mingled as their hands played deep inside each other.

*Unison. Harmony. Accord.* From nowhere, musical terms appeared in Vivian's mind, and she knew this was how she felt about Mike. She kissed her tenderly and whispered, "I love you, *cara*, and I want to make you feel so good. I want you to stay like this, in my arms. I need you, so...much...Mike! Mike...oh...oh..."

Mike kept rolling her hips, and Vivian felt sweat stream down Mike's temples and onto her own face as Mike leaned over her. "Then kiss me again. Make me yours..."

Vivian buried the fingers of her free hand in Mike's damp hair and kissed her thoroughly, deeply, and with all the love she now felt entitled to show. As if the truth about their mutual feelings set Mike free enough to enjoy the physical aspect of love, Mike came with a loud whimper, her body rigid from her toes to her head, which was thrown back over Vivian's arm. "Vivi! Oh, my God...ah!" Deep moans followed as her body convulsed repeatedly.

Vivian felt an unusual, but rather pleasant, soreness when she cradled Mike and allowed her to catch her breath and find her bearings. The room was quiet except for their labored breathing. When they calmed down, Mike raised her head and kissed the tip of Vivian's nose.

"I love you." She said it without hesitation, and yet Vivian got the impression that Mike was holding her breath.

"I love you right back." Vivian felt Mike relax and put her head on Vivian's shoulder.

"I'm happy. And afraid. I've never been this happy," Mike explained, "so I'm not sure how to make it last. Does that make sense?"

"Yes, in a way. But if it makes you feel better, I've never been this happy either, and I have no clue where to go from here. All I know is that wherever I go, or whatever I do, I want you to be there. If you want to be."

"Of course I do." Mike sighed. "But I can't just go places. I have the café."

"I know." Vivian kissed Mike in a slow, deep way and hoped her kiss conveyed all the emotions that defied words.

"You need to go home to Perry and Mason sooner or later." Mike became silent for a moment, and Vivian waited patiently for what was about to come. "If I throw a few things in a bag, can I come with you? I can walk the boys and spend a few nights. What do you think?" She shrugged and sounded a little embarrassed.

"Would you? Really?" Vivian smiled. "That'd be great. I've worried about the dogs lately. I can still walk them during the day but have problems when it's dark."

"I understand," Mike said, the embarrassment gone from her voice. "So, it's a deal, then?"

Vivian's chest filled with an expanding balloon of happiness. "Deal."

## CHAPTER TWENTY-FOUR

Manon stood by her window and watched the sun set over her beloved hometown. East Quay possessed a special beauty any time of year, but the autumn sun's glow on the red and yellow maple leaves in the park not far from her building was breathtaking. Still, she wasn't thinking about the view but about the woman downstairs. After spending four nights in Boston, Manon was torn between dread and anticipation when she thought of Eryn.

*I can't believe I'm this nervous.* She stared at her trembling hands. *But I have every reason to be.* Manon knew Eryn was bound to have her ire up, thinking Manon had ignored her messages. However, for the first time in her life, she hadn't checked in with the office. When Dennis finally heard from her only ten minutes earlier, he'd sounded ready to call the police.

Manon had thought about calling Eryn, but she couldn't tell her how she felt over the phone. Eryn would have realized she was hiding something and interpreted it in the worst way possible. *For good reason.* Now, Eryn might think Manon had ignored her, but she might possibly blame Dennis. *Let's hope for the latter.*

She had made arrangements for Marjorie's funeral and, because guests were expected from all over the world, had decided on two ceremonies: one large and official, the other small and intimate.

*Enough procrastination.* Manon smoothed her black turtleneck and pressed a hand against the flutters in her stomach. It was time to face Eryn.

❖

Eryn was putting what was left of her microwave lasagna away when the doorbell rang. Muttering a curse—*please, not Sandy this evening*—she headed for the door. The previous night yet another family member, her older sister Kelly, had stopped by. Eryn had enjoyed their visit, but she was a little tired of talking about her mother's miraculous olive branch. As happy as Eryn was, she couldn't stop thinking about Manon, though she wasn't going to chase her to Boston or leave the ten messages a day she felt like leaving.

Pushing loose hair from her face, she jerked the door open and snapped her jaw shut so hard it hurt.

Manon stood there, aristocratically perfect posture and eyes aglow. Still, her laced fingers fiddled with each other, and she swayed back and forth.

"Eryn? May I come in?" Manon's throaty, velvet voice sounded a bit unsteady.

"What? Yes. Come in, come in." *Breathe. Breathe. That's it. She's here.* "Did you have a good trip to Boston?" Eryn was impressed with how casual she managed to sound. But after two seconds her usual straightforwardness poked its head up. "I missed you."

"I missed you too, very much."

"I couldn't tell." *Stop, stop. Bitterness alert.*

"I know. Could you be patient a little longer while I try to explain something?"

Though Manon was asking a lot, what alternative did Eryn have? "Coffee?"

"No. I had some in the limo and it upset my stomach. Or it could be nerves." Manon smiled. "That's my guess."

"You're nervous?" *I wasn't imagining, then.* "I can't understand why." *Unless you're finally going to tell me to get lost.* Eryn gestured for Manon to sit on the couch and then joined her.

"A lot depends on how you react to what I say." Manon turned toward Eryn and propped her elbow on the backrest. Pushing her hair away, she rubbed the base of her neck.

Finally Eryn noticed that Manon wore her hair down, for once. *Reminds me of shiny chocolate sauce…delicious.*

"I went to Boston to talk to Faith, my oldest friend. Before you, Vivian, and Mike, she was my only real friend," Manon continued. "She's very straightforward, rather like you, and I trust her judgment. I asked her how on earth I could manage a relationship with you and still devote myself to the foundation."

Eryn jerked but bit her lip. Manon's words hurt already and made her feel like a liability.

"Faith asked me to describe you, which I did, easily enough. As I mentioned each of your wonderful traits, I discovered answers to questions I didn't even know I had." Manon reached for a small embroidered pillow and held it against her stomach. "My brother Jack and I were very different. He was artistic, softhearted, and loved animals."

Eryn wondered about the sudden switch of topic, but stayed true to her promise and didn't ask. Manon now gazed just above Eryn's shoulder, and she wondered if Manon saw her brother.

"Jack had gone to a friend's house to see his new puppy and was riding his bike home when a car hit him from behind. He was on the bicycle path, and the impact threw him fifty feet, headfirst into a tree." Manon's eyes darkened and she blinked repeatedly.

"They told me he didn't feel anything. The sad part is, neither did I. For years. Mother left us two years later, ironically after drinking her way through our wine cellar. I visited her occasionally, to keep up appearances." She frowned. "As you can see, I started early."

"Manon…" Eryn scooted closer, unable to watch Manon go through this experience without at least holding her hand. She wasn't surprised to find Manon's fingers cold and trembling.

"I've already told you about the boarding-school fiasco. And when I started being homeschooled, the only classes I took at the local high school were phys ed, chemistry, and physics. During phys ed, when the other girls talked about their latest crush on a boy, I felt nothing.

"Instead, there was a girl." Manon smiled as if she could see her. "Funny, I can't even remember her name, but she was shy and really pretty. I liked to watch her play basketball—the way her body moved, and how she beamed after she scored. I exchanged maybe ten words with her, but the fact that I found her cute and attractive…and had nobody to talk to about it scared me to death. So much had happened in my family: death, loss, and then the unspoken mourning that just lay sodden over our household for years…"

Eryn warmed Manon's hand between her own. She ached for the young Manon, the serious girl who'd not only lost her twin, but her mother and, in a way, her youth as well.

"In college I went on many innocent dates, which was an effective and fairly easy cover, since boys love to brag and stretch the truth. The boyfriend I did keep for a while, and finally tried sex with, was nice and caring. The sex wasn't bad, but nothing I wanted, and it certainly wasn't satisfying, though I did appreciate the closeness. My only adult relationship with a man, with Garrison Hollingsworth, ended not only because of my orientation but also because he became abusive when he drank."

"Oh, damn," Eryn said softly. "And since a drunk driver killed Jack—"

"Exactly." Manon made no move to sit any closer, but she clung to Eryn's hands, still hiding her other hand under her hair, massaging her neck. "I broke up with him and that's the last time I dated a man. My escorts served a purpose, as you know, and they were safe."

Eryn thought of Dustin. They had made a stunning couple, and she assumed that was partially why Manon had chosen him in the first place.

"Well," Manon smiled carefully, "I'm starting to figure myself out."

Eryn looked at her skeptically.

"I'm realizing why I'm so adamant about...being perfect. I grew up trying to be both my brother and myself because I saw it as my responsibility. When I noticed my interest in girls, I knew being different would cause new problems. By then my mother had already left, so I just suppressed my emotions." Manon sighed and hugged the pillow closer. "She never tried to have me live with her or even get shared custody. She just left everything in East Quay, including me."

Eryn wondered how it would have been to have lost her own mother like that, to not have a mother to come out to, no matter how badly Harriet had taken it.

"And I kept going. I put my education and, later, the foundation first. I wanted so much to please my grandfather and make him proud. But most of all I wanted to lessen his grief for Jack. Even after he died and my father had his stroke, I worked myself to a frazzle to stay on track. It became a way of life."

"And then I came along and challenged all that."

"Then you came along..." Manon's eyes softened. "You pushed and infuriated me, but you were delightful—so fresh and beautiful."

"Oh." *Beautiful? Me?* Nobody had ever called her beautiful.

*Where are you going with this, Manon?* Was Manon going to reject her once and for all? Or was she going to finally make her happy?

"I know I've acted like a coward." Manon smiled ruefully. "And I've probably been driving you crazy. I'm sorry." She let go of Eryn's hand and folded both of hers in her lap. "I'm probably going to make you crazier...but I just can't change overnight."

"Manon."

"No, let me get this out." Manon took a breath. "I'm gay. I know that now and I accept it. It's a relief to finally just admit it."

"But..." Eryn said cautiously.

"I can't just come jumping out of the closet as if my past doesn't count. I'm not even sure where to start."

Eryn smiled encouragingly. She knew it must be difficult for Manon to admit how uncertain she felt.

"I won't be much longer." Manon blushed faintly. "I just want to say this. If you're still interested in some sort of relationship with me...I'd be delighted."

"You would?" Eryn flinched. "Why? And under what circumstances?" She hated to ask, but needed to protect herself.

"Surely you must know I'm in love with you." Manon reached out to Eryn with both hands, her voice unsteady. "Am I too late?"

"In love?" Eryn repeated. "You're in love with me?"

"Yes."

"And you want to be with me? Like lovers?"

Manon nodded, her breath uneven as she slid closer and took Eryn by the shoulders.

"In secret?" Eryn continued.

"No. But not broadcasting it either. As I said, no coming-out party." Manon was slightly awkward as she tried to joke.

"I never asked for anything more than no secrets. I'd never ask you to put out a press release regarding your personal life, gay or straight." Eryn tugged at Manon and pulled her up on her lap. "I want to be with you, and if we have to be discreet, that's okay, as long as I don't have to sneak around."

"No sneaking." Manon hid her face in Eryn's hair. "Oh, God, just hold me, Eryn. I've been so cold for so long."

They sat in silence for a moment, as Eryn stroked steadily up and down Manon's back. "You haven't asked how I feel," Eryn murmured, placing a hand on Manon's stomach and moving it in small circles.

"Arrogant of me, isn't it?"

"I think you're a little scared what I might say."

"Also true."

Eryn moved her hand up, cupping a breast. "I love you. I love you with all of your past, and I'm so proud that you've come this far. You're very brave."

Manon tipped Eryn's head back. "Really?"

"Yes." With that, Eryn moved and slid Manon off her lap. She rose and extended a hand. "Come with me?"

"Where to?" A nervous smile played on Manon's lips.

"To my bed. We don't have to make love, if you're not ready. I just want to hold you."

"All right. I'd like that." Manon took Eryn's hand and they walked toward the bedroom.

Eryn's heart drummed a fast rhythm in her chest. To finally hold Manon without massive persuasion and maneuvering. Could there be more happiness in her world?

❖

Mike stood on the patio, wrapped in a wool blanket, and listened to the waves crash into shore as she inhaled the salty night air greedily. She had awakened with a start, not sure what she had dreamt but glad she was in Vivian's beach house. Mike wondered about her sudden need for air and space but refused to read too much into it. Instead she gave in to her feelings and stepped farther out on the patio.

Something cool and wet hit the back of her knee. "Perry!" She could easily tell the dogs apart, not so much from their looks as their behavior. Perry placed his nose on her very gently, but insistently, and Mason, the more direct type, stuck his head under her arm and pushed it up. "You startled me, boy," Mike said and scratched his ear. "Were you looking for me?"

Perry sat down next to her and scanned the beach as if he understood. Mike laughed and patted his head. "Good dog." Perry gave her a quick lick and then resumed his regal position: chin up, full attention on his surroundings, tail wagging slowly.

"Mike?" Vivian's drowsy voice reached her through the half-closed French doors leading into the bedroom.

"Right here, Vivi. On the patio."

"You all right?"

"I'm fine. Perry's with me. I just needed some air, but I'll come in now." Mike stepped inside and closed the doors. "It's so crisp and starry tonight."

"What woke you up?" Vivian leaned on her elbow and extended a hand.

"I think I dreamt something." Mike took Vivian's hand and slid into bed. "No clue, really. Something odd happened, though."

"What?"

"For the first time in ages, it felt okay to be out in the open and not have four massive basement walls surrounding me after a dream." Mike scooted down in bed and placed her head on Vivian's shoulder. Vivian wrapped her arms around her and remained silent. "I didn't understand very much about the media frenzy after my father killed that boy. I heard the other children in the foster home and in school whispering. The grownups around me, the foster parents and even some of the teachers, always talked about it. Or at least that's how it felt to me."

"Why was it such a big deal? Granted, it was horrible, but people drive under the influence every day and a lot of people get injured. Why was this so…"

Vivian quieted for a moment, and Mike knew that she had figured it out.

"Oh, my God. Your father hit and killed young Jack Belmont, didn't he? That was headline news even in New York. No wonder there was a media frenzy."

"And people have a long memory. They commented on it all through my teens, asking if I was his daughter. I was reduced to being *only* that—the daughter of Richard Collins, the drunken child killer. That's why I took my mother's maiden name. Josie thought it was a good idea too, because she knew how cruel people can be. As the saying goes, the Belmonts were the closest thing East Quay has to royalty, and my father killed the crown prince."

"Surely you never felt responsible?"

"I did when I was little. If you only knew how many bottles of beer and booze I stole from my father and poured down the toilet, even when he got furious. Josie explained that this response is common among children of alcoholic parents. We feel a responsibility and a deep shame that's hard to shake."

"Darling." Vivian kissed Mike's forehead. "And when Jack

Belmont was killed, in your way of thinking as an eight-year-old, you shared the responsibility?"

"Yes. Not anymore, though. I worked it out with Josie."

"Thank God."

Another kiss made it possible for Mike to relax.

"Does Manon know?"

Mike shook her head. "No. Well, I don't know. I'm going to have to tell her before someone else figures it out."

"She won't hold it against you. I know Manon. She's the epitome of fairness."

Mike pressed closer into Vivian's embrace. Outside, the winds had cleansed her of the nightmare, and in here, Vivian soothed her. "I hope so," she whispered against the velvet skin under her lips. She kissed it lingeringly, over and over. "Vivian…my love…"

"*Cara.*"

Their need for each other was insatiable, and soon the night filled with whispers and moans that drowned out the sound of the sea.

❖

Manon stood motionless as Eryn lit four tea candles on her bedroom dresser. She looked nervously at the cast-iron bed that took up most of the room and was covered with pillows of all sizes on its maroon velvet bedspread.

"May I undress you?" Eryn asked, and slowly walked up to Manon. "If you'd rather not, just say so. It's fine."

"No, no. I want you to."

"You sure? Just tell me if it doesn't feel right." Eryn fingered the button of Manon's pants. Within seconds, she had unzipped them and they pooled around Manon's feet. She stepped out of them and watched Eryn hang them on the back of a small wooden chair.

"Up," Eryn said as she turned to Manon again.

Manon raised her arms and Eryn pulled the turtleneck off, completely disheveling Manon's hair.

"God, you're stunning…" Eryn sighed, and Manon could almost feel her eyes rake over her half-naked body. "Want to stop here?"

"Yes. I think so. For now."

"Okay. Slip into bed. I'll be there in a sec."

Manon shivered between the cool cotton sheets, but other parts of her were hotter than she thought possible. She hungrily watched Eryn remove her clothes, and since she wasn't wearing a bra, Eryn came to bed in only her skimpy blue lace panties.

"There. Warmer, huh?" Eryn grinned. Her eyes sparkled with dancing green flames. "Come here." Eryn slid her arms around Manon and drew her close. "Yes. That's it. Just relax. You're fine."

Manon couldn't relax. This fairy creature sent tremors through her body, and she moved restlessly. Wherever her skin met Eryn's, small bonfires of desire erupted. "Eryn, this might not work out as planned," Manon said through gritted teeth.

Eryn flinched. "Why?"

"You're far too sexy and beautiful. I can't lie still next to you."

"Then do what you need to do, Manon. I'm all yours."

Hesitatingly, Manon slid a hand along Eryn's stomach. Eryn inhaled deeply and held her breath as Manon closed her hand over her breast. The rigid nipple prodding her palm made Manon hot, and her center hardened, a new surge of wetness coating the inside of her thighs. The deep feelings of lust and arousal were all about Eryn. Manon's legs parted of their own volition as she examined Eryn's body with increasing delight.

"Am I doing this right?" Manon whispered. "Feel good?"

"More than good." Eryn sighed. "Kiss me."

Manon moved up and covered Eryn's mouth with hers, and it wasn't difficult at all. Eryn's taste was familiar, and Manon deepened the kiss without hesitation, eager to prolong it. Since Manon considered kissing the most intimate form of touch, she felt they were joining their souls as well as their bodies, Eryn's kisses met every one of Manon's secret dreams, and Manon knew that she would always crave this expression of love.

As Eryn reached around Manon and unhooked her bra, Manon moaned into the kiss and pressed against Eryn, arousal permeating every cell when their breasts touched. Their hard nipples pressed into pliant skin and rubbed against their counterparts. Manon let her tongue examine Eryn's mouth over and over, until she was out of breath and had to pull back. When she looked down at their breasts naked together, where their bodies met, the sight stole what little breath she had left.

Eryn took one of Manon's breasts in her hand and slid down just enough to suck the nipple into her mouth.

Unprepared for the stab of pleasure, Manon tossed her head

back and whimpered. "Eryn...oh, my God..." She arched into the excruciating caress, a red haze of pent-up lust and love covering her field of vision. She rubbed her legs together and recognized the heat from that night not so long ago when she had come against her will while thinking of Eryn. *And now I'm here...in her bed. Eryn, what are you doing to me?*

It was obvious what Eryn had in mind when she slid her hands inside Manon's panties. She pushed them down, and Manon helped by kicking them off when Eryn couldn't reach any farther.

"Manon, you're so damn beautiful, so hot and sexy," Eryn murmured against her neck. "I want all of you. I've dreamt of making love with you, of this..." She slid her hand down and cupped Manon's hip. "Of touching you like this." Slowly Eryn continued to the wet delta between Manon's thighs.

Manon parted her legs, and her fear equaled her desire as she waited for the intimate caresses she knew were coming. To her surprise, Eryn merely covered her sex in a protective gesture. Manon moved her hips restlessly and moaned. "Eryn...I need you to touch me." The ache inside Manon and the fundamental need to become one with Eryn all brought a flood of moisture between her swollen folds.

"I can feel how you want me." Eryn carefully slid her fingers in to find Manon's engorged clitoris. "Oh, sweetheart, you're so wet, so ready. I think you've been ready for me for quite some time."

"Ever since I left for Boston," Manon confessed. She couldn't keep her eyes open as Eryn's fingers traced small circles in the wetness. "I tried to satisfy myself, but it was...impossible. You weren't there—"

"But I'm here now. Just let it happen. Just let go. I'm here," Eryn cooed. "That's right."

Manon rode the gentle fingers that were suddenly too gentle when they touched her. "Eryn, please. More."

"More? Oh, sweetie...my pleasure." Eryn's voice was thick with passion, and she scooted down while pushing Manon onto her back.

Dizzy, Manon spread her legs to accommodate Eryn, who now placed lingering open-mouth kisses down Manon's stomach. She didn't stop when she reached the dark brown curls, but parted Manon's wet sex and exposed the delicate folds.

"Eryn!"

When Manon felt Eryn's mouth close over her clitoris, she cried out and arched her back, shivering. Her orgasm washed over her with every caress of the agile tongue that licked in an increasingly faster pattern. She could hardly breathe as the convulsions shook her body. *Eryn, Eryn...* She couldn't form one coherent thought. All that mattered was the woman between her thighs, wonderful, extraordinary.

When the overwhelming contractions ceased, Eryn climbed up Manon's body, straddling her left leg. "You're amazing, absolutely amazing," Eryn murmured. "You turn me on so much. I need to come too. Kiss me…"

Manon reached blindly for Eryn and kissed her. "Tell me—"

"Reach your hand down. Touch me. Any way you want, just touch me, quick."

Manon pushed her right hand down between them and cupped Eryn's sex, mimicking Eryn's caresses. As Eryn wrapped her left hand around Manon's shoulders, Manon rolled them onto their sides. Then Eryn bent her knee and whispered, "Go inside. Please."

Manon circled Eryn's wet opening and found it definitely lubricated enough for her to enter. When she pushed first one, then two, fingers inside she immediately felt slick walls pull her farther in. Eryn moaned and rolled her hips, and Manon tried to establish a steady rhythm. Her thumb accidentally brushed Eryn's clitoris, and after a few thrusts, Eryn was reduced to a shivering bundle clutching at Manon's shoulders.

"Now, oh, now…there…" Eryn cried.

Manon felt Eryn's muscles contract, over and over, around her fingers. She pushed even deeper inside, and another gush of wetness dampened her hand. Eryn's body shook for precious seconds, and then she lurched forward into Manon's embrace. Wracked with sobs, she cried against Manon's shoulder.

Afraid and taken aback, Manon gradually realized that Eryn had reacted so strongly because she had finally released her stress and fear.

"I love you, Eryn," Manon whispered, and gently pulled her hand free. She cradled Eryn and rocked her as her tears fell. Eryn's long hair covered them both, and its signature scent of citrus and vanilla made everything familiar and safe.

"I love you too," Eryn sobbed, and reached for a tissue. She curled up back into Manon's arms and blew her nose. "Wow…didn't see *that* one coming."

"Good?" Manon held her breath, even though she was fairly sure Eryn's orgasm had been overwhelming.

"You're kidding, right?" A red eyebrow rose and Eryn smiled broadly through her tears. "I went into orbit, I think. And you were wonderful. Wonderful to touch and the way you touched me…" Eryn brushed her lips over Manon's. "Magic."

Manon's head whirled with emotions and the last week's turn of events. "Magic" wasn't the word she'd have chosen. She pulled the covers over their glistening bodies, content to stay in their warm cocoon. "I'm not a fatalist," she said slowly. "But this…you…could change my mind about that."

"Really, Belmont? You? Change your opinion about something?" Eryn winked mischievously. "Utterly uncharacteristic, my dear."

"Funny." Manon smiled. "Jokes aside, the last few weeks have been, like you said, magical. But more than that. Like providence… fate, I guess."

"Whatever word you decide on, sweetheart." Eryn snuggled closer.

"Words are your business." Manon held her tenderly. I'll leave it to you."

"Fine. Works for me," Eryn said in a sleepy voice.

"Relax. I'm not going anywhere."

Within minutes, Eryn showed the greatest trust a person can demonstrate, by falling asleep in Manon's arms.

# CHAPTER TWENTY-FIVE

Vivian's voice rose and fell at the Belmont Foundation Charity Concert, proving that East Quay's most celebrated daughter was one of the world's best mezzo-sopranos.

When she appeared center stage, her hair up in an intricate twist that allowed it to billow out in rich curls down her back, the applause resonated for several minutes before the conductor raised his baton for silence. The orchestra sat in a muted light at the feet of the beautiful woman dressed in a cobalt velvet dress that trailed several feet behind her.

Mike sat next to Manon and Eryn and absorbed every moment of Vivian's personal triumph. She doubted that anyone in the audience realized that Vivian couldn't see them. She stood there, radiating strength and vocal beauty, at least three feet away from the microphone and sang in a way that entranced Mike.

After the third and last aria, new applause erupted, and this time it lasted more than five minutes. Mike could see Vivian's cheeks color and knew what a personal victory this was for Vivian, who also was trying to lessen her guilt for shunning everything to do with East Quay.

Mike applauded until her arms ached and tears streamed down her cheeks, as did Eryn and Manon. Eryn's relatives sat on the same row, and obviously Mr. and Mrs. Goddard were also taken by the performance.

"*Da capo!*" a male voice called out from behind them. "*Da capo, bellissima!*"

To Mike's surprise, Vivian raised her hands, palms out, until the applause had died out.

"Thank you," Vivian said, her voice filling the concert hall. "You're very kind. I want to dedicate this song, a lullaby, to a young woman who holds my heart." She turned toward the conductor. "'Summertime,' Maestro, please."

As the conductor nodded and tapped his stick against his podium, the audience held its breath as one, exhaling only when Vivian began to sing the famous song from *Porgy and Bess*.

Mike pulled out a tissue. She had guessed she'd become emotional, but to hear Vivian sing this song, this famous lullaby, to *her*, was almost too much. As if Vivian by some miracle knew exactly where Mike sat in the audience, she easily homed in on her, and Mike couldn't look away for a second.

Vivian Harding, world famous and loved by millions, loved Mike Stone, unheard of and unknown, living in little East Quay. For a moment, Mike felt nervous, but Vivian's tender version of the song melted her fears.

When the song was over, Mike was certain the applause would tear the roof off the old concert hall. She watched Vivian curtsey deeply several times, with perfect balance, before she turned to the right side of the stage and reached out. A handsome young man in a white tuxedo offered Vivian his arm, which she took and allowed him to escort her off stage.

The applause still boomed, and Vivian came out to thank the audience three more times, each time the young man accompanying her. Mike realized this fact alone, together with the remarkable performance, would create a buzz throughout the opera world.

Her palms stung from clapping, but this sign that Vivian was unashamed to let her disability show made Mike applaud even harder.

❖

The sold-out concert had raised $700,000 for the new hospital wing, and now ticket sales to the cocktail party at the hotel added another $75,000.

Manon felt happy and content, primarily because of Eryn. A few curls framed Eryn's face, and the rest of her abundant hair was secured with two large ebony pins. Manon remembered how Eryn's locks had fanned out across the pillows as they had reached for each other numerous times during their first heated night together. *She's sheer beauty and honesty. No secrets or hidden agendas.* Manon surreptitiously admired Eryn's long sleeveless dress, hinting at her curves as the forest green fabric whispered around her.

Manon squeezed Eryn's hand furtively as Eryn's parents approached them. Manon had briefly met Harriet and David Goddard in the concert hall, and now they approached her and Eryn with careful smiles.

"Ms. Belmont," Harriet said. "I hear we have you to thank for such a wonderful evening."

"Not entirely true," Manon said. "The late Mrs. Dodd Endicott contributed to it as well. I'm delighted you could attend. And please, call me Manon. Did you get to talk to Vivian?"

"We did," David said. "And she was very gracious. She signed a CD for us to auction at the church and one she insisted we keep."

Manon smiled. "I'm glad the evening was a success."

"And most of all we're glad to meet you," said Harriet. "I've never seen Eryn this happy."

Manon winced but knew this was just one of a series of tests she'd face while feeling her way with her lover. "That's mutual," Manon managed, and received a surprised and happy smile from Eryn.

When Harriet and David said good night, Eryn turned to Manon and scrutinized her through narrow eyes. "Well, now, Belmont," she said slowly. "If I didn't know any better, I'd say you're sweet on me or something."

Manon tossed her head back and laughed. "Or something. Oh, here come Mike and Vivian now. Guess Vivian could finally tear herself away from the fans. Mike was a good bodyguard, though."

"Oh, damn," Eryn sighed. "Mike looks fabulous in those black leather slacks."

"Hey, there." Manon smiled. "Remember who you're talking to."

"Yeah, I know. I intend to stick to brunettes in deep red evening dresses that leave *very* little to the imagination."

When Mike and Vivian walked up to them, Manon saw traces of fatigue around Vivian's eyes, but other than that, she was obviously thriving on her performance and the audience reaction. *Who can blame her? They worship the stage she walks on.*

Mike, on the other hand, looked almost ill.

"You all right, Mike?" Eryn asked.

"Yes. I'm fine, thanks. Are you ready to leave? Vivian's a little tired."

Vivian waved her hand. "If you want to stay longer, perhaps Benjamin can make two trips?"

"No, I'm ready," Manon said, and turned to Eryn. "How about you?"

"Whenever you want to, sweetheart," Eryn said and quickly covered her mouth with her hand.

Manon couldn't help but smile at Eryn's dismay.

"Don't freak out, Eryn. You're among friends." Manon gestured toward the door. "Looks like we're some of the last to leave, actually."

Manon was relieved to get into the limousine, and she leaned back and closed her eyes briefly as Benjamin pulled out into the late-Saturday-evening traffic. When she relaxed, she realized she was exhausted.

"Manon?" Mike's voice broke her out of her reverie.

"Hey, there, what's wrong? Do you feel bad?" Manon reached out and took Mike's hand. Vivian held on to the other, and now it was obvious that Mike was close to tears.

"I have something to tell you. Especially since I've been in the limelight several times now, kind of by accident, because I'm with Vivian."

Manon, at a loss, kept Mike's cold hand in hers.

"There's no easy way to say this, so I'll just tell you up front." Mike looked at Vivian and then redirected her attention to Manon. "Stone is my mother's maiden name. My name was Michaela Collins."

"Yes? I knew that." Manon slid over to the opposite seat and sat next to Mike. "What's this about?"

"Surely you must understand…make the connection?" Mike whispered. "I'm Richard Collins's daughter." It was clear that she was bracing herself since she didn't even blink once when she stared at Manon.

"I know that too." Manon's heart constricted painfully, but her tenderness for Mike grew.

"You do?" Mike croaked. "How…when and how long…" She stopped stuttering and stared at Manon.

"Oh, Mike," Eryn murmured from her corner. "You never said anything."

"I knew when you applied for a grant the first time, as soon as I read your file. Belmont Foundation conducts thorough research into the people we decide to help. I always cosign for grants of that size handed out to a single person."

"And you still okayed the grants. Twice." Mike squeezed Manon's hand hard. "You—"

"I never, ever blamed you for what you father did," Manon said, tears running down her cheeks. "Not for a second. You lost your father and ended up in an endless circle of foster homes. I lost my brother, and all because of senseless drinking and poor judgment. We both paid the price for your father's irresponsibility."

Mike flung her arms around Manon's neck. "I'm so sorry," she said. "I used to hide as many of his bottles as I could, but—"

"You were a child. So was Jack. Both of you victims. You weren't responsible."

"I know that, intellectually, but it might take me a while yet to really feel it." Mike clung to Manon. "I was so afraid you wouldn't understand. I should've known better. Vivian told me to trust you. I'm sorry."

Manon pressed her eyes together in a futile attempt to stop the tears that soaked Mike's black satin shirt. She glanced over at Eryn and saw her wiping her eyes as well.

"We're a sight," Eryn said, between laughter and tears. "Why don't we redirect Benjamin to the café and help Mike make us some killer lattes? We're all too emotional to go home."

"A brilliant idea, Eryn," Vivian said.

Mike slowly let go of Manon and reached for Vivian's hand. "I'd love to make four lattes. We close in a few minutes and will have the place to ourselves."

"Excellent. I'll tell Ben." Manon sighed and anticipated the energy kick Mike's coffee always provided. Moving back to sit next to Eryn, she laced her fingers with her lover's. "It's never too late for coffee, if you ask me."

"I wonder if I should be concerned," Eryn teased. "Since I know what caffeine does to you."

"I have no idea what you're talking about, Goddard." Manon smiled. "Coffee is energizing, and I just never know when I'll need my energy."

Surprised, Eryn hugged Manon. "My mother was right. I've never been this happy."

Manon gazed into the depths of the sparkling eyes of the woman she loved. *Mon amour.* "Neither have I."

Silence settled among the four women as Benjamin turned the car into the road leading to the marina. Manon studied the serene faces around her. She was so proud of Vivian, of how she'd mastered her fears and persevered. Mike was perhaps the one among them who'd come the farthest from where life had tossed her as a child.

And Eryn. Manon sighed and merely looked at her lover. *I adore everything about you. You're the only one for me.*

The limousine stopped and Benjamin opened the door. "We've arrived at the Sea Stone Café, ladies. Someone really buffed up this place."

"Why, thank you, Benjamin." Mike shot him an enigmatic grin. "What about a latte, or do you take it black?"

"Coffee? Yes, ma'am. Black and strong and sweet enough to float the spoon."

They all laughed and entered the café as the last regular patrons left. Manon sat on a stool by the bar while Eryn stood with an arm around her shoulder.

"Like a second home, isn't it?" said Eryn.

"Since you're here," Manon agreed, "I couldn't agree more."

# EPILOGUE

*One and a half years later*

L adies and gentlemen," the announcer said, his voice indicating that the gathered crowd of East Quayers was in for a treat, "for the first time live in front of an audience, to commemorate the opening of this fantastic new state-of-the-art East Quay Memorial Hospital wing…" The man paused effectively, and there wasn't a sound in the large hallway to the Marjorie Dodd Memorial Wing, where several hundred locals had gathered.

"A new group is going to play something I can guarantee you've never heard before. These performers need no introduction, so without further ado, here they are, the Chicory Ariose!"

Applause thundered, only to briefly falter when the audience realized who sat on the stool by the microphone.

Eryn grinned when she heard the whispers skitter among the crowd. "It's Vivian Harding!"

Eryn plugged in her Les Paul and waited for Mike to settle in behind the drums and Manon to take her place at the digital piano. After another silence, Eryn knew just how to begin. She let her fingers caress the neck of her guitar, and then a softly climbing note filled the entire hallway, alone for a few shimmering seconds before another one followed, this time from the piano.

Eryn and Manon bounced the notes back and forth, followed each other in the dance, until Mike let the hi-hat join in. She caressed the melodies that Manon and Eryn created, and the music rose until it came to a full stop. The silence, which Eryn thought was beautiful in itself, reached a point where the listeners seemed to hold their breath, and then all three instruments and Vivian's voice pushed toward the same goal. The notes rose and fell in harmonies, sometimes struggling, and at other times carrying each other.

Vivian's voice had never been as full or charismatic. Without the restraint of having to form words, she created melodies that no one had ever heard or might never hear again, since they always improvised. They played music in the moment, which Malcolm thought was a great title for their first CD. It was going to be recorded in two months, when they played in Boston.

Twenty minutes later, Eryn let her guitar take the lead again, feeling that Vivian had given all she could this time. This was a special concert, emotional for all of them, since the hospital wing was ready just as Eryn's biography of the Dodd women's accomplishments through nine generations hit the stores.

Eryn slowed the tempo, drew Mike with her into a suggestive, almost buzzing melody that reminded her of an autumn forest in New England, when the maple trees burned against the blue sky. Soft high tones fell from Manon's fingertips, like rain, as the music came to a fading halt when Mike let the cymbal crash ring out.

Eryn thought the applause was going to lift the ceiling of the already tall white and gold hall. Glass stretched all the way up the four floors so that many of the patients' rooms had indoor balconies overlooking the entrance hall, as well as a breathtaking view of East Quay.

"Thank you, Chicory Ariose," the announcer bellowed. "If you're interested in buying the upcoming CD, you can register for a copy by the reception desk. All profits will go to the Belmont Foundation. On Monday these doors will open to staff and patients…"

The enthusiastic man continued, but Eryn tuned out his voice and walked off the stage with her friends. Manon waited for her by the small temporary stairs. "Think they like us?" She smiled and quickly brushed Eryn's cheek.

"At first they were too stunned to like us, but after a while they were hooked."

"You surprised me with the soft intro. That's new."

"It struck me that this is a hospital where hardworking people save other people's lives, help them live better or die in peace. It just felt right."

"I agree. It was so moving that I forgot to listen for a good place to join in. I just did."

A blonde appeared next to Eryn. "Ms. Goddard? I'm Lisa Reardon, a reporter for KDL-TV. Would you and your group members do an interview for us? We taped some of the performance today and would like to do an exclusive, including showing some of our footage."

Eryn exchanged a glance with Manon, who signaled, "Why not?"

"Sure, that'll be good PR for the foundation," Eryn said. "What did you have in mind? And when? We're not available tonight."

"We have a morning news show. Is seven o'clock tomorrow morning okay?"

Eryn grimaced. "That early, huh? Well, I guess we can manage." They exchanged business cards, and the smiling blonde returned to her cameraman.

"TV already. Who knew? Let's go tell Mike and Vivian." Eryn motioned toward them, sipping from champagne flutes. "They've found the buffet, I see."

"We're off to our fifteen minutes of fame tomorrow." Manon laughed as she reached for some champagne. "Well, except for you, Vivian. Your fame is like fifteen times two—years! And then some."

"What's happening tomorrow?"

As Eryn filled the others in, Mike said, "Great. Tomorrow's Sunday. I don't have to be back till brunch."

"Okay," said Manon. "I think we've fulfilled our duties here today. Why don't we locate Benjamin and go home."

"Speaking of that, I miss the limousine," Eryn groused. "It's not the same with a minivan."

"I know, but it draws less attention. And it's just as luxurious, even more so." Manon patted Eryn's arm. "You'll get used to it."

"If you say so." Eryn pouted and then dropped the act. "Actually, I don't care if we ride a bicycle, as long as we're together."

"Hey," Mike interrupted, "aren't we always together? When we're not working, we're living in the same house." She raised an eyebrow at Manon and Eryn. "Any more together we'd be Siamese quadruplets!"

"You make it sound like we live in a two-bedroom apartment," Vivian said as they approached the minivan where Benjamin faithfully waited. Vivian felt her way with a white cane and entered first. "Hi, boys. Did you have nice walk while Mommy sang?"

Perry and Mason wagged their tails and sniffed Vivian's hand through the bars that kept them separated from the backseats.

"Of course I know we have more space than we can use, but unless we start looking for more tenants to fill out the Dodd Mansion, I think we'll just have to live with it. After all, Mrs. Dodd Endicott lived there alone most of her life." Mike sat down next to Vivian and gave her a quick kiss. "You all right? The light in there was pretty bright."

"I'm fine, *cara*. I haven't had any pain in six months, and today was no exception."

"Good. Just checking." Mike smiled faintly.

Eryn sat next to Manon and, mindful of the people crowding outside the car trying to catch a glimpse of Vivian, she didn't lean in for a kiss. Instead she took Manon's hand, surprised when Manon rubbed her thumb along Eryn's palm. "Manon!"

"Just so you know," Manon replied blithely. "I've missed you."

"I know, and I've missed you terribly. I'm so glad I made it back for today. It was touch and go for a while since the fog in Boston nearly made the plane head for Newark. I'm not going away again for months." Eryn knew her book-signing tour throughout New England had kept her away far too much. She was relieved she would be able to work from home again. Her publisher wanted her to write a fictional novel about a settler's family and perhaps turn it into a series of five. "I can't wait to have you to myself."

"I love you," Manon whispered, and as usual her throaty voice sent shivers through Eryn's system.

"I love you too." Eryn leaned her head against the backrest and admitted to herself how tired she was. "Mom and Dad were there. I saw them just before the show began, and they said they'd stop by later in the week. I have ten more books signed for them to auction off at the church bazaar."

"They're very proud of you."

"Yes." It was a source of constant happiness and occasional disbelief, but Eryn was finally ready to accept that her parents were doing their best to understand her. She couldn't ask for more.

"Hey, where's the bag with the thermoses?" Vivian called out from the back. "Can you see it in the front?"

"Is it red?" Eryn asked, and looked between the seats.

"Yup, that's the one." Mike reached for it. "I made some regular black coffee with our new house blend before we left. It should still be hot." She opened the first thermos and sniffed. "Mmm, it is." Quickly, Mike produced five stainless steel mugs and poured some coffee. "Here, hand some to Benny, please."

As usual, "Benny" frowned at his nickname in the rearview mirror, but as always, his eyes softened when he looked at the four women. "Thanks, Mike," he responded, and carefully reached for the mug.

"You're welcome." She looked around at her friends and took Vivian by the hand. "I propose a toast."

"A toast." Vivian beamed. "Wonderful. Go on, *cara*."

"To Manon, whose work saves lives and helps people help themselves. To Eryn, who writes women's stories and gives them visibility. And to Vivian, who touches us with her voice."

There was a brief silence.

"To Mike," Manon said, "who is proof to so many young people that it's possible to overcome adversities beyond belief and…I have a couple of surprises for you, Michaela."

The use of Mike's real name made them all listen. Eryn looked from Manon to Mike. She could tell from her lover's face that this was going to be good.

"You'll hear it officially tomorrow, but our new chairman of the East Quay Chamber of Commerce gave me permission to let you know that you're this year's winner of the Business Person of the Year. Congratulations, Mike."

Mike paled, and then two burning spots of red appeared on her cheeks. "Me? They chose me?"

"Yes. Unanimously."

"I…I never…" Mike stopped talking and stared down into her mug.

"You never thought it, but we all hoped and guessed," Vivian said, and scooted closer. "What's the next surprise, Manon?"

"An even better one." Manon smiled broadly. "I hired a private investigator a few months ago, but I didn't want to say anything to get your hopes up prematurely."

"A PI?" Mike moved her hands to Vivian's upper arm and pressed closer to her partner. "And?"

"And he sent me his report yesterday. Here. Read out loud."

Mike accepted a thin folder and opened it with unsteady hands. "Josephine Quinn, counselor. New address: 2105 Gardener Street, East Quay…East Quay…" she whispered. Mike's eyes flew down the page.

"She moved here only a month ago! Oh, Vivi, she might've beaten the cancer, don't you think? I mean, it's been more than two years—"

"Now you can go see her and make sure." Vivian laughed. "That's wonderful news. Manon...you made our day in so many ways." She raised her coffee mug again. "So here's to all of us!" As Ben turned the car off Main Street and headed toward home, Vivian kissed Mike's cheek before she sipped her coffee. A content smile spread over her face. "Oh, *cara*, this is an excellent blend."

# About the Author

Gun Brooke is a native of Sweden. A former NICU nurse, she has always enjoyed writing, and her first love was poetry in her native language. In 2001, she received an international award for her poem, "The Taste of Your Name." She is a 2006 Golden Crown Literary Society Award finalist for *Course of Action* in the Romance and Debut Author categories and for *Protector of the Realm* in the Sci-Fi/Fantasy category.

She first explored Internet writing when *Star Trek: Voyager* and fan fiction captured her imagination. Since most fan fiction was written in English, this experience led to her interest in creating original novels for the English reading population. Her first published novel was *Course of Action* (Bold Strokes Books, 2005), a high-stakes romance among the jet-set crowd of actresses, producers, and world-famous entrepreneurs. Her second novel, *Protector of the Realm—Supreme Constellations: Book One* (Bold Strokes Books, 2005), is the first in a series featuring an intergalactic adventure filled with suspense and romance. Her upcoming works include the next in the Supreme Constellations series and a new romance novel.

Gun also has selections in the anthologies *Erotic Interludes 2* and *3*: *Stolen Moments* and *Lessons in Love* (Bold Strokes Books 2005/2006) and *First-Timers: True Stories of Lesbian Sex* (Alyson 2006).

Gun's Web site, www.gbrooke-fiction.com, is filled with mystery, adventure, and romance stories as well as a popular message board and chat room where Gun hosts her "guests" from around the world. Besides writing, Gun enjoys graphics and Web design, as well as spending time with her family and friends in the Land of the Midnight Sun.

You may e-mail her at fiction@gbrooke-fiction.com.

# Books Available From Bold Strokes Books

**Whitewater Rendezvous** by Kim Baldwin. Two women on a wilderness kayak adventure—Chaz Herrick, a laid-back outdoorswoman, and Megan Maxwell, a workaholic news executive—discover that true love may be nothing at all like they imagined. (1-933110-38-4)

**Erotic Interludes 3: Lessons in Love** ed. by Radclyffe and Stacia Seaman. Sign on for a class in love...the best lesbian erotica writers take us to "school." (1-933110-39-2)

**Punk Like Me** by JD Glass. Twenty-one-year-old Nina writes lyrics and plays guitar in the rock band Adam's Rib, and she doesn't always play by the rules. And oh yeah—she has a way with the girls. (1-933110-40-6)

**Coffee Sonata** by Gun Brooke. Four women whose lives unexpectedly intersect in a small town by the sea share one thing in common—they all have secrets. (1-933110-41-4)

**The Clinic: Tristaine Book One** by Cate Culpepper. Brenna, a prison medic, finds herself deeply conflicted by her growing feelings for her patient Jesstin, a wild and rebellious warrior reputed to be descended from ancient Amazons. (1-933110-42-2)

**Forever Found** by JLee Meyer. Can time, tragedy, and shattered trust destroy a love that seemed destined? When chance reunites two childhood friends separated by tragedy, the past resurfaces to determine the shape of their future. (1-933110-37-6)

**Sword of the Guardian** by Merry Shannon. Princess Shasta's bold new bodyguard has a secret that could change both of their lives. *He* is actually a *she*. A passionate romance filled with courtly intrigue, chivalry, and devotion. (1-933110-36-8)

**Wild Abandon** by Ronica Black. From their first tumultuous meeting, Dr. Chandler Brogan and Officer Sarah Monroe are drawn together by their common obsessions—sex, speed, and danger. (1-933110-35-X)

**Turn Back Time** by Radclyffe. Pearce Rifkin and Wynter Thompson have nothing in common but a shared passion for surgery. They clash at every opportunity, especially when matters of the heart are suddenly at stake. (1-933110-34-1)

**Chance** by Grace Lennox. At twenty-six, Chance Delaney decides her life isn't working so she swaps it for a different one. What follows is the sexy, funny, touching story of two women who, in finding themselves, also find one another. (1-933110-31-7)

**The Exile and the Sorcerer** by Jane Fletcher. First in the Lyremouth Chronicles. Tevi, wounded and adrift, arrives in the courtyard of a shy young sorcerer. Together they face monsters, magic, and the challenge of loving despite their differences. (1-933110-32-5)

**A Matter of Trust** by Radclyffe. JT Sloan is a cybersleuth who doesn't like attachments. Michael Lassiter is leaving her husband, and she needs Sloan's expertise to safeguard her company. It should just be business—but it turns into much more. (1-933110-33-3)

**Sweet Creek** by Lee Lynch. A celebration of the enduring nature of love, friendship, and community in the quirky, heart-warming lesbian community of Waterfall Falls. (1-933110-29-5)

**The Devil Inside** by Ali Vali. Derby Cain Casey, head of a New Orleans crime organization, runs the family business with guts and grit, and no one crosses her. No one, that is, until Emma Verde claims her heart and turns her world upside down. (1-933110-30-9)

**Grave Silence** by Rose Beecham. Detective Jude Devine's investigation of a series of ritual murders is complicated by her torrid affair with the golden girl of Southwestern forensic pathology, Dr. Mercy Westmoreland. (1-933110-25-2)

**Honor Reclaimed** by Radclyffe. In the aftermath of 9/11, Secret Service Agent Cameron Roberts and Blair Powell close ranks with a trusted few to find the would-be assassins who nearly claimed Blair's life. (1-933110-18-X)

**Honor Bound** by Radclyffe. Secret Service Agent Cameron Roberts and Blair Powell face political intrigue, a clandestine threat to Blair's safety, and the seemingly irreconcilable personal differences that force them ever farther apart. (1-933110-20-1)

**Protector of the Realm: Supreme Constellations Book One** by Gun Brooke. A space adventure filled with suspense and a daring intergalactic romance featuring Commodore Rae Jacelon and the stunning, but decidedly lethal, Kellen O'Dal. (1-933110-26-0)

**Innocent Hearts** by Radclyffe. In a wild and unforgiving land, two women learn about love, passion, and the wonders of the heart. (1-933110-21-X)

**The Temple at Landfall** by Jane Fletcher. An imprinter, one of Celaeno's most revered servants of the Goddess, is also a prisoner to the faith—until a Ranger frees her by claiming her heart. The Celaeno series. (1-933110-27-9)

**Force of Nature** by Kim Baldwin. From tornados to forest fires, the forces of nature conspire to bring Gable McCoy and Erin Richards close to danger, and closer to each other. (1-933110-23-6)

**In Too Deep** by Ronica Black. Undercover homicide cop Erin McKenzie tracks a femme fatale who just might be a real killer…with love and danger hot on her heels. (1-933110-17-1)

**Stolen Moments: Erotic Interludes 2** by Stacia Seaman and Radclyffe, eds. Love on the run, in the office, in the shadows…Fast, furious, and almost too hot to handle. (1-933110-16-3)

**Course of Action** by Gun Brooke. Actress Carolyn Black desperately wants the starring role in an upcoming film produced by Annelie Peterson. Just how far will she go for the dream part of a lifetime? (1-933110-22-8)

**Rangers at Roadsend** by Jane Fletcher. Sergeant Chip Coppelli has learned to spot trouble coming, and that is exactly what she sees in her new recruit, Katryn Nagata. The Celaeno series. (1-933110-28-7)

**Justice Served** by Radclyffe. Lieutenant Rebecca Frye and her lover, Dr. Catherine Rawlings, embark on a deadly game of hide-and-seek with an underworld kingpin who traffics in human souls. (1-933110-15-5)

**Distant Shores, Silent Thunder** by Radclyffe. Dr. Tory King—along with the women who love her—is forced to examine the boundaries of love, friendship, and the ties that transcend time. (1-933110-08-2)

**Hunter's Pursuit** by Kim Baldwin. A raging blizzard, a mountain hideaway, and a killer-for-hire set a scene for disaster—or desire—when Katarzyna Demetrious rescues a beautiful stranger. (1-933110-09-0)

**The Walls of Westernfort** by Jane Fletcher. All Temple Guard Natasha Ionadis wants is to serve the Goddess—until she falls in love with one of the rebels she is sworn to destroy. The Celaeno series. (1-933110-24-4)

**Change Of Pace:** *Erotic Interludes* by Radclyffe. Twenty-five hot-wired encounters guaranteed to spark more than just your imagination. Erotica as you've always dreamed of it. (1-933110-07-4)

**Honor Guards** by Radclyffe. In a wild flight for their lives, the president's daughter and those who are sworn to protect her wage a desperate struggle for survival. (1-933110-01-5)

**Fated Love** by Radclyffe. Amidst the chaos and drama of a busy emergency room, two women must contend not only with the fragile nature of life, but also with the irresistible forces of fate. (1-933110-05-8)

**Justice in the Shadows** by Radclyffe. In a shadow world of secrets and lies, Detective Sergeant Rebecca Frye and her lover, Dr. Catherine Rawlings, join forces in the elusive search for justice. (1-933110-03-1)

**shadowland** by Radclyffe. In a world on the far edge of desire, two women are drawn together by power, passion, and dark pleasures. An erotic romance. (1-933110-11-2)

**Love's Masquerade** by Radclyffe. Plunged into the indistinguishable realms of fiction, fantasy, and hidden desires, Auden Frost is forced to question all she believes about the nature of love. (1-933110-14-7)

**Love & Honor** by Radclyffe. The president's daughter and her lover are faced with difficult choices as they battle a tangled web of Washington intrigue for...love and honor. (1-933110-10-4)

**Beyond the Breakwater** by Radclyffe. One Provincetown summer, three women learn the true meaning of love, friendship, and family. (1-933110-06-6)

**Tomorrow's Promise** by Radclyffe. One timeless summer, two very different women discover the power of passion to heal and the promise of hope that only love can bestow. (1-933110-12-0)

**Love's Tender Warriors** by Radclyffe. Two women who have accepted loneliness as a way of life learn that love is worth fighting for and a battle they cannot afford to lose. (1-933110-02-3)

**Love's Melody Lost** by Radclyffe. A secretive artist with a haunted past and a young woman escaping a life that has proved to be a lie find their destinies entwined. (1-933110-00-7)

**Safe Harbor** by Radclyffe. A mysterious newcomer, a reclusive doctor, and a troubled gay teenager learn about love, friendship, and trust during one tumultuous summer in Provincetown. (1-933110-13-9)

**Above All, Honor** by Radclyffe. Secret Service Agent Cameron Roberts fights her desire for the one woman she can't have—Blair Powell, the daughter of the president of the United States. (1-933110-04-X)